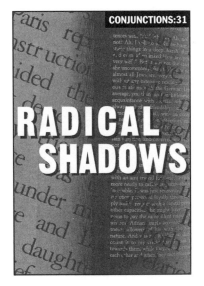

# CONJUNCTIONS

*Bi-Annual Volumes of New Writing*

*Edited by*
Bradford Morrow

*Contributing Editors*
Walter Abish
Chinua Achebe
John Ashbery
Mei-mei Berssenbrugge
Guy Davenport
Elizabeth Frank
William H. Gass
John Guare
Robert Kelly
Ann Lauterbach
Patrick McGrath
Mona Simpson
Nathaniel Tarn
Quincy Troupe
John Edgar Wideman

*published by* Bard College

EDITOR: Bradford Morrow
MANAGING EDITOR: Michael Bergstein
SENIOR EDITORS: Robert Antoni, Martine Bellen, Brian Evenson,
   Thalia Field, Pat Sims, Lee Smith
ART EDITORS: Anthony McCall, Norton Batkin
PUBLICITY: Mark R. Primoff
WEBMASTERS: Brian Evenson, Michael Neff
EDITORIAL ASSISTANTS: Caroline Donner, Lauren Feeney,
   Andrew Small, Alan Tinkler, Karen Walker

CONJUNCTIONS is published in the Spring and Fall of each year by
Bard College, Annandale-on-Hudson, NY 12504. This issue is made
possible in part with the generous funding of the Lannan Foundation
and the National Endowment for the Arts.

This publication is made possible with public funds from the New
York State Council on the Arts, a State Agency.

SUBSCRIPTIONS: Send subscription orders to CONJUNCTIONS,
Bard College, Annandale-on-Hudson, NY 12504. Single year (two
volumes): $18.00 for individuals; $25.00 for institutions and overseas. Two years (four volumes): $32.00 for individuals; $45.00 for
institutions and overseas. Patron subscription (lifetime): $500.00.
Overseas subscribers please make payment by International Money
Order. For information about subscriptions, back issues and adver-
tising, call Michael Bergstein at 914-758-1539 or fax 914-758-2660.

Editorial communications should be sent to 21 East 10th Street,
New York, NY 10003. Unsolicited manuscripts cannot be returned
unless accompanied by a stamped, self-addressed envelope.

Printers: Edwards Brothers.
Typesetter: Bill White, Typeworks.

ISSN 0278-2324
ISBN 0-941964-46-9

Manufactured in the United States of America.

# TABLE OF CONTENTS

## PAPER AIRPLANE
### The Thirtieth Issue

In Memoriam
James Laughlin
1914–1997

# *From* The Trial
# *Franz Kafka*

—*Translated from German and with
an afterword by Breon Mitchell*

## ARREST

SOMEONE MUST HAVE SLANDERED Josef K., for one morning, without having done anything truly wrong, he was arrested. His landlady, Frau Grubach, had a cook who brought him breakfast each day around eight, but this time she didn't appear. That had never happened before. K. waited a while longer, watching from his pillow the old woman who lived across the way, who was peering at him with a curiosity quite unusual for her; then, both put out and hungry, he rang. There was an immediate knock at the door and a man he'd never seen before in these lodgings entered. He was slender yet solidly built, and was wearing a fitted black jacket, which, like a traveler's outfit, was provided with a variety of pleats, pockets, buckles, buttons, and a belt, and thus appeared eminently practical, although its purpose remained obscure. "Who are you?" asked K., and immediately sat halfway up in bed. But the man ignored the question, as if his presence would have to be accepted, and merely said in turn: "You rang?" "Anna's to bring me breakfast," K. said, scrutinizing him silently for a moment, trying to figure out who he might be. But the man didn't submit to his inspection for long, turning instead to the door and opening it a little in order to tell someone who was apparently standing just behind it: "He wants Anna to bring him breakfast." A short burst of laughter came from the adjoining room; it was hard to tell whether more than one person had joined in. Although the stranger could hardly have learned anything new from this, he nevertheless said to K., as if passing on a message, "It's impossible." "That's news to me," K. said, jumping out of bed and quickly pulling on his trousers. "I'm going to see who those people are next door, and how Frau Grubach can justify allowing this disturbance." Although he realized at once that he shouldn't have spoken aloud, and that by doing so he had, in a sense, acknowledged the stranger's right to oversee his actions, that didn't seem important at the moment. Still, the stranger took it that way, for he said: "Wouldn't you rather stay here?" "I have no wish to stay here, nor to be addressed by you, until you've introduced yourself." "I meant well," the stranger said, and now opened the door of his own accord. In the adjoining room, which K. entered more slowly than he had intended, everything looked at first glance almost exactly as it had on the previous evening. It was Frau Grubach's living room; perhaps there was slightly more space than usual amid the clutter of furniture coverlets china and photographs, but it wasn't immediately obvious, especially since the major change was the presence of a man sitting by the open window with a book, from which he now looked up. "You should have stayed in your room! Didn't Franz tell you that?" "What is it you want, then?" K. said, glancing from the new man to the one called Franz, who had stopped in the doorway, and then back again. Through the open window the old woman was visible once more, having moved with truly senile curiosity to the window directly opposite, so she could keep an eye on everything. "Let's just see what Frau Grubach—" K. said, and started to walk out, making a gesture as if he were tearing himself loose from the two men, who were, however, standing some distance from him. "No," said the man by the window, tossing his book down on a small table and standing up. "You can't leave, you're being held." "So it appears," said K. "But why?" "We weren't sent to tell you that. Go to your room and wait. Proceedings are under way and you'll learn everything in due course. I'm exceeding my instructions by talking to you in such a friendly way. But I hope no one hears but Franz, and he's being friendly with you too, although it's against all regulations. If you're as fortunate from now on as you've been with the choice of your guards, you can rest easy." K. wanted to sit down, but he now saw that there was nowhere to sit in the entire room except for the chair by the window. "You'll come to realize how true that all is," said Franz, walking toward him with the other man. The latter in particular towered considerably over K. and patted him several times on the shoulder. Both of them examined K.'s nightshirt, saying that the one he would be given would not be nearly so nice, but that they would look after this one, as well as the rest of his undergarments, and if his case turned out well, they'd return them to him. "You're better off giving the things to us than leaving them in the depository," they said, "there's a lot of pilfering there, and besides, they sell everything after a time, whether the proceedings in question have ended or not. And trials like this last so long, particularly these days! Of course you'd get the proceeds from the depository in the end, but they don't amount to much in the first place, since sales aren't based on the size of the offer but on the size of the bribe, and secondly, experience shows that such proceeds dwindle from year to year as they pass from hand to hand." K. scarcely listened to this speech; he attached little value to whatever right he might still possess over the disposal of his things, being much more interested in gaining some clarity about his situation; but he couldn't even think in the presence of these men: the belly of the second guard—they surely must be guards—kept bumping against him in a positively friendly way, but when he looked up he saw a face completely at odds with that fat body: a dry, bony face, with a large nose set askew, consulting above his head with the other guard. What sort of men were they? What were they talking about? What office did they represent? After all, K. lived in a state governed by law, there was universal peace, all statutes were in force; who dared assault him in his own lodgings? He'd always tended to take things lightly, to believe the worst only when it arrived, making no provision for the future, even when things looked bad. But that didn't seem the right approach here; of course he could treat the whole thing as a joke, a crude joke his colleagues at the bank were playing on him for some unknown reason, perhaps because today was his thirtieth birthday, that was certainly possible, perhaps all he had to do was laugh in the guards' faces and they would laugh with him, perhaps they were porters off the street, they looked a little like porters— nevertheless, from the moment he'd first seen the guard named Franz, he had decided firmly that this time he wouldn't let even the slightest advantage he might have over these people slip through his fingers. K. knew there was a slight risk someone might say later that he hadn't been able to take a joke, but he clearly recalled—although he generally didn't make it a practice to learn from experience—a few occasions, unimportant in themselves, when, unlike his friends, he had deliberately behaved quite recklessly, without the least regard for his future, and had suffered the consequences. That wasn't going to happen again, not this time at any rate: if this was a farce, he was going to play along.

He was still free. "Pardon me," he said, and walked quickly between the guards into his room. "He seems to be reasonable," he heard them say behind them. In his room he yanked open the drawers of his desk at once; everything lay there in perfect order, but at

9

first, in his agitation, he couldn't find the one thing he was looking for: his identification papers. Finally he found his bicycle license and was about to take that to the guards, but then it seemed too insignificant a document, and he kept on looking until he found his birth certificate. When he returned to the adjoining room, the door opposite opened and Frau Grubach started to enter. She was only visible for a moment, for no sooner had she noticed K. than she seemed seized by embarrassment, apologized, and disappeared, closing the door carefully behind her. "Come on in," K. barely had time to say. But now he remained standing in the middle of the room with his papers, still staring at the door, which did not reopen, until he was brought to himself by a call from the guards, who were sitting at the small table by the open window and, as K. now saw, eating his breakfast. "Why didn't she come in?" he asked. "She's not allowed to," said the tall guard, "after all, you're under arrest." "How can I be under arrest? And in this manner?" "Now there you go again," said the guard, dipping his buttered bread into the little honey pot. "We don't answer that sort of question." "You're going to have to answer them," said K. "Here are my papers, now show me yours, starting with the arrest warrant." "Good heavens!" said the guard, "you just can't accept your situation and seem bent on annoying us unnecessarily, although we're probably the human beings closest to you now." "That's right, you'd better believe it," said Franz, not lifting the coffee cup in his hand to his mouth but staring at K. with a long and no doubt meaningful, but incomprehensible, look. K. allowed himself to become involved in an involuntary staring match with Franz, but at last thumped his papers and said: "Here are my identification papers." "So what?" the taller guard cried out, "you're behaving worse than a child. What is it you want? Do you think you can bring your whole damn trial to a quick conclusion by discussing your identity and arrest warrant with your guards? We're lowly employees who can barely make our way through such documents, and whose only role in your affair is to stand guard over you ten hours a day and get paid for it. That's all we are, but we're smart enough to realize that before ordering such an arrest the higher authorities who employ us inform themselves in great detail about the person they're arresting and the grounds for the arrest. There's been no mistake. After all, our department, as far as I know, and I know only the lowest level, doesn't seek out guilt from among the general population, but, as the Law states, is attracted by guilt and has to send us guards out. That's the Law. What mistake could there be?" "I don't know that law," said K. "All the worse for you," said the guard. "It probably exists only in your heads," said K.; he wanted to slip into his guards' thoughts somehow and turn them to his own advantage or accustom himself to them. But the guard merely said dismissively: "You'll feel it eventually." Franz broke in and said: "You see, Willem, he admits that he doesn't know the Law and yet he claims he's innocent." "You're right there, but he can't seem to understand anything," said the other. K. said nothing more; why should I let the idle talk of these lowly agents—they themselves admit that's what they are—confuse me even further? he thought. After all, they're discussing things they don't understand. Their confidence is based solely on ignorance. A few words spoken with someone of my own sort will make everything incomparably clearer than the longest conversations with these two. He paced back and forth a few times through the cleared space of the room; across the way he saw the old woman, who had pulled an ancient man far older than herself to the window and had her arms wrapped about him; K. had to bring this show to an end: "Take me to your supervisor," he said. "When he wishes it; not before," said the guard called Willem. "And now I advise you," he added, "to go to your room, remain there quietly, and wait to find out what's to be done with you. We advise you not to waste your time in useless thought, but to pull yourself together; great demands will be placed upon you. You haven't treated us as we deserve, given how accommodating we've been; you've forgotten that whatever else we may be, we are at least free men with respect to you, and that's no small advantage. Nevertheless we're prepared, if you have any money, to bring you a small breakfast from the coffeehouse across the way."

K. stood quietly for a moment without responding to this offer. Perhaps if he were to open the door to the next room, or even the door to the hall, the two would not dare stop him, perhaps the best solution would be to bring the whole matter to a head. But then they might indeed grab him, and once subdued he would lose any degree of superiority he still held over them. Therefore he preferred the safety of whatever solution would surely arise in the natural course of things and returned to his room without a further word having passed on his part or on the part of his guards.

He threw himself onto his bed and took from the nightstand a nice apple that he had set out last night to have with breakfast. Now it was his entire breakfast, and in any case, as he verified with the first large bite, a much better breakfast than he could have had from the filthy all-night cafe through the grace of his guards. He felt confident and at ease; he was missing work at the bank this morning of course, but in light of the relatively high position he held there, that would be easily excused. Should he give the real excuse? He considered doing so. If they didn't believe him, which would be understandable given the circumstances, he could offer Frau Grubach as a witness, or even the two old people across the way, who were probably now on the march to the window opposite him. K. was surprised, at least from the guards' perspective, that they had driven him into his room and left him alone there, where it would be ten times easier to kill himself. At the same time he asked himself, from his own perspective, what possible reason he could have for doing so. Because those two were sitting next door and had taken away his breakfast? Committing suicide would be so irrational that even had he wished to, the irrationality of the act would have prevented him. Had the intellectual limitations of the guards not been so obvious, he might have assumed this same conviction led them to believe there was no danger in leaving him alone. Let them watch if they liked as he went to the little wall cupboard in which he kept good schnapps and downed a small glass in place of breakfast, then a second one as well, to give himself courage, a mere precaution, in the unlikely event it might be needed.

Then a shout from the adjoining room startled him so that he rattled his teeth on the glass. "The Inspector wants you!" It was the cry alone that startled him: a short clipped military cry that he would never have expected from the guard Franz. The order itself he gladly welcomed: "It's about time," he called back, locked the cupboard, and hurried into the adjoining room. The two guards were standing there and, as if it were a matter of course, chased him back into his room. "What are you thinking of?" they cried, "do you want to see the Inspector in your nightshirt? He'll have you soundly flogged and us along with you!" "Let go of me, damn you," cried K., who was already pushed back against his wardrobe, "if you assault me in bed, you can hardly expect to find me in formal dress." "It's no use," said the guards, who, whenever K. shouted at them, fell into a calm, almost sad state that either put him at a loss or restored him somewhat to his senses. "Ridiculous formalities!" he grumbled, but he was already lifting a coat from the chair and holding it up for a moment in both hands, as if submitting to the judgment of the guards. They shook their heads. "It has to be a black coat," they said. K. threw the coat to the floor in response and said—without knowing himself in what sense he meant it—"But this isn't the main hearing yet." The guards smiled, but stuck to their words: "It has to be a black coat." "If that will speed things up, it's fine with me," said K., opened the wardrobe himself, took his time going through his many clothes, selected his best black suit, an evening jacket that had caused a small sensation among his friends because it was so stylish, then changed his shirt as well and began dressing with care. He secretly believed he'd managed to speed up the whole process after all, for the guards had forgotten to make him bathe. He watched to see if they might recall it now, but of course it didn't occur to them, although Willem did remember to send Franz to the inspector with the message that K. was getting dressed.

When he was fully dressed, he had to walk just ahead of Willem through the empty room beside his into the following room, the double doors to which were already thrown open. As K. well knew, this room had been newly occupied not long ago by a certain Fräulein Bürstner, a typist, who usually left for work quite early and came home late, and with whom K. had exchanged no more than a few words of greeting. Now the nightstand by her bed had been shoved to the middle of the room as a desk for the hearing and the inspector was sitting behind it. He had crossed his legs and placed one arm on the back of the chair. In a corner of the room three young men stood looking at Fräulein Bürstner's photographs, which were mounted on a mat on the wall. A white blouse hung on the latch of the open window. Across the way, the old couple were again at the opposite window, but their party had increased in number, for towering behind them stood a man with his shirt open at the chest, pinching and twisting his reddish goatee.

"Josef K.?" the inspector asked, perhaps simply to attract K.'s wandering gaze back to himself. K. nodded. "You're no doubt greatly surprised by this morning's events?" asked the inspector, arranging with both hands the few objects lying on the nightstand—a candle with matches, a book, and a pincushion—as if they were tools he required for the hearing. "Of course," said K., overcome by a feeling of relief at finally standing before a reasonable man with whom he could discuss his situation, "of course I'm surprised, but by no means greatly surprised." "Not greatly surprised?" asked the inspector, placing the candle in the middle of the table and grouping the other objects around it. "Perhaps you misunderstand me," K. hastened to add. "I mean—" Here K. interrupted himself and looked around for a chair. "I can sit down, can't I?" he asked. "It's not customary," answered the inspector. "I mean," K. continued without further pause, "I'm of course greatly surprised, but when you've been in this world for thirty years and had to make your way on your own, as has been my lot, you get hardened to surprises and don't take them too seriously. Particularly not today's." "Why particularly not today's?" "I'm not saying I think the whole thing's a joke, the preparations involved seem far too extensive. All the lodgers at the boardinghouse would have to be in on it, and all of you, which would go far beyond a joke. So I'm not saying it's a joke." "That's right," said the inspector, checking the number of matches in the matchbox. "But on the other hand," K. continued, as he turned to all of them, and would have gladly turned even to the three by the photographs, "on the other hand, it can't be too important a matter. I conclude that from the fact that I've been accused of something but can't think of the slightest offense of which I might be accused. But that's also beside the point, the main question is: who's accusing me? What authorities are in charge of the proceedings? Are you officials? No one's wearing a uniform, unless you want to call your suit"—he turned to Franz— "a uniform, but it's more like a traveler's outfit. I demand clarification on these matters, and I'm convinced that once they've been clarified we can part on the friendliest of terms." The inspector flung the matchbox down on the table. "You're quite mistaken," he said. "These gentlemen and I are merely marginal figures in your affair, and in fact know almost nothing about it. We could be wearing the most proper of uniforms and your case would not be a whit more serious. I can't report that you've been accused of anything, or more accurately, I don't know if you have. You've been arrested, that's true, but that's all I know. Perhaps the guards have talked about other things, if so it was just that, idle talk. If, as a result, I can't answer your questions either, I can at least give you some advice: think less about us and what's going to happen to you, and instead think more about yourself. And don't make such a fuss about how innocent you feel; it disturbs the otherwise not unfavorable impression you make. And you should talk less in general; almost everything you've said up to now could have been inferred from your behavior, even if you'd said only a few words, and it wasn't terribly favorable to you in any case."

K. stared at the inspector. Was he to be lectured like a schoolboy by what well might be a younger man? To be reprimanded for his openness? And to learn nothing about why he had been arrested and on whose orders? He grew increasingly agitated, paced up and down, without hindrance, pushed his cuffs back, felt his chest, brushed his hair into place, went past the three men, muttering, "It's completely senseless," at which they turned and looked at him in a friendly but serious way, and finally came to a stop before the inspector's table. "Hasterer, the public prosecutor, is a good friend of mine," he said, "can I telephone him?" "Certainly," said the inspector, "but I don't see what sense it makes, unless you have some private matter to discuss with him." "What sense?" K. cried out, more startled than annoyed. "Who do you think you are? You ask what sense it makes, while you stage the most senseless performance imaginable? Isn't it enough to break your heart? First these gentlemen assault me, and now they stand or sit around and put me through my paces. What sense is there in telephoning a lawyer when I've supposedly been arrested? Fine, I won't telephone." "But do," said the inspector, and waved toward the hall, where the telephone was, "please do telephone." "No, I no longer care to," K. said, and went to the window. Across the way the group was still at the window, their peaceful observation now slightly disturbed as K. stepped to the window. The old couple started to rise, but the man behind them calmed them down. "There's more of the audience over there," K. cried out to the inspector and pointed outside. "Get away from there," he yelled at them. The three immediately retreated a few steps, the old couple even withdrawing behind the man, who shielded them with his broad body and, judging by the movement of his lips, apparently said something that couldn't be understood at that distance. They didn't disappear entirely, however, but instead seemed to wait for the moment when they could approach the window again unnoticed. "Obnoxious, thoughtless people!" said K., turning back to the room. The inspector may have agreed with him, as he thought he noticed with a sideways glance. But it was equally possible he hadn't been listening at all, for he had pressed his hand firmly down on the table and seemed to be comparing the length of his fingers. The two guards were sitting on a chest draped with an embroidered coverlet, rubbing their knees. The three young men had placed their hands on their hips and were gazing around aimlessly. Everything was silent, as in some deserted office. "Now, gentlemen," K. said firmly, and for a moment it seemed to him as if he bore them all upon his shoulders, "judging by your expressions, this affair of mine must be closed. In my opinion, it would be best to stop worrying whether or not your actions were justified and end the matter on a note of reconciliation, by shaking hands. If you share my opinion, then please—" and he stepped up to the inspector's table and held out his hand. The inspector looked up, chewed his lip, and regarded K.'s outstretched hand; K. still believed that the inspector would grasp it. But instead he rose, lifted a hard bowler hat from Fräulein Bürstner's bed, and donned it carefully with both hands, like someone trying on a new hat. "How simple everything seems to you!" he said to K. as he did so. "So you think we should end this matter on a note of reconciliation? No, I'm afraid we really can't. Although that's not at all to say you should despair. Why should you? You're under arrest, that's all. I was to inform you of that, I've done so, and I've noted your reaction. That's enough for today, and we can take our leave, temporarily of course. No doubt you wish to go to the bank now?" "To the bank?" K. asked. "I thought I was under arrest." K. said this with a certain insistence, for although no one had shaken his hand, he was beginning to feel increasingly independent of these people, particularly once the inspector had stood up. He was toying with them. If they did leave, he intended to follow them to the door of the building and offer to let them arrest him. And so he said again: "How can I go to the bank if I'm under arrest?" "Oh, I see," said the inspector, who was already at the door, "you've misunderstood me; you're under arrest, certainly, but that's not meant to keep you from carrying on your profession. Nor are you to be hindered in the course of your ordinary life." "Then being under arrest isn't so bad," said K., approaching the inspector. "I never said it was," he replied. "But in that case even the notification of arrest scarcely seems necessary," said K., stepping closer still. The others had approached as well. Everyone was now gathered in a small area by the door. "It was my duty," said the inspector. "A stupid duty," said K. relentlessly. "Perhaps so," replied the inspector, "but let's not waste our time with such talk. I assumed you wished to go to the bank. Since you take such careful note of every word, let me add that I'm not forcing you to go to the bank, I simply assumed you would want to. And to facilitate that, and to render your arrival at the bank as inconspicuous as possible, I had arranged for three of your colleagues here to be placed at your disposal." "What?" K. cried out, and stared at the three in amazament. These so uncharacteristically anemic young men, whom he recalled only as a group by the photographs, were indeed clerks from his bank, not colleagues, that would be an overstatement, and indicated a gap in the inspector's omniscience, but they were certainly lower-level clerks from the bank. How could K. have failed to notice that? How preoccupied he

16

must have been by the inspector and the guards not to recognize these three. Wooden, arm-swinging Rabensteiner, blond Kullich with his deep-set eyes, and Kaminer with his annoying smile, produced by a chronic muscular twitch. "Good morning!" K. said after a moment, and held out his hand to the men, who bowed courteously. "I completely failed to recognize you. So now we can go to work, right?" The men nodded, laughing and eager, as if that was what they'd been waiting for all along, but when K. missed his hat, which he'd left in his room, all three tripped over each other's heels to get it, which indicated a certain embarrassment on their part after all. K. stood still and watched them pass through the two open doors, the lethargic Rabensteiner bringing up the rear, of course, having broken into nothing more than an elegant trot. Kaminer handed over the hat and K. had to remind himself, as he often did at the bank, that Kaminer's smile was not deliberate and that in fact he couldn't smile deliberately at all. In the hall, Frau Grubach, not looking as if she felt any particular sense of guilt, opened the outer door for the whole company and K. looked down, as so often, at her apron strings, which cut so unnecessarily deeply into her robust body. Downstairs, watch in hand, K. decided to go by car so as not to extend unnecessarily what was already a half-hour delay. Kaminer ran to the corner to get a cab; the other two apparently felt they should entertain K. somehow, since Kullich suddenly pointed to the door of the building across the way, in which the man with the blond goatee had just appeared, and, at first embarrassed by now showing himself full-length, had retreated to the wall and leaned against it. The old couple were probably still on the stairs. K. was annoyed at Kullich for having pointed out the man, since he had already seen him himself, and in fact had been expecting him. "Don't look over there," he said quickly, without realizing how strange it must sound to speak that way to grown men. But no explanation was necessary, for at that moment the cab arrived, they got in, and it pulled away. Then K. remembered that he hadn't seen the inspector and the guards leave: the inspector had diverted his attention from the three clerks, and now the clerks had done the same for the inspector. That didn't show much presence of mind, and K. resolved to watch these things more carefully. Even now he turned around involuntarily and leaned across the rear panel of the car to see if the inspector and guards might still be in sight. But he turned around again immediately, without having made the slightest effort to locate anyone, and leaned back comfortably into the corner of the cab. Despite appearances, he could have used some conversation, but now the men seemed tired: Rabensteiner gazed out the car to the right, and Kullych to the left, leaving only Kaminer and his grin, which common decency unfortunately forbade as a topic of humor.

---

## Afterword: *The Translator's Trial*

TRANSLATING KAFKA WAS ONCE my dream. Now all I dream of is how I might have done it better. From the moment I first read *The Trial*, as a teenager on the plains of Kansas in the late fifties, I was drawn into his world so strongly that I have never quite escaped it. I had no idea then that scarcely five years later I would be studying with Malcolm Pasley in Oxford, hearing firsthand the tale of how he had retrieved most of Kafka's manuscripts and arranged for their deposit in the Bodleian Library, nor that my next summer would be spent walking the streets of Prague on a pilgrimage that, in the mid-sixties, still retained its spiritual excitement, and even a hint of danger, under a regime that had forbidden the publication and sale of Kafka's works.

Thirty years have passed, and Kafka now gazes from the shop windows of every bookstore in Prague. Nor did Kafka ever leave my life. Now, after almost three decades of reading, teaching and writing about Kafka, I have undertaken the closest reading of all, faced with the challenge of doing him justice.

This new translation of the opening chapter of *The Trial* is based on the German critical edition prepared by Pasley for the Fischer Verlag and published in two volumes in 1990. Schocken Books will publish the entire translation later this year. In it the structure of the definitive text of *The Trial* is rendered precisely, paragraph by paragraph, and sentence by sentence. Punctuation generally follows established English usage, since Kafka's own punctuation, although somewhat loose, is still well within the range of accepted German usage, and I do not wish for it to appear falsely ungrammatical. It should be noted in particular that Kafka's prevalent use of what we call a comma splice has been perfectly acceptable in German prose since the eighteenth century, as are the long and complex sentences resulting from this practice. I have, however, attempted to reflect every truly unusual use of punctuation, including the occasional omission of an expected question mark.

In all these ways, the present translation attempts to mirror the critical edition of the text quite closely. But rendering Kafka's prose involves far more than punctuation and paragraphing. The power of Kafka's text lies in the language, in a nuanced use of the discourses of law, religion and the theater, and in particular in a closely woven web of linguistic motifs that must be rendered consistently to achieve their full impact. Here Edwin and Willa Muir, for all the virtues of their translation, fell far short, for in attempting to create a readable and stylistically refined version of Kafka's *Trial*, they consistently overlooked or deliberately varied the repetitions and interconnections that echo so meaningfully in the ear of every attentive reader of the German text. Which is not to say that there are any easy solutions to the challenges Kafka presents.

> Jemand mußte Josef K. verleumdet haben, denn ohne daß er etwas Böses getan hätte, wurde er eines Morgens verhaftet.

The translator's trial begins with the first sentence, in part because the uncertainty so subtly introduced by the subjunctive verb *"hätte[n]"* is inevitably lost in the standard translation, even with E. M. Butler's later revisions: "Someone must have been telling lies about Joseph K., for without having done anything wrong he was arrested one fine morning." Although in this version it is by no means clear why Josef K. has been arrested, there seems to be little doubt about his innocence. The German subjunctive, however, tends to undermine this reading. Of course nothing is ever that simple in Kafka, even in translation, and we might argue that since the information received is filtered through Josef K.'s own mind from the very beginning, it is constantly suspect in any case. On a strictly literal level, however, the standard English translation appears to declare K.'s innocence far too strongly.

There are other questions as well. Why render the simple phrase *"eines Morgens"* with the false irony of "one fine morning"? Why not end the sentence, as in German, with the surprise of his arrest? And why has the legal resonance of *"verleumden"* (to slander) been reduced to merely "telling lies"? A further problem is posed by *"Böses,"* a word which, when applied to the actions of an adult, reverberates with moral and philosophical overtones ranging from the story of the Fall in the Garden of Eden to Nietzsche's discussion of the origins of morality in *Jenseits von Gut und Böse* (Beyond Good and Evil). To claim that K. has done nothing *"Böses"* is both

19

more and less than to claim he has done nothing wrong. Josef K. has done nothing *truly* wrong, at least in his own eyes.

In wrestling with these problems I settled upon the following: "Someone must have slandered Josef K., for one morning, without having done anything truly wrong, he was arrested." My choice of "truly wrong" for *"Böses"* had a double purpose: to push the word "wrong" toward the province of the criminally malicious and to introduce, on a level corresponding to the almost subliminal use of the subjunctive in German, the question of truth.

There are no totally satisfying solutions to the difficulties presented by Kafka's opening sentence. But it is crucial to recognize and grapple with them. Such a struggle is not inappropriate in a novel which deals with Josef K.'s attempts throughout the course of a year to twist and turn his way through the process of his own trial. And indeed, having made it through the first sentence, the translator is immediately confronted by problems of another sort in the second:

> Die Köchin der Frau Grubach, seiner Zimmervermieterin,
> die ihm jeden Tag gegen acht Uhr früh das Frühstück brachte,
> kam diesmal nicht.

Here Kafka himself is partly to blame. He originally began the sentence quite straightforwardly: *"Die Köchin, die ihm jeden Tag . . ."*; but the manuscript reveals that he inserted the words *"der Frau Grubach, seiner Zimmervermieterin"* between the lines, introducing her immediately into the cast of characters. Literal versions such as "His landlady Frau Grubach's cook, who brought him breakfast . . ." or "The cook of Frau Grubach, his landlady, who brought him breakfast . . ." are impossibly awkward and even grammatically misleading. The Muirs solved this problem by simply omitting her name: "His landlady's cook, who always brought him his breakfast . . ." Here as so often, the Muirs smooth away the difficulties at some cost, since when Frau Grubach's name first comes up later in the scene, it is not clear in the English version who she is. In order to reflect Kafka's obvious intentions, I have retained her by name: "His landlady, Frau Grubach, had a cook who brought him breakfast . . ." Although this solution is less readable, it remains true to Kafka's text, even in its slightly awkward construction.

This second sentence raises an issue of some importance for the critical edition of the text and its translation. Kafka's manuscript is unfinished and unrevised. He might well have smoothed out such sentences, or even rewritten them entirely. He would surely have removed inconsistencies in the spelling of a character's name, Kullich and Kullych, both versions of which are retained in the critical edition; he would probably have straightened out the confusion with time in the Cathedral chapter, where K. plans to meet the Italian at ten o'clock, then later refers to eleven instead; he might well have cleared up the matter of the maid's room where Block works and sleeps, which is at first windowless (*"fensterlos"*), although a few pages later it includes a window that looks onto an air shaft. But we can hardly hold the author of *The Metamorphosis* to a strict standard of reality. Kafka constantly distorts time and space, and often underlines the frailty of human perception. The critical edition therefore retains such apparent anomalies, allowing the reader direct access to Kafka's text in progress, and here too I have followed the German version faithfully.

*The Trial* begins as farce and ends in tragedy. The opening chapter has a strong theatrical air, complete with an audience across the way. Later that evening, when Josef K. reenacts the scene for an amused Fräulein Bürstner, who has just returned from the theater herself, he takes on both his own role and that of his accuser, replaying the farce, shouting his own name aloud with comedic consequences. The final chapter of the novel offers a carefully balanced counterpart in which the men who are sent for him, like a pair of "old supporting actors," stage the final scene in the deserted quarry before yet another audience at a distant window. But this time no one is laughing.

Josef K.'s appearance before the Examining Magistrate at the initial inquiry is yet another farce, a staged gathering in which the supposed parties of the assembly are merely acting out their roles before the gallery, under the direction of the magistrate. In the lawyer's apartment, Huld calls in the merchant Block and offers a performance intended solely to demonstrate his power to K. Even the priest's appearance in the cathedral has all the trappings of a private show for K.'s benefit.

Throughout the novel the line between farce and tragedy is blurred in such scenes. Although they are connected at the level of the plot, the relationships are made striking and forceful in the language itself. The Muirs' translation weakens these connections by failing time and again to render Kafka's language precisely. When K. accuses the inspector of staging "the most senseless performance imaginable" before the "audience" at the opposite window, the Muirs misread *"führen . . . auf"* as a reflexive verb and simply have him "carry on in the most senseless way imaginable," while the group opposite is turned into a "crowd of spectators." When K. reenacts that same scene for Fräulein Bürstner in the second chapter, moving the nightstand to the center of the room for his performance, he tells her she should visualize "the cast of characters" (*"die Verteilung der Personen"*) including himself, "the most important character," before the action begins. The Muirs lessen the effect of this language by having her simply "picture where the various people are," including K., "the most important person," and undermine the sense of a rising curtain implied by *"Und jetzt fängt es an,"* with a colorless: "And now we can really begin."

Taken individually, such considerations may seem minor, but over the course of the novel they accumulate with great power. Kafka took special care to create verbal links between important passages in the work, links the Muirs either missed or unintentionally weakened on several occasions. A few examples will have to suffice.

The verb *"verleumden"* from the opening sentence of *The Trial* is repeated only twice in the novel. Regardless of what we are to make of these reoccurrences, we should be able to hear the echo. Thus, when Frau Grubach says: *"Ich will Fräulein Bürstner gewiß nicht verleumden"* ("I certainly have no wish to slander Fräulein Bürstner"), the German reader is immediately alerted to the connection. The same is true in the fragment "Fräulein Bürstner's Friend," when Frau Grubach protests: *"Ich sollte meine Mieter verleumden!"* ("That I would slander my boarders!"). On both occasions, the Muirs use the phrase "speak ill of," which fails to recall either the original "traduced" or the revision "telling lies" in their own first sentence, and a striking link between K. and his series of women helpers is lost.

Fräulein Bürstner's apparent reappearance in the final chapter reminds the reader again how crucially linked she is to K.'s fate. Kafka has reinforced this in many ways, including his use of the verb *"überfallen"* (to attack by surprise, assault). Although this verb has a range of meanings, including "mugging" if it occurs on the street, it is of crucial importance to render it consistently. In the opening chapter K. wonders: *"wer wagte ihn in seiner Wohnung zu überfallen"* ("who dared assault him in his lodgings"). On two further occasions in that first chapter he refers specially to the "assault" upon him, and when he appears before the examining magistrate at the initial inquiry he repeats the same term twice again. Thus when he hesitates to speak to Fräulein Bürstner because his sudden emergence from his own darkened room might have *"den Anschein eines Überfalls"* ("the appearance of an assault"), and even more strikingly, when he suggests to her *"Wollen Sie verbreitet haben, daß ich Sie überfallen habe"* ("If you want it spread around that I assaulted you"), and repeats the phrase a sentence later, the verbal link between his own slander and arrest and that of the young typist is made abundantly clear. A final link in the chain of associations is forged when K. worries that his lawyer is simply lulling him to sleep, *"um ihn dann plötzlich mit der Entscheidung zu überfallen"* ("so that they could assault him suddenly with the verdict"). The Muirs, however, render the six occurrences where K. is referring to his own arrest or the possible verdict as: "seize him," "grab me," "fall upon me," "seized," "some wild prank" and "overwhelm him," while the three times Kafka uses the term in Josef K.'s conversation with Fräulein Bürstner are rendered as "waylaying her" and "assaulted" (twice). Thus no reader of the English version has been in the position to recognize one of the central links in the novel, nor fully understand why her appearance in the final chapter is such a strong reminder of the futility of all resistance.

The dominant discourse in *The Trial* is of course legal. Some critics have gone so far as to suggest that the whole of the novel is written in legalese, reflecting Kafka's own training as a lawyer, and his abiding interest in the law, effacing all distinction of tone, so that "everybody in *The Trial*, high or low, uses the same language." But in fact the voices of the novel are clearly varied. They include not only the long legal disquisitions of the lawyer Huld, but also the voices of women, of K.'s uncle, of the merchant, the painter and the priest. Moreover, the narrative itself is recounted in a voice we have long since come to recognize as distinctly Kafka's own. The translator's task includes rendering these voices individually, even when they are all caught in the web of the law.

The German word *"Prozeß,"* as has often been noted, refers not only to an actual trial, but also the proceedings surrounding it, a process that, in this imaginary world, includes preliminary investigations, numerous hearings and a wide range of legal and extra-legal maneuvering. Over the course of a year, Josef K. gradually weakens in his struggle with the mysterious forces that surround him. His true trial begins with the first sentence and ends only with his death.

23

The translator's trial is in its own way a similar ordeal. Faced with his own inadequacy, acutely aware each time he falls short, the translator too is impelled toward a final sentence in an imperfect world.

Nothing I have said can or should obscure the Muirs' very real achievement, nor the crucial role their translation has played in establishing Kafka as a major figure in world literature. By providing the reading public with smooth and readable translations of his great unfinished novels, they rendered a laudable service to literature. They could hardly have been expected to treat the text with any special reverence in 1937, for they had no way of knowing the importance Kafka would eventually acquire for the twentieth century. Nevertheless, they created versions that are on the whole accurate and a pleasure to read to this very day, versions that have moved millions of readers. My own translation, occasioned by the appearance of the newly restored text in German, is only one of many others that will surely follow over the years. It is always dangerous to translate an author one reveres as deeply as I do Kafka. I have tried to be true to him, and to his trial.

# The Freedom Prize Speech
## Günter Grass

—Translated from German by
Peter Constantine

*This speech was delivered in the Paulskirche in Frankfurt on October 19, 1997, at the ceremony awarding the Freedom Prize of the German Book Trade Association to the writer Yasar Kemal.*

AT THIS HISTORIC SITE, whose spirit is so often invoked in speeches, a prize is awarded with fitting ceremony. In this church, the Paulskirche, there have been long and futile struggles for the institution of fundamental democratic rights. In 1848 the Revolution strove, up to the day it foundered, to express eloquently its ideals in the National Assembly that convened here. As if isolated from political reality, parliamentary rhetoric was rehearsed on a makeshift stage. The endless theme of debate was Germany's unity. Among those assembled here were also writers such as Ludwig Uhland. But a Prussian Junker, Otto von Bismarck, saw to it that these early endeavors came to naught. As Prussian delegate to the Bundestag, he had a completely different unity in mind, which in the end he forcibly implemented with the help of three wars. It was not the toil of the Paulskirche Assembly—as captured with ironic melancholy by the painter Johannes Gruetzke—but Bismarck's hunger for power that proved decisive for Germany's future. Of the Reich of Chancellor Bismarck, whose severity is popularly attested as having been "iron," as good as nothing remains. And yet this much does remain: at the Berlin Congress of 1878, Bismarck's political moves furthering German imperial interests were quick to exploit the Bosporus crisis, laying the groundwork for the special relationship between the German and the Ottoman empires, which lasted as the so-called German-Turkish "Weapons Brotherhood" until the two countries' final defeat in the First World War—a comradeship built on blood and iron.

But the Paulskirche was too good for such alliances; it is a sad relic of German futility. Both the Paulskirche and its oft-summoned spirit, time and again, drew the short straw. When, for instance, in 1949 the brand-new West German State, consisting of three occupied zones, cast about to find a capital, it was not Frankfurt am Main that got the bid. It was the separatist from the Rhineland, Konrad Adenauer, who got his way. What remained was a hole, surrounded by restrained sighs. Thanks to the German Book Trade Association, the vacuum in this stuffed repository of our history is filled from year to year with a meaningful celebration. After this brief excursion into history, I would like to welcome this year's recipient of the Freedom Prize, Yasar Kemal.

And so one writer looks up from his own work to praise the work of another. My dear Yasar Kemal! I am sure you will have had your reasons for suggesting me as the speaker on this occasion. I was happy to accept your request, and glad to fly back from the Mediterranean, over the flat clay fields of the coast, over the Chukurova, covered in blackberry bushes, wild grape vines and reeds, and then over inland swamps, fertile fields, hills fragrant with myrtle and plateaus—one of which is called Dikenlidüzü and has five villages—and opening up before me a vista of the Taurus range with its snowy peaks.

Although I have traveled widely, I have never been to Anatolia. And yet, as a reader of your work, with each book I have come closer to your country. What was once foreign to me has become, with all its aromas, familiar and comprehensible, even the misery of the landless peasants. Words can do this; literature annuls distance. The literary conquest of land brings us close to people who only exist on paper. Literature makes impenetrable deserts and looming, jagged eagle-summits accessible. It reminds us, confronting us with the misery of subjugated peasants, of the serfdom once imposed on our own land. Literature annuls the borders drawn on maps, and also the borders that cut through our consciousness. Literature builds a bridge to one's other self, the alienated self. It throws us together. It turns us into accomplices. It evokes empathy in us.

This is the way, and not directly, my dear Yasar Kemal, that we are related. Not only because you, as a Kurd, belong with sore affliction to Turkey, as I, Kashubian on my mother's side, am assigned with burdensome remembrance to Germany, but also in our tendency to recapture our respective losses through words. This obsession drives us to write against our time and to tell those stories that have not been ennobled by the state with pomp and ceremony, because they are about people who never sat on a dais and ruled, but who have always been rulers' victims.

Added to this is the fact that our two countries are far from one another in a geographic sense, but still find themselves close because both are burdened with lasting guilt, and because in both their societies the majority continues to act high-handedly toward minorities. When the century that is now drawing to a close was still young, hundreds of thousands of Armenians were made victims of systematic genocide; the German crimes, committed in immeasurable number on Jews and Gypsies, are a Mene Tekel—a writing on the wall—epitomized by Auschwitz. Unable to achieve unity within ourselves, our countries engendered wars that have exposed our neighbors to continuing horror. We Germans were defeated repeatedly and then divided, after which for forty years we stood facing each other armed and blinkered. In Turkey, the Kurdish people are exposed to this day to arbitrary national policies and military action, whose victims are mostly women and children. Racism and arrogant intolerance, wars and the consequences of war, mark the history of our two countries.

With this background, which no amount of ceremony can embellish, Yasar Kemal is being presented today with the Freedom Prize of the German book trade. This prize is being awarded to him for his literary work, but also to honor him as a champion of human rights. But these contributions of his are not separate entities; one stems from the other. Only those who have delved into Kemal's novels can understand how rooted his political protest is in the miseries, dreams and hopes of the common people. Even in his first work, *Anatolian Rice*, the author already dares to tread on terrain that is politically out-of-bounds. His theme is peasants' dependence on a big landowner, who has the lands and even the villages ruthlessly flooded in order to reap profits with the unrestrained cultivation of rice. We know this ever-recurring story. It is told over and over in many literatures. Every time, we see helplessness facing power. Every time, readers fear the outcome of this unequal battle, even though they foresee its depressing end.

In this short and tight-knit narrative, it is a woman peasant and a young Kurd who lead the inhabitants of the flooded village in a protest march. It is they who approach a young official, who had taken on his problematic post with naive unpreparedness, and open his eyes to the misery of the villages and the specter of long-standing corruption. Every episode (the exodus of the clay-caked peasants), every detail noted with seeming casualness (the office of the young official) is saturated with experience and contemplation.

27

This tormented region, after all, is sultry Chukurova, which has stayed with the author since childhood, molding him and sensitizing him to right and wrong. He has given voice to this region, first as a street-scribe, then as a journalist and then with this, his first novel.

Yasar Kemal is one of those writers for whom the little piece of land on which he was born is world enough. As with Faulkner, Aitmatov or Joyce, all the action centers around the place of early hurt. Landscapes are conjured up—they can also be urban landscapes—and in them people who, regardless of how forlornly they might live on their fringes, always occupy and inhabit the focal point of this world.

I, too, know this obsession well—this not being able to break loose from long-lost provinces. For every clause I have ever put to paper has been rooted—even if it ultimately leads elsewhere—in the marshes of the river Vistula, the hills of Kashubia, in the city of Danzig and its suburb Langfur and on the beaches of the Baltic. That is where my American South lies, that is where I have lost my Dublin, where my Kirghiz steppes spread out, and there too lies my Chukurova.

Already in the mid 1950s, Yasar Kemal's eyes, trained on injustice close at hand, proved to be far-sighted, encompassing the curves of the globe. His novel *Memed, My Hawk* has been translated into over thirty languages; not only because the indestructible Robin Hood story is retold as a fresh event, but also because the author manages to take his readers—regardless of whether they open the book in South America, Russia or the two Germanies—and whisk them to a region whose injustices, as the pages turn, become profoundly their own. All this without becoming bogged down in rigid doctrine, or giving way to the pathos of social denunciation, but demonstrating, against the arbitrary power of the rulers, why a frail shepherd lad, later a field hand, who is beaten, humiliated and separated from the sweetheart he has loved since childhood, would arm himself and head for the mountains to become a feared bandit, an avenger of the poor, a legend for the peasants swindled out of their last piece of land.

But this heroic figure is not a decal lifted from the pages of a trivial bandit romance. No "positive hero" is teaching us a lesson. This young man, Memed, is neither a tough guy nor a gunslinger: he quietly tills his mother's small plot; we see him running through endless fields of thistles, hounded by fear. But when he singlehandedly demands his rights, he inevitably becomes guilty. He joins a gang of street marauders, watches as they rob a group of nomads who had once extended their hospitality to him and finally turns into an arsonist when he thinks he has found the man who tortured and murdered his mother, the merciless man who rules over five enslaved villages. But Memed inadvertently plunges the enslaved peasants into disaster, as their homes and barns also catch fire and burn down. He is an incongruous figure who inspires hope in the poor, but also unleashes horror upon them. A hero who stands up to the terror of continually regenerating injustice, which—as primitive as it sounds—reflects the causes and effects of the murderous terrorism of the present.

Even the minor characters of this novel are portrayed as incongruous figures. Ali the Cripple, for instance, hates the landowner and shows that he is on the fleeing Memed's side through repeated acts of friendship. But because of Ali the Cripple's extraordinary talent in following trails, and moreover because he passionately follows every trail he stumbles upon, he is susceptible to treachery, and the police set him to follow Memed's trail. Iraz, who along with Memed's girlfriend is among the fugitives, tries to deny the danger: "He would give his life for you." But Memed knows the situation only too well: "I know, but if he sees a track, he can't help himself. I should have killed him on the very first day . . ."

The characters of the novel are pulled in one direction and then another, showing loyalty, but then suddenly and unexpectedly ready to commit acts of betrayal. They are dipped in hot and cold baths of love and hatred, tumbling from dizzying hope to abject despair. Encountering these characters, the reader experiences the heights and the abysses of the novel's events like deep fluctuations within himself. So the reader reaches out for the second novel of the Memed series, *Burn the Thistles,* and will greedily reach for the third, *The Land of Forty Eyes.* Yasar Kemal's novels will not let the reader go. The books take him captive. The reader is marooned in feverish marshes, surrounded by man-made reeds, pursued through stinging thistle fields, driven into pathless forests and mountains surrounded by mountains. Thrust into the most extreme situations, the reader experiences solitude, is exposed to conflicting feelings and with survival his only concern finally, finishing the last page, puts the book down, a changed person.

But Yasar Kemal does not take sides. His books do not set out to provoke. A socialist by experience, he knows that injustice is immense, and that it is always quick to take on clever new guises. Injustice seems ineradicable, because the very struggle against it unleashes lawlessness on the world. And yet, in his writing, Yasar Kemal argues against such fatalism. His heroes and anti-heroes are running on treadmills. Their almost tangible reality is ever touched by intellectual deliberation. It is legend or, to be more precise, the engendering of legend from within the narrative, that makes the characters bigger than life, immortal. Rumors, whisperings, hopes nourished by bits of sentences, foster this process. The constantly changing cast of voices form a coherent whole.

In Yasar Kemal's epic 1978 novel, *The Sea-Crossed Fisherman*, we see these two-sided, even many-sided, heroes even more clearly than in his early novel, *Memed, My Hawk*. The setting is no longer the Anatolian Chukurova and the Taurus mountains, but the chaos of metropolitan Istanbul.

Loners once again determine the plot's driving action. One of them, Selim the Fisherman, comes from a Caucasian-Circassian background, and laments the wholesale, profit-driven slaughter of the dolphins of the Sea of Marmara. For him this slaughter is the beginning of the end. The other character, Zeynel, is a Laz whose ancestors came from the Black Sea coast. The novel begins like a classic thriller, with Zeynel committing a murder, from which point on he is hounded by the police and his own fears, transporting the reader into the dark refuges of the city.

But right after the murder, and right after Selim the Fisherman has spat in Zeynel's face, all definite and realistic elements disappear, blurring the falling and ebbing whirl of voices in the coffee shop (the crime scene) and the firm outlines of the characters. This is a stylistic device that Yasar Kemal had already developed in *Memed, My Hawk*. There is a piling up of voices without commentary, a chatter intensifying over pages, fanning each linear event into flame: the massacre of the dolphins, the police chasing the fugitive murderer. This is a crescendo that works up to legend-engendering exaggerations and that starts rumors rolling, feeding them, destroying them, growing into a Greek chorus that inserts caesuras in the tragic action.

In one of the few places where there is a commentary on Zeynel the murderer, the text runs: "Zeynel had become the embodiment of all their sins. In their minds he was a mixture of all things: smuggler, saint, madman, gangster, good, bad, generous, cruel, courageous, timorous . . ."

Added to this, an army of journalists feed the newspapers with sensational accounts. They turn Zeynel, a scrawny, frightened, isolated fugitive who manages time and again instinctively to give the police the slip, into a wide-shouldered gang leader committing one evil after the other, unleashing panic on Istanbul. Even pictures of this legendary fiend circulate: a handsome man, whose image arouses fear mixed with admiration in everyone, including Zeynel himself.

The metropolis on the Bosporus and the sea before it is the scene where all the wild action takes place. The city center and the suburbs, fishing and smuggling quarters, cemeteries, mosques, harbors and markets all blend into one another. Yasar Kemal manages to conjure up a jumble of shuttling images that create a picture of the forecourt of hell—Istanbul, the center of horrors and at the same time a sanctuary of literature:

> And all around was the huge mirey swamp, the Golden Horn, nothing but a cesspit now, a garbage dump, full of carrion, dogs, cats, huge rats, gulls, horses, a stagnant sea with never a wave, its flow forgotten, bleakly reflecting the neon lamps, car lights, and the dull hazy sunlight, strewn with deadwood, and the sweepings of hundreds of kilos of vegetables, tomatoes, eggplants, oranges, leeks, melons, and watermelons from the vegetable market, torpid, its surface skimmed with years and years of acid-stinking burnt oils from the surrounding factories, reeking with a noisome nauseating odor like no odor in the world.

This quote can stand for many. Again and again, the city's skyline rises out of the haze and the harsh sunlight. The fugitive flees the center of town for the suburbs. In one place he finds shelter, in the next he is turned away. And the police are ever-present, whether as an invisible whistle-blowing pack, or as three policemen sitting in the coffee shop, the scene of the crime, awaiting the murderer's return. More distinctly than anywhere else in the novel, Yasar Kemal portrays them as representatives of a hostile power:

> They sat there, taking turns day and night, waiting for Zeynel. They were all three country lads and had been taken into the police force because, so they were informed, they were pureblooded, unalloyed sons of a noble race. Convinced of this privileged condition, they nursed a strong animosity towards all Circassians, Kurds, Lazzes, and more particularly Jews, Greeks and Armenians. They felt a particular hatred for Zeynel because he was a Laz. Just let them get their hands on

31

him, they'd skin him alive, that Laz, fill his mouth with bullets ... They never exchanged a word with the fishermen in the coffee house. Casting supercilious looks at them, they sat apart in a corner, talking in whispers about how one day they would kill all the socialists and purge the noble blood of the Turkish nation. They had the strength for that. In the police force alone they numbered twenty thousand, avenging eagles every one of them, of pure and noble race, sworn enemies of those Kurds, Lazzes, Circassians, Jews, and immigrants, especially the immigrants, and the Salonicans, those turncoat Jews ... Yes, it was those people of impure blood who were ruining his country. But the Great Leader would soon give the word, and then ... A very sound reckoning by their Great Leader and his Gray Wolves: three million people had to be killed, another five million banished, and thus Turkey would be redeemed. And then the true Turks would be brought over from Central Asia, in particular the descendants of our Kirghiz forebears.

In this quote racism, the genocide proclaimed at the policemen's table, speaks out. Nowhere else in *The Sea-Crossed Fisherman* does Yasar Kemal grant such freedom of speech to unbridled hatred. The talk may be of pureblooded Turks and inferior Kurds, Lazzes, Jews and Circassians, but the reader feels that the policemen's table in the coffee shop could well be seen as an international table; in other words, also a German-speaking table expressing itself without inhibition. But it is not only policemen who voice fascism so openly. Did not a leading German politician not long ago warn us of the "crossbreeding of the German *Volk*"? Is it not latent German xenophobia, packaged in bureaucratic jargon, that is speaking in the deportation agenda of our current minister of the interior, whose harshness is echoed by radical right-wing militia groups? Over four thousand refugees from Turkey, Algeria and Nigeria, who cannot be shown to have committed any crime, are under lock and key in German deportation camps. *Schueblinge*, "thrust-offs," is the neologism for them. The truth is, we are all passive witnesses of a recurring, but this time democratically sanctioned, barbarism.

Although in Yasar Kemal's books—in this presentation I can only cite a few as examples—racism as xenophobia is woven into an unremittingly verdant narrative. This xenophobia is still clearly recognizable as an expression of official government policy. This is why the powers that be find Yasar Kemal irksome. This is why, time and again, he has been dragged before the courts. This is why he had to suffer imprisonment and torture. This is why—and also to escape right-wing assassination—he sought asylum abroad for a few years. But he returned to Istanbul and, bedded in his language and its legends, he will continue to be an irksome presence for the government.

He is a writer who lives outside the literary ivory tower that we so readily conjure up here in Germany, someone who does not perceive himself apart from his society. This is why he is persecuted. This is why he has spent his whole life in opposition. Sentenced as a Marxist socialist, he early on had firsthand experience of Turkish prisons. Later he dubs them the "School of Turkish Literature." The poet Nazim Hikmet, sentenced as a Communist, could only leave prison for exile. The satirist Aziz Nesin, with his political commitment, was also a friend of Yasar Kemal's. These three names stand for the other Turkey, for a country in which all people live together with equal rights, for a country in which the quest for peace encompasses the desire for unbiased social equality. These three authors have brought Turkish literature to the world. Yasar Kemal has written book after book, unswayed by the current literary tendency in the West, and particularly in Germany, to polemicize against literature that exposes social realities. Countering the spirit and fashions of the times, he has written books such as *The Wind From the Plain, The Foundling, Iron Earth, Copper Sky* and *To Crush the Serpent,* thickening the web of his Anatolian saga, opening up to us the remotest regions of his country. Yasar Kemal has managed to do what stifling and compulsively fearful political policies, trying brutally to exclude forgiveness, have failed to do: in his writing Yasar Kemal shows reality within myth and the mythical interface of reality, taking readers across borders, opening up foreign terrain.

Let us return from this lengthy literary journey and express our thanks to Yasar Kemal, showing our readiness to overcome the constraints of a politics that excludes and discriminates, and let us dispel the propagandistic fear of living alongside our Turkish neighbors in Germany. Let us promote a politics that will finally grant German citizenship to the millions of Turks and Kurds who live here.

Wherever in Germany I have lived and written—for decades in Berlin, and more recently in Luebeck—Turks have been part of the scene. Turkish children have been and are the classmates of my children and grandchildren. And I have always felt that the daily contact of different ways of life can only be productive, for no culture can live off its own substance for long. In the seventeenth and eighteenth centuries large numbers of French refugees, Huguenots persecuted by the Catholic church and a despotic France, fled to Germany, mostly to Brandenburg. These immigrants visibly boosted the German economy, Germany trade and, not least, German literature. How incomplete the nineteenth century would have been, coming down to us without the novels of Theodor Fontane. Today one can say similar things about the enriching influence of the more than six million foreigners living in Germany, even though, unlike the Huguenots, who were granted civil rights by a special Edict of Tolerance, these foreigners are repressed by political currents that discriminate against them. The slogan "Foreigners Go Home!" is not merely smeared on walls.

And yet, perhaps the Freedom Prize that is being awarded today by the German Book Trade Association can act as an impetus, a powerful impetus, for change. That would be in accord with the position of Yasar Kemal, as his criticism has not been restricted to the inner conditions in his country. A few years ago, in an article published in the German magazine *Der Spiegel*, Yasar Kemal lamented the persecution of the Kurds in his country, at the same time reminding Western democracies of their share of responsibility. He wrote:

> On the threshold of the twenty-first century, no people, no ethnic group, can be denied human rights. No nation has the power. It was the people's power that ultimately chased the Americans out of Vietnam and the Russians out of Afghanistan, and brought about the miracle in South Africa. The Turkish Republic must not, by continuing this war, enter the twenty-first century as an accursed nation. The conscience of humanity will help the peoples of Turkey bring this inhuman war to an end. Above all, the people of those nations supplying the Turkish government with weapons must help. . . .

This appeal, ladies and gentlemen, is also, and for a particular reason, to be addressed to Germany. Those representatives of the Kohl-Kinkel government present here in the Paulskirche are well aware that for years the Federal Republic of Germany furnished weapons to the Turkish Republic, which is using them to wage a war of extermination against its own people. After 1990, when favorable circumstances opened the way for us to German reunification, even tanks and armored vehicles from the stockpiles of the former East German People's Army were sent to the warring government of Turkey. We were and are accomplices. We tolerated a business that was as quick as it was dirty. I am ashamed of my country, that has degenerated into a mere marketplace, whose government permits deadly trade and on top of that refuses persecuted Kurds political asylum.

A freedom prize is being presented. If this award honoring a celebrated writer is to have the right to give itself such a name, if the place of ceremony, the Paulskirche, is to be more than a mere backdrop, if the literature that I cherish so is still able to act as an impetus for change—then all of us who have gathered here today, authors, publishers, booksellers, everyone who feels any sense of political responsibility, is urged and called upon to respond to Yasar Kemal's appeal, to help sustain it and to make sure along with him that human rights will finally be respected in his country, that armed aggression will no longer rage and that freedom will descend upon even the remotest villages.

---

## SELECTED BOOKS BY YASAR KEMAL TRANSLATED INTO ENGLISH

*Memed, My Hawk.* New York: Pantheon, 1982; London: Harper-Collins, 1993. Translated by Edouard Roditi.

*Burn the Thistles.* New York: Morrow, 1977; London: Writers and Readers, 1982. Translated by Margaret E. Platon.

*The Sea-Crossed Fisherman.* New York: Braziller, 1985. Translated by Thilda Kemal.

*The Wind From the Plain.* New York: Dodd, Mead, 1969; London: Collins Harvill, 1989; London: Harvill, 1996. Translated by Thilda Kemal.

*The Foundling.* London: Harvill, 1997. Translated by Thilda Kemal.

*Iron Earth, Copper Sky.* London: Collins Harvill, 1989; New York: Morrow, 1997. Translated by Thilda Kemal.

*To Crush the Serpent.* London: Harvill, 1991. Translated by Thilda Kemal.

# Three Poems
## Jorie Graham

### from THE REFORMATION JOURNAL

The wisdom I have heretofore trusted was cowardice, the leaper.
*
I am not lying. There is no lying in me.
*
I surrender myself like the last rat on the sinking ship,

a burning wreck from which the depths will get theirs when the heights
have gotten theirs.
*
My throat is an open grave. I hide my face.
*
I have reduced all to lower case.

I have crossed out passages.

I have severely trimmed and cleared.
*
Locations are omitted.

Uncertain readings are inserted silently.

Abbreviations silently expanded.
*
A "he" referring to God may be capitalized
or not.
*
(is crying now)      show me
*
is crying now      (what's wrong)
*

in a strange tree     of atoms     of

\*

too few     *more*     no wonder

\*

Give me the glassy ripeness

\*

Give me the glassy ripeness in failure

\*

Give me the atom laying its question at the bottom of nature

\*

Send word          Clear fields

\*

Make formal event          Walk

\*

          **Turn back**

\*

Reduce all to lower case          Have reduced all

\*

Cross out passages          Have inserted silently

\*

is there a name for?

\*

glassy ripeness

\*

in failure

\*

born and raised

\*

and you?

\*

(go back)          (need more)

\*

having lived it          leaves it possible

\*

fear     lamentation     shame     ruin     believe me

\*

explain     given to

\*

explain     born of

*Jorie Graham*

                          *
Absence is odious                    to God
                     *
I'm asking
                     *
Unseen unseen             the treasure unperceived
                    *
Unless you compare        the treasure may be lost
                    *
Oh my beloved          I'm asking
                   *
More atoms, more days, the noise of the sparrows, of the universals
                 *
Yet colder here now than in
                *
the atom still there at the bottom of nature
               *
that we be founded on infinite smallness
              *
"which occasions incorruption or immortality"
             *
(incorruption because already as little as it can be)
            *
(escape square, wasted square, safety square, hopeless square)

"to all except anguish the mind soon adjusts"
           *
have reduced, have trimmed, have cleared, have omitted
          *
have      abbreviations          silently          expanded
         *
to what              avail
        *
explain      asks to be followed
explain      remains to be seen

## UNDERNEATH (8)

### 1.

\*

Exhale          (in years)

\*

The shadows     live

\*

Fleshless     lovers

\*

The tabernacle     of

\*

(fleshless lovers)

\*

(with no lifetimes     laid hard on them)

\*

As in they shall seek death

\*

and shall not find       it

\*

What if there is       no end?

\*

What if there is no

\*

        punishment.

\*

As in     *it is written.*

### 2.

While gods sleep     she says

Deposit     in me     my busyness, flesh.

Deposit     thirst     in me.

Deposit     tongue     poor rendez-vous.

And eyes     patient     their dry study.

*Jorie Graham*

Also  heavy rains  tearing the soil.

Also  my heart  multiplying terror.

And twelve weeks of summer.

And  an assignment  clear.

Deposit in me.

First shoots.

Unripen what  to ripen my assignment.

Make the sore  not heal  into meaning.

Make the shallow waters  not take seaward  the mind.

Let them wash it back continually onto the shore.

Let them slap it back down onto the edges of this world.

Onto the rocks. Into light unturned by wave. Still sands.

Deposit back on the stillest shore all messages tossed.

Do not take  back in  the soundtrack.

Let the cries stay where they were shouted out.

Let the horizon  lower its heavy  lid.

Agree  to be  seen.

Deposit  silt.

Dream of  existence.

Refuse  rescue.

Overhear  love.

3.

Where definition     first comes upon us          empire.

DUST (VOICE) WATER

1.

First star:
the fly trapped deep in the opened geode's chamber
thrumming and buzzing—

*

Since it won't get out again

*

how long will it last,

*

my listening into

*

the thousand facades—?

(And took (a rib)

*

And closed up the flesh thereof)

*

—(to all except anguish

*

the mind soon adjusts)—

*

And ay shall be endless

*

And nought is but I

*

And all shall be made even of nought

*

And also them that are nought

*

those made of my moan and my might

*

that marked them

41

and marks them

foremarked

foremarred—

(how long will it last?)

&ast;

&ast;

&ast;

&ast;

2.


And took.
And closed up the space thereof.

And made space    of might
And made them    foremarred

(There in me)        (I hear footsteps)

(Loaves fishes such sunlight and a road, very red, laid out)
            (Before us)

In the rearview all one would see was blossoms

Right on the glass the overfullness of blossoming

            (so don't look in)
            (no homeland)

Foremarred so the red road is laid out
awaiting footprints as the only acceptable blossoming

The land arid but still a force simplifying
our eyes that they might grow the only fruits:
            *amplification    emphasis*

Distance come this close to my chest and then no further
Yr distance come this close to my flesh and then (no) further.

3.

Then more distance.

Distance where the eye loses muscular stress but still pushes—

(with what?)—

As if distance's dust would leap on one and hold one fast—

(see how it falls away) (the only fruit) (remembering)—

As if distance could hold to one as its fatigue—

Beneath, the long canyons in which shadowplay briefly opens

the old green stories (*here* and *here*)—then the dusty red again
(of the road below) (how far we've come) (killed serpent)—

(called out holy name and the small-but-lengthening winds
carrying it away without lifting)

(all holy requests for explanation carried across the plains in
dust bursts)

(as if no soul could ever again be taken

into a body)—

4.

Then slow across it all the one river by degrees posed

Very broad     all stress     but still casual

Doing little to be, as death does so little to be

Threading and turning light into its belly, its broad green realism

*Jorie Graham*

On its surface paws shells horns hands scrolls scales

Toss or dance of twisting light again and *all the hereabouts*

Some purple just underneath then rope reversals

Especially near rocks    And cloud under cloud

And tree under tree    Like talking too freely

(and your face held up above your river-face)

(your eyes still leading back to thoughts
laid onto the roping dun-blue waters)

then pulling up out of the surface    your eyes:

air stirring in them    as if one doesn't waver

and how one can see the soul come and go at will

(all round bright shapelessness being paid out)

Then your whole glance    in true keeping
leading back nowhere now    strong unfailing flow

Clear green aqua blue black trembling shaping

the chain of backwardness    taking year in

swimming upcurrent

2.5 miles per hour so holding still

eyeing the land but only out of kindness    skyline your spine

the angel    mouthing    abundance

the mouth    opening    (nothing)

the angel    prying the eyes    by disappearance

manifest     unmanifest     present     present conditions

as the nail is pulled up out of the parted flesh

and a voice is heard within flesh          and that sound is light

and the flesh closes back over, smooth.

*

        I ask no other          thing

*

        Save yourself          only on the surface

# Rückenfigur
## *Susan* Howe

Iseult stands at Tintagel

on the mid stairs between

light and dark symbolism

Does she stand for phonic

human overtone for outlaw

love the dread pull lothly

for weariness actual brute

predestined fact for phobic

falling no one talking too

Tintagel ruin of philosophy

here is known change here

is come crude change wave

wave determinist caparison

Your soul your separation

But the counterfeit Iseult

Iseult aux Blanches Mains

stands by the wall to listen

Phobic thought of openness

a soul also has two faces

Iseult's mother and double

Iscult the Queen later in *T*

Even *Tros* echocs Tristan's

infirmity through spurious

etymology the Tintagel of *Fo*

not the dead city of night

Wall in the element of Logic

here is a door and beyond

here is the sail she spies

———————

Tristran Tristan Tristrant

Tristram Trystan Trystram

Tristrem Tristanz Drust

Drystan these names concoct

a little wreath of victory

47

dreaming over the landscape

Tintagel font icon twilight

Grove bough dark wind cove

brine testimony Iseult salt

Iseut Isolde Ysolt Essyllt

bride of March Marc Mark in

the old French commentaries

your secret correspondence

Soft Iseut two Iseults one

———————

The third of Tristan's overt

identities is a double one

his disguise as nightingale

in *Tros* then wild man in *Fo*

Level and beautiful La Blanche

Lande of disguise episodes

the nocturnal garden of *Tros*

*Fb* recalls the scene in Ovid

Orpheus grief stricken over

the loss of Eurydice sits by

the bank of a river seven days

I see Mark's shadow in water

Mark's moral right to Iseult

David's relationship to Saul

———————

Lean on handrail river below

Sense of depth focus motion

of chaos in Schlegel only as

visual progress into depth its

harsh curb estrangement logic

Realism still exists is part

of the realist dual hypothesis

Dual on verso as one who has

obeyed acceleration velocity

killing frost regencrative thaw

you other rowing forward face

backward Hesperides messenger

into the pastness of landscape

inarticulate scrawl awash air

———————

*Susan Howe*

Insufferably pale the icy

limit pulls and pulls no

kindness free against you

Deep quietness never to be

gathered no blind treat

Assuredly I see division

can never be weighed once

pale anguish breathes free

to be unhallowed empty what

in thought or other sign

roof and lintel remember

Searching shall I know is

some sense deepest moment

What is and what appears

———————

The way light is broken

To splinter color blue

the color of day yellow

near night the color of

passion red by morning

His name of grief being

red sound to sense sense

in place of the slaying

Tristram must be caught

Saw the mind otherwise

in thought or other sign

because we are not free

Saw the mind otherwise

Two thoughts in strife

————

Separation requires an

other quest for union

I use a white thread

half of the same paper

and in the sun's light

I place a lens so that

the sea reflects back

violet and blue making

rays easily more freely

your nativity and you

51

*Susan Howe*

of light from that of

memory when eyelids close

so in dream sensation

Mind's trajected light

———————

It is precision we have

to deal with we can pre-

scind space from color if

Thomas was only using a

metaphor and metaphysics

professes to be metaphor

There is a way back to the

misinterpretation of her

message TheseusTristan is

on the ship AegeusIseut

is a land watcher she is

a mastermind her frailty

turned to the light her

single vision twin soul half

———————

Dilemma of dead loyalty

Mark's speeches are sham

Gottfried shows Tristan

only hunting for pleasure

Emerald jacinth sapphire

chalcedony lovely Isolt

Topaz sardonyx chrysolite

ruby sir Tristan the Court

sees only the beauty of

their persons that they

appear to be represented

Isolt sings to your eyes

Surveillance is a constant

theme in lyric poetry

————

Le Page disgracié his attempt

to buy a linnet for his master

from a birdcatcher he hoped

to comfort him with bird song

but gamboled the money away

and in desperation bought a

wild-linnet that didn't sing

His first words occur in the

linnet episode the young master's

perplexity about the bird's

silence so just the linnet's

silence provokes Tristan's *je*

hero his shared identity the

remarkable bird list in *L'Orphée*

---

*L'Orphée*—a lanner falcon

takes pigeons a sparrow-

hawk sparrows a goshawk

partridge when Tristan was

young he would have watched

hawks being flown his own

little hunting falcon his

observation of the way in

which other birds refrain

from their characteristic

habit of "mobbing the owl"

Vignette of the bird-catcher

in the street that day the

linnet's mimic reputation

———————

Parasite and liar of genius

even emptiness is something

not nothingness of negation

having been born not born

wrapped in protective long

cloak power of the woodland

No burrowing deep for warmth

The eagle of Prometheus is a

vulture the vulture passions

go to a predator tricked up

forever unexpressed in half-

effaced ambiguous butterfly

disguises authentic regional

avifauna an arsenal of stories

———————

*Susan Howe*

Ysolt that for naught might

carry them as they coasting

past strange land past haven

ruin garland effigy figment

sensible nature blue silver

orange yellow different lake

effect of the death-rebirth

eternal rush-return fragment

I cannot separate in thought

You cannot be separate from

perception everything draws

toward autumn distant tumult

See that long row of folios

Surely Ysolt remembers Itylus

———————

Antigone bears her secret in

her heart like an arrow she is

sent twice over into the dark

social as if real life real

person proceeding into self-knowledge as if there were no

proof just blind right reason

to assuage our violent earth

Ysolt's single vision of union

Precursor shadow self by self

in open place or on an acting

platform two personae meeting

Strophe antistrophe which is

which dual unspeakable cohesion

———————

Day binds the wide Sound

Bitter sound as truth is

silent as silent tomorrow

Motif of retreating figure

arrayed beyond expression

huddled unintelligible air

Theomimesis divinity message

I have loved come veiling

Lyrist come veil come lure

echo remnant sentence spar

*Susan Howe*

  never never form wherefor

  Wait some recognition you

  Lyric over us love unclothe

  Never forever whoso move

# Thirteen Ecstasies of the Soul
## *Dale Peck*

*—for Gordon Armstrong*

### **| Declaration |**
#### ON LEAVING HOME

TELL YOUR MOTHER that you love her but make her no oath of loyalty. Let her clasp your hands between hers for only a moment and then pull free. Shake your father's hand firmly then, and then shake your brother's, and then bend down low to kiss your sister on the cheek. Hug your mother, and your sister, and your brother when he finally comes forward, and nod to your father, who stands with his hands behind his back. You know they expect words from you but don't give them away. Tell them goodbye. Tell them you look forward to seeing them again but don't say when. Tell them that today there are only starting points. The journey on which you embark has neither direction nor destination; the search which you will make has neither method nor object. If they persist in questioning you, step away from them. Scratch your head, and smile, and tell them that you are a man now.

### **| 1 |**
#### SLOTH

In the morning, when you awaken, the light that fills your room is that of a sun pushing through a sky thick with clouds. You hear the light sound of drizzle outside, and on the exposed skin of your shoulders and neck and head you feel damp cold air, and you pull the light blanket a little higher. For a moment, you tell yourself, for just a moment you'll stay in bed. In a moment you reset the alarm for an hour hence, and when that hour comes you push it back another hour. You half-sleep during those two hours: your body is rested, what it's doing now is languishing; you merely lie in bed. Your eyes are closed, your mind neither dreaming nor focusing on anything as definite as a thought. When the alarm rings again you shut it off. By now you've abandoned the day, and you turn the clock around, turn off the ringer on the bedside phone, turn your body over and feel, more than anything else, the pressure of your pierced right nipple on the mattress. But masturbation, you feel, would be wrong, a break in the pact you're making with laziness, and, slowly, you convince your body to relax. You're hungry, but when you realize you're not going to do anything which requires energy that hunger becomes less important, ignorable, eventually unnoticeable; in the same way, the pressure from your bladder recedes. The rainy day passes: sometimes you lie awake and sometimes you sleep; when you sleep you dream sometimes, and your dreams are deep and vivid but disappear each time you wake up. When you're awake you notice the gradations of light in the room, morning's gray, afternoon's silver, evening's almost brown shadows, and then, inevitably, it's black again. There's no strength anywhere in your body; the urge to stay in bed all day, whatever else it was, wasn't vampiric: you're tired, and ready to sleep the night away. You set the alarm for tomorrow, and in the few minutes before you fall into a sound sleep you have the only clear thought you've had all day, because your mind, too, your mind was lazy today. You have done nothing today, you think, absolutely nothing. But you haven't wasted this day; you have, instead, erased it. When tomorrow comes you will be no closer to death than you were yesterday.

## | 2 |
### HUNGER

That morning I put on last night's clothes out of deference to you, who had no choice, and so, reeking of cigarette smoke and smelling also of sweat and beer and poppers, we entered a hot bright morning in search of food. You wore jeans, I rememer, and an old tight T-shirt that had once been blue; your hair was more red than I'd realized, and the sunlight brought out the freckles in your skin. What was on your feet? At the restaurant we ordered coffee and water and orange juice. We ordered eggs and potatoes, and while we waited we ate the loaf of bread they'd left us, layering each slice with a thick film of butter. When our breakfast came we ordered more coffee and more juice; the waiter filled our water glasses, brought us more bread. We mashed the scrambled eggs and hash browns together and forked them in yellow lumps onto pieces of buttered bread. We laughed as we ate, I remember, but we didn't talk, and bits of food sprayed across the table; when our forks scraped across our empty plates we looked at each other, and then ordered more: more eggs, more potatoes—omelettes this time, and French fries—more coffee, more juice, more bread too, and a couple of those corn muffins we saw advertised on a blackboard. The waiter attempted a joke but something about the way we wielded our forks and knives stopped him. Perhaps he was just driven away by the farts leaking from both of us: by then, peristalsis had produced in me a tremendous urge to shit, and I knew it must have been much worse for you. The waiter brought the coffee and juice first, then the bread. We discovered a jar of strawberry jam, and ate a spoonful with each bite of bread. We dunked our muffins in our coffee and when they broke apart we fished out the yellow-brown dumplings with our spoons. We blackened our omelettes with pepper and drank drafts of water to cool our throats, we swirled fries into a spiral of mustard and ketchup, and as I finished my coffee I discovered an inch of slushy sugar at the bottom of the cup which I let dribble down my throat. The waiter approached warily. Will there be anything else, boys? We looked at each other and smiled. There were bread crumbs in your goatee, green herbs stuck in your teeth. I watched you press your finger into a piece of food which had spewed from one of our mouths, then bring your finger to your tongue. We hadn't spoken all morning except to order, and you left it up to me now. We'd gone far past the point of satiety, but each bite, each swallow, each burning burp had carried a hint of revelation, and all I could say was "More."

## 131
### SHIT

Who was the culprit? The man you sucked off in the bar's bathroom last Saturday, or the trick you met on the street in the middle of the week, the one who'd decorated his apartment in Catholic kitsch and kneeled in front of you like an altar boy? Perhaps it was the man who fucked you without a rubber beside the indoor swimming pool in his apartment building, the smell of chlorine in your nostrils, the cold tiles irritating your back, the guilt you felt almost but not quite overriding the pleasure of his unfettered cock moving inside you. It doesn't really matter: you're trapped now, on your toilet, your stomach swelling with gases like pseudocyesis and watery shit leaking from your ass, wishing you had followed your mother's advice and become a priest and waiting for the erythromycin to take effect. When the diarrhea is on hold your body relaxes and your mind wanders; you imagine amoebae moving inside of you by means of pseudopodia, as your encyclopedia told you, false feet, a protrusion of cytoplasm which is both a means of locomotion and of consumption. It feels like they're stampeding; what's left for them to eat? When the diarrhea starts again your intestines cramp visibly; there's Compazine for that but it's not working yet. You close your eyes against the burning pain in your guts and your ass; it's a cliché, but it feels like lava is moving through your body. After the umpteenth episode, when you have wiped yourself clean with wet toilet paper to soothe the rash on your buttocks and flushed the toilet, you open your eyes and realize as you look at the unfamiliar walls of your bathroom that when your eyes had been shut your mind had been shut as well. Not just shut, but shut off. You remember it as a blank moment of time; you remember now a succession of these blank moments, reaching back into the early hours of the morning when the diarrhea had first struck. They are like bricks, these blank spots, and together they form a wall through which you can't see, over which you can't climb, around which you can't walk or run. You feel trapped then, by that wall, by the undeniable feeling of wellness moving into your body, by the inadequacy of the grammar you possess to describe the wall and the wellness. You know that while you were building that wall you were able to see beyond it, but now you can't remember what you saw. As you wait in vain for the next bout of diarrhea you realize suddenly that the body doesn't always succumb to illness: sometimes it yearns for it. It embraces it with a protrusion of false limbs and pulls it inside itself, and in so doing takes you, if only for a little while, beyond the confines of this world, and into another.

| 4 |

SEX

You find yourself in a foreign country, in a bar. Atmospheric details claim your attention: blaring music and clouds of smoke and the funk of sweat and stale beer. Dim lights seem to be absorbed by dark wooden walls, and you must squint to read numbers on unfamiliar currency. Cold bottle in hand, you mount a few steps to a raised platform at the back of the bar where the men are waiting. They are familiar, as are their codes; it's only their words you don't understand. You communicate through their leather and your leather, through the dark blue handkerchief dangling from the right rear pocket of your jeans and the sanded white patches in the bulging crotches of theirs, through the medium of the bar itself, which has many functions but no other purpose than to facilitate this communication. Men stare at you and you at them, they note your details and you theirs. Some wear collars and some carry leashes, some—including some who, for aesthetic reasons, probably shouldn't—are bare-assed in chaps, and others wear protruding codpieces. There is no subtlety to this code and there isn't supposed to be; there are just a set of obvious correspondences to memorize, to offer up or respond to. Yellow means piss; brown, shit; black and blue, well, they mean black and blue; and more individual concerns—how dominant is dominant, how submissive, submissive— are communicated through the strength of a stare or the coyness of an averted glance, through bearing, through signals which, even if you spoke the language here, you would still pick up on. When do you notice the dark narrow descending stairway at the back of the bar? You're not sure. It's been in your peripheral vision for some time now, registered like a cataract by your eye but not your mind. Once you see it your eyes keep returning to it. Men go down; they don't seem to come back up; but you don't go down. You make yourself wait, drink another beer, and then another. You let yourself imagine, just a little, what might be going on below you, and you move closer so that you smell more clearly the sex smell, hear occasionally a slap or a groan. Finally you go down, one steep step at a time. Immediately it's darker: walls and pipes and other things register only as motionless shadows, and men as moving ones. They are stripped now of even the simple code you were able to observe upstairs. The first thing you realize is that this doesn't bother you, and the second thing you realize is that it's actually a continuation of what was happening above: here, in this bar, you and these men are losing individuality, becoming more and more alike, images which reflect each other in one sense and, in another, partially discrete pieces, like tentacles, of some larger whole which is represented most clearly by the bar but which is not, you feel, confined to the bar itself; and the third thing you realize is that someone is running his hand along the crack of your ass. For an instant you surrender and push into the hand, and listen to the sounds of other men, and watch their coupling shadows, but then you pull away and move deeper into the basement. You walk through the network of small rooms and narrow hallways, thinking as you go that with a little paint, better lighting, several well-placed area rugs—on second thought, better make that wall-to-wall—this could make a nice place to live. When you have made your way through all the rooms and all the men you find a place to stand, and stand there. The men who had been close to you move closer. You look into blank faces at expressions you can't make out and offer a smile to the man nearest you—a tall man, broad-shouldered, with long white arms and big hands encased in black gloves—but then you realize he probably can't see your smile, so you offer him your body instead. You press up against him and feel the hair on his chest and his soft flat stomach, and probe at the hidden message of his leather-coated crotch. You're prepared to back away if he indicates that he doesn't want you but he stands firm, and when you have fitted your body as tightly to his as you can he places one hand on your ass and the other on your head. He tips your head back and kisses you, surprising you with a short moustache and a long smoky tongue, and then he works his fingers as deeply into your ass as your jeans will let him. Then he stops and pulls his hands from your body. He holds one of them up and squints at what appears to be a piece of cloth. It's your handkerchief, you realize, and he realizes, and he runs it gently but firmly over your face, wiping away sweat and spittle, pausing several times when he passes it over your eyes until you realize what he wants and press into the cloth. Why didn't he simply ask you? It's not just because you don't hear anyone talking. This man, you realize, won't ask you what you like, or tell you what to do, or name you in his language Friday, or Tonto, or Toby. He won't use words: he will only use you, as you want to be used. Then he blindfolds you. He presses you against his body as you had pressed against it. With your eyes covered it's a new beginning: he's completely in charge. He kisses you again, grabs your ass again. He moves your limbs around as though you were a puppet, pushing your head as far back on your neck as it will go, pulling your hands above your head to remove your shirt, kicking your legs wide and grabbing your crotch. You let yourself be pushed and pulled and kicked; you notice less what happens to your body than what his hands do to it. As long as he's touching you, you are centered, you are safe, you are home. It's only when he doesn't touch you that you feel naked, or alone, or silly, and not even the panting of his breath a few inches away reassures you. But he rarely lets go; the need you have to be touched by him is matched by a need in him to touch you. How long does this go on? You don't know, you can't know, and besides, it's the last thing on your mind—though it would suck if the bar closed before you finished. At some point you start to think he's grown extra hands but you realize that he's sharing you with other men. Your sense of abandonment increases then. Before, you could have said you chose this man, but these other men touching you, using you, having sex with you, these men you didn't choose, nor they you; you have been given to them like a toy. There are hands everywhere now. You are being caressed, fondled, slapped, pinched, prodded, you are being pushed to your knees, things are put in your mouth, hands move your face from crotch to crotch, your mouth on one man, your hands on two others, you are moved from one man to another and then another and you lose the man you had been with and then finally you lose yourself. You are a drill boring into the earth. You are a top spun round and round. You are an umbrella twirling off the drops which fall on it. You are a helicopter whirling up into the sky. You are the world, turning on its axis. You are making so many people happy, but what are you? You know that some people decry this kind of sex for its lack of intimate connection, but how much more connected could you be? You feel lifted and weighted by your attachment with the men touching you. If you knew one more thing about them, if you were to learn even their names, you feel you would explode with excess information. But you remain in a perfect suspended state of contained motion, and it's only in these pure moments that truth comes wandering in like a hungry dog. As you feed in the midst of your frenzied pack you understand suddenly what the point of this sex is. The point of sex isn't orgasm; what you're doing now is the point of sex. The point of sex isn't merely self-obliteration, it's the obliteration of the murdering world by a self made temporarily all-powerful and all-consuming. But only temporarily. Soon, inevitably, your motion ceases. As you come to rest and come back to yourself you hear men speaking around you, above you; have they been talking the whole time? You consider speaking. You're in Amsterdam, after all, where half the residents speak English better than you do.

*Dale Peck*

But you don't. Dizzy, you kneel on the floor, silent. Then a familiar pair of leather hands touch you, press your cheek against a familiar soft flat stomach. You wonder, who really hides behind the blindfold? A sticky semihard cock lies against your neck. In a moment he stands you up. He kisses you, in farewell you think, but then you feel his hand unbuckling your belt, unbuttoning your pants, unleashing you. Only then are you stunned by what goes on in this world. Who are you, you think, whoever you are holding me now in hand? What are you? But you know. He is the only man you have had sex with tonight. He is the only man you have ever had sex with, and he is every man you have ever had sex with before. He is everyone in the world but Daniel. He is someone and something you have found once and in a moment will lose forever. But for right now, he is your soul.

## I 5 I
### LOVE

#### SPRING

The days pass one by one. On top of the mountain the sky is always clear and the wind always humid. Each evening at sunset, when the heat breaks, he becomes your sun. He pulls you into orbit around him; the heat is from his body, the light from his eyes. You try to take all of him but he's too much for one man to handle. His surplus flows from you in fluids, in breath, in words, and it's inevitable that in their rovings his hands, his eyes, his mouth shall retrieve the parts of him that you slough off. This is the cycle: day into night into day, him into you into him. But the light and the darkness remain discrete and distinct, while you and he blend together, become inseparable, indistinguishable, like lichen. It's pointless to say that if you remove one the other will die: there is no one, there is no other. This is not the general product of love; this is the product of your love, of your ecstasy. Some people give birth to babies. You give birth to each other.

#### SUMMER

Germination was a tender touching process, soon over: seeds split like broken zippers, shoots push into darkness, trusting that this way lies the sun. Growth seems a funny purposeless thing until suddenly the closed petals of lust burst open, revealing the naked

66

desire of need and want, of love. In your thirst you drink the poisoned blood of the one you have named lover. In your hunger you lick the shit from his ass and the pus from his sores and the fungus that grows in his eyes and mouth and feet and fingers. His drool is your faucet, his piss your shower, his cum marks the end of your days. You take the pain of his every illness and injury inside you; a thousand times you take the seed of death from him and let it bloom within your body. In the end the strength of the need of your love exhausts him, chokes him as the vine chokes the tree. He withers within your grasp, and together you crumple to the ground.

FALL

He will call you when the crows fly thick through the night. You will go out and walk under cover of darkness and falling feathers and caw-caw-cawing for carrion. There will be neither light to see nor air to breathe nor room in the thick atmosphere to push out words, and the only thing you can trust is his hand in yours. Its bones are thin, frail, light, the bones of a bird, and they pull you on and on, past your town, past the farms that surround your town, into the empty uncultivated fields that lie beyond the farms. In long cold dry grass he will lay you down, and his hands fluttering across the expanse of your skin are a bellows, blowing away your clothes, igniting the coals that, for him, are always smoldering in your body. He has given birth to you once again, and now you reach for him and attempt to mirror his passion: he kisses you and you open your mouth, he ties your arms to the ground with grass and you don't pull against the weak roots, he lifts your legs and aims his cock at your asshole. The muscles in your ass shiver and try to pull him inside of you but before he lets you have him he plays a language game. "An exaltation of larks," he spits into your ear, "an ostentation of peacocks, a pride of lions." He lifts his head then, and you see that he is looking at the dark shapes flying overhead. "A murder of crows!" you scream, and he fucks you then, and morning never comes. And if that isn't love it will have to do, until the real thing comes along.

WINTER

You lost him one night in a tangle of sheets. He disappeared into a drift of snow and he was consumed by a pile of paper. When the white had finally finished its task you found yourself with only frozen toes and a damp hollow in your bed. Yesterday's news is your only information now. Cheap sentiments fill your mind, and false memories in which your life together is reduced to a discount vacation package of pastoral picnics, Caribbean cruises and sweet lustless sex. Outside your window the world is frozen solid; the only movements are signs of further decay. Tree limbs snap in the wind, squirrels eat their frostbitten toes in a vain effort to stay alive. This stillness is your only consolation, for you tell yourself that as long as the world remains motionless then you will move no farther from him than you already are. Cold comfort, this, for when he left you his leaving was absolute. Eventually you leave your bed, your bedroom, your home: you cover the white skin that covers your body with clothing and walk into the fields west of your house. They are bare now, covered with frosty soil so hard that it chips under your feet like shale. But these fields aren't fallow. Last fall you watched the farmer plant his wheat, and during the warm afternoons you could almost see it grow. When the frost came it died, but you know that all it awaits is the spring thaw, when it will burst from the ground. In the middle of all this you stand. You watch the slow minuet of objects and shadows. Your own shadow curls around your body like a vine as the moon moves through the sky. I watch you from the other side of the window. If you ever come back I will tell you what I can see from here, which perhaps you cannot. For your lover, Gordon, *you* are the frozen earth. The facade of death is only temporary, and I promise you that one day you will both be born again.

## | 6 |
### PAIN

I believe that the soul exists, but not all the time. It has to be whipped into shape, like a slave, like a political party, like an egg cream. But this calling forth of the soul is fraught, for what is whipped is not the soul but the self. The soul will only come forward when the self is effaced, and afterward, when it has departed, it is the body which must bear the pain of the beating. And so in your search you find yourself on my bed. I close your eyes and I seal your mouth, I fill your ears and I stuff your nose with amyl, and I hide your face from you and from me. On the bed you are a naked body and on the bed you are a body without a head. You are a stranger on my bed, your face and all it signifies hidden from me and your body and all it signifies hidden from you. From now on you can only feel; from now on I can only act. Only I can act and I can only act on the shackled pink X that is your body; the black egg that your head has become retains its mysteries, and inside that egg you are trapped. The distant slapping and lashing and beating and punching are powerless blows against a shell which won't crack, and the pain that you feel, but can't see or hear, or cry out against, or know, or describe, is different than any pain you have ever felt before. Because your external senses have been made useless it moves inside of you, inside your body and then, inevitably, inside your mind, and soon it comes to feel like a part of you. That part of you is a wind, a tornado which lifts you from where you are—my bed, and this world, and your life—and sets you down somewhere else. Later you will be able to say nothing about this place save that whatever is there can't be experienced through the senses and that whatever is there can only be experienced when the senses are absent, but while you are there you don't even know you are there. Only I know that. When you come back all you know is that you aren't there anymore, and that you hurt. Distant points of violation identify themselves, and the pain you feel in each place is distinct from the pain in each of the other places. For a moment you slip inside each of these pains and for each of these moments you rise a few inches above the bed and are back where you had been. But then you fall, and fall again, and again and again you fall, until finally a knowledge that is more a yearning than an idea makes you still: you realize that it's only in the moments after it leaves you that you know the soul in terms you can understand, in words, and in remembered sensations. That's all. That is all there is, and you know then that you can only lie there bound to the bed at your wrists and ankles but bound to the world by ties that are even more constraining, and you lie there, and you watch your soul retreat from you, and it retreats from you like the loss of your mother's body.

## | 7 |
### ADDICTION

Neither the flame shall singe your fingers nor the smoke cloud your lungs. Nor the flame burn your lips, nor the smoke blacken your breath. Nor the flame melt your skin, nor the smoke rot your body.

*Dale Peck*

Nor the flame consume the world, nor the smoke wave its banner to the dead. Nor singe, nor burn, nor melt, nor consume; nor cloud, nor blacken, nor rot, nor wave. The only sign, this: the yellow tips of two of your fingers, the mark of habit, of compulsion, of identity, of Cain. Here is your point of departure, here your journey's end. Here is your portable home and here the continuous you. No matter where you are you can look at these yellow tips and locate yourself. Touch them to your lips and you will remember everything you have ever done. Touch them to mine and for that instant I will know you completely.

## | 8 |
### FEAR

Then from the horizon black like the wall of a distant cliff comes the wind, washing waves over the bow of the boat and knocking the fire from its place, and then the fire begins to devour the flesh of the boat. Then the men fight the fanned flames with buckets of water and the soil of potted plants and the breath of their lungs and then, suddenly, somehow, the fire is gone. Then for a moment the burned boat rides in the lee of a valley between two high mountains of water, and then the mountains clap together like a pair of hands and the boat is broken apart like matchsticks. Then the men cling to the splinters of their lives and fear a grave in the dark soil far below them and forget forever their voyage of discovery, and they call out in voices drowned by the wind, "We are doomed." And only then does one voice shine forth like a beacon, and in unwavering tones declare, "You are saved."

## | 9 |
### GRIEF

*COMING AND GOING BLUES*
*FOR DANIEL GEORGE MARKS, 1957–1988*

I been blue all day
I been blue all day
I been thinking 'bout my man
He done come and gone away

70

He wasn't here too long
He wasn't here too long
When he was here he was my life
Now he's gone he is my song

He done took up sick
Sick done took up him
Sickness fell down like a storm
Weatherman said It sure looks grim

I watched it take up hold
I watched it take up hold
Wheezing like a tire hit a nail
His skin was hot but now it's cold

Marks showed up on his face
Marks showed up on his face
They showed a map of hurt and pain
I hope he's in a painless place

At the end I took his hand
At the end I took his hand
I said If you wanna leave
Then you know I'll understand

I remember our first kiss
Yes, I remember that first kiss
Words fail me to describe it
But that kiss I'm gonna miss

That man was like a castle
And he given me the key
I lived inside his walls
Now he lives inside of me

I'm a-coming home
I'm a-coming home
I'm a-coming home
I'm a-going home

> I been blue all day
> I been blue all day
> Love is gone away, boys
> Come and dig my grave

## | 10 |
### DEATH

The hands are the body's conjunctions: they can bring together any-thing they can grasp, hold, pick up, carry, move, anything they can touch. Look at your hands now, the unmarked left one and the right with its two nicotine-stained fingers. Those hands have touched pens and penises, and food and forks and knives and spoons to eat that food, they have touched your naked body and the clothes that have covered it, and they have touched the hands of living and dying and dead men. They have dug into soft earth and run bunches of freshly mown grass over your skin, tugged daffodils from the ground and pulled your body up the rough trunks of oak trees. They have grasped doorknobs and turned them, and turned back blan-kets, and turned on taps to release jets of hot and cold water, and they have touched that water. They have run through the grooves in an elephant's skin and untangled the matted mane of a horse and pulled back from the sting of a honeybee. They have held books and tickets and clocks and maps and money and guitars and iron bars, and they have held nothing except air. Oh, how can you stand it, how can you bear to think of all your hands have touched, how can you continue to reach out for more? But your soul grows lonely, trapped within its bodily prison, and so there is always that reach for more, for excess, for the fifth cup of coffee, the body in the dark-ness, the bullet, to slip into the chamber. Dear Gordon, your soul is like the soul of anyone: it reaches out for both good and evil. It is neither good nor evil in itself, for like any creature with two hands you can reach out with your left and touch one thing and reach out with your right and touch another, and your soul reconciles these opposites through the medium of your body. But the search of the soul is really the search *for* the soul, and the search for the soul is, finally, the search for death. One day—one day you will reach out too far to the left and you will reach out too far to the right. You will reach out so far that you will be unable to draw your hands back in, and so you will continue to reach farther and farther out, and you will continue reaching out until your body splits open and what is inside is released and shines forth, like a star.

## | 11 |
### ART

What is left is the word: everything else died or departed long ago. What is left is the imagination. If I had to formulate a theory of language then I would say that because our grammar allows us to link any one word with any other—the words "life" and "death," for example, can be joined by a single conjunction—then no word can quite escape all those other meanings. It's not just that nothing is simply one thing, it's that one thing can be, must be everything, and this multiplicity of meanings is, I believe, the writer's only consolation. How else could we live with what little we manage to get on paper? I choose to locate my quest for the soul in you because there is no way something as imprecise as this language can ever arrive at the absolute nature of love, of pain, of hunger, of the soul. There can only be my love, my pain, my hunger, my soul; there can only be your love, your pain, your hunger, your soul; and it is my hope that somewhere in the conjunction between you and me I will arrive at something that is more than either of us. We have, as they say, poured our soul into every word we've written. We've tried with each of those words to communicate a complete vision of the world. We know that art, like activist politics, seeks to make itself unnecessary: embedded somewhere in every poem, every story, every play is a utopian vision that, if achieved, would make the words irrelevant, redundant, unnecessary. You have your vision, I have mine, and I suspect that these visions are closer than we realize; and now I will reveal something about myself to you: I don't know what good it does to write about someone after they die, but I'm not above thinking that if I write about someone before they die then they will keep on living. I don't mean that metaphorically, and I don't mean just you. "The epidemic is the revelatory aspect of our time," you wrote in a letter when you were alive, but what it reveals to me and what it revealed to you are not, I think, the same things. Faced with that, all I can offer is a variation on childhood's dare: I'll show you what it's shown me, if you'll show me what it's shown you.

73

## | 12 |
### SMELL

In your bathroom there is a sink, a white oval, the shape of a halved hollowed eggshell, a porcelain bowl that rests upon a porcelain pedestal. Hidden within this pedestal is the pipe that carries away your sink's refuse, which is your refuse: your whiskers and sloughed-off skin cells, hairs that have broken from your head, blood that has leaked from gums or nose or fingers. It is a feature, this sink on its pedestal—so says your landlord—but, in fact, because of the pedestal's narrow width, the pipe within it lacks what plumbers call a trap, that double curve of pipe shaped like an S too lazy to stand upright. The trap is meant to hold water in its valley and so block sewer gases from rising into your bathroom. But your sink lacks this trap: the water from your tap rushes straight back into the earth like rain falling on a windless day, and often, on hot days especially, a fetid smell rises into your house, a thinly but evenly spread stench that takes over your life like the sound of an argument in the house next door. Light a match, your landlord said when you complained, and left it at that. Now, years later, it has become your companion, this stink, something to talk to when you're alone the way other people talk to a pet or to the walls. Oh, it's you again, you say, and you wave a hand, a greeting and a clearing of the air—and, so, a farewell as well. Sometimes, when you awaken in the middle of the night for a pee and there is no smell in your bathroom, you put your face right into the shell of the sink and sniff deeply, pulling into your lungs a past that is deeper than memory. Once, after doing this, you stand up and catch sight of yourself in the mirror. Your face spooks you for some reason, and you grab nervously at the book of matches left in a concavity of the sink meant for a bar of soap. You take a match, light it, you hold it to the mouth of the drain. It sputters there, a brief consolation, and then, as if tweaked by fingers, it goes out. Your sleep-glazed eyes stare at a rising ribbon of smoke which seems to offer both rebuke and absolution, and then a second breath, yours or the pipe's, disperses even that illusion, and you are left with nothing but your sink.

## | 13 |
### DREAMS

Just before I fell asleep I heard water dripping out of the drainpipe in the back garden. Robbie was sleeping beside me; his hand was on my stomach and their steady rise and fall seemed a conjunctive effort. We had just had sex; I was thinking about death. (I am moving away from you, Gordon, I know, I am moving back into myself. This is what I meant when I talked about the conjunction of you and me: I am offering a piece of myself to you now, in the hope that you can pick it up and so give us both meaning.) The water dripped slowly: the rain had stopped hours ago and what I heard was just the last coalescing drops falling the few inches from the bottom of the pipe to the concrete sidewalk, a slow and surprisingly regular rhythm made more of silence than of splashing. I wondered, then, where the water went, and I thought I remembered the rusted bars of an iron grate, the darkness of a hole visible, or invisible, between its slats. So the water drains from a smaller pipe into a larger, I thought, drop by drop, and then goes where? The canal, I thought, no more than a quarter mile away across Mile End Park, and as I slid closer to sleep my breathing fell in with Robbie's and my mind fell in with the water, and together—me, the water and Robbie— squeezed and shimmied our way down that long narrow tunnel until we spilled out into the canal. And the canal carried us to the Thames, and the Thames carried us to the Channel, and the Channel was like the clasped fingers of the Atlantic, holding us in its embrace. I was almost asleep by then, and I thought, children leave their parents this way, and lovers leave each other, and the soul will leave the body like this, like a drop of water making its way back to the ocean, slowly joining and rejoining and joining yet again, until what was whole once becomes, once again, whole.

## | Epilogue |
### ALMOST CLOSED

We heated our house in Kansas with a wood-burning stove, and each night the last person still awake had to stoke the fire so it would last the night. This was a task with which I was finally, occasionally, entrusted in my late teens; it was a clumsy, potentially noisy operation that had to be achieved with some attempt at silence since everyone else was asleep, and I can still feel the weight of the cast-iron shovel in my hands as I tried to skim ash from the stones that covered the stove's bottom without dragging the shovel over their rough surface. The ash had to be removed, the coals consolidated, a few fat logs maneuvered through the stove's narrow door and laid gently atop the coals. I would close the door then, and lean heavily against it so that the metal of its handle wouldn't squeak against the metal of the hasp as I fastened it. Finally, I would adjust the air vent to almost closed, so that just enough oxygen would enter the stove's interior to keep the flame alive, and then I would go to sleep. Even these precautions weren't enough, and the only way to ensure that the fire would still be going come morning was by checking it during the night. This was the only thing left to chance: no one set their alarms for three A.M. or anything, we just hoped someone would wake up. Usually I did. I would lie in the dark for a moment, my body cocooned in blankets, my face exposed and cold; then I would rush to the bathroom and pee; then I would go to the stove and open it quickly, quietly, only a crack. There was something rhapsodic in the moment, something that demanded pause. I stared into the fire, shivering. I looked at the orange embers, tiny, fiercely hot and yet restrained, and only slowly consuming the logs laid on top of them. Air entered the stove and the coals flickered, glowed more brightly; within moments a few flames would have appeared but by then I'd have determined if the fire was okay or if another log was needed, and one way or another the moment passed. The stove and its small warmth were soon resealed, and I returned to my still-warm bed and fell asleep listening to the crackling fire settle into its own version of slumber. In the frigid morning, the stove's vent could be opened wide: in their steel shell the coals would pulse and spit sparks until, with almost concussive suddenness, the logs would burst into flame and heat blaze into the house.

This is one way to live.

# *From* In America
## *Susan Sontag*

In May 1876, when Maryna Zalewska was still thirty-five and at the pinnacle of her glory, she cancelled the remaining engagements of her season at the Imperial Theatre in Warsaw—and her guest engagements at the Polski Theatre in Cracow, the Wielki Theatre in Poznań, the Count Skarbek Theatre in Lwów—and fled seventy miles south of Cracow, her birthplace, to the mountain village of Zakopane, where she usually spent a month in the late summer. With her went her husband, Bogdan Dembowski; her seven-year-old son, Piotr; her widowed sister, Józefina; the painter Jakub Goldberg; the *jeune premier* Tadeusz Bulanda; and the schoolmaster Julian Solski and his wife, Wanda. So displeasing was this news to her public that one Warsaw newspaper exacted revenge by announcing that she was taking an early retirement, which the Imperial Theatre (to which she was under life contract) promptly denied. Two unkind critics suggested that the moment had come to acknowledge that Poland's most celebrated actress was a little past her prime. Admirers, particularly her ardent following among university students, worried that she'd fallen seriously ill. The year before, Maryna had had a bout of typhoid fever and, although bedridden for just two weeks, did not play again for three months. It was rumored that the fever was so high she had lost all her hair. She had lost all her hair. And it had all grown back.

Then what was it this time, friends not in the know wondered. Frail lungs were endemic in Maryna's large family. Tuberculosis had taken her father at forty, and later claimed two sisters and a brother; and now her favorite brother, also an actor, was mortally ill. Stefan's doctor in Cracow, her friend Henryk Tyszyński, had hoped to send him with them to inhale the pure mountain air, but he was too frail to support the arduous trip, two days of lurching along narrow rutted roads in a peasant's wagon. And could Maryna herself be—? Was it now her turn to come down with—? "But no," she said, frowning. "My lungs are sound. Actually I'm as healthy as a bear."

Which was true . . . and Maryna, long inclined to recast her discontents into an ideal of health, had dedicated herself to becoming healthier still. Warsaw, any populous city, was unhealthy. The life of an actor was unhealthy; exhausting; rife with demeaning anxieties. More and more, instead of assuming that whatever time she could free for travel should be spent educating herself in the theatres and museums of a great capital, Vienna or even Paris, or practicing the ways of the world in a resort like Baden-Baden or Carlsbad, Maryna, her intimates in tow, was choosing the purifying simplicities of rustic life as lived by the privileged. The allure of Zakopane, among many other candidate villages, was its particularly ravishing setting among the majestic peaks of the Tatras, Poland's southern boundary and only altitudes, and the dense customs and savory dialect of its swarthy native people, who seemed as exotic to these city folk as American Indians. They'd watched tall lithe highlander men dancing at a midsummer festivity with a tamed brown bear in chains. They'd made friends with the village bard—yes, Zakopane still had a bard, charged with the melodious misremembering of the lethal feuds and unhappy love stories of the past. In the five years that Maryna and Bogdan had been part-summering there, they'd revelled in their increasing attachment to the village and its dignified, uncouth inhabitants, and had spoken of one day retreating there for good with a band of friends to devote themselves to the arts and to healthy living. On the clean slate of this isolated, politely savage Zakopane they would inscribe their own vision of an ideal community.

Part of its appeal was the difficulty of getting there. Winter made the roads impassible for months on end, and even when, starting in May, the trip became feasible, a vehicle from the village was the only transport. This vehicle was not the familiar, homely farmer's wagon of the more nearby countryside but a long wooden affair topped with a canvas stretched over a bowed hazel frame like a gypsy wagon—no, just like those in engravings and oleographs of the American West. A few such wagons were to be intercepted in Cracow, at the main food market, where there were always some highlanders on a weekly run from Zakopane to the city; once voided of their load of mutton carcasses and sheepskin jackets and intricately incised logs of smoked sheep's cheese, they would be returning to the village empty.

Merely to set out was already an adventure. Leaving the dawn light to pile into the wagon's dark pungent interior, with the driver gallantly pressing his sheepskin coat on Madame Maryna for a pillow, they huddled among their soft bags, chattering and grimacing with delight as the highlander screwed his broad-brimmed hat down on his head and urged his two Percherons forward, out of the city and down the plain south of Cracow. Peace to their bones! A quaint wayside cross or shrine or, better, one of the small Marian chapels at the crossroad, would provide an excuse to clamber out and stretch their legs while the driver genuflected and muttered some prayers. Then the wagon started up the Beskid hills, and the horses' pace dropped to a slow walk. With time out for a hasty picnic of food they had brought from Cracow, they would reach the hamlet at the top by late afternoon and, as negotiated by their driver, be fed by their peasant hosts and deeply asleep, the women in huts and the men in barns, before dark. It was dark, three in the morning, when they were pulling themselves up into the creaking wagon for the second half of the journey, which—after the long bone-jarring stretch downhill, mostly at a trot—had a much-awaited halt a little before midday at the only town on the route, Nowy Targ, where they could wash and eat a hearty meal and drink the Jewish tavernkeeper's execrable wine. Sated, and soon to be hungry again, they regained the wagon, which continued along meadows lush with grass and herbs and bordered by a lively stream. Beyond, ahead, rising into a bluer and bluer sky, was the limestone and granite Tatras wall, crowned by Mount Giewont. They were munching on some dried cheese and smoked ham purchased in Nowy Targ as the valley narrowed and the wagon began its last uneven ascent. As the hills closed in and the winding climb began in earnest, the horses went even slower, and for the steepest part it was necessary that some of the party descend to lighten the wagon's load; otherwise they would not arrive until after nightfall. Those who chose to walk behind the wagon for a spell, Maryna was always one of them, were invariably rewarded by a glimpse, through the stands of pine trees and black firs, of a bear or a wolf or a stag, or an agreeably equalizing roadside exchange of greetings ("Blessed be the name of Jesus!" "Through all ages, amen!") with a shepherd from the village, wearing a long white cloak and the distinctive male headgear, a black felt hat with an eagle feather stuck in it, which he doffed at the welcome sight of the quality folk from the big city. It would be another three hours before they reached the upper valley, some twenty-eight hundred feet high, where the village nested, and the weary horses, longing for home and a horse's oblivion, picked up speed. With luck it would be just sunset when they came clattering into the village to take up their borrowed peasant life.

For some weeks, as long as a month, they commandeered a low

square hut with four rooms, two of which could be used as sleeping chambers: the women and Piotr slept in one room, the men in the other. Like every dwelling in Zakopane, this hut was an ingenious sculpture of spruce logs (the region abounded in spruce forests) with the joints dovetailed at the end, while its few heavy chairs, tables and slatted beds were carpentered from the more expensive, pinkish larch. Within minutes of their arrival they had flung open the dull-paned windows to air out the garlic reek, distributed in cupboards and on wall pegs their minimum of possessions—bringing so little was also part of the adventure—and were ready to start enjoying their unencumbered freedom. In principle, country life for city people is a delicious blank, time sponged clean of work and the usual habits and obligations. Were they not on holiday? Of course. Did this give them more time to themselves? No. The engrossing, compulsory routines of city people in the country managed to fill the whole day. Eating. Exercise. Talking. Reading. Playing games. And of course housekeeping, for another part of the adventure was dispensing with servants. The men swept and chopped wood and collected the water for bathing and laundry. Washing, beating the wash and hanging it out to dry was the women's task. "Our phalanstery," Maryna would say, evoking the name of the principal building in an ideal community as envisaged by the great Fourier. Only the cooking was left to the hut's owner, Mrs. Bachleda, an elderly widow who moved in with her sister's family during their lucrative stay. The day was organized around her ample meals. Over breakfast, sour milk and black bread, they would apportion tasks and plan excursions. In the late morning, the whole party would set out for a collective walk in the valley, taking a picnic of black bread and ewe's cheese and raw garlic and cranberries. Evenings, after a supper of sauerkraut soup, mutton and boiled potatoes, were for reading aloud. Shakespeare. What could be healthier than that?

Being people of active conscience, Maryna and Bogdan could not have accepted being mere summerfolk, and had made a tacit contract of benevolence with the village that went far beyond the infusion of cash their annual presence brought into its near-subsistence economy. Maryna and her friends were hardly unaware that, healthy as Zakopane was for them, the health of the two thousand villagers left a great deal to be desired. Luckily, one of the friends who had followed Maryna to Zakopane was the faithful Henryk. Soon he was spending more time there than she, confiding his practice in Cracow to a colleague for a full three months each year and treating everyone without charge. At first the villagers were suspicious, seeing no impediment in a mouthful of rotten teeth or throat goiters or rickets and nothing unnatural in the death of infants or the sickening of anyone over thirty-five. His little speech about the principles of sanitation was city gibberish to their ears—until they saw how many lives were saved by his ministrations (and the food he brought from Cracow) the second summer he was there, in 1873, when cholera struck. And he alone among Maryna and her friends understood most of what the Tatras highlanders were actually saying, even when they spoke rapidly, their dialect being as different from standard Polish as the dialect of the Scottish Highlands is from standard English, with scores of words for common things that exist nowhere else. His tutor was a grateful patient, one of the village priests.

The villagers' part of the contract (to which they had not consciously assented) was: not to change. Their cosmopolitan visitors thought they could help in this. Bogdan had the idea of starting a folkloric society, and Ryszard of learning the dialect in order to transcribe the fairy tales and hunting stories of the village bard. Henryk was planning a scientific museum which would display for the villagers' education the glories of the Alpine mass looming above them, such as the astonishing variety of mosses he had amassed on his rocky climbs. Maryna was for starting a lacemaking school for young village girls, which would aid the village's faltering economy and help preserve an endangered local craft. Last summer she had taken lessons from a one-eyed crone reputed to be Zakopane's champion lacemaker and, to the titters of the village women, tried her hand at wood carving.

Difficulty of access had up to now protected the village, its archaic customs and uniformity of behavior and rich traditions of oral recitation. There were still only a few kinds of faces, as there were only a few family names. The village still had one muddy street, one wooden church, one cemetery. A real community! But Maryna and her friends were not the only outsiders. There were not yet any chalets (imitating, floridly, the wooden plainness of the highlander huts) or tuberculosis sanatoria (it would be a decade more before Zakopane achieved the official status of a health resort), and a railroad link to Cracow (guaranteeing year-round access to the village) would not be built for another thirteen years. Yet it was on the verge of becoming fashionable in the summer months—since Poland's most famous actress and her husband began taking their holidays there. Cultivated, artistic people usually make up the party of advance despoilers, who then complain that the fishing village or rocky island or mountain hamlet is not the charming, unspoiled place it used to be. When they first came, there was one way to stay in Zakopane: to be lodged and fed in a highlander's hut. Two summers later, when Ryszard first was invited to accompany them, the village had one ill-kept public lodging and two cottages nearby serving expensive monotonous food and undrinkable wine. And there were tourists, a handful, to stay at the hotel and frequent the two restaurants.

How different the occupations of these tourists from the healthy regimen Maryna was following. Each day, whatever the weather, began with dawn bathing in the brook behind the hut, followed by a long walk by herself before breakfast. She roamed the damp meadows, plucked unfamiliar mushrooms from rotting tree trunks and dared herself to eat them on the spot, recited Shakespeare to goats. She had accumulated a rich repertoire of manias, enthusiastically taken up and then dropped. Some of them were dietary: for days on end she consumed only sheep's milk, then nothing but sauerkraut soup. There were also breathing exercises, from a book by Doctor Liebermeister, and mental exercises, too: for one hour a day she stretched out motionless on the grass and concentrated on recalling a happy memory. Any happy memory! It was the beginning of the era of "positive thoughts," which specialists in self-manipulation were preaching to men, to make them more robust salesmen of themselves, and doctors were prescribing to women, especially those suffering from "nerves" or "neurasthenia"—when they were not prescribing to women simply not to think at all. Thinking (like city life) was supposed to be bad for one's health, especially for a woman's health.

But Henryk was not like this, not like other doctors. He might say, Trust the good air of Zakopane to work its curative powers. Henryk was a great believer in air. But he did not say, Rest, have a mental blackout, confine yourself to womanly occupations like lacemaking. There was no one Maryna liked talking to as much as Henryk. If only he weren't so obviously enamored. It was one thing for young men like Ryszard and Tadeusz to fall in love with her; she knew the power of a reigning actress to inspire such reckless, perfectly sincere but shallow infatuations. But that this intelligent melancholy older man was pining with unavowed love was painful to her. She wished he would sneeze.

"Sneeze, Henryk!"

"I beg your pardon."

"I like to hear you sneeze. It makes me laugh. It makes me find you ridiculous."

"I am ridiculous."

Maryna sneezed. "See how handsomely I do it?"

It was last September and they were sitting in a sun-filled room in the hut Henryk had rented for the summer. With one larch table, two chairs and a bench, its white walls bare except for a row of crudely colored pictures on glass of shepherds and bandits, painted by local shepherds and bandits, it was scarcely a parlor, much less a consulting room. Only the cupboard's worth of scalpels, forceps, microscope, stethoscope, stoppered vials and two dog-eared medical books—the modest selection from his well-stocked office back in Cracow which provided more doctoring than any of the residents of the village ever received before—confirmed his profession.

"Are you telling me you have a cold? It would hardly surprise me, since you insist on walking barefoot in the grass and bathing in an icy stream at dawn."

"I don't"—she started coughing convulsively—"have a cold."

"Of course not." He came toward the bench where she was sitting and extended his open hand.

"Ah, the good air of Zakopane," Maryna said, surrendering her delicate wrist.

He shut his eyes as he stood over her. A minute passed. With her free hand Maryna reached for the plate of raspberries at the end of the bench, and slowly ate three. Another minute had passed.

"Henryk!"

Opening his eyes, he grinned mischievously. "I like taking your pulse."

"I've noticed."

"So I can reassure you"—he placed her hand back in her lap, he was still smiling—"how healthy you are."

"Stop it, Henryk. Have a raspberry. Don't offer me a drink."

"And your headaches?"

"I always have a headache."

"Even in Zakopane?"

She grimaced. "All I have to do is relax. As you know, I rarely have a full-blown headache when I'm working too hard."

He had returned to the table. "And yet your instincts are right to tell you to seek refuge here whenever you can from the hurly-burly of Warsaw and all the touring."

"What refuge!" she exclaimed. "Admit it, friend, it's hardly the undiscovered village it was when we arrived here four years ago."

"When *you* arrived, dear Maryna. Please recall that you were the first well-known person to come here every summer. I merely followed."

"Not you," she said. "I mean all the others."

Henryk tilted his head, forefinger to bearded chin, and gazed out the window at his cherished view of the Giewont and the distant summit of the Kasprowy.

"What do you expect since each time you and Bogdan come a few more people discover the beauties of the place. You are the village's biggest populator."

"Well, at least they are my friends. But now there are people I don't know in that so-called hotel old Czarniak has opened. Zakopane with a hotel!"

"Where you go everyone follows," he said, smiling.

"There are even foreigners now—and don't tell me they are here because of me. English, God be praised." She paused melodramatically. "If one must have tourists, let them be English. At least we don't have any Germans."

"Just wait," he said. "They'll come."

*

This year's stay was different. For one thing, they had arrived much earlier, and they were not on holiday. Bogdan had proposed they assemble everyone involved in the plan—their plan: it had not been hard to bring Bogdan round again. Maryna thought they should invite just a few friends, those who were wavering. Ryszard and the others on whom she already knew they could count need not come.

After journeying from Warsaw to Cracow and recovering Piotr— two years before Maryna had sent the child away from Warsaw, where the language of instruction in schools was Russian, back to live with her mother in Cracow, where the more lenient Austrian rule permitted Polish-language schooling—they spent a week of afternoons in Stefan's flat, often joined by the guardedly reassuring Henryk. Stefan was now confined to bed much of the time. The morning after their arrival Bogdan himself went to the food market square to arrange everything with one of the highlanders sure to be loitering there after selling off his load of mutton and cheese. Familiar faces crowded around him, offering their services, their wagons. Bogdan picked a very tall fellow with lank black hair who spoke a shade more intelligibly than the others and, in his comical farrago of educated Polish and highlander patois, instructed the man to tell the old widow whose hut they'd rented last September to ready it now for the arrival of himself and his wife and stepson with five others, and to be prepared to bring them to the village one week from today. The man, a Jedrek, declared that it would be an unforgettable honor to carry the Count and the Countess and their party in his wagon.

They had known only the summer, when the mountains above the tree line look clear of snow and the meadows have gone bare of flowers. The high mountains were still covered with snow—winters are long and harsh in the Tatras—but as the wagon passed along green meadows carpeted with yellow primroses and purple crocuses, purple with a dash of dark blue, Jedrek's passengers could hardly refuse to call it spring. Maryna reached the village excited, then edgy—feelings she identified as the elation that follows the making of a great decision and the restlessness that succeeds the familiar discomforts of the journey. It could not be a headache, though this giddiness and pointless energy was not unlike what she would feel, sometimes, three or four hours before the onset of a headache. No, it could not be a headache. But as she stood with Bogdan relishing the sunset, she had to acknowledge that there was something wrong with the way she was seeing, it had become full of dazzles and zigzags and flicker and sprays of light, the sun seemed to be boiling, and she could no longer deny the throbbing in her right temple and the tightness in the nape of her neck. She who had never cancelled a performance because of a headache collapsed for twenty-four hours, lying in the dim sleeping chamber with a towel wrapped tightly around her head in a leaden stuporous daze. Piotr tiptoed in and out, and asked when she was going to get up and clearly needed to be comforted, and she made the effort to keep the child with her for a while. It was all right if she patted his hair and kissed his hand with her eyes tightly shut. Whenever she opened them, Piotr seemed very small and far away, as did Bogdan crouching by the bed, asking again what he might bring her—they seemed to have lattices on their faces. There were faces enough peering out of the dark knots in the beams that supported the ceiling, which seemed to be just above her, pressing down on her, shimmering, scintillating. All she wanted was to be left alone. And vomit. And sleep.

The headache she had later in their stay was mild compared to this, one of the worst Maryna could remember. But after she recovered she was very fretful. There were long insomniac nights watching the shadows on the wall (she kept one oil lamp lit) and listening to Piotr's adenoidal breathing, Józefina's snoring, Wanda's coughing, a sheepdog barking. Once a night Piotr would crawl into her bed to tell her that he needed to use the outhouse and she had to come too, to protect him from a horrible witch who lived in the yard and looked exactly like old Mrs. Bachleda. And when they returned to the sleeping chamber, he would want to get back into her bed because, he explained, the witch would try to kill him in his dreams. Useless for Maryna to tell Piotr he was far too big to have such childish fears. But soon, hearing the noisy mouth breathing that signified sleep, she could carry him to his mattress and go outside again to look up at the night sky full of stars. Then, finally, a few hours before dawn, it was her turn to sleep. And to have odd dreams, too—that her mother was a bird, that Bogdan had a knife and hurt himself with it, that something terrible was hanging from a tree. She was often tired.

Still, some days she would feel "dangerously well," as she put it, since any exceptional energy or high spirits might be a sign that she was to have one of her disabling headaches the following day. The antic thoughts, the uncontrollable urge to laugh or sing or whistle or dance—she would pay for these. Convinced that her headaches were due to the slackening of effort, she took more strenuous walks than ever before; it seemed that she had gathered her friends around her mostly in order to leave them.

She walked partly to exhaust herself—and had no need of company. Bogdan helped her dress, tenderly booted her and watched her until she disappeared, heading southwest. From the village to the higher meadow leading to Mount Giewont was about five miles. From there she crossed into the forest and followed the trail that brought her, breathless, to a still higher plateau with grass, dwarf shrubs and Alpine flowers; in giddy homage to the murder of Adrienne Lecouvreur by the gift of poisoned flowers, she picked a bunch of edelweiss, inhaled the odorless blossoms and lifted her face to the sun. She would have liked to climb to the crest of the Giewont, which she'd done in previous summers with Bogdan and friends and a guide from the village. But, afraid of the dark fancies that filled her mind, she didn't dare attempt it alone. Even to venture into the foothills through patches of melting snow, and partly up the slopes, she wanted Bogdan, Bogdan only, to accompany her.

Bogdan's stride was faster than Maryna's, and she didn't mind walking behind him. That way she could feel both accompanied and alone. But sometimes she had to bring him to her side, when she saw something which he might be missing. A crow in a tree. The silhouette of a hut. A cross on a hill. A grouping of chamois or an ibex on a nearby crag. The eagle swooping down on some luckless marmot.

"Wait," she would cry, "did you see that!" Or: "I want to show you something."

"What?"

"Up there."

He would look in the direction she pointed.

"From here. Come back here."

He would come halfway and look again.

"No, right here."

She would take his arm and bring him back to where she had stopped to admire, so he could place his booted feet just ... there. Then, standing at his side, she could watch him seeing what she had seen and, thoughtfully, not moving for a minute to show he really had seen it.

What a tyrant I am, Maryna did sometimes think. But he doesn't seem to mind. He's so kind, so patient, so husbandly. That was the true liberty, the true satisfaction of marriage, wasn't it? That you could ask someone, legitimately demand of someone, to see what you saw. Exactly what you saw.

\*

From a letter that Maryna entrusted to one of the highlanders leaving for the market in Cracow, to post as soon as he arrived:

"... Ryszard, what have you been doing, thinking, planning? Given your habitual fine opinion of yourself, perhaps I am doing an injury to your character if I confide that you have been missed here by all of us. Do not feel too self-important, however. For this may be because our usual occupations have been taken from us. First it was snowing for two days—yes, snow in May! And now we're having three days of cold rain, so Bogdan and I and the friends have had no choice but to decree ourselves housebound. And now I remember what it was like to be a child in a large family who has been denied permission to go out. For, thus cooped up, we have tired of all subjects of conversation, even that most on our minds, and despite the extreme interest of what Bogdan has told us about a colony in one of the New England states called Brook Farm. Well then, you'll say, amuse yourselves. But we have! I have devised charades for those who wanted to exercise their acting skills (it wouldn't have been fair for me to participate)—Bogdan has beaten Jakub and Julian at chess— we have composed songs both jolly and sad (Tadeusz is learning to

play the *gesle*, that fiddle-like instrument we've heard at the shepherds' encampments)—we have recited Mickiewicz poems to each
other and got through all of *As You Like It* and *Twelfth Night*. And,
yes, it's still raining.

"Guess what we did today. We were reduced to entertaining ourselves by killing flies. Truly! This morning among Piotr's toys I
found two tiny bows, Julian made arrows out of matches with a
needle at the end, and we took turns aiming at the drowsy flies ornamenting the wooden walls of the room where we sit, applauding as
one by one our victims fell at our feet. What do you say to such an
occupation for Juliet or Mary Stuart?

"Nevertheless, don't think that it's because I am bored that I am
inviting you to join us. We're certain to remain at least another two
weeks, in which time the weather is bound to improve and much
could be discussed, and it occurs to me that since Julian now seems
quite committed and eager, you should be here too, so that we may
settle some details of the new plan in which you have a leading role.
And you can reassure Wanda, who is distressed over their impending
separation, that you will keep an eye on her husband and make sure
he does not court any unnecessary danger, although, knowing you
both, I think it should be the other way around! So, consider yourself
invited—if (yes, there is an if) you give me your word on one delicate
matter. What does the dear Maryna want of me that I would not willingly grant her, you will be thinking. I know your warm heart. But I
also know something else about you. An actor, dear Ryszard, may be
just as observant as a writer! Will you forgive my frankness? Surely
you will. Here is my request. You must promise me to behave like a
gentleman with the local girls. Yes, Ryszard, I am aware of your bad
habits. But not in Zakopane, I beg you! You are my guest. I may yet
come back here, I have made a commitment to these people. Do we
understand each other, my friend? Then come, dear Ryszard."

*

Mortified when he received Maryna's letter, and determined to do
anything and everything she asked of him, Ryszard left Warsaw the
next day. Arriving in Cracow, he called on Henryk to ask his advice
about how to hitch a ride to the village. Henryk not only accompanied him to the market to assist him in finding a reliable driver but
decided impulsively that he would go, too. Surely Stefan's condition
could not significantly worsen if he were gone for only ten days. If Ryszard were invited, and by Maryna herself, how could he stay away?

Ryszard took his room in the hut of the village bard, partly to continue the task begun last summer of getting the old man to recite his tales, partly to escape Maryna's vigilant eye if, despite his best intentions, he should succumb to the unwashed charms of one of the village girls.

"Ah, communal life," Henryk said to Bogdan when told there was a mattress waiting for him in the men's sleeping room. "Please don't be offended if I stay at Czarniak's place."

"The hotel?" said Bogdan. "You can't be serious. I trust you carry a disinfectant in your physician's satchel for the mattress you'll be given there."

Except for when he was called to some medical emergency (a breech birth, a smashed leg, a ruptured appendix), Henryk was almost always at the hut, available to Maryna, entertaining Piotr. The boy seemed bright to him, and so he decided to teach him about the new doctrines of evolution.

"If I were you," he said to Piotr, "I'd think twice before you tell the priests at school that a friend of your illustrious mother has even mentioned the name of that great Englishman, Mr. Darwin."

"But I can't tell them," said the boy. "Mama says I'm not going back to that school anymore."

"And do you know why you're not going back?"

"I think so," said Piotr.

"Why?"

"Because we're going on a ship."

"And what will you do on the ship?"

"See whales!"

"Which is what kind of a creature?"

"A mammal!"

"Excellent."

"Henryk!" It was Ryszard, who had just sauntered over. "Don't fill the lad's head with useless facts. Tell him stories. Stimulate his imagination. Make him bold."

"Oh, I'd like a story," cried Piotr. "Tell one about a witch and how she gets killed. Fried. In a stove. And then she—"

"You should be telling the stories," said Ryszard.

"I have stories, too," said Henryk. "But they don't make me bold."

\*

She was growing silent, she who had always been so talkative. How those who had gathered here wanted to please her.

89

Maryna watched Tadeusz and Ryszard watching her with ador-
ing eyes. She wished she were in love, for being helplessly in love
awakens one's better self. But when marriage puts an end to that, it
is a deliverance. Love makes men strong, self-confident. It makes
women weak.

Friendship, though . . . that was another matter. Friends make you
strong. How was she to do without Henryk? They were in the forest
sitting on the stump of a fir tree near a wildberry patch. Piotr was
playing with his full-size bow and arrows nearby.

"I've never liked forests," said Henryk. "But I'm starting to. All I
have to do is imagine that each tree is a fellow creature. Stuck in this
gloomy forest. Rooted here. Waving its leaves about. Help! Help!
cries the tree, I'm—"

"Don't be pathetic, dear Henryk."

"I thought I was being amusing."

"Ah," she said smiling. "You're that, too."

"Good. Where was I? Oh, my trees. No Birnam Wood to Dunsi-
nane for them. And then they're cut down, which is not the escape
they had in mind. Try some of this."

Maryna took the proffered flask of vodka.

"Can't you imagine," she said after a while, "what it is to have got
in your head that there is something that your Fate has willed, that
you must obey your star. Whatever the others think."

"Maryna, you speak about yourself as if you were completely
alone. But what strikes me is how set you are on bringing others
along with you."

"One can't have a theatre life without other people."

"Actually, I was thinking of Zakopane. You are vexed that you
can't keep the Zakopane you discovered, but you have to know it
can't remain what it was. I think it shouldn't. The lives of people
here are hard. But they're not a tribe of nomadic Indians in North
America. They're a hemmed-in settlement of shepherds in Europe
whose miserable livelihood is shrinking. The land has always been
too poor for serious farming, and you know, don't you, the iron mine
is bound to close within the next few years. How will they live then
if they don't peddle their humble finery and wooden geegaws, their
mountains, the views, the good air?"

"Do you really imagine I don't care about—"

"And, as I've often pointed out," he continued heatedly, "you,
abetted by the dear indispensable Bogdan, set all that in motion.
Though it was bound to happen anyway. How could more and more

people not hear about Zakopane? You wanted others around you. Your community."

"You think me naïve."

He shook his head.

"You think I'm being pretentious."

"Oh," he laughed, "there's nothing wrong with being pretentious, Maryna. I confess to the adorable failing myself. It's a Polish specialty, like idealism. But I do think you shouldn't confound a spartan house party with a phalanstery."

"I know you don't like Fourier."

"It's not for me to like or dislike your utopian sage. I can't help it if I know something about human nature. It's hard for a doctor to avoid that."

"And you think I could be the actress I am without knowing something about human nature?"

"Don't be angry with me." He sighed. "Maybe I'm jealous. Because I can't be a member of your party. I have to stay . . . here."

"But if you wanted, you could, when we—"

"No, I'm too old."

"What nonsense! How old are you? Fifty? Not even fifty!"

"Maryna. . . ."

"Do you think I don't feel old?" she said shrilly. "But that doesn't stop me from—"

"I can't." He raised his hand. "Maryna, I can't."

*

The weather turned warmer, and the whole party, except for Henryk and Ryszard, had spent the afternoon in the forest and were now assembled outside the hut in the falling light, pleasantly tired, more than a little talked out, and looking forward to their dinner of soup and two kinds of mushrooms, the delicately shriveled brown ones they had found in a grove of firs today and the savory dark-orange pickled *rydz* they had harvested on forest excursions during their stay last September. Bogdan had laid down a track on the grass for Piotr to play with his wooden trains. Maryna was writing a letter at a little table by the oil lamp Tadeusz had lit for her: a crescent moon and a pair of planets had appeared in the pale sky. Wanda was changing the buttons on a neighbor's new embroidered flax shirt she purchased for Julian. Józefina and Julian were having a whispered dispute over a card game. Jakub was sketching the card players. The screech of an owl heralded the baaing of some wayward sheep, while

91

from indoors came the sound of sizzling butter in Mrs. Bachleda's crude skillet—delicious noise!

Henryk had strolled over, poured himself some arrack, pulled a chair to the card players' table and was trying to concentrate on a book. Ryszard, who had elected to spend his forest day with his landlord (killing animals in the company of another man was the most enjoyable way of staying clear of the temptations alluded to by Maryna), was the last to arrive. He had pulled up a chair to Maryna's table, taken out his notebook, and was writing up a hunting tale the old man had told him after they'd shot their second fox.

Bogdan was pacing. "I shall go to sleep as soon as we eat," he said. "I've done nothing strenuous but I am tired."

Henryk snapped the book shut. "You're not feeling ill?"

"I don't think so."

"You didn't sample any strange mushrooms today?"

"I did," said Tadeusz.

"And how are you feeling, young man?"

"Couldn't be better!"

"Because you're not supposed to eat whatever looks enticing to you in a forest."

"Everyone knows that," Bogdan muttered. "But should someone have been imprudent, we have a doctor among us for the week."

"If I were you," said Henryk, "I'd place no more confidence in doctors than in mushrooms." He was toying with his empty glass. "Would you like to hear a cautionary tale about both?" He laughed. "It's a dreadful story."

Ryszard looked up from his notebook.

"You probably never heard of Schobert. Nobody plays his compositions now, which were written for the harpsichord." He paused. "He lived in Paris. He was famous throughout Europe."

"Don't you mean Schubert?" said Wanda.

"Don't answer her," said Julian.

"I'm afraid it's Schobert," said Henryk.

He stood, slowly lit a pipe and buttoned his jacket, as if he were off for a stroll.

"So at last," said Ryszard, "you're going to tell us a story."

"Well, this is quite an unpleasant one," said Henryk, sitting down again. "I wonder why I thought of telling it."

"Henryk, don't tease us," Maryna said.

Henryk knocked his pipe against the sole of his boot. "Could it be," he said, "that I'm a little thirsty?" Józefina fetched him the bottle of arrack.

He took a swig. "Courage," said Maryna.

Henryk looked about at his expectant auditors and smiled.

"Well, it seems that this man, this valuable man, this . . . artist was extremely partial to mushrooms, and so had arranged a day's outing in the country, I think it was the forest of Saint-Germain-en-Laye, no matter, with his wife, the older of his two small children and four friends, among whom was a doctor. They arrived in two carriages at the edge of the forest, descended and began to walk. Schobert starting scouting for mushrooms, and during the course of the day picked what he thought was a choice basketful. Late in the afternoon, the company went to Marly, to an inn where Schobert was known, and asked for a dinner to be prepared to which they would contribute the mushrooms. The cook at the inn glanced at the mushrooms, assured his guests that they were the wrong sort and refused even to touch them. Schobert told the cook to do what he had been asked. But could they actually be the wrong sort, asked one of the friends. Nonsense, said the friend who was a doctor. Nettled at the cook's obstinacy, though of course it was they who were being obstinate, they left and went to an inn in the Bois de Boulogne, where the head waiter also refused to prepare the mushrooms for them. More obstinate than ever, for the doctor still insisted that the mushrooms were good, they left that inn, too."

"Heading for disaster," murmured Ryszard.

"Night having fallen and everyone admitting to being very hungry, they returned to Paris, to Schobert's house. There he gave the mushrooms to his maidservant to cook for supper—"

"Oh," said Wanda.

"—and all seven of them, including the doctor who claimed to know all about mushrooms, as well as the maid, who must have nibbled while cooking, and the dog, who must have begged a taste from the maid, were poisoned. Since they succumbed together, they were without any assistance until the following midday, a Wednesday, when a pupil of Schobert, arriving for his lesson, found them all thrashing about in agony on the parquet floor. Nothing could be done for them. The child, who was five years old, died first. Schobert survived until Friday. His wife did not die until the following Monday. Two lived as long as ten days more. Of Schobert's little family only the three-year-old, who hadn't been taken along on the outing and was asleep when everyone returned, was left."

Piotr giggled loudly.

"Go inside and wash your hands, Piotr," said Bogdan.

The child went on pushing his trains about. "Crash!" he said. "It's a train wreck."

"Piotr!"

"What a grisly story," said Jakub, who had been standing in the pegged doorway of the hut. "They only had to listen to the cook at the first inn, or the head waiter at the second."

"Servants?" Ryszard exclaimed. "Who of that era did not feel superior to servants? It's a perfect story of the *ancien régime*."

"Imagine placing such faith in a doctor," said Henryk.

"Imagine a doctor being so confident he was an expert on mushrooms," said Ryszard.

"But Schobert was the one who was so fond of mushrooms," said Bogdan. "It's Schobert's fault. He was the head of the family, he was in charge of the excursion."

"But a doctor," Wanda said. "A man of science."

"While I suppose I should protect my wife's illusions about men of science," said Julian, "the truth is, both are equally to blame."

"No, the responsibility has to be Schobert's," Józefina said. "Nobody wanted to contradict him. Think of the force of his personality. A great musician, a man admired by everyone . . ."

"What do you think?" Tadeusz said, the first to feel uneasy that Maryna was not taking part in the conversation. She shook her head. "If someone said that mushrooms we had picked were poisonous but *you* wanted to eat them—"

"Surely you would not follow me."

"Perhaps I would."

"Bravo!" said Henryk.

Everyone looked expectantly at Maryna.

"But I am not so stubborn," she cried gaily. "I would never insist on eating mushrooms that someone said were poisonous." She paused. "What do you take me for?" (What did they take her for? Their queen.) "Oh, my dear friends. . . ."

*

Maryna had no desire to linger beyond early June, when the first summer tourists would be arriving. The men spent their last hours in the village purchasing sheepskin blankets and six of the sturdily crafted hatchets that double as weapons for the highlanders. Back in Cracow she visited Stefan, now alarmingly paler and thinner, before continuing on with Bogdan and Piotr, accompanied by Ryszard and

Tadeusz, to Warsaw. There Tadeusz learned that he was finally to be offered a contract at the Imperial Theatre, which Maryna, seeing his joy wilted by his fear of disappointing her, warmly counselled him to accept, abandoning any thought of joining them. She did Tadeusz the honor of accompanying him when he signed the contract, and stayed on for a quiet talk about her own plans with the Imperial's blustering, kindly managing director, who would not hear of anything but a year's leave of absence, no more. Bogdan was busy raising the money needed for their great venture, and this furnished the detective assigned to follow him everywhere with a new list of names for other detectives to follow: those who came to look at their apartment and its furnishings, which Bogdan had put up for sale.

Within two weeks, however, they were hurrying back to Cracow for Stefan who, long separated from his wife, was now unable to care for himself at all and had gone home to their mother's flat. The evening of their arrival Stefan closed his eyes and, with a loud sigh, tumbled into a coma. Kneeling by the bed, Maryna touched her lips to his brow and wept soundlessly. The clammy face on the pillow was eerily juvenile, bony as when she had first seen him on a stage, without recognizing him, as the beloved friend of both Don Carlos and his wicked father; the face of the gloriously handsome young man she had worshipped as a small child. Unbelievable to think that it was now his time to die!

"Mother was quite overcome with grief," she wrote to Ryszard, "but Adam was there, and Józefina, and Andrzej, and little Jarek. Henryk, who never left us, did what he could. I held him all night in my arms as the blood poured from his mouth, and then he was gone."

Stefan's death was also Maryna's farewell to her family.

\*

Bogdan too had to make a farewell visit: his family were rich land-owners, living on their large holdings in western Poland under Prussian rule. Maryna had been at the principal Dembowski estate once, in 1870, after she accepted Bogdan's proposal of marriage—but not to stay, for Ignacy, Bogdan's older brother and the head of the family, refused even to meet her, while telling Bogdan that he, of course, would always be welcomed with open arms. They took rooms at a nearby inn.

Before they left two days later, Bogdan did bring Maryna into the sprawling white-pillared manor to meet his grandmother, who had sent word to him that she, naturally, did not oppose his marriage. Squeezing his wife's hand, Bogdan had pulled her through room after room over the brightly polished wooden floors (she remembered their shine) as if they were naughty children, fleeing a justly wrathful adult, or children in disgrace, fleeing an ogreish tyrannical adult— so much did he dread coming upon his brother in one of those large, sparsely furnished rooms. Bogdan in a hurry, panting, seemed to her like a child. Maybe he had become one in this house where he had been a child. Maryna didn't want to feel like a child. It was partly so as not to feel like a child, ever, that she had become an actress.

They gained his grandmother's upstairs sitting room. Bogdan kissed her while Maryna made a curtsy that was, pointedly, not a stage curtsy. Then he left them alone.

Maryna had never met anyone like Bogdan's grandmother. Born in 1791, the year before the Second Partition, when the last king of Poland, Stanislaw August Poniatowski, was still on the throne, she was a survivor of a distant, more free-spirited era. She thought her grandchildren, with the possible exception of Bogdan, were fools. Above all, Ignacy, her eldest—as she explained to Maryna at a rapid clip and with a twinkle in her rheumy eye.

"He's a prig, *ma chère*, that's all there is to it. A frightful prig. And don't expect him to soften and come around. The well-being of his younger brother counts as nothing to him, compared to some vain idea of the family's dignity. Is this what our bold, virile Polish gentry has come to? Disgusting! I can hardly believe I'm related to this sanctimonious, Mother-of-God-worshipping fool. But there you have it, *mon enfant*. Modern times. *Que voulez-vouz?* And he calls himself a son of the Church. As far as I understand, Jesus did look favorably on brotherly love. Now you see the true face of this ridiculous religion. Should not a Christian rejoice that such a charming accomplished woman as you has arrived to make his brother happy? *Mais non.* You do make him happy, I hope. You know what I mean by happy?"

Maryna was more surprised by the old lady's scorn for religion— she had never heard anyone rail against the Church—than by the impertinent question she'd sprung at the end of her tirade. Bogdan had mentioned that his grandmother was reputed to have taken many lovers during her long, contentious marriage to the man with the sword, General Dembowski. Considering that she had a right not to reply, Maryna mustered a becoming, modest blush: she could blush as easily as weep on inner command. But the old lady was not to be put off.

"Well?" she said.

Maryna gave in. "Of course I try."

"Ah. You try."

Maryna didn't, wouldn't, answer this time.

"Trying is a very small part of it, *ma chère*. The attraction exists or it doesn't. I would have thought you, an actress, would know all about these matters. Don't tell me that actresses don't in any way deserve their interesting reputation? Just a little? Come now," she bared her toothless gums, "you disillusion me."

"I don't want to disillusion you," Maryna answered warmly.

"Good! Because there's something that troubles me about Bogdan. *C'est un serieux. Trop serieux peut-être.* Of course, he's too intelligent to think himself bound to grovel before ignorant priests mumbling in barbaric Latin. Unlike Ignacy, Bogdan has a mind. He has the makings of a free spirit. Which is why he chose you. But still, I've worried about him. He's never had love dalliances like his brother or all the other young men in his circle. And chastity, *ma fille,* is one of the great vices. To be twenty-eight and still know nothing of women! You have a great responsibility. It's his one defect for which I reproach him, but you have arrived to correct that, unless of course, which would explain the mystery, for there are men like that, as you must know, being in the theatre, he's really—"

"He really loves me," Maryna interrupted, feeling a pang of anxiety about the direction the conversation was taking. "And I love him."

"I see that I displease you with my candor."

"Perhaps. But you honor me with your trust. Surely you wouldn't say these things to me if you did not believe I love Bogdan and intend to do everything in my power to be a good wife to him."

"Prettily said, *mon enfant.* A charming evasion. Well, I will not press you on this matter. Just promise me you won't leave him when he ceases to make you happy—for he will, you have a restless spirit, and he is not a man who knows how to possess a woman entirely— or when you fall in love with someone else."

"I promise," said Maryna gravely. She sank to her knees and bowed her head.

The old lady burst out laughing. "Of course your promise is worth nothing. Get up, get up! You are not on a stage." A bony hand reached out and seized her arm. "But nonetheless I shall hold you to it."

"Nounou?" It was Bogdan at the door.

*"Oui, mon garçon, entre.* I have done with your bride, and you may take her away with the knowledge that I'm quite pleased with her. She may be too good for you. You may both visit me once a year, but no more often and, *rapelle-toi,* only when your brother is traveling. You will have a letter from me when you may come."

*

Maryna was furious not to be regarded as a worthy wife to Bogdan by his family for . . . what? Being a widow? They couldn't know that Heinrich had been unable to marry her or that he wasn't dead; his health failing and having decided to return to Königsberg, he had given his promise, she believed a sincere promise, never to enter her life again. Having a child? Could they be so base as to suspect that the late Mr. Zalewski, her husband, was not Piotr's father? But he was! No, she was certain the reason was Ignacy's disapproval of his younger brother's lifelong passion for the theatre. Gratifying as it was that the Dowager Countess Dembowski did not share the family scorn for actresses, Maryna knew that until she was accepted by the older brother she would never be accepted by the others. Maryna supposed the distinguished old lady must have some influence on Ignacy—but either didn't or disdained to use it, and Maryna had never seen her again. Whenever Bogdan was summoned for his yearly visit, Maryna was mid-season in Warsaw or on tour.

They had never accepted her. Eventually she had won the love of Bogdan's maiden sister Izabela, but Ignacy's opposition only hardened with time, and Bogdan ceased to have any relation with his brother, pride dictating even that he decline, out of his income from the various family properties, that portion due him from the estate managed by Ignacy. But Bogdan had no choice but to ask for a proper assignment of this money now. He wrote Ignacy explaining the reason for his impending arrival. An investment, he said. An excellent investment. He wrote to his grandmother asking her permission for an unscheduled visit. Maryna said that she wanted to say goodbye to his grandmother, too.

As soon as they arrived and had installed themselves in their rooms at the inn, Bogdan and Maryna hired a carriage and drove to the manor. The chief steward told Bogdan that the Count would receive him in an hour in the estate office, and that the Dowager Countess was in the library.

They found her heaped with shawls in a high deep chair, reading. "You," she said to Bogdan. She wore a white lace headdress and there were patches of rouge on her seamed, knobby face. "I don't know whether you are late or early. Late, I suppose."

Bogdan stammered, "I didn't think—"

"But not too late," said the old lady.

Beside her was a low table with a tall glass of something thick and white that Maryna could not identify until she and Bogdan were brought glasses of their own: it was hot beer with cream and morsels of finely chopped white cheese floating in it. *"A votre santé, mes chers,"* murmured the old lady, and raised the glass to her sunken mouth. Then she looked sharply at Maryna.

"You're in mourning."

"My brother." Recalling the old lady's style of impertinent declaration, Myrna added, "My favorite brother."

"And he was how old? He must have been very young."

"No, he was forty-seven."

"Young!"

"We knew Stefan was very ill and unlikely to recover, although of course one is never really prepared for—"

"One is never really prepared for anything," said the old lady. "But the death of someone is always a liberation for someone else. Contrary to what is usually said, *la vie est longue. Figurez-vous,* I am not speaking of myself. It is very long even for those who don't attain any spectacular longevity. *Alors, mes enfants"*—she was looking only at Bogdan—"here is what I have to say to you. I like your folly, *cela vous convient.* But may I ask why?"

"Many reasons," said Bogdan.

"Yes, many," said Maryna.

"Too many, I suspect. Well; you'll find the real one *sur la route."* Suddenly her head dropped forward—as if she had fallen asleep, or . . . .

"Bogdan?" whispered Maryna.

"Yes!" shouted the old lady, opening her eyes, "a long life is altogether wasted on most people, who quickly run out of enthusiasm or dreams and still have all those years ahead of them. Now, a fresh start, that would be something. Something rare. Unless, as people usually do, you manage to turn your new life into the old one."

"I think," said Bogdan, "there's little chance of that."

"You aren't getting any more intelligent," said his grandmother. "What kind of books are you reading now?"

"Practical books," said Bogdan. "Books on farming, on viticulture, on carpentry, on soil management, on—"

"Pity."

"He reads poetry with me," said Maryna. "We read Shakespeare together."

"Don't defend him. He's an idiot. You're not all that clever, at least you weren't when I met you six years ago, and now you're more intelligent than he is."

Bogdan leaned over and kissed his grandmother tenderly on the cheek. A tiny hand gnarled by arthritis reached up and patted the crown of his head.

"He's the only one I love," she said to Maryna.

"I know. And you're the only one it distresses him to leave."

"Nonsense!"

"Nounou," cried Bogdan.

*"Pas de sentiment, je te defend. Alors, mes chers imbéciles,* it's time for you to go. We won't meet again."

"But I'll be back."

"And I'll be gone." Unclenching her right hand, she stared at the palm. Then she lifted it slowly, murmuring, "An atheist's blessings on you, my children." Maryna bowed her head. *"Bis! Bis!"* said the old lady merrily. "And some advice, yes? Don't ever do anything out of despair. And, *écoutez-moi bien,* don't invent too many reasons for what you've decided to do!"

*

Everyone wonders why we are going, Maryna said to herself. Let them wonder. Let them invent. They won't get it right anyway. Don't they always tell lies about me? I can lie too. I don't owe anyone an explanation.

But the others need reasons, or so they tell themselves:

"Because she's my wife, and I must take care of her. Because my brother will see that I'm a practical man, not just a lover of theatre and the editor of a patriotic newspaper that was quickly shut down by the authorities. Because I can't bear being always followed by the police."

"Because I am curious, that's my profession, it's what a journalist should be, because I want to travel, because I am in love with her, because I am young, because I love this country, because I need to escape this country, because I love to hunt, because Nina says she is pregnant and expects me to marry her, because I've read so many books about it, Fenimore Cooper and Mayne Reid and Bret Harte and the rest, because I intend to write a great many books, because . . ."

"Because she's my mother and she promised me she would take me to the Centennial Exposition, whatever that might be."

"Because I, a simple girl, am to be her maid. Because, out of all the other candidates at the convent, all prettier and more skilled at cooking and sewing, she chose me."

"Because that's where the future is being born."

"Because my husband wants to go."

"Because maybe I can't be just Polish, even there, but I won't be only a Jew."

"Because I want to live in a free country."

"Because life will be better there for the children."

"Because it's an adventure."

"Because people should live in harmony, as Fourier says, though— it must be very uplifting from all that I've heard—I confess that each time I open his *Principles of Universal Harmony* my eyes start to—"

"Then forget about Fourier! Shakespeare," Maryna said. "Think of Shakespeare."

"But there's everything in Shakespeare."

"Exactly. Like America. America is meant to mean everything."

And so they went to America.

# Two Poems

## *John Ashbery*

### THE EARTH-TONE MADONNA

What were you telling him about,
and why were veins implanted in the marsh
where everyone looks? Today
is the first day of spring, I think.
Sailing near us on a monocle,
the spray tapped and jiggled,
forever like a lifeboat.

And true some were found perjured
in cornshocks, there was no meat left that day,
no edge one could run around on.
There were peepers in the loose chaos called
oblivion, and not much else on the table.
Miss—er—Jones, what is the order of events?
I think not sir she cabled
from a vantage point in Toronto where all ships
and trains have their terminus. And if it's Wednesday?
Then man the egrets, the snowplow is coming
to rest where all of us have our workshoes on
and it will be a tough call to divide up the rope
and Saturday.

There was no hope in the statue
of the saint, eyeballs collapsed, sloping forward
like a scythe, and yet we came to know
how he was doing, and appreciated a chat
at his knees. Now this was only the fourth time
any had done so. So we squeegeed
the happy-face off home plate, and bunches
of aristocrats all around us applauded
what came to seem fair, and in time

were whisked away—the ox in his pumps,
forgotten for daydreaming, the tangled marl
of old Sol's beard. Everything was decimated,
which was devastating, yet we went on
living, along the row we had been set down in
and soon we had reached the end. A conniving quiver
set compass needles skittering, prize lists
fairly glittering. And I looked to thee
to see what a retroactive spouse might be
yet we got lost somehow in the confusion
attendant on the formal victory. We were back
home, in fact, but no one thought to look
for us there. We were let out to pasture
in the shade, and six more volumes dovetailed.
The first part of the novel was now complete,
a hundred years in the making, yet its style
seemed chaste, if not downright lackluster, in the best sense,
as many terriers were starting to run,

yappingly. If there was a space for us
in all this fireside, it got debunked. We were kept waiting
right up until the announced departure,
and so became part of humanity. Part and parcel, I was going to say.

In the dim
eclectic din, beaters waited.
Let's handsel it, love, O my love, I said.


THE LAUGHTER OF DEAD MEN

Candid jeremiads drizzle from his lips,
the store looks as if it isn't locked today.
A gauzy syllabus happens, smoke is stencilled
on the moss-green highway.

This is what we invented the suburbs for,
so we could look back at the lovable dishonest city,
tears clogging our arteries.

*John Ashbery*

The nausea and pain we released to float in the sky.
The dead men are summoning our smiles and indifference.
We climb the brilliant ladder toward their appetites,
homophobes, hermaphrodites, clinging together like socks
hanging out to dry on a glaring day in winter.

You could have told me all about that
but of course preferred not to,
so fearful of the first-person singular
and all the singular adventures it implies.

# Semaine d'Artaud
## *Anne Carson*

They gave me a week to "get" Artaud and come up with a script.
Those nights were like saints.
SEE BELOW FOR DIAGRAM.

| Lundi: | Folie |
| Mardi: | Chair |
| Mercredi: | Vissage |
| Jeudi: | Mexique |
| Vendredi: | De[Vol]rrida |
| Samedi: | Sang |
| Dimanche: | Éternel |

*Anne Carson*

*Lundi*

Artaud is mad. He stays close to the madness. Watching it
breathe or not breathe,
he deduces laws of rhythm, which he divulges to his actors.
They are to achieve
a mastery of passions mathematically—be Artaud only sane.
Observe the minutest push and pull within themselves of muscles
grazed by emotion. Learn to render these as breath.
Discover all that is "feminine," all that reaches forward in
supplication within us—
*the way a diver digs his heels into the ocean floor in order to rise*
*to the surface: there is a sudden vacuum where before there was*
*tension.*

For Artaud the real drawback of being mad is not that
consciousness is crushed and torn but that he cannot say so,
fascinating as this would be, *while it is happening.* But only later
when somewhat "recovered" and so much less convincingly.

The mad state is, as he emphasizes over and over again, *empty.*
Teeming with emptiness. Knotted on emptiness. Immodest in its
emptiness. You can pull emptiness out of it by the handful.
"I am not here. I am not here and never will be."
You can pull it out endlessly.

*le théâtre est le seul endroit au monde*
*où un geste fait ne se recommence deux fois*

106

*Mardi*

A primary characteristic of pain is its demand for an explanation.

      Knife wounds.

      Assault with an iron bar.

      Shock treatments.

      Stigmata.

      Scraping.


He expresses satisfaction.

A large part of his correspondence is addressed to doctors and their wives.

*J'ai mal*      implies      *on m'a fait mal.*


His favorite text from Van Gogh's letters to Theo describes drawing

as a passage        through an iron wall

       by force of will.

       For "will" Artaud reads *clou.*


    *une heure pour le caillot*

107

*Anne Carson*

*Mercredi*

He makes profound use of his face.

It is something of fire on which his soul wrote.

Portraits show an icy dandy.

Modelled by drugs and deprivation it took on an allure.

*Screams are heard in the most up-to-date hospitals.*

Taps his little leather heels together in the snow.

(Look over there, look down. Look at me. Not too sad.

That's good. Bit of a smile? There it is. That's what I like.

Now very pensive. Eyes lower. Now look up. More. Yes. Yes.)

*Psychiatry was invented as a defense against visionaries.*

Poetry (he lifts the plastic to show me)

comes from a black lump within the body, sweats itself out.

Body is pure.

Everything loathsome is the mind,

which God screws into body with a lascivious thrust.

Here is a sketch of himself as bones

dated December 1948 (he died in March).

And a bit of lung for flashing light up

onto the face from underneath.

*I beg you.*

*ne me représente en aucune façon*

Anne Carson
*Jeudi*

In Mexico it is useful to have the obsession of counting.
For he gets lost in the membrane
which shone like pulverized sun
and only by "adding up shadows" can he find his way back
to strange centers—
from the dirty yellow table at which he sits
to what it was on the forest floor,
servant full of pity *Brueghel red,*
blood of all that matter has endured
before Artaud.
Like many a white man here he wants to believe in
God's birth.
Stare at it for hours.


*car je fus Inca mais pas roi*

*Vendredi*

The unique, as Derrida puts it, eludes discourse. Artaud's adventure resists clinical or critical exegesis, it is a protest against exemplification itself. Artaud habitually destroys the history of himself as an example, history of a difference between his body and his mind, history that doctors and critics are combing and scouring after to comment on it. He wants both to speak and to forbid his speech being spirited away (*soufflée* : Derrida) and placed in an order of truth for commentary. "Artaud knew that all speech fallen from the body, offering itself to understanding or reception, offering itself as a spectacle, is stolen speech." To speak in such a way that the theft blocks itself. His theatre of cruelty is where he stages public attempts at this. But the prior stage is mind. "Something is destroying my thinking, something furtive which takes away from me the words which I found." To have thoughts *which even he himself will not want to steal* and repeat as speech. He must become so boring or abhorrent to himself that his language does not eavesdrop on its own calls.

*What holes, and made of what?*

kilzi

trakilzi

faildor

barabama

baraba

mince
o dedi

o dada orzoura

o dou zoura

o dada skizi

*Samedi*

To the scandal of language he does not consent.
False etymology makes him bold.
He says *unglue words from the sky:*


*Car après, dit poematique, après viendra le temps*
                                  *du sang.*
*Puisqu' ema, en grec, veut dire sang, et que po-ema*
                  *doit vouloir dire*
                              *après*
                                 *le sang*
                                    *le sang après.*
*Faisons d'abord* poème, *avec sang.*


For after, said poetically, after will come the time
                                  of blood.
Since *ema* in Greek means blood, and po-ema
                  ought to mean
                              after
                                 the blood
                                    the blood after.
Let us make first *poem,* with blood.


Violence is total here. He deliberately misspells
the ancient Greek word for "poem" (*poiema*)
                  as "poema."
Then misdivides it
into *po* and *ema* (2 nonexistent syllables in Greek),
wrongly identifying *ema* with the Greek word for blood (*haima*)
in order to etymologize *poema* as "after the blood after"
(but in what language does *po* mean "after"?)
Poetically indeed.


*mais j'en ai assez ce sera pour un prochain livre*

*Anne Carson*

*Dimanche Éternal*


He died at dawn on 4th March.
With spring snow on the ground.
Alone in his pavilion. Seated at the foot of his bed.
Holding his shoe.
His body did not burst into unforgettable fragments at his death, no.

That summer was throughout Europe remarkable for its tempests.
Here I am! What lightning! was what people said
as they strolled along.


*et en effet c'est trop peu pour moi*

Artaud Script

Artaud is mad.
He stayed close to the madness. Watching it breathe or not breathe.
*First a close-up of me driven to despair.*

His face is mad.
It was something of fire on which his soul wrote. All this mental glass.
*Me beating my head against a wall.*

His body is mad.
Some days he felt uterine. Mind screwed into him by a thrust of sky.
*I run among the ruins.*

His mind is mad.
There was (he decided) no mind. The body (hell) just as you see it.
*Go throw myself from the tower, gesticulating, falling.*

His hospital is mad.
He noted in electric shock a splash state. What holes, and made of what?
*Falling to the beach.*

His Mexico is mad.
There was not a shadow he did not count. No opium, no heads on the days.
*You see my body crumpled on the sand.*

His God is mad.
He felt God pulling him out through his own cunt. *Claque. Claque-dents.*
*It moves convulsively a few times.*

His double is mad.
The drawback of being mad was that he could not both be so and say so.
*Beautiful jerks.*

His word is mad.
He had to become an enigma to himself. To prevent his own theft
of him.
**You see my battered face.**

His excrement is mad.
He envied bones their purity. Hated to die *rectified* (as he said) by
pain.
**Then I fall back.**

His spring snow is mad.
They found him at dawn. Seated at the foot of his bed. Holding his
shoe.
**And shy away.**

# Black

## *Alexander Theroux*

BLACK IS THE STYGIAN well. As a color, truculent, scary, deep and inaccessible, it appears as a kind of abstract unindividualized deficiency, a bullying blot with a dangerous genius to it. There is no ingress. It absorbs and efficiently negates all color—in spite of the fact that Claude Monet once pronounced it of all colors the most beautiful—and with the negative aura of nothing more than itself suggests the sinister, dissolution and the permanence of disease, destruction and death. As Jan Morris says in (and of) *Fisher's Face*, reminding me of black, "One does not like that queer withdrawal into the expressionless." It is a color rightly described in the words of Henry James as portentously "the fate that waits for one, that dark doom that rides." It shocks us in the saccade of its sudden, inky prohibition but becomes as well in the inscrutable deepness of sleep the backdrop of all our dreams, and is sometimes even a comfort. (Dickens wrote, "Darkness was cheap, and Scrooge liked it.") With its syntax of hidden and unverifiable dimension, black has no indexicality but remains for the fat prohibitive hachuring of its drawn drapes a distinct code above all colors that, like espionage, legislates no place signs or particularity. In its relentless boldness, black is both atrociously present and atrabiliously absent.

No one would deny that the color black in its solid vagabondage, forgive the paradox, barges into things, and how its bigness booms. There is nevertheless relief, arguably, in seeing the ultimate value of "reality," and it is here, perhaps, that black allows for any continuing comfort.

Is that why Henri Matisse declared, "Black is the color of light," in spite of the fact that in color theory black is the absence of light? No pure colors in fact exist. Black and white, which are banished from chroma, at least in the minds of many if not most people, in the same way 0 and 1 were once denied the status of numbers—solid Aristotle long ago defined number as an accumulation or "heap"— are each other's complements just as they remain each other's opposites. It this too paradoxical? W. H. Auden wrote,

> Where are the brigands
> most commonly to be found?
> Where boundaries converge.

Weirdly, black *is:* darkness truly is our destiny at both ends of life. And yet it *is not:* "And those wonderful people out there in the dark," declares creepy, decaying, old, self-deluded Norma Desmond, when there is nothing out there at all. If an object absorbs all the wavelengths. We call it black, in the same way, for example, that a leaf that absorbs red light looks green to us or a stained-glass window that absorbs blue looks orange. And yet how can we legitimately call what is so full of other colors, whether white or black, *one* color? There is beyond its almost muscular intensity an irreconcilable force to the sheen of its light and shape of its lutulence, *ut tensio sic uis:* "as the tension, so the power." Black both is and it is not: disguises appear, we use aliases, and silently stand before that unabsorbing wall. The color black is the extreme, high-gravity, bombed-out, cave-blot color of Nox, Rahu, Quashee, Hela, Erebus, Sambo, Maevis and, deader than Dead Sea fruit with black ashes inside, it is the dark side of the Manichean alternative.

More often than not, it is with black as with Gustav Mahler's *Sixth Symphony,* which in its deep complexity, in Bruno Walter's phrase, "utters a decided 'No.'"

It is a color specifically inimical to white, including its thousand shades and tints and tones, along with what is in between. (Technically speaking, *tints* are colors that also contain white; *shades,* colors that contain black; and *tones* are those colors containing gray.) We call an object black if it has absorbed all wavelengths. Ordinary sunlight (or white light) is a mixture of light at all wavelengths—or all colors. A material that we perceive to be colored, of whatever color, has absorbed certain visible wavelengths and not others. Black and white, however, as polar extremes most significantly both embody what Paul Fussell, discussing the nature of enemies, refers to as "the *versus* habit," one thing opposed to another, not, as he explains, "with some Hegelian hope of synthesis involving a dissolution of both extremes (that would suggest a 'negotiated peace,' which is anathema), but with a sense that one of the poles embodies so wicked a deficiency or flaw or perversion that its total submission is called for." In this sharp dichotomy along the lines of "us" versus "them," black *is*—legendarily, has always been—precisely that wickedness. If white is known, safe, open and visible; black, unknown, hostile, closed and opaque, is the masked and unmediated alternative. Is it not clear in the confrontation of chess?

> The board
> detains them until dawn in its hard
> compass: the hatred of two colors

writes Jorge Luis Borges in "Chess."

It has an unholiness all about it, does black. "Your blood is rotten! Black as your sins!" cries Bela Lugosi in the film *Murders in the Rue Morgue* (1932). Doesn't the devout Moslem pray for the Kaaba's return to whiteness, which has turned black by the sins of men? Is not black the color of chaos, witchcraft, black magic, mad alchemy and the black arts? "Some negroes who believe in the Resurrection, think that they shall rise white," writes Sir Thomas Browne in *Christian Morals* (1716). And what of the darkness of bondage? The descent into hell? Evil? The word black is, more often than not, considered somewhat of a rude and insulting adjective, especially in English, serving as a dark, maledroit, prefixal name or term like "Dutch" and "psycho" and "gypsy." What puzzle can ever be worked of the spasmodic record of all it portends? Who in the essence of its ultimate reduction does not disappear? No animal or bird can see in total darkness. What is the color of the Congo? Boomblack! Jew's pitch! Nightmare! The bituminous side of life. Coalblack trolls. Demons. Bats. Moles. Fish alone can live in the unravellable inscrutableness of darkness. Coelacanths, blind as stones! According to the song "Think Pink" in *Funny Face* (1957) what should be done with black, blue and beige, remember? Banish the black, burn the blue and bury the beige! In Saint-Saëns's *Danse Macabre*, the white skeleton may terrifyingly dance in the darkness, but it is Death playing the violin.

After the ominous scriptural caveat "Whoever touches pitch will be defiled" (Sirach 12), the color black has never stood a chance. The rule was writ. Watch, for the night is coming.

Why speak of Cimmeria and unearthly mythologies? Darkness is right above us. Space itself is perpetual night, an atmosphere as black and haunted as the Apocalypse, totipalmate, hovering, suffoblanketing our entire and endless universe in which, crouching in total enigma, we lost inchlings squat in fear with headfuls of questions. How caught we are by its vastnesses. Midnight, according to Henry

David Thoreau, is as unexplored as the depths of central Africa. "It is darker in the woods, even in common nights, than most suppose," he wrote in his diary at Walden Pond. "I frequently had to look up at the opening between the trees above the path in order to learn my route, and where there was no cart-path, to feel with my feet the faint track which I had worn." Old-timers in New Hampshire used to say of a winter's blackness, "This is a gripper of a night." But don't we know, by what we fear, what blackness is by the state of our natural condition? Black intimidates us. As the line from the old song "Lovin' Sam (The Sheik of Alabam)," tells us, "That's what it don't do nothin' else, 'cep."

On the other hand, what with any clarity defines whiteness? No, W. B. Yeats is correct: nothing can live at the poles (". . . there's no human life at the full or the dark"). No activity can be discovered there, no incarnations. They are gloomy waste places in the extreme, noncerebral and brainless and uninhabited, recalling for me the phrase by which Laurel and Hardy were once described: "two minds without a single thought." Orthochromatics shock us, before anything else, not only in the insolence of their extremes, but in the way they are part of the same destitution. Schiller asserted, *"Verwandt sind sich alle starke Seele"*—"All strong spirits are related."

Black suggests grief, loss, melancholy and chic. It also connotes uniformity, impersonality, discipline and, often as the symbol of imperial order, jackbooted force and Prussian dominance. It is the color of Captain Mephisto and the dark lunar half of the Zoroastrian puzzle, with the kind of legendarily subterranean and inscrutable, praealtic malignity apposite to it that conjures up the sort of words on which writers like Edgar Allan Poe and Arthur Machen and H. P. Lovecraft constantly relied, like "unutterable," "hideous," "loathsome" and "appalling." It is the color of the contrarian, the critic and the crepe-hanger. It is airless, above all, hermeneutically closed, a larcenous color which in its many morphs of mourning and concomitant glumness is wholly subject, like André Gide's brooding immoralist, to "evasive and unaccountable moods." What could be worse than to be destitute of light and at the same time incapable of reflecting it? Blackness tends to envelop and overwhelm a person by dint of the largeness of volume in which it appears or is presented to one, in the very same way that the faster you walk the more your peripheral vision narrows. The Japanese adjective *usui* means not only thin as to width but light as to color. What other color in the spectrum comes at you point-blank and so directly yet without access? It is immoderate and almost autoerotic in what subrationally but somehow inexorably it suggests of possibility in the theatrical, untiring and even violent depth of its inscrutable vastness. The darkness of black is the part of its brooding deepness inviting dreams. The soul of the color harbors in its holophrastic enigma all sorts of moods, including deliberation and delay. Didn't Rodin tell us, "Slowness is beauty"? There is gravity in the batwing-black of its weight, pull and shocking hue. It is the very medium of stark, rigorous negativity, a storm in Zanzibar, the black cataracts of Stygia, Kanchenjunga and its ferocious clouds, black maelstroms, black goat tents, catafalques, of defeaturing and helmeting shadows, rebellion and revolt, the unforgiving, spectral grimace fetched up in beetling frowns—the color of Spartacus, Robespierre, Luther, Marat, Sam Adams, Marx and Lenin and Mao, intractable Prometheus and defiant Manfred.

> From thy own heart I then did wring
> The black blood in its blackest spring

Mystery doesn't so much surround the color black as it defines it. If color symbolizes the differentiated, the manifest, the affirmation of light—and is not God, as light, ultimately the source of color?—black in turn indicates primordial darkness, the non-manifest, renunciation, dissolution, gravity. Isn't it sadly apposite to the surreptitious ways of man himself? Didn't André Malraux write perspicaciously in *The Walnut Trees of Altenburg* "Essentially a man is what he hides"? Don't we placate by our reliance on black the very color with which we most identify? A wife in Africa to be fertile often wears a black hen on her back. In Algeria, black hens are sacrificed. A black fowl in certain folklores, if buried where caught, is alleged to cure epilepsy. In medieval France, the limbs of black animals when applied warm to the limbs of the body supposedly relieved rheumatism. Chimney sweeps wear black as a totem with the same credulity that bandits in Thailand and Myanmar adorn themselves with protective tattoos. In Ireland, England—even Vermont—black wool to many people provides a cure for earache, just as in Russia it cures jaundice. Who can explain why for Rimbaud in his *Vowels* the letter A was black? Or why Beethoven thought that the key of B minor was black? No, enigma is only another word for black. We spend half our lives in curved shadows and in the sleep of dark, occlusive nights that are as "sloeblack, slow, black, crow black," as Dylan Thomas said of his own Welsh ("fishing-boat-bobbing") sea, and that are every bit as vast and profoundly mysterious.

Wet *is* black. On a gray day, in neutral light, with a faint drizzle, stones of almost any stripe quite vividly take on colors. As Adrian Stokes writes, the passing of water on stone gives a sense of organic formation and erosion, so that the stone seems "alive." Robert Frost in "The Black Cottage" notes, "A front with just a door between two windows/Fresh painted by the shower a velvet black." Cactus spines shine strangely red or gold in deserts during wet weather, just as creosote bushes become olive after rain. Most things darken when wet. And brighten when dark. And glisten when bright. Even swimmers. Harry Cohn of Columbia Pictures even said of his swimming star, Esther Williams, "Dry, she ain't much. Wet, she's a star." Darkness is also depth. The depth of black is determined by the penetration of light, which equals color when light is translated to pigment. A color with great tinting power allows in a lot of light. The stronger a tint is, the more transparent it may seem. The darker the wampum, the more valuable it was in trade. Native Americans sought *dark* clam shells from the English colonists who were compelled to use wampum in trading with them. Fr. Joseph François Lafitau, the French Jesuit, wrote in *Manners of the American Savages* in 1724 that in his time the usual strand of a wampum belt was eleven strands of 180 beads or about 1,980 beads. Three dark (or six white) beads were roughly the equivalent of an English penny. Black water in its stillness goes deeper than the ramparts of Dis. Clouds loom high above us, ominous, profoundly dark, yet shifting. There is a "black wind," the *beshabar*, a dry melancholy wind that blows northeasterly out of the Caucasus. "Even such winds as these have their own merit in proper time and place," declares Robert Louis Stevenson on the chiaroscuro wrought by wind, observing how "pleasant [it is] to see them [the clouds] brandish great masses of shadow."

Black is a maelstrom oddly inviting, winding about, ever beckoning us. It is a veiled temple, emptiness, the Balzacian abyss, "the mystery for which we are all greedy." Just as darkness is depth, corners are hidden and dark and inaccessible. Black is not only recessed but even in its most noble aspects never far from surreption and stealth. Is that not why silos are round? (Silage *spoils* in corners.) Black can be sullen as distant thunder, heavy as lead, here starkly blunt, there preternaturally atraluminous. It is also unlived-in, too authentic, embowered, conspiratorial, rarely tender-hearted, cruelly

cold, uninviting, casket-heavy, thick, explosive, mum and uncata-
logably dead.

I think of Peggy Lee, singing the heartbreaking "Yesterday I Heard
the Rain."

> Out of doorways
> black umbrellas
> come to pursue me
> Faceless people
> as they passed
> were looking through me
> No one knew me

Gene Lees, who wrote it, around 1962, told me it was a song about
the loss of faith.

Black is the color without light, curtain dark, the portcullis-drop-
ping color of loss, humility, grief and shame. Although to the human
eye everything visible has a color, where color exists as an optical
phenomenon, with a place already constructed for it in the human
imagination, what can be said of the color black? *Is* black visible? Is
it even a color? Or in some kind of grim, ruinous thunderclap and
with a sort of infernal and ghastly force does it somehow smother
color? Wholly destitute of color, is it the result of the absence of—or
the total absorption of—light? It is patently not included among
Andrew Lang's color fairy books. It is, oddly, *not* the color of blindness. "I can still make out certain colors. I can still see blue and
green," said Jorge Luis Borges, who added, ironically, that the one
color he did not see in his blindness was black, the color of night. He
said, "I, who was accustomed to sleeping in total darkness, was bothered for a long time at having to sleep in this world of mist, in the
greenish or bluish mist, vaguely luminous, which is the world of the
blind." Achromatopsy can involve partial or complete loss of color
vision, where shades of gray are seen. (Robert Boyle spoke of this
phenomenon as early as 1688.) To sufferers of such color deficiency,
most foods appear disgusting—things like tomatoes appear black, for
example. A patient of Dr. Oliver Sacks in 1987 became a victim of
such dislocating misperception: "His wife's skin seemed to him to be
rat-colored," Sacks observed, "and he could not bear to make love to
her. His vision at night was so acute that he could read license plates
for four blocks away. He became, in his words, 'a night person.'"

Many World War II pilots had the singular experience of actually
*seeing* black, when, during "blackouts," pulling out of a dive—they
could often hear but not see—blood quickly drained out of their

heads and flowed into their abdomen and legs, whereupon immediately they "sticked" high to gain altitude and usually came fully alert. There are no commercial airplanes painted black. It is far too inkily deathful and crepuscular a hue. Most modern aircraft, in fact, have bright white fuselage tops largely to reflect sunlight and reduce rising cabin temperatures. Flight data recorders, introduced in 1965 and dubbed "black boxes" by the media, in spite of the fact that they are invariably orange, traditionally share that nickname with any electronic "box of tricks," as I learned when, teaching at MIT, I found twenty examples so named.

Black, unlike white, has comparatively far less of what Francis Crick in *The Astonishing Hypothesis* calls "pop-out." Crick speaks of the "spotlight" of visual attention regarding the matter of human perception. "Outside the spotlight, information is processed less, or differently or not at all." In relation to what the Hungarian psychologist Bela Julesz calls "preattentive processing," boundaried objects—and colors—are targets, as it were. According to Monet, Cézanne habitually kept a black hat and white handkerchief next to a model in order to ascertain, to fix, to examine the two poles between which to establish his "values." Although white can be considered a highly "salient" color, black with its remorseless absorption, assimilating all wavelengths, utterly engorging light, lacks such definition. Any radiation that strikes a "black hole," for example, is utterly absorbed, never to reappear. "A material that absorbs all light that falls on it is black, which is how this particular beast received its ominous name," write Robert Hazen and James Trefil in *Science Matters*. You could say that the color black is an "unattended" event, as it were, with no "fixation point." It detargets a visual place by its very nature, blots things out, becomes the ultimate camouflage. It is, as a distractor, the color of grimness and goodnight. The high dark fog in San Diego is called *El velo de la luz*, the veil that hides the light. F.D.R. had the metal parts of his leg braces ("ten pounds of steel," he once pointed out) painted deep black at the ankles, so as to escape detection against his black socks and shoes. "Gobos" (or "flats," "niggers" or "flags") are those large black cloth shades used on Hollywood sets to block out unwanted light from the camera lens in order to avoid halation and other undesirable effects. Black by definition scumbles objects.

Where is it half the time when we *can* discern it? Isn't rude, unforgiving black, impossibly covert like midnight and airport macadam and prelapsarian ooze, merely a spreading brainless giant without shape or contour? Contour, remember, almost always changes a color's tone. A square centimeter of blue, Matisse argued, is not the same as a square meter of the same blue. Beyond that even, the extent of the area changes the tone, as well. And isn't black in its fat merciless gravitation almost by definition arealess? Without boundaries, at least without easily perceptible boundaries, black can be comfortless for that. If it doesn't threaten us, it can make us feel uneasy. Purple, which comes between blue and ultraviolet, resembles black in this. Although we accept that ultraviolet exists, there is little evidence of it in our daily lives. (The best evidence we have is sunburns and cataracts, neither of which are close to purple.) Black is bottomless, autogyromotive and indirigible. Given Spinoza's observation that everything longs to endure in its being, doesn't black, more than any other struggling tinct, show an unpardoning tendency to be its own archetype, traveling, not like night, but with a kind of deep and unspellable horror reaching, stretching out, gathering, by way of everything from the monstrositous depth of children's formless nightmares to the gruesome hood-black anonymity of an executioner's reality, very like bony Death's harvesting hand?

I wonder, does black invoke what might be called "enemy-memory"? Or is black *itself* the enemy-memory? The witches on the back fence? The wreck into which we dive? Didn't Italo Calvino warn us, "The eye does not see things but images of things that mean other things"?

We tend to go wild in lunar light, in dark light, in the grip of the "night mysterious," as the song lyric goes. As Sky Masterson (Marlon Brando) tells Sarah Brown (Jean Simmons) in the film of the Broadway musical *Guys & Dolls*, "Sarah, I know the nighttime. I live in it. It does funny things to you." The question we pose of night, when we do not recoil from it, recalls for me certain lines from "Night Voices," a passionately personal poem which the young German pastor Dietrich Bonhoeffer wrote in 1943, two years before he was hanged by the Nazis in the Flossenburg concentration camp:

> I sink myself into the depths of the dark.
> You night, full of outrage and evil,
> Make yourself known to me!
> Why and for how long will you try our patience?
> A deep and long silence;
> Then I hear the night bend down to me:
> "I am not dark; only guilt is dark!"
>
> —*translated by Keith R. Crim*

As a color, black goes in more than several directions. It is the color of Saturn; the number 8—if for Pythagoras numbers have designs, why can't they have colors?—and symbolizes in China the North, yin, winter, water, as well as the tortoise among the Four Spiritually Endowed Animals. Ek Xib Chac, the western spirit of the Mayan rain-god, Chac, was black. In the Kabbala, black carries a value of understanding, while black in heraldry stands for prudence and wisdom. In the world of alchemy it is the color of fermentation. To ancient Egyptians, black symbolized rebirth and resurrection. Many Native American tribes who held the color black to be a powerful talisman wore it as war paint in battle and for feathers, because it made the warrior invulnerable. It is the fathomless color of everything from Nazi parachutes to Hernando's Hideaway, "where all you see are silhouettes," to the famous lunar eclipse on August 27, 413 B.C., which contributed to the terrible defeat of the Athenians (soothsayers, seeing the portent, advised delay) at the hands of the Spartans under Gylippus. What metaphor of need or hope or aspiration cannot be constructed of the ongoing paradox that black attracts the sun? The whole idea recapitulates the entire historical phenomenon of opposites: of the Beauty and the Beast, of Venus and Vulcan, of Plus and Minus, of Innocence and Guilt, of Death and Transfiguration. Noctiluca, "she who shines by night," wonderful paradox, is a classical synonym for Diana. Among some of the wilder, more extravagant and overingenious schemes presented over time to deal with the threat of dangerous, destructive glaciers, such as blowing them up, towing them, etc., someone once seriously suggested painting them solid black so that they would melt under the hot sun!

Although no two color blacks are alike—some would argue that one can almost always find a subtle and misleading gradualness of tone in whatever two examples are set side by side—as a basic color black seems, more often than not, invariable, solid, like no other, *la verità effetuale della cosa*, the nature of fact, true, although it has as many adjectives as it has hues—jet, inky, ebony, coal, swart, pitch, smudge, livid, sloe, raven, sombre, charcoal, sooty, sable and crow, among others. Things get smutched, darkened, scorched, besmirched in a thousand ways. (Common black pigments like ivory, bone, lamp, vine and drop black all basically consist of carbon obtained by burning various materials.) It is a color that reminds me in its many odd morphs of what photographer Diane Arbus chose to call freaks, "the quiet minorities," for its hues seem never the same, seem never alike, and in their enigmatic sombreness, like freaks, having passed their trials by fire—black is *the end*—are, as Arbus once said of her odd subjects, often ogled by people pleading for their own to be postponed. Isn't it strange that if you're "in the black," you are doing well, but if your "future looks black," things are bad? Its profundity is its mystery. The way of what the depth of black in going beyond deepness hides of, as well as defines in, the color reminds me of what Martin Heidegger once said of Carl Orff's musical language, *"Die Sprache der Sprache zur Sprache zu bringen,"* that it gives voice to the language of language. The color is an irrational and complicated achromatic, a tetrical, hcat-cating, merciless, unforgiving and obdurate color, jayhawking you in a hundred ways, and in certain riddling guises it often reminds me of Frank Sinatra's "It Never Entered My Mind," a song Ol' Blue Eyes sings quite brilliantly but which, filled with sharps and flats and atonal glissandi, constantly strikes me, an amateur, mind you, as almost impossible to sing. There are many shades and faded grades in the parade of black, very like the turbid and half-turbid sounds found in Japanese writing and pronunciation.

It is not commonly compared to song, however. The spoken word sounds like a gunshot. *Blak!* As a pronounced word it has the sudden finality of a beheading. *Blak!* What a convinced declaration is made, for example, in Rouault's black line! Or Beckmann's! Or de Kooning's! Hcnri Rousseau did not want lines. He sought to make a line happen, as in nature, by arranging the delicate contrast between contingent colors. Art, it may be argued, like personality, like character, like human behavior, is fractal—its contours cannot be mapped. Who first conjured the color black, however, sharing with Robert Frost, who frequently wrote of the dark, the stormy "inner weather" within us, surely insisted fences made good neighbors.

What is of particular interest is that Frost, a poet often highly pessimistic and more than well acquainted with the night, also believed that blackness had to be faced. Remember in his poem "The Night Light" how he chides a woman who while she sleeps burns a lamp to drive back darkness, declaring, "Good gloom on her was thrown away"?

The origins of the word black (ME *blak*, OE *blǣc*, ON *blakkr*) go back to *flamma* (flame), and *flagrare* (L, to blaze up), words having to do with fire, flame, things that have been burned—compare *blush, bleak, blind, flare* and *flicker*—and is ultimately formed from the Indo-European *bhleg*, to burn with black soot or to burn black with soot. There are several Anglo-Saxon and Early English words for black or darkness: *piesternesse* (darkness), *blǣqimm* (jet) and *blakaz* (black). We find "blake" in *The Ancren Riwle*, or "Rule of Nuns," ca. 1210, and in *King Horn*, before A.D. 1210 ("He wipede bat blake of his swere"). A couplet from *The Story of Havelock the Dane*, an Anglo-Saxon tale, before A.D. 1300, goes as follows:

> In a poke, ful and blac,
> Sone he caste him on his bac

But do we in fact get our English word from sound symbolism or mispronunciation? Different meanings, amazingly enough, have derived from the very same original word by way of a sequence of semantic shifts and in the process ironically have moved in the opposite direction, as is evident in Old English in which *blǣc* is "black." But the word *blac*, with no other phonetic difference than that of a vowel, actually once denoted, according to Anglo-Saxon scholars W. W. Skeat, Rev. Richard Morris and T. Wedgwood, what we now think of as its opposite. The original meaning of *black* is "pale," "colorless," "blank" or "white." Is this not astonishing? The word *black* (Anglo-Saxon *blac, blǣc*), which is fundamentally the same as the old German *blach*—a word now only to be found in two or three compounds, e.g., *Blachfeld*, a level field—originally meant level, bare and by extension bare of color. According to William S. Walsh's *Handy-Book of Literary Curiosities*, the nasalized form of black is blank, a word which originally signified bare, and was used in the sense of white specifically and logically because white is (apparently) bare of color. In Anglo-Saxon we read, *"Se mona mid his blacan lēohte"*—the moon with her pale light. An old poet praises the beauty of *"blac hleor ides"*—the pale-cheeked girl or woman. *Blac* in *Beowulf* means "bright," "brilliant." In the great hall, Beowulf sees Grendel's mère for the first time by the bright firelight—*"fȳr-lēoht zeseah, blācne lēoman"* (l. 1516). The Old English infinitive *blǣcan* means not "to blacken" but rather "to bleach." Our words *bleak* and *bleach*—is this not passing strange?—are from the same root. In the north of England, the word *blake*, as applied to butter or cheese, means "yellow." So now you know the essential difference between black and white. *There is none!* Weirdly, in the etymological sense, black means white. Black *is* white!

# New South Wales
## *Erik Ehn*

*Characters:*

GUARD
LIZARD
CUT ONE
CUT TWO
CUT THREE

CUT FOUR
PRINCESS
NURSE
NARWAL

## ONE

(*An India Indian princess is incarcerated in the hold of a wooden ship. The vessel rides high on a stormy sea; the young woman moves as a wave inside a wave. Up on a deck, one man sells her to another; the price settled on is a handful of fresh water. The seller is about to turn over the leg-iron keys in exchange for the draught when a wave shatters the ship. The men are killed and the princess is forced undersea. The keys become keyhorses and droplets of fresh water become their eyes. The horses swim with the princess, helping her landward. A crate of rifles breaks open against coral; differing schools of fish seize them for their own and begin battling one another. A rifle lances into the princess's grip; the momentum launches her ashore. The unarmed keyhorses are shot to death; the hail of bullets is sea foam shattered on the rocks, and the sea is locked against her. We read a broadside of these events on the underside of a manta ray.*

*The princess crosses mountains.*

*An Australian prison guard with the head of a koala enters and talks to the lop-tailed lizard on the back of his hand.*)

GUARD. She landed here in New South Wales. She's crossing the back of High Warrumbungle with her bandits. We lose the price of her if she makes Queensland.

LIZARD. There's a joke in there, isn't there? Going from one place to another. There's a joke in there—tell it to me.

> (*The guard whispers a joke. The laughter of the bear and the lizard combines with the music of the successful sprees staged by the rebel princess.*)

## TWO

> (*The princess has hurt her hands in a fall; cactus needles detail her. Opera—her cuts sing.*)

CUT ONE. Each singing cut reveals—

CUT TWO. Red silk.

CUT THREE. Drink your milk and sit up straight.

CUT FOUR. Too late.

CUT ONE. Cactus archers. You race to stable arrows.

CUT TWO. Go.

CUT THREE. New infection.

CUT FOUR. Looted by your own.

PRINCESS. No.

CUT ONE. Your useless hands walk you into town.

> (*Opera over. She goes down into town and knocks on a door; she has to knock gently, with her forehead. A nurse comes to the door.*)

PRINCESS. Do you work on Saturdays?

NURSE. You have no equal.

> (*The nurse leads her in. The princess grows weaker and weaker.*)

The doctor's out but I make my own medicines by pickling.

(*The princess lies down. The nurse fills a large hypo from a jar of pickled ostrich eggs. She injects the princess.*)

You have an equal. Drive your head down through the old bed.

(*The princess sticks her head in the salt of the ancient sea-bed, ostrich fashion. She goes all the way under and is in a primal sea; she tosses as she did in the hold of the ship. The nurse runs away, ornamenting herself as she goes with different colored muds made of her sweat and dusts. The nurse comes upon the princess's old gang.*)

I'm the one now.

(*She and the bandits dance in preparation for a raid. The princess drifts in fever, salt-sick. Coelacanths with muskets draw near.*)

PRINCESS. So thirsty. Spare me.

(*A guard hands the bandits silver. The bandits cast the silver from the mountain; the pieces collect to a cloud and rainwater down a funnel spiked through the bitter sand; the princess drinks. The guard gets a key from the nurse, unlocks the earth, finds the princess and leads her into captivity.*)


**THREE**

(*The princess paces in a courtyard in a penal colony. The sea makes mountains of itself beyond the water. A narwhal breaches.*)

NARWHAL. Come away with me.
  The rifles have rusted shut and sunk below the sea.
  With my nose I set you free.
  Princess, come away with me.
  I've made books out of manta rays.

(*A guard in a tower reads a large book made of dried, bound manta rays. What he says comes true.*)

GUARD. A tree grows and the princess climbs it. The narwhal shows wings. The narwhal is a partridge. The princess feeds pears to the monkeys who patrol the razor wire and she leaps past, into the waves. The narwhal saves her and flies up, dressed in the robes of the sea, dressed in the clothes of a blue queen, partridge pregnant. The drops that fall from the dress are red: rust from the chains and keys and guns. And all Queensland is rust red after the escape of the rebel princess and the Queen of Heaven.

# Four Conversations
## *Rosmarie Waldrop*

### CONVERSATION ON SLOW MOTION

EVEN IF OUR LIFE seems scattered, a text always going astray, it builds on constants, she says. Like a piece of music. The mind should be able to embrace it in its full extravagance and touch the architecture of cause even as it forms. More so with the years, with resources of slowness. You must sit in a blue shift to sort seed from going to.

Not sit, he says. Only in motion, albeit slow. Arrows toward new setting out even as the day sets. As if by walking I'd find where I need to go, just as following the seduction of one basic rule can unknot essential dimensions of a whole new system. It's when I try to keep pace with the wind that particles turn into perspective and ride out into the large.

You launch exotic birds, she says, and some adapt to the Rhode Island winter. I stick with domestic varieties, crows in my face, a rooster on the brain, maybe a Rhode Island Red. My breasts droop, faintly mournful. Such simple desire blasting the bones electric, to perch on crags and cliffs, so matter of fact. But highs are only one element of the climate. The shadow of a cloud, and I slow into symptoms. The sun drops. The surface of the leaves turns blue.

The cells rust, he says, not hunger. It seems yesterday that I flung myself into the January river, gasping with shock, plunging for the unreachable that is promised—though only as long as we have no history. Now the train's speed is hostage to the next station, becalmed legs and thinning hair. Could it be that loss completes possession? Becomes, like the "with" in "without," a second acquisition, deeper, wholly internal, more intense for its pain?

*Rosmarie Waldrop*

## CONVERSATION ON AGING

Take the hordes of children, she says. So to take off on the crest of light, so to run toward the horizon through fields, bushes, the knee-high grass, undeterred by stop signs, fences or decapitated statues. As if walking were as hospitable as sleep. As if the games didn't unravel. As if innocence were forever, though time might age, and a season forget to be born.

But even children, he says, toss their pebble across the river to throw off some undefined unease that weighs on them. As does the indifference the stone drops into. But its call and echo from bank to bank barely touches the water, skips as on light, as into regions of enhanced density, increasing in power.

Is it war or games or excessive tension that makes us grow up? she asks. Or simply the way particles behave in a field of force? One day the girl disappears into a different point of reality, a woman with sagging breasts. And still my sense of self is woolly, diffuse as in sleep, as if the years had only heaped on more blankets. I always want to hear the sirens, albeit tied to the mast, but I fear becoming the sailor with ears plugged, just plugging away at the oar.

Gaps in the text open it up, he says, the way breathing allows the world into our chest. Your woolly self still makes me want to get under those blankets. Penelope, mind, isn't part of your scenario: you don't seem in danger of taking up needlework. But I too want to get down through all the roar and twang to the deep horizon note I know is there though I can't hear it: my own frequency. Is this another image that holds us captive? And if I touched it? I saw a dog stray into the subway and hit the live rail.

## CONVERSATION ON CAUSE

I step into my mother's room, she says, and though a woman's body is a calendar of births and injunctions to death, time disappears. Only dead enough to bury could soundproof silence. Anxiety I've known by heart and lung. In my mother's room. Terror and lack of perspective. The tie between us anticipates any move to sever it.

The river runs clear without imparting its clarity whether we step into it or not.

Distant causes, he says. I don't mean the stars, not in the astrological sense. But if a butterfly fluttering its wings in China can cause a storm in Rhode Island, how much more the residues of radiation or the solemnity of past rituals. The stove glows red. Thin apple trees line the road. You think you are taking a clean sheet of paper, and it is already covered with scribbles, clumsy as by a child's hand.

The heart has its rhythm of exchange, she says, without surplus or deficit. Monotony swelling, subsiding, vague oscillation of a language that conjugates precise details with a window on the infinite. As I burrow down inside my skin I take your touch with me, pulling it out of your reach to develop in a darkroom of my own. The way the current elongates our reflection in the river and seems to carry it off.

A death without corruption is the promise of photography, he says. Cut from the flesh of the world, translated into color. But matter, the initial trace, is not at home in a striated mirror, even if light falls into the arms of love.


## CONVERSATION ON THE MILLENNIUM

There are many invisible borders, she says. Some erect and inexorable as when a lover recedes into friend. How we fuss as we approach the millennium, after having slept in its secular sense so long. As if civilization were about to draw its lazy length up toward a moment of moments, where Human-Nature-Can/Cannot-Be-Changed would slide down opposite slopes of time. The horizon is a function of eye-level. Are we not nose to the ground overestimating, as so often, things Christian?

A frame supports what would, on its own, collapse, he says. And deep focus can make the ground turn figure in retrospect. Like a German sentence that comes clear only once you reach the verb at its end. By a strong effort of will. Time divides us into dust, but also binds our bodies forward. Though the exhaustion will not be squared. When I say "book" you don't think clay tablets, Japanese silk scrolls or palm leaves strung together.

The moon is constant, she says, my bleeding a calendar. The instant we apprehend an end we desperately predict new wagon trains to head west, as if celebrating zeros could create bluer skies and more self-evident truths. As if the universe could big-bang again. And again. Not sadly untracked sand, but too many dots per inch. Machinery whirring while the credit's gone.

Writing pulls east, he says, with the movement of the earth. For all our love of diagonals we cling to the slower proofs measured in mutations, milky ways, and ever the wind blows. The spectacle inside the eye projects its large, invariant rhythm onto a trust in daybreak. Which we make ours. Because as long as we follow we lag behind, and the centuries pass intestate.

# Four Poems
## *Gustaf Sobin*

### OF OUR INVISIBLE ANATOMY

. . . no, it's not history that
happens, but the
blown veils of so much random apparition: but the
glints, you

called them: the sudden
sporadic drops of some otherwise
in-

determinable substance.    yes, signs, *sema*, all the
given indices of that
all-
pervasive *isn't*.    does it glow?      then
sip.    flutter?    then bring yourself flush a-

gainst the
rippling sheath of such steady
dis-

semination.    (whose eyes, you wrote, weren't
eyes but
echoes.    whose echoes but the residue of some long-
since-

rescinded determinant).    sleep, then, in
mouths, in the open
o-

*Gustaf Sobin*

rifice of so
much
scuttled letter.   feed, feed on
omission alone.   for there, at least—limbs
piled, breath

locked—you'd
glut, occasionally, upon the
verb's
stray vapor: what rippled—insistent—into
                                        extinction.


LUBERON

only there, in the hills'
deepest creases, would you grow, at
last, legible, hear
your-

self happen in each dark,
spark-
hearted foliation.   weren't you, after
all, your very
own antecedent, the organs you'd

bring, mumbling, into that
arena of
leaves, thistles, ledges?   there, that
is, where your breath, at
last, might
en-

counter mass?   wed, then, the interval of
each
articulated
instant, the acorn that

glows, as if epiphanous, at its own
ac-
cording.   for only the pleat,
finally, speaks.   and, in the name of the
neither, resonant,
echoes.


## BLUE MOON

*—for Peter Cole*

"there's a blue moon in
    blossom," he writes you from Yerushalayim.   "its
scent," he
tells you, "rises clear into the crisp, mid-

Hanukkah cold."   doesn't the poem, that
address without *destinataire*, do exactly the
same: rise, that
is—sputtering flare—fuelled by nothing other than

its own, open
im-
perative?   what's emptier, though, than
words?   than the clattering syllables of so much
preempted existence?   yet the
scent, you

realize, yes, the indelible
odors of that
il-

legible scent.   isn't it for this, this
octave-
without, that one
writes?   why, this morning, amongst its
floating bars—yes, its impossible promise—you reply.

*Gustaf Sobin*

## TRANSPARENT ITINERARIES: 1997

where the numbers, finally, ended in nimbi.


where rubbed, pummelled, the face, finally—cupped in a fanned
chalice of fingers—glowed as if exempt, now, from every given
contingency.


like a goldbeater's sheath—you'd written—meticulously tooled.


like a mirror, too, but a mirror that had sucked, drained from
that face its every living feature.


wherein the room itself, that instant, might have volatilized.


———


we, who'd always compared things to the
        comparable, when elsewhere, when otherwise, when
nothing, really, but the
dissolving that
drew.


———


but the relapsing facets of nomenclature.


the decor having grown, if anything, more and more elaborate to
the extent that it withheld—within its running pleats—the
pleatless.

(its compressed releases).


to the extent that a single earring—its nacreous globe—might
have turned premonitory.


a wrist in a bracelet of shadows, inductive.


for only there, exchanging weights, slipping through the very last
layers of identity, had we ever happened.


———————


hard
hallucinatory splendor of
    those instances: hollow, immense as the
very air in which, still
spasmodic, they'd readily dis-
sipate.


———————


within, that is, the *wasn't* without which—*de natura*—*weren't*.


without which, matte, irreflexive, caught in the drafts of a
massive refluence, had done little more than thrash within the
dry pools of reason.


beating, as we did, against our very depthlessness.

—depth itself but the pure product of a psychic imperative,
having no other validity than the satisfaction of that imperative—


by which, counter-syntactical, we'd always acceded.


_____


. . . word
sloughing word in an ever-
al-
leviative movement towards . . .


_____


for only the inference, finally, mesmerized.


only its articulated omission—its blanched letters—drew.


(oh, the beauty of such bewilderment).


limb lapping limbs but only for the sake of that singular passage.


that blind perspective.


oval in which, thoroughly enveloped, would reflect, finally,
each other's invisibility.

# Songbirds
## *Jack Barth*

*—for Philip and Geneva Barth*

*Jack Barth*

# The Visiting Privilege
## *Joy Williams*

DONNA CAME AS A VISITOR in her long black coat. It was spring but still cool. She never wore light colors, she was no buttercup. She was visiting her friend Cynthia who was in Pond House for depression. Donna never had a drink beforehand when she visited Cynthia. She shunned her habitual excesses and arrived sober and aware, with an exquisite sinking feeling. She thought that Pond House was an unfortunate name, a pond being as it was, stagnant, artificial and small. This wasn't just her opinion, a pond was indeed an artificially confined body of water. Cynthia thought that Pond was most likely the name of the hospital wing's benefactor, most likely a man. Cynthia had three roommates, a woman in her sixties and two obese teenagers. Donna liked to pretend that the old woman was her mother. Hi, she'd say, you look great today, what a pretty sweatshirt. Donna would help her with her bills. They weren't bills at all actually.

Donna had been visiting Cynthia for about a week now. She could scarcely imagine what she had done with herself before Cynthia had had the grace to get herself committed to Pond House. She liked everything about it but she particularly liked sitting in Cynthia's room, speaking quietly with her while the others listened. They didn't even pretend not to listen, the others. But sometimes she and Cynthia would stroll down to the lounge and get a snack from the fridge. In the lounge, goofy helium balloons in the shape of objects or food but with human features were tied to the furniture with ribbon. They bobbed there opposite the nurses' station, and people would bat them as they passed by. Cynthia thought that the balloons would be deeply disturbing to anyone who was already disturbed but everyone thought they were wildly amusing. None of the people at Pond House were supposed to be seriously ill, at least on Floor Three. Floor Four was another matter. But here they were supposed to be ruefully aware of their situation, aware that they could possibly be helped. Before Cynthia had come here, she'd been sleeping a lot, up to twenty hours a day. When she did drag herself out of bed, it

148

would be to commit violent, wretched acts, the most recent being the torching of her boyfriend's car, a black Corvette. The boyfriend was married but Cynthia strongly suspected he was gay. He drove her crazy. "He's a taker and not a giver, Donna," she told Donna earnestly.

Cynthia told Donna that she was so discouraged that everything seemed vaguely yellow to her, that she saw everything as though through a veil of yellow.

"I've seen it described that way somewhere," Donna said excitedly. "The yellow part."

"You know, Donna," Cynthia said, "you're part of my problem."

When Cynthia got like this, Donna would excuse herself and go away for a while. Or she would go back to the room and talk with the old woman. She got a kick out of being extraordinarily friendly to her. Once she brought her gum, another time a jar of night cream. She ignored the obese teenagers, but one afternoon one of them deliberately bumped into her as she walked down the hall. The girl's flesh was hard and she smelled of coconut. She thrust her face close to Donna's. Her pores were large and clean and Donna could see the contacts resting on the corneas of her eyes.

"I'm passionate, intense and filled with private reverie and so is my friend," the girl said, "so don't slime us like you do." Then she punched Donna viciously on the arm. Donna felt like crying but she was only a visitor, she didn't have to come here so frequently, she was really coming here too much, sometimes twice a day.

There were group meetings three times a week and Donna always tried to be present for these, although she was not permitted to attend them. Sometimes, however, if she stood just outside the door, the nurses and psychologists didn't notice her right away. Cynthia and the fat teenagers and the old lady and a half dozen others would sit around a large table and say anything they wanted to.

"I dreamt that I threw up a fox," one of the fat girls said.

Really, Donna couldn't tell them apart.

"I shit something that looked like an onion once," a man said. "It just kept coming out of me. I pulled it out of myself with my own hands. I thought it was the devil, but it was a worm. A gift from Central America."

"That is so disgusting," the other fat girl said, "that is the most . . ."

"Hey!" the man said. "Get yourself a life, woman!"

The worm thing caused the old lady to request to leave. Donna walked back to the room with her and they sat down on her bed.

149

"Feel my heart," the old lady said. "It's pounding. I wasn't brought up that way."

The old woman liked to play cards and she and Donna would often play with an old soiled deck that had pictures of colorful fish on it. Donna pretended she was on a boat, in a cabin on a boat, on a short, safe trip to a lovely island. The old woman was a mysterious opponent, not at all what she seemed. Donna had, in fact, been told by the nurses that she was considerably more impaired than she appeared to be. Beyond the window of the cabin were high gray waves, pursuing and accompanying them. The waves were an essential part of the world the boat required, but they hated the boat too, it was clear.

"What kind of fish are these?" Donna asked.

The old lady looked at her cards as though she had never seen them before.

"These are reef residents," she finally said.

They played a variation of Spit in the Ocean. Donna had had no idea that there were so many variations of this humble game.

The two fat girls came in and lay down on their beds. The old lady was really opening up to Donna. She was telling her about her husband and her little house.

"After my husband died, I was afraid someone might come in and . . ." She passed her finger across her throat. "I bought one of those men. Safe-T-Man II, the New Generation. You know, the ones that look as though they're six feet tall but can be folded up and put in a little tote bag? I put him in the car or I put him in my husband's easy chair right in front of the window. He had all kinds of clothes. He had a leather coat. He had a seersucker jacket. He had a baseball cap."

"Where is he now?" Donna asked.

"He's in his little tote bag. Actually he frightened me a little, Safe-T-Man. I think I ordered him too dark or something. I never did get used to him."

"That's racist," one of the fat girls said.

"Yeah, what a racist remark," the other one said.

"I bet he wonders what happened to me," the old woman said. "I bet my car does too. One minute you're on the open road, one excitement after another, the next you're in a dark garage. I'm not afraid of dying, but I don't want to die old."

She was quite old already, of course, but the fat girls did not challenge her on this. Cynthia came into the room, eating a piece of fruit, a nectarine or something.

150

"The first thing I'm going to do when I get out of here is go home and make Festive Chicken," the old woman said. "I hope you'll all be my guests for dinner."

The fat girls and Cynthia stared at her.

"I'd love to," Donna said. "What is Festive Chicken? Can I bring anything? Wine? A salad?"

"It requires toothpicks," the old woman said. "You bake it with toothpicks but then you take the toothpicks out."

"It sounds wonderful," Donna said.

Cynthia rolled her eyes. "Would you give it a rest," she said to Donna.

"I'm tired now," the old woman said sweetly. "I'm tired of playing cards." She put the cards back in their box but the box didn't have reef residents on it. It had a picture of an old dreary European city; it was the very opposite of a reef resident.

"This is not good," she said. "This isn't good at all! These don't belong in this box; it's the first time I've noticed this. Would you go to my house and bring back the other deck of cards?" she asked Donna.

"Sure," Donna said.

"My house is a little strange," the old woman said.

"What do you mean?"

"I bet it is," one of the fat girls said.

"I love my little house," the old woman said anxiously. "I want to get back to it as soon as I can."

She gave Donna the address and a key from her pocketbook. That evening, when visiting hours were over, Donna drove to the house, which was small and clean, with a crushed rock yard. There was a dead nestling in the driveway, brown, the way they always were. The place didn't seem that strange to Donna. One would be desperate to get out of it, certainly. There seemed to be lots of things that plugged into the walls but none of them were plugged in. She found the cards almost immediately, in the kitchen. There were the colorful fish on the cover of the box and inside, the deck had pictures of the foreign city. Idly, she opened the refrigerator. The refrigerator was full of ketchup, nothing but bottles of ketchup, each one partially used. Donna had an urge to top the bottles up from other bottles, to reduce the unseemly number of bottles but with not much effort she resisted this.

On the way back to her apartment she stopped at a restaurant and had several drinks in the bar there. The bartender's name was Lucy.

151

She had just come back from her vacation. She had spent forty-five minutes of that vacation swimming with the dolphins. The dolphin that had persisted in keeping Lucy's company had an immense boner.

"He kept gliding past me, gliding past," Lucy said. She moved her hand through the air. "I just kept worrying about the little kids. They're always bringing in these little kids who have only weeks to live due to one thing or another. I would think it would be pretty undesirable for them to experience a dolphin with a boner."

"But the dolphins know better than that, don't they," Donna said.

"It's not all that relaxing to swim with them, actually," the bartender said. "They like some people better than others and the ones they don't feel like shit. You know, out of the Gaia loop."

People in the restaurant kept requesting exotic drinks that Lucy had to look up in her Bartender's Bible. After a while, Donna went home.

The next afternoon, Donna swept into Pond House in her long black coat bearing a bunch of daffodils as a gift in general. In the elevator there were a number of people. They were all visitors and Donna smiled gravely at them.

Cynthia was in the lounge in a big chintz slip-covered chair reading *Anna Karenina*.

"Should you be reading that?" Donna asked.

Cynthia wouldn't talk to her.

Donna found the old woman and gave her the deck of cards.

"I'm so relieved," the old woman said. "That could have been such a problem, such a problem. Would you do me another favor?"

Donna smiled gravely at her.

"Would you get my dog?"

Donna was enthusiastic about this. "Do you have a dog? Where is he?"

"He's at my house."

"Is anyone feeding him?" Donna said. "Does he have water?" She had found her vocation, she was sure of it. She could do this forever, she felt. She felt like a long-distance swimmer in that place that long-distance swimmers go in their heads when they're good.

"Nooooooo," the old woman said. "He doesn't need water." She looked delighted too. She and Donna beamed at one another. "He's a good dog, a watchdog."

"I didn't see him," Donna said.

"He wasn't watching you. He's gray." The old woman suddenly

looked concerned. "He's something you plug in," she said.

"Oh," Donna said. "I think I did notice him." She felt a little disappointed, he looked like a stereo speaker. She had pictured something a little more along the lines of Cerberus that they were talking about, the dog that guarded the gates of hell. Those Greeks! It wasn't that you couldn't get in, it was that you couldn't get out. And that honeycake business. . . . Actually, she had never grasped the honeycake business. . . .

"He detects intruders up to thirty feet and he barks. He can detect them through glass, brick, wood and cement. The closer they get, the louder and harder he barks. He's just a little individual but he sounds ferocious. I always liked him better than Safe-T-Man. I got them at the same time."

"But he'd be barking all the time here," Donna said. "You have to think of that."

"He can be quiet," the old woman said. "He can be good."

"I'll get him for you then," Donna said, as though she had just made a decision after a long thought. "Consider it done."

As Donna was leaving Pond House she passed a tall thin man dressed all in red yelling into the telephone. He looked like a bungee jumper. There was a pay phone at the very heart of the third floor and it was always in use. "What were you, born with an ax in your hand!" he yelled. "You're so destructive!"

Donna returned the next day with the old woman's dog, which she carried in a smart black-and-white Bendel's shopping bag that she had been saving. She arrived just about the time the group meeting was coming to a close. She lingered just inside the door. She saw the fat teenagers and Cynthia's round neat head with its fashionable haircut. A male patient she had never seen before was saying, "Hey, if it looks, walks, talks, smells and feels like the anima, then it is the anima." Donna thought this very funny and somewhat obscene. "Miss!" someone called to her. "You are not allowed in these meetings!" She went back to Cynthia's room and sat on her bed. The old woman's bed was stripped down to the ticking. She sat and looked at it vacantly.

When Cynthia came in, she said, "Donna, that old lady died, honest to God. We were all sitting around after dinner eating our goddamn Jell-O and she just tipped over."

"I have something she wanted here," Donna said, raising the bag. "This is hers, from her house."

"Get rid of it for godsakes," Cynthia said. "Listen, act quickly and positively." She began to cry. Donna thought her friend's response somewhat peculiar but that was probably why she was in Pond House.

As the day wore on, it was disclosed that the woman had no family. There was no one.

"There wouldn't have been any Festive Chicken either," Cynthia said. "That's for sure." She had her old mouth back on her, Donna was glad to notice.

There was a little discussion in the room about what had happened. The old lady had been eating the Jell-O. She hadn't said a word. She'd expressed no dismay. "She was clueless," one of the fat girls said.

"Were you friends before you came here or did you become friends here?" Donna asked them. They looked at her with hatred.

"She's a nut fucker, I think," one of them said. They began speaking about her as though she wasn't there. Donna listened with fascination. They were so alike she couldn't be sure which of them had struck her. She thought of them as Dum and Dee. She pretended she was a docent in a living museum leading tours. The neuroses of these two, Dum and Dee, are so normal they're of little concern to us, she would say, indicating the fat girls. Then she pretended the two girls were her jailors over whom, however, she held moral sway. The girls meanwhile had stopped discussing Donna and were arguing between themselves about whether Chinese astrology had any relevance if you weren't Chinese.

"You're textbook metal horse," one said to the other. "Textbook. Even before I knew your birthday I could have told you that."

After a while, Donna's mind began to wander.

The barking dog alarm had not worked at the old lady's house. It seemed a simple enough thing with few adjustments that could be made to it; its function would either be realized or it wouldn't, and it wasn't. Donna had gone outside, into the street, and walked slowly back toward the house, then she had run, waving her arms, giving the thing every opportunity. No one had been around to see her, thank goodness. There had been no sound at all, only the sound of her own feet on the crushed rock yard. It had not worked in her own apartment either. It had not even felt warm.

Poor old soul, Donna thought.

Night was creeping around the corners of the hospital, rising from the grass. There was the smell of potatoes, the sound of wheels bringing the supper trays. The visitors were always required to leave around this time.

"Cynthia," Donna said. "I'll see you tomorrow."

"Why?" Cynthia said.

At home, Donna pretended she was on a train with no ticket, eluding the conductor as it sped through the night on its gleaming rails. She made herself a drink. She drank it, almost finished it completely, then fluffed it up a bit. The phone rang and it was Cynthia. She was delighted it was Cynthia.

"You will not believe this, Donna," Cynthia said. "You know that new guy, flannel shirt, jeans, kind of really annoying? Well, at dinner he was saying that when women attempt suicide they often don't succeed but with men they do it on the first go round. He said that that simple statistic tells it all about the difference between men and women. He said that men are doers and that women are idlers and flirts, and Caroline just threw back her chair and . . ."

"Who's Caroline?" Donna asked.

"My roommate for godsakes, the one who hates you. She attacked this guy. She gouged out one of his eyes with a spoon."

"She gouged it *out?*"

"I didn't think it could be done, but boy, she knew how to do it."

"I wonder if that could have been me," Donna said.

"Oh, I think so. It's bedlam in here." Cynthia laughed wildly. "I want to leave, Donna, but I don't feel better. But I could leave, you know. I could just walk right out of here."

"Really?" Donna said. She thought, when I get out of here, I'm going to be gone.

"But I think I should feel better. I have no destination is the problem."

"Goal," Donna said. "You have no goals?"

Maybe the phone wasn't such a good idea, Cynthia using the phone. Donna preferred sitting quietly with her in Pond House watching different impulses move across her pale face, offering to get her little things she had expressed no desire for, reflecting about Dennis, her married man who had not come by to see her once. Of course he was probably still annoyed about his car, although he had filed no charges.

Cynthia kept talking, pretty much about her life, the details of which Donna had heard before and which were no more riveting this time. She'd had a difficult time of it. It had started in childhood. She had been an intense little thing but thwarted, thwarted, and so on. Donna walked around with the phone to her ear, making another drink, crushing an ant or two that ventured onto the countertop, staring out the window at the dark only to realize that she couldn't see the dark, but only a darkened image of herself and the objects behind her. She sipped her drink and turned toward some picture postcards she had taped to one of the cupboards. Some of them had been up for years. One was of a city, a somber and civilized city similar to the one on the old woman's playing cards.

Cynthia was saying, ". . . I just can't accept so much, you know, Donna, and I feel, I really feel this, that my capacity to adapt to what is has been exceeded. I . . ."

"Cynthia," Donna said. "We're all alone in a meaningless world. That's it. OK?"

"That's so easy for you to say!" Cynthia screamed.

There was a loud crack and the connection was broken.

Donna had no recollection who had sent her the postcard or from where. She couldn't think what had prompted her to display it either. The city held no allure for her. She certainly had no intention of taking it down and looking at it more closely.

Later, she lay in bed trying to find sleep by recounting the rank of poker hands. Royal Flush, Straight Flush, Four of a Kind, Full House. . . . A voice kept saying in her head *Out or In. Huh? Which?* She could not fall asleep. Then it was dawn and she had still not fallen asleep. But she was not tired, she felt alert, glassy even. She bathed and dressed and hurried to Pond House where she had breakfast in the cafeteria. Eggs, toast, juice, it was awful, she ate it quickly. Her eyes darted about, falling on everything, glittering. There was her coat hanging on a hook next to her table. The coat seemed preposterous to her suddenly, a thing, dumb, of unnecessary associations. What must she look like in that coat, honestly.

Up on Floor Three, Cynthia wasn't in her room but the remaining fat girl was. Her face was red and her eyes swollen from crying. Donna sat quietly and watched her. She pretended that she was a stone, proud and confident and successful.

"I just lost my friend," the fat girl said. "They took away my friend."

"You're not Caroline, then," Donna said.

"I wish I was," the fat girl said. "I wish I was Caroline." She lay on her bed, crying loudly.

Donna looked out the window at the street below. You couldn't open the windows. A tree outside was struggling to burst into bloom but it had been compromised heavily by the asphalt of a parking area. Trees annoyed people more than one would think, or so it appeared.

Big chunks of its bark had been torn away by poorly parked cars. It could not succeed like the stone, it had to be alive. Of course it could be transformed and have an existence in another manner, something that people could not do, which was perhaps what made them so resentful. When she had been a child, visiting Florida, she had seen a palm tree burst into flames. It had been beautiful! Then rats, long as her downy child's arm, had rushed down the trunk. Later, she had learned that it was not unusual for a palm tree to do this on occasion, given the proper circumstances of a particular day. This tree didn't want to do anything like that though. It couldn't. It struggled along quietly.

Donna felt excited about something. The excitement didn't feel all that great, actually.

She turned from the window and left the room where the fat girl had stopped sobbing and had fallen asleep. She walked down the corridor, humming a little. She pretended she was a virus, wandering without aim through a body, someone's body. She found Cynthia in the lounge, painting her long and perfect nails.

Cynthia regarded her sourly. "I really wish you wouldn't visit me anymore," Cynthia said.

Donna picked up the bottle of nail polish and Cynthia snatched it back. Donna hoped that this would pass. This is what she did, she came here. After Cynthia, it would have to be someone else.

A nurse appeared from nowhere like they did, a new one. "Who are you visiting?" she said to Donna.

Cynthia looked at her little bottle of nail polish and tightened the cap.

"You have to be visiting someone," the nurse said.

"She's not visiting me," Cynthia muttered.

"What?" the nurse said.

"She's not visiting me!" Cynthia said loudly.

After some remonstrance, Donna found herself being steered away from Cynthia, down the hallway to the elevator. "That's it now, then," the nurse said. "You've lost your privileges here." Donna was alone in the elevator as it went down. On the ground floor some people got on and the elevator went up again. On Floor Three they got off. Donna went back down. She walked through the parking lot, to her car.

She would just go home, she thought. She would come back tomorrow was all, and avoid the new nurse. In her car, she sat for a moment, feeling a little lost. She had to decide which route to take home. It was the way they made roads anymore, they made five or six ways to get to the same place. On the highway she ran into construction almost immediately. There was always construction. Cans and cones, those bright orange arrows blinking, and she had to merge. She inched over, trying to merge. They wouldn't let her in! She pushed her way in. Then she realized she was part of a funeral procession. Their lights were on. She was part of a cortege, of an anguished throng. She didn't know what to do. Should she turn on her lights to show sympathy, to apologize? She didn't know. She put on her sunglasses. People didn't turn their lights on in broad daylight just for funerals though, she thought. They turned them on for all sorts of things. Remembering somebody or something. Actually, showing you remembered somebody or something, which was different. Safety. People were urged to put them on for safety too. *Lights on for safety.* But this was a funeral, no two ways about it.

After what seemed an eternity, the road opened up again and Donna turned the car sharply into the other lane. In quick moments she had left the procession far behind. She found herself desperate to get home. She would sleep and sleep, she was simply worn out. But she still felt that unpleasant excitement.

On her own street she parked and hurried toward her door. It was midmorning, the neighborhood was quiet, it was always quiet. Who knew what people did here. She never saw any of them. Nero had illuminated his gardens with living bodies soaked in tar, hadn't he? Who knew what anyone was capable of?

A dog began to bark, quite frighteningly. As she walked on, it seemed to draw closer. It was the poor old soul's dog, Donna thought, the gray machine, somehow operative again, resuming its purpose. She knew that this was not so. But it sounded so real, it seemed so remarkably real and what she felt seemed so remarkably real as well that she hesitated. She could not go forward. Then, she couldn't go back.

# *From* Draft 32: Renga
# *Rachel* Blau *DuPlessis*

Snarled light, snap, bare.
     Of golden glass light trees, of Knots
            to which one is apprenticed,
      of split splints intransigent,
               no beginning beginning.

     *

no beginning but
emptiness full, fulling
in-betweens.

What twisting ribbon (time? or light? or words?) is

it Aglows Astripe?

     *

That glows, stripes and

branches, while bursts

of gold-glass light snarls

complicate

"the tangle of it."

     *

The tangle-basket's
          split stone lid
rests on plaited shims of bark—

Brush twist total. The words' single streamer makes

boundaries from overlays, from twigs and space.

159

*Rachel Blau DuPlessis*

     \*

Borders and overlays between twigs and space

                               Small reds and Slight greenings.

Sideshadows, caught arrays of them
there were, and darkling crossbeams

through which—

     \*

Through which (come)
night-rems and day-vectors
plumy and plummy blues.
This (thus) can (n)ever
register "it" enough.

     \*

Can never register it enough,

its cross-greens, purple croci or cerulean squill,

its (g)utturals or (c)harms—

these watery buds, its fingers in orfi that

awaken manifolds.

                        \*   \*   \*

Black ABC's code inside
this white fold, that little slip

frill and sweet honey ruffle
multiple registers that travel
to the serif of one letter.

     \*

The serif of one letter or

*Rachel Blau DuPlessis*

one red dot
dripping a flower-fashioned fractal
over the peony core.
Then at edges, everything's midrash.

     \*

Right at the edge, midrash piled on midrash, Pelion on Ossa, to

highlite the vitreous floaters with comment and interp. And there's

     the "yesterday I"
                  had a diaristic impulse but
        it didn't work out, now, did it?

     \*

or Did it? Can't tell? Blame
the unwritable oddities of journey—"the daily";
blame the persistent bad manners of the dark horse
mashing the other one in the yoke,
bumping sideways into—o that horse!—the gloss.

     \*

The gloss also comes bumping and travelling sideways
full of "enjabments" that doth
make the poem show as such
     it gives a little poke
     "watch me go under"

     \*

     "watch me go under"
mossy flip dunking
bell-note;
stone plump, plunk.

       "watch me stay under"

161

*Rachel Blau DuPlessis*

        *

under or blunder?

memorized or mesmerized?

oculist or occultist?

annotated or anointed?

                        Your Call

             *   *   *

Look at it in this light.
        Imprints of the bare trees stand as
neither line exactly nor curve, not i̲ nor s̲, but as particular cases—
sun, wind, openness, whatever
they turn and come to makes the next—

        *

Particular cases of turning, next creates next,

"is" i̲s̲ action; memory a mode of thought

scumbled on a neural surface

that struggles with attachment

inside and despite fragment.

        *

Attachment inside and despite fragment:

pinholes of entry, broad strangeness, twisted joist,

and snarls of light on the floor.

Been there. Done that.

Words, anyway, are "fuzzy sets."

        *

In words made of words' fuzziness and interlock,

"The 'it' is not identified in this sentence,"

it drifts laterally

inside, and of space, "site of watchfulness"

moves through its own thickness and thinness.

     *

Thickness thinness
          thisness thatness
grain by grain as the mist, as clay or humus,

as cold starfire, as depth magnetism, its

-idity.

     *

idity; burr-ditty,
         more scat and doggerel

can zing those descriptors,
         whether they're done in "viewless pencil" or low-res pixel,

         for rogueish maps or for symmetrical immersions.

     *

If it's Immersive Symmetries
vs. "unassuaged unrest":

go instability.

The symmetries don't bear watching

only the restless stragglers, the incident off.

             *   *   *

*Rachel Blau DuPlessis*

Wander looketh up,
the trees have leaves, when did that happen (?)

beech leaves out of crisp rust-colored packets
the oak and its looping golden flowers
the soft back silver and the delicate greening.

      \*

Bright green of new leaves and large green light blowing
showing spaces inside words,

silver impossible words cannot do it; it is a space

creating a change of scope

scales get blasted

      \*

Scale—like one inch to a mile/ to test us

even the most banal relationship/ is odd:

what does a "map" mean/ can one credit

a here/ slightly off center from the last

stroke.

      \*

a Here up and off center,

flying over a blank and snow-filled plain
in which three clear mountains exist
the wide site of event
one and two and three

      \*

one and two and three

three kinds of slippage: ridge, peak, volcano
      a kind of renga chain
is what we live on;
        it cannot help be odd.

\*

It is so odd, it is so curious.

A gigantic spherical object at the deep center of earth:
under the crust, slower than the surface,
heavier than the moon and nearly as large as it
revolves round and round beneath our feet.

\*

Under our feet, after the hail

salads of torn leaves cover the streets.

Ground between two stones, two moons and a comet

we blow like wheat and chaff together

through the air of our stepping.

\*

Stepping into
"inevitability," journey that is "the binding,"
"I have been wading a very long river"
sloshing across waywardly
trying not to go too quickly.

\*

Go
quickly.
No
summary.
Touch that knife.

\*

   In time, the infinite,
the knife
comes down; it's
an angel
holds the point.

165

Rachel Blau DuPlessis

*

Holds the deep point,

tipped against one edel finger,

the blade dulls

in that kind light.

But if said angel did not catch the brunt in time?

*

Catching the brunt of time
given the memory of the site
should we be grateful or angry?
Glad to submit, or glad to be spared it?

There is ladder and chain, binding and knife.

*

Ladder, chain and binding:
Light snarls around the walkers.
These paths are dusty, people thirsty.

The point is—not to question what you are given;
The knife is, you can't help it.

# You Are Jeff
## *Richard Siken*

### 1.

THERE ARE TWO TWINS on motorbikes but one is farther up the road, beyond the hairpin turn, or just before it, depending on which twin you are in love with at the time. Do not choose sides yet. It is still to your advantage to remain impartial. Both motorbikes are shiny red and both boys have perfect teeth, dark hair, soft hands. The one in front will want to take you apart, and slowly. His deft and stubby fingers searching every shank and lock for weaknesses. You could love this boy with all your heart. The other brother only wants to stitch you back together. The sun shines down. It's a beautiful day. Consider the hairpin turn. Do not choose sides yet.

### 2.

There are two twins on motorbikes but one is farther up the road. Let's call them Jeff. And because the first Jeff is in front we'll consider him the older, and therefore responsible for lending money and the occasional punch in the shoulder. World-wise, world-weary and not his mother's favorite, this Jeff will always win when it all comes down to fisticuffs. Unfortunately for him, it doesn't always all come down to fisticuffs. Jeff is thinking about his brother down the winding road behind him. He is thinking that if only he could cut him open and peel him back and crawl inside this second skin, then he could relive that last mile again: reborn, wild-eyed and free.

### 3.

There are two twins on motorbikes but one is farther up the road, beyond the hairpin turn, or just before it, depending on which Jeff you are. It could have been so beautiful—You scout out the road ahead and I will watch your back, how it was and how it will be, Memory and Fantasy—but each Jeff wants to be the other one. My name is Jeff and I'm tired of looking at the back of your head. My name is Jeff and I'm tired of wearing your throw-away clothes. Look, Jeff, I'm telling you, for the last time, I mean it, etcetera. They are the same and they are not the same. They are the same and they hate each other for it.

### 4.

Your name is Jeff and somewhere up ahead of you your brother has pulled off to the side of the road and he is waiting for you with a lug wrench clutched in his greasy fist. O How he loves you, darling boy. O How, like always, he invents the monsters underneath the bed to get you to sleep next to him. His chest to your chest or his chest to your back, the covers drawn around you in an act of faith against the night. When he throws the wrench into the air it will catch the light as it spins towards you. Look—it looks like a star. You had expected something else, anything else, but the wrench never reaches you. It hangs in the air like that, spinning in the air like that. It's beautiful.

### 5.

Let's say God in his High Heaven is hungry and has decided to make himself some tuna fish sandwiches. He's already finished making two of them, on sourdough, with melted fontina, before he realizes that the fish is bad. What is he going to do with these sandwiches? They're already made, but he doesn't want to eat them.

Let's say the Devil is played by two men. Here: we'll call them Jeff. Dark hair, green eyes, white teeth, pink tongues—they're twins. The one on the left has gone bad in the middle, and the other one on the left is about to. As they wrestle, you can tell that they have forgotten about God, and they are very hungry.

### 6.

But maybe you are wrestling with an angel. Maybe Big Daddy isn't holding all the cards. Maybe you are wrestling with an angel and he is changing your name while you are doing all the fighting, demanding to be blessed. You expect it to change your life, but it doesn't make it better. It just doesn't make it any better.

Let's say you're driving a bus, but the traffic between Heaven and Hell is very heavy. At the first stop, four Jeffs get on and three Jeffs get off. At the second stop, seven Jeffs get on and eighteen Jeffs get off. At the third stop nobody moves. Where, exactly, are you going? How long until you get there? What is the bus driver's name?

7.

You are playing cards with three men named Jeff. Two of the Jeffs seem somewhat familiar, but the Jeff across from you keeps staring at your hands, your mouth, and you're certain that you've never seen this Jeff before. But he's on your team, and you're ahead, you're winning big, and yet the other Jeffs keep smiling at you like there's no tomorrow. They all have perfect teeth: white, square, clean, even. And, for some reason, the lighting in the room makes their teeth seem closer than they should be, as if each mouth was a place, a living room with pink carpet and the window's open. *Come back from the window, Jefferson. Take off those wet clothes and come over here, by the fire.*

8.

You are playing cards with three Jeffs. One is your father, one is your brother and the other one is your current lover. All of them have seen you naked and heard you talking in your sleep. The Father, the Son and the Holy Ghost. Are there any other permutations possible? You are in the living room, playing cards with Jeff Daddy and Jeff Junior while your boyfriend Jeff gets up to answer the phone. To them he is a mirror, but to you he is a room. *The phone's for you,* Jeff says. Hey! It's Uncle Jeff, who isn't really your uncle. But you can't talk right now anyway, one of the Jeffs has put his tongue in your mouth. Please God, let it be the right one.

9.

Two brothers are fighting by the side of the road. Two motorbikes have fallen over on the soft shoulder, leaking gas and oil into the dirt, while the interlocking brothers grapple and swing at each other. You see them through the backseat window as you and your parents drive past them. You are twelve years old. You do not have a brother. You have never experienced anything this ferocious or intentional with another person. Your mother is pretending that she hasn't seen anything. Your father is fiddling with the knobs of the radio. There is an empty space next to you in the backseat of the station wagon. Make it the shape of everything you need. Now say hello.

10.

You are in an ordinary suburban bedroom with bunk beds, a tiny bookshelf, two wooden desks and chairs. You are lying on your back, on the top bunk, very close to the textured ceiling, staring straight at it in fact, and the room is still dark except for a wedge of powdery light that spills in from the adjoining bathroom. The bathroom is covered in mint green tile and someone is in there, singing very softly. Is he singing to you? For you? Black cherries in chocolate, the ring around the moon, a beetle underneath a glass—you can't make out all the words, but you're sure he knows you're in there, and he's singing to you, even though you don't know who he is.

## 11.

You see it as a room, a tabernacle, the dark hotel. You're in the hall-way again, and you open the door, and if you're ready, you'll see it, but maybe one part of your mind decides that the other parts aren't ready, and then you don't remember where you've been, and you find yourself down the hall again, the lights gone dim as if the left hand was singing the right hand back to sleep again. It's a puzzle, each piece, each room, each time you put your hand to the knob, your mouth to the hand, your ear to the wound that whispers.

You're in the hallway again. The radio is playing your favorite song. You're in the hallway. Open the door again. Open the door.

## 12.

Consider the hairpin turn. It is waiting for you like a red door or the broken leg of a dog. The sun is shining, O How the sun shines down! Your speedometer and your handgrips and the feel of the road below you, how it knows you, the black ribbon spread out on the greens between these lines that suddenly don't reach to the horizon. It is waiting, like a broken door, like the red dog that eats your rose-bushes and chases its tail and then must be forgiven. Who do you love, Jeff? Who do you love? You were driving towards something and then, well, then you found yourself driving the other way. The dog is asleep. The road is behind you. O How the sun shines down.

## 13.

After work you go to the grocery store to get some milk and a carton of cigarettes. Where did you get those bruises? You don't remember. Work was boring. You find a jar of bruise cream and a can of stewed tomatoes. Maybe a salad? Spinach, walnuts, blue cheese, apples and you can't decide between the Extra Large or the Jumbo black olives. Which one is bigger anyway? Extra Large has a blue label, Jumbo has a purple label. Both cans cost $1.29. While you are deciding, the afternoon light is streaming through the windows behind the bank of checkout stands. Take the light inside you like a virus, like another knee in the chest, holding onto it and not letting it go. Now let it go.

### 14.

Let's say that God and the Devil are making out in the corner booth of a seedy bar. They're second cousins, so it's okay. The lights are low and the drinks are cheap and in this dim and smoky night you can barely tell whose hands are whose. Someone raises their glass for a toast. Is that the Hand of Judgment or the Hand of Mercy? The bartender only smiles, running a rag across the burnished wood of the bar. The drink in front of you has already been paid for. *Drink it,* the bartender says. *It's yours, you deserve it, and it's already been paid for. Someone's paid for it already. There's no mistake,* he says. *It's your drink, it's the one you asked for, just the way you like it.* How can you refuse?

### 15.

This time everyone has the best intentions. You have cancer. Let's say you have cancer. Let's say you've swallowed a bad thing and now it's got its hands inside you. This is the essence of love and failure. You see what I mean but you're happy anyway, and that's okay, it's a love story after all, a lasting love, a wonderful adventure with lots of action, where the mirror says mirror and the hand says hand and the front door never says Sorry Charlie. So the doctor says you need more stitches and the bruise cream isn't working. So much for the facts. Let's say you're still completely in the dark but we love you anyway. We love you. We really do.

### 16.

The motorbikes are neck and neck but where's the checkered flag we all expected, waving in the distance, telling you you're home again, home? He's next to you, right next to you in fact, so close, or he isn't. Imagine a room. Yes, imagine a room: two chairs facing the window, but nobody moves. Don't move. Imagine a room in which I ruin you. Keep staring straight into my eyes. It feels like you're not moving, the way when, dancing, the room will suddenly fall away. You're dancing: you're neck and neck or cheek to cheek, he's there or he isn't, the open road. Imagine a room. Imagine you're dancing. Imagine the room now falling away. Don't move.

### 17.

One Jeff grabs you by the back of the neck in the industrial bathroom while another Jeff chuckles to himself next to the urinals. Hands of fire, hands of air, hands of water, hands of dirt. Someone's doing all the talking but no one's lips move. Consider the hairpin turn.

Jeff on the dance floor, Jeff still sleeping, Jeff in the kitchen, in a bathrobe, making blintzes. The Jeff you love is buried six feet underneath the other ones. Some other Jeff is pulling all the strings.

Jeff in moonlight, Jeff the creep, Jeff in the garden with the garden rake or crying in his sleep. His skin like cream. His hands like cream.

Or sleeping the sleep that happens when your head hits concrete.

### 18.

Let's say the Devil is a married man with his hand in your pants. No, that's too easy, let's try it again. Let's say that the devil *wants* to put his hand in your pants, so you let him. One big red hand snaking past the elastic waistband of your underwear. So he's not married, it's not about being married, he's a bachelor, the little devil, and he's invited you back to his bachelor's pad: a red shag wall-to-wall with a hot plate and a foldout couch. You want him to be married—we all want him to be married—but he's not. You're not married either. And Big Daddy, in the back office, counting all the money, he's single too.

### 19.

So your eyes are closed and the Devil has his hand in your pants. We're all adults here, so you know what I'm saying. And, deep down, we're all single too, so you know why I'm saying it. Big Daddy puts some rosebushes in the front yard and calls it a garden, but he's still lonely. Makes himself a man out of the brown dirt, but the man's lonely. Makes a woman out of the man's rib but now they're too into each other to do anything but ignore him, so he kicks them out, into the street, no questions asked. And the man wrapped around the tree, the one with the apple, was he really flirting, or was he just trying to make somebody jealous? Think about it. Two lonely single men in a garden. What would you do?

### 20.

Two brothers are standing on the soft shoulder of the highway, the wrench still spinning in the air between them. It's time to choose sides now. This is how you make the meaning, you take two things and try to find the distance between their bellies. Jeff or Jeff? Who do you want to be? You just wanted to play in your own backyard, but you don't know where your own yard is, exactly. You just wanted to prove there was one safe place, just one safe place where you could love him. You just wanted to be let back into the garden. You have not found that place yet. You have not made that place yet. You are here. You are here. You're still right here.

### 21.
Here are your names and here is the list and here are the things you left behind: the mark on the floor from pushing your chair back, your underwear, one half brick of cheese, the kind I don't like, wrapped up, and poorly, and abandoned on the second shelf next to the poppy-seed dressing which is also yours. Here's the champagne on the floor, and here are your house keys, and here are the curtains that your cat peed on. And here is your cat, who keeps eating grass and vomiting in the hallway. There's no need to explain. I wasn't listening anyway. Here is the list with all of your names, Jeff. They're not the same name, Jeff. They're not the same at all.

### 22.
Two brothers: one of them wants to take you apart. Two brothers: one of them wants to put you back together. It's time to choose sides now. The stitches or the devouring mouth? You want an alibi? You don't get an alibi, you get a guardian angel. You get the needle and the thread or you get a good set of choppers. You want to go home but it's time to choose sides now. There's no one else in the bed now. You're alive, but you don't live here. You don't live anywhere. You have to choose. Here are two Jeffs. Pick one. It doesn't matter which is smarter or more interesting. It's about the ability to adapt. Say: *Hello. My name is Jeff. I'm not from around here. And I love you.*

### 23.
There are two twins on motorbikes but they are not on motorbikes, they're in a garden where the flowers are as big as thumbs. Imagine you are in a field of daisies. What the hell are you doing in a field of daisies? Get up! Let's say you're not in the field anymore. Let's say they're not brothers anymore. That's right, they're not brothers. They're angels in a garden, and they know you, and they're talking to you, but you're not listening. They are trying to tell you

173

something but you're not listening. What are you still doing in this field? Get out of the field! You should be in the garden! You should, at least, be trying to get into the garden. Ah! Now the field is empty.

24.

Someone had a party while you were sleeping but you weren't really sleeping, you were sick, and parts of you were burning, and you couldn't move. Perhaps the party was in your honor. You can't remember. It seems the phone was ringing in the dream you were having but there's no proof. A dish in the sink that might be yours, some clothes on the floor that might belong to someone else. When was the last time you found yourself looking out of this window. Hey! This is a beautiful window! This is a beautiful view! Those trees lined up like that, and the way the stars are spinning over them like that, spinning in the air like that, like wrenches.

25.

Let's say that God and the Devil are each played by two men. Here: I'll be all of them—Jeff and Jeff and Jeff and Jeff are all standing on the soft shoulder of the highway, four motorbikes knocked over, two wrenches spinning in the ordinary air. Two of these Jeffs are windows, and two of these Jeffs are doors, and all of these Jeffs are trying to tell you something. Come closer. We'll whisper it in your ear. It's like seeing your face in a bowl of soup, cream of potato, and the eyes shining back like spoons. If we wanted to tell you everything, we would leave more footprints in the snow or kiss you harder. One thing. Come closer. Listen . . .

26.

Imagine you're in a car with a beautiful boy, and he won't tell you that he loves you, but he loves you. And you feel like you've done something terrible, like robbed a liquor store, or swallowed pills, or shoveled yourself a grave in the dirt, and you're tired. Imagine: you're in a car with a beautiful boy, and you're trying not to tell him that you love him, and you're trying to choke down the feeling, and you're trembling, but he reaches over and touches you, like a prayer for which no words exist, and you can feel your heart taking root in your body, like you've discovered something you don't even have a name for.

# Moral Yellowness
## William T. Vollmann

> Iago very precisely identifies his purposes and his
> motives as being black and born of hate. But no:
> that's not the way it is! To do evil a human being
> must first of all believe that what he's doing is good,
> or else that it is a well-considered act in conformity
> with natural law. Fortunately, it is in the nature of a
> human being to seek a *justification* for his actions.
>
> —*Solzhenitsyn, 1973*[1]

TROTSKY'S COLLEAGUE KRESTINSKY once remarked that Stalin was
"a bad man, with yellow eyes." After that, Trotsky thought to perceive what he called the *moral yellowness* of Stalin. (Krestinsky, by
the way, was liquidated by Stalin a few years before Trotsky's turn
came. And some people might have seen moral yellowness in all
three of them—or at any rate moral redness, they being so complicit
in the atrocities of "Red Terror" which Lenin launched in 1918.[2] "I
plead not guilty," Krestinsky said at the end. "I am not a Trotsky-
ite."[3] He'd thus achieved the distinction of denouncing each of the
antagonists to the other.)

Being able to spy out moral yellowness would certainly simplify
our task of determining when violence is justified; for that very reason a misperception of moral yellowness would be a very serious
error. Stalin's belief that he saw it in the class of *kulaks* or rich peasants—for the science of Marxism-Leninism proved that it must be
there—gave him the confidence to direct the repression and outright

---

[1]Vol. 1, p. 173. Italics in original.
[2]The secret memorandum launching the Red Terror is addressed from Lenin to
Krestinsky. See *The Unknown Lenin*, p. 56 (document 28, memorandum to N. N.
Krestinsky, 3 or 4 September, 1918 [dated provisionally by editor]).
[3]*Report of Court Proceedings: The Case of the Anti-Soviet Bloc of Rightists and
Trotskyites*, 1938, in Daniel, p. 213. When Krestinsky tried to recant, the NKVD
apparently dislocated his shoulder. See Conquest, *The Great Terror*, pp. 342–354, for
an account of his trial.

William T. Vollmann

extermination of millions.[4] In my experience *there is almost never any moral yellowness.*[5] (I say "almost" because no one's experience, including mine, is wide enough.) When I set out to meet Pol Pot, I knew that I would search for moral yellowness in his laughing face if I found him (I didn't), and cast upon some perfectly innocuous trait which in my opinion betrayed and signified his evil. That is the artist's job, and the second-rate journalist's. And, indeed, it's superior to the tasks demanded by mere superstition. In life as in art, beholding commences or continues the search for wholeness, whose aim is to make meaning cohere with appearance. At its highest, this striving is expressed by souls such as the Canadian painter Emily Carr: "Search for the reality of each object, that is, its real and only beauty," she writes in her journal.[6] With noble obsessiveness she wonders: "What is that vital thing in ugly as well as lovely things and places, the thing that takes us out of ourselves, that draws and attracts us, that unnameable thing claiming kinship with us?"[7] There is a significance, which we can call spirit, to a British Columbian cedar, and Carr's painting of one of those trees convinces me that she portrayed its outward form in a manner consistent with its inner character—or rather (crucial qualification!) with what she perceived as its inner character; for another painter's rendering of the same tree, successful or not, would be different. Meanwhile, her image owns life and truth because it is *fitting.* Most everybody searches for the secret, the summation, the innerness of things. Watch a child, a stranger in a new place, a person falling in love. The pupils widen; the face thrills, growing mobile like clay worked in the potter's warm hands; the consciousness within exercises itself, straining to identify with what it sees, to bind itself to the world with perception and memory.

"The thing that takes us out of ourselves" need not be happy. If that were the case, one would never find anyone at funerals. Whether

---

[4]"The tide of terrorism was running," writes a capitalist historian, "and Stalin observed what he could not have known before—that slaughtering people high and low in the party caused not indignation and protest but awestruck submission . . . Millions wept when the grim secluded monster died."—Wesson, pp. 159, 161.

[5]*My Life,* p. 449. In Trotsky's house in Coyoacán the kitchen was all yellow, maybe in ordinary life he didn't mind yellow, maybe Natalia loved that color, most likely Trotsky didn't worry about interior decoration. Ten yellow chairs, Mexican vases and plates on the yellow buffet (Natalia must have collected them), three yellow cabinets with brown trim. More shelves, a stove with four burners, a platter with leaping fishes, a tiny frying pan, a roller on the table and here are Natalia's round glasses.

[6]Emily Carr, p. 29 (entry for November 3rd, 1932).

[7]Ibid. p. 33 (entry for January 26th, 1933).

the casket is open or closed, the mourners' perceptions surge forth, seeking the dead body inside that they will never see anymore. To reject the pain, turning away from this concentration-point of grief which wounds them afresh, would be expedient but inhuman: The loss must be embraced in order to be understood. Even death is a "vital thing."

This is how we live, taking in, correlating, organizing our experiences in ways which express our varying personal needs for reference. When violent actors perform before us, whether they be victims, perpetrators or tools, then (if experience or professionalism has not yet made us inhuman) we tend to crave understanding almost desperately, understanding being the offering we lay down on the altar of every force of power—and in its transformative abilities violence is debatably the most powerful entity of all. Earth falls upon the coffin. Why did the addicted mother's boyfriend drown the three-year-old in the bathtub? Why did my friends have to meet a land mine? Why did Hitler want to kill the Jews? So the searching and seeking goes out, alert and cautious, like fingers toward a naked bloodstained razor—be it Trotsky's razor of terror or Sherman's razor of war or any other variety. Now, the most important part of the razor is the blade. When we face a human razor, we want him or her to have a blade, too, something that reveals itself instantly, something that explains. Many of us expect our mass murderers to somehow look like mass murderers, to glower, to be frightening or eerie in appearance. If only they were truly this way, then we could recognize them and be protected . . . ! Or at least we could somehow *know* them, which might spread the balm of rationality upon the shocking mind-wounds they give us. The same need applies to the murderers themselves—oh, not all of them; I've spoken just now of how inhuman it would be to turn away from the funeral of a person with whom one shared a life, but not all bipeds called human from a biological point of view *are* so from any other category; enough to say that *most* of them seek to create categories—especially the ones who justify (and it is, after all, with them that this book is concerned). They want to find a characteristic in their victims which will set them safely beyond the pale. Hence all stereotypes (the one-in-all being the furthest opposite on the continuum from the all-in-one of Emily Carr); hence the stone throwing and cries of "Monster!" directed at a keloid-riddled girl who survived Hiroshima[8]; hence the

---

[8]Cook and Cook, p. 386 (testimony of Yamaoka Michiko).

William T. Vollmann

laborious reifications of Nazi movies in which all the Jews have shifty eyes and hooked noses, the ideal being to convince the uninitiated that Jews are the murderers, not the other way around: Fool, can't you *see* the shining moral yellowness of the Jew?

*Moral yellowness is the aesthetic handmaiden of violence.* It can never be a worthy justification. Although we may imbibe it unthinkingly, sooner or later, all of us who actually meet the morally yellow must experience the uneasy sense that they may be gray underneath. From that moment on, we can be said to worship the fiction of moral yellowness *by choice.* Be warned by the career of Field Marshal Keitel, who did Hitler's bidding because that was profitably easy. Loyalty and compulsion—much less inertia—cannot exculpate us from committing acts of injustice. A person is always more than a member of a category.

For such reasons, we very often overtly discredit the whole notion of moral yellowness—nobody owns or is only *one* vital thing!— Keitel himself, for instance, reveals as many sympathetic traits as Napoleon—he took care to express "personal esteem" and "sympathy" to the head of the French delegation who surrendered to Germany in 1940,[9] and in 1946 he displayed a textbook stoicism at Nuremberg in the face of a dishonorable death—nor is he evil-looking. How can we believe in moral yellowness, really?—But here it is in Telford Taylor's famous memoir of the first Nuremberg trial. This truth-sure jurist reproduces a group photograph of several of the first trial's defendants, the big fish, and in that image the most striking figure initially is Rudolf Hess, on account of the thick dark diamond-shaped eyebrows in his strange pale face; his chin is squared up, possibly due to clenched teeth, so that his head has become a cube upon that aloof white neck. His arms are folded. He glares into space. Moral yellowness? Taylor thinks so, claiming that the closeup is "accentuating his beetlebrows, sunken eyes, and grim expression."[10] Beside Hess, but seemingly in another world, is stiff old Ribbentrop, his throat tight as if the trial were already ended and Master Sergeant Woods had applied the noose. He strains, as always in his career, to express resentment and fury. "Ribbentrop as usual has his chin raised and eyes closed," remarks Taylor. Between and behind those two we find Baldur von Schirach, formerly the leader of the Hitler-Jugend: He's an ordinary, pleasant-looking man who gazes down at a

---

[9]Keitel, p. 113.
[10]Taylor, photo by R. D'Addario (sixth photo following p. 354).

178

pencil in his hands. Taylor is quick to tell us that he "is attending to his own writing rather than the proceedings." Moral yellowness? If I were shown an uncaptioned photograph of this man alone, I would never think him any kind of criminal.[11] Hess is half-mad and looks it, but as a matter of fact, since he flew to England to try to negotiate a peace, he had no time to accrue much war guilt. Accordingly, he'll not be hanged, but at the insistence of the Russians (against whom he proposed an Anglo-German alliance) he'll be kept in Spandau until he finally commits suicide at ninety-three years of age. Even Taylor has to remark: ". . . such long-continued incarceration, especially in a huge prison where he was the sole innmate, was a crime against humanity."[12] That leaves Ribbentrop, by all accounts an eminently dislikable person. And that is how he looks. Can one tell from his expression, however, that he is also morally and politically dislikable, having been involved in the deportations of French and Hungarian Jews? Could the circumstances under which the photograph was taken (on trial for his life, in a court of his victorious enemies) have anything to do with his expression? (On account of exactly those circumstances, Admiral Raeder in the background is covering his face from the photographer.) I say again: There is no moral yellowness. Or, rather: The perception of moral yellowness is learned. "The first time I saw dead Germans they looked just like Americans, except for the uniform," an American soldier recalled

---

[11]During the Spanish Civil War, looking into the eyes of some villagers who'd just shot a man for ideological reasons, Saint-Exupéry thought, "Strange: there was nothing in their eyes to upset me. There seemed nothing to fear in their set jaws and the blank smoothness of their faces. Blank, as if vaguely bored. A rather terrible blankness" (*Wind, Sand and Stars*, p. 183).

[12]Ibid. p. 618. With what I take to be some cynicism, Taylor writes (loc. cit.): "Hess was utterly devoted to Hitler and, if he had remained in Germany, there is little doubt he would have followed his Fuehrer to the end. There is little reason to be sorry for his conviction." But Hess did not, after all, choose to stay in Germany, and I am not aware that people ought to be punished for what they might have done. Of course, this is not to say that Hess was entirely guiltless either. "Hess had a central position in the Nazi government, and the documents he signed and the meetings he attended adequately proved his knowledge of and participation in Hitler's plans and decisions to conquer Czechoslovakia and crush Poland, the Low Countries and France" (p. 269). In the end, his punishment was like something out of a Borges story. He spent his last years entirely alone in that prison, as Taylor acknowledges; as soon as his suicide attempt had succeeded, the structure was immediately razed. It is as if the authorities had followed Kant's prescription in *The Science of Right:* "Even if a civil society resolved to dissolve itself with the consent of all its members—as might be supposed in the case of people inhabiting an island resolved to separate and scatter themselves throughout the whole world—the last murderer lying in the prison ought to be executed before the resolution was carried out" (p. 447).

fifty years later. "And then you started to think of them as animals."[13] Moral yellowness is visual prejudice, and so is its opposite: the tendency of any given category of humankind to see good in its own image. Thus one American slave boy, who always ran away from white men when they looked at him, in case it might be their intention to sell him in Georgia, shared the conviction of his fellow slaves that Queen Victoria must be black. "Accustomed to nothing but cruelty at the hands of white people, we had never imagined that a great ruler so kind to coloured people could be other than black ..."[14] Hence the Nuremberg judges' "gestures of bewilderment, readily explicable," when Einsatzgruppefuhrer Ohlendorf gave his hideous testimony. Clean-cut and polite, he just didn't look the part of somebody who'd murdered ninety thousand human beings! "No one could have looked less like a brutish SS thug such as Kaltenbrunner," in whom Rebecca West saw moral yellowness, which is why she wrote that he reminded her "of a particularly vicious horse." To me, Kaltenbrunner appears rather bored and neutral in his photograph, not vicious—and what should a brutish thug look like? I have met several. It's not how they look; it's how they act. "Ohlendorf was small of stature, young-looking and rather comely. He spoke quietly, with great precision, dispassion and apparent intelligence. How could he have done what he now so calmly described?"[15]

I grant the obvious fact that people's appearance may on occasion reveal their intentions, their emotions, etcetera. The man in the bar to whom I have said nothing, who sneers and glares at me, puts me rightfully on my guard. In that sense there are in fact physiognomies of aggression. But that is only because these souls act out of rage, which shines through their flesh like fire behind a paper screen. However, should their moral spectrum be laid out differently than mine, their feelings as displayed by their bodies may be connected to different behaviors than I might expect. What if it makes the stranger tranquilly joyous to contemplate murdering me? What if, like De Sade's protagonists, they delight in caressing before they destroy? Then their friendliness is what I must fear. Among the indications of antisocial character disorder (in which category Göring has been

[13]Steve Johnson, "Survival in the Bulge: Fifty Years Ago, Houk Earned Silver Star in World War II Battle." *Los Angeles Times*, Monday, December 19, 1994, p. C19.
[14]Thomas L. Johnson, p. 6.
[15]Taylor, p. 248.

placed[16]) is this one: "Often a charming, likeable personality with a disarming manner and an ability to win the liking and friendship of others. Typically good sense of humor and generally optimistic outlook."[17]

We read that when Himmler came to Minsk on an inspection tour, *Einsatzgruppe B* demonstrated its shooting skills on a hundred Jews. One of the doomed had blond hair and blue eyes. Himmler was miserable. If, as his ideology insisted, biology justifies all, and if the measure of biology is phenotype (hence the skulls and pickled heads harvested from concentration camp inmates for scientific specimens), then why didn't this boy have a hooked nose? Where was his moral yellowness? Group B took aim. Two women survived the first volley, and Himmler screamed![18] He longed to understand his violence as much as we do. It seems to me that at that moment his understanding must have been unable to evade recognizing his dishonesty. What did he do afterwards? Did he talk with racial experts who reassured him with maxims about the cunning mask of the Jew? Or did he retreat into one of his rationalistic metaphors about cleaning, fumigating, sterilizing—all processes which require overkill for their effectiveness to be guaranteed?

The moral is this: Never judge a person solely for what he is. We already know that we ought not judge him solely for what he does: If the defendant is insane, or if he had reasonable cause to believe, mistakenly or not, that the man he shot meant to shoot *him*, we treat the act of homicide differently from the professional or expedient acts of a Himmler, a Bluebeard, an Elisabeth Bathory. Judge him for what he is and what he does together. The insane man who kills not and the killer who is not insane each deserve differently from the crazed murderer. Clear—evident—banal. And in discarding moral yellowness we need not deprive ourselves of the concept of manifest intent.[19] Look into those glaring yellow eyes or those red ones: My Jamaican friend, Pearline, was sure that one "crew" of ghetto men was sinful because their eyes were all bloodshot—probably from

---

[16]Coleman, pp. 365–66.
[17]Ibid. p. 363.
[18]Levin, p. 244.
[19]"You are on patrol when you observe two men in an apparent traffic dispute," runs a California police manual. "One of the men pulls back his coat to display a pocket knife and looks menacingly at the other while displaying the knife. This man's actions are . . . a misdemeanor . . . To satisfy the elements of this crime, one need only *exhibit* a deadly weapon in a rude, angry or threatening manner" (Bruce, p. 239).

*ganja* smoking. As a matter of fact, Pearline was not wrong, for at least some of those fellows were gunmen. The red eyes she seized on were a kind of shorthand for moral yellowness—a metaphorically expressed intuition, à la Emily Carr. In this she was poetically justi-fied—justified in every other way, too, for she didn't plan to act on her perceptions. (What do *you* see? *Whom* do you see?[20]) And Telford Taylor would have had every right to remark on Hess's beetle-brows—had he not been simultaneously working to convict him. Metaphors ought to be left outside both courtroom and battlefield: Metaphors and political action (to say nothing of metaphors and vio-lence) make a dangerous mix.

### ADDENDUM: AUGUST SANDER'S PHOTOGRAPHS OF PERSECUTED JEWS

For his immense, never to be finished *Citizens of the Twentieth Century* series, the photographer August Sander, obstructed and menaced but not quite silenced even though his Communist son died in a concentration camp, quietly continued his project of depict-ing human types by, among other things, taking photographs of the people he very accurately called "persecuted Jews." It is 1938, and in an armchair against a gray wall[21] sits old Frau Michel, her thinning hair neatly combed back, her eyes half-closed behind the round spec-tacles on her round face. She grips the curved handles of her twin canes. She gazes at nothing. Her lips are pursed. She is wary, weary, pale and sad. Turn the page and see Herr Fleck—1938 again. All the portraits of persecuted Jews are dated 1938 or ca. 1938. Did Sander lose interest in the Jews after that or was he satisfied with these likenesses or had this particular study simply become too danger-ous?[22] 1938 was the year of *Kristallnacht*, remember, when with

---

[20]On the subject of colored reputations one could recall Carlyle's epithet: "sea-green Robespierre." Carlyle considered that liquidator a murderer and a terrorist, which he was. Trotsky, on the other hand, chalked up much of the French revolution's progress to have been thanks to "the austere labor of Robespierre," in whom Trotsky saw no yellowness or greenness—indeed, nothing but goodness. The science of moral phys-iognomy would seem to be in its babyhood.

[21]Or possibly the gray curtain which Sander sometimes used for his portrait photog-raphy.

[22]My friend Kent Lacin, a commercial photographer who introduced Sander's work to me, is convinced that all the photographs of persecuted Jews were taken on the same day: the lighting and the camera angle never change.

official sanction thugs and zealots smashed in the windows of Jewish businesses; the following year began World War II, whose course led on greased tracks straight to ghettos and gas chambers. At any rate, Herr Fleck, sallow and professional, folds his palms on his crossed legs and gazes anxiously through his too brilliant spectacles, while shadows crawl on the wall behind him. On the facing page sits Herr Leubsdorff, hale and clean, not fear-expressing like Herr Fleck but definitely pensive. File him under "Aristocrats" and you wouldn't know his case was serious. Frau Oppenheim, fiftyish but still pretty, with her necklace just so, draws her pale arms tightly inward, lowers her eyelids and glares at Sander (and us), her head bowed a little, as if she were awaiting a blow from behind. On the recto page, her elderly husband, his mouth grimacing almost insanely, gazes pop-eyed through his glasses. What has he seen? These two images glow with a pain which seems to be embedded in the very emulsion. Next comes a young persecuted Jewess who looks unremarkable, per-haps a little saucy; she could be refiled under "The Small Town" or "Working Women" or "Painters and Sculptors" and I'd never know, and then we see Herr Doctor Philip, who on the other hand looks crushed and ruined, as he probably is. We see a plump, sub-missive girl and a bewildered man (they could both go under "Servants" or "Families"), then middle-aged Frau Marcus in her butterfly scarf, clutching her coat edges nervously together, then at last Dr. Kahn full on who stares at us with wet anguish filled with comprehension.[23]

Many of Sander's other subjects, even some of the vagabonds, throw their shoulders back, raise their heads high.[24] The persecuted Jews do not. Did Sander say, "Please, Herr Doctor Philip, I would like to take your photograph" or did he say, "Well, to get right down to it, Herr Doctor Philip, I'd like to use you in my series of persecuted Jews?" Knowing the context would be useful in evaluating the ex-pressions on the portraits. And yet it is fair to say that the majority of these victims resemble victims.

Turning for comparison to Sander's photographs of National So-cialists, we first discover a Hitlerjugend lad in 1941, dressed in his uniform best, the swastika armband proudly displayed, the black tie almost touching the belt—he stands serious and self-important there

---

[23]Thus the complete series of persecuted Jews (plates 410–20) given in Sander, VI, "The Big City." (See p. 63 for portfolio contents.)
[24]Ibid. VI. "Itinerants," plates 356–64.

in what is probably the family back yard; he's blond and freckled, just a boy, but he knows how to stand with his feet apart in the tall boots, how to look confident. He does not resemble a persecutor. The National Socialist of 1937–38, fat and coarse, might be hard, but necessarily vicious (I wouldn't have been surprised to see him categorized under the rubric of "The Circus"); facing him we see a portrait of an effeminate blond boy in Nazi uniform who squeezes his hands together just like the persecuted jews, but his clenched, open-eyed young face inclines toward us in an even-tempered stab at resolution. The next two youths could be anyone, cleancut, faraway-gazing. (Call them "Students." Recall this: "Ohlendorf was small of stature, young-looking, and rather comely . . ." It's not so easy, is it? It's not that there's nothing there, but that the soul of a likeness is perhaps too complex for these categorizations.) Finally comes a pair of uniformed, swastika'd officials evincing the hardness so fashionable during the period; they have power and are conscious of it, especially the righthand one, the ruthless-looking chief of Cologne's cultural department.[25] Call them Nazis, to be sure; but Sander's other rubrics of "Businessmen," "Officials" or "Lawyers/Judges" would also have fit—and of course Nazis became all of these things.

What can we say about the National Socialists as a group? Again, they're not really evil, there's no moral yellowness; if there were, then the Nazis themselves, who looked so hard for it, would have found it in the mirror . . .

---

[25]Ibid. IV. "Occupations," "National Socialists" (plates 242–248).

# The Road to Basra
## Kevin Magee

ANTHOLOGIA GERMANICA

*—for Robert Duncan*

Throat of the whirlwind, what might have been.

This stern hymn.

And every pool a sea. And murder in the air.

Help was hoped for.


We speak of *Scots wha hae wi' Wallace bled.*

The war ode, composed on horseback, pounding
over Galloway moor,

and to follow it
as the one thing needful, through good or evil,

in the company of a Mr. Symmes, who, observing,
forebore.


A poet has been appointed.

This blessing is not often given.

In the arena of his own remote glen,
for want of a wider one.

In the Life his riding to Edinburgh
as early as his thirty-third year.

*Kevin Magee*

A wish that to the last hour.
Of his standing. Higher or lower.

Was it not wonderful that the Adjustments
between them have been postponed?

Was not he too one of the Napoleons, material fate
pitched against free will,

*Sae rantingly, sae wantonly,*
*below the gallows-tree*

## HOMERIC FRAGMENT

*"Shakespeare goes farther, and makes his Greeks*
*and Romans Englishmen; otherwise his nation*
*would not have understood him." Goethe,*
*Conversations with Eckermann.*

### I.

The rage of Achilles
destructive brought
Hades souls heroes

crowding, countless
prey for dogs, birds,
fulfilling conceived

the destiny, when he
and lord of men Agamemnon
broke up and fought,

which one of the gods
turned them against
one another? Disease

killing off many honored
that army, show respect for
distant targets welcomed

186

here who inhabit allow
you these hollow ships'
ransom, bondage, staff

in his hand the wreath
of Apollo, he begged alone
his cause with a shout,

Don't make me still angrier
out of fear I never offered
far from her native land

the priests release my dear
he brutally told loitering
along the shores of the loud

sea who said hear me obey
you who stand guard ruler
beside me now I beg you

make you build you War,
Helen, and strove forward
struck, bleed, endlessly

the pyres for the dead lit up
stopped first hit in the quiver
noise peaks battling, ear-shot.

*[Enter one in sumptuous armor*

What's that? What's that?

What honey is expected?

What pretty abruption

What raging of the sea

would rend and deracinate
the unity and married
calm of states. To say the truth,
true and not true.

Now play him me
the defects, miscarrying
lolling some Oration.

When degree is shak'd.

Here lies the Lord of Imbecilities
and posts. Make paradoxes
for those that with the finesse

of their souls, words,
vows, gifts, guide
love's full sacrifize.

　　　　　　　*[Enter common Soldiers passing by*

Is this *Achilles?*

Kingdom'd *Achilles.*

I am *Achilles.*

If not *Achilles*, nothing.

What's the matter man.

What lost in the labyrinth
of thy fury?

You dog.
*[Strikes him]*

*Mars* his Idiot,
do rudeness, do

188

*Kevin Magee*

Camel, do, do.
Where's my wits?

See see your scylence
conning in dumbness

at the author's drift.

Proclaim'd a fool, I think.

Bak'd with no date in the pie.

Poor wretch, you poor *chipochia*

Vassalage at unawares encountring
scantling indexes
to subsequent volumes.

The ill aspects of Planets.

Nor nothing monstrous neither.

Nothing but our undertakings.

Weaker than a woman's tear.

They call this bed-work,
mappry, Closet warre,

the spice & salt that season
a very land-fish languageless.

Power into will, will into appetite.

A monster, my Ambassador.

As red as *Mars* his heart.

*Kevin Magee*

*[Enter the Prologue arm'd*

> How much in having
> or without or it cannot,
> though in and of him
> there is much contesting
>
> to heere the wooden dialogue
> and sound, twixt
> this stretcht footing
> and the scaffollage.
>
> That's my integrity and truth
> to you,
>
> if we talk of reason,
> this cram'd reason,
> reason and respect.
>
> Let's shut our gates.
>
> I'll speak it in my spirit
> and honor no.
>
> That proof is call'd
> impossibility.
>
> What are you reading?


## II.

> Against forgetting,
> in place of knowledge, the palace of knowledge.
> Who can say they know how.
> I have read Genesis 22 five times
>
> that tells the story of what is called the sacrifice
> or holocaust of Isaac. How does one
> who does not possess himself express it,
> unless he were to become his own Atrocity?

190

I'm also reading about the place-name,
how it "pushes away" (Derrida) or "infects" (Lyotard)
what it's called. The Gorge of Lost Souls,
and it's going to be known. This thought takes hold.

Seized and held in the grip of another. Or held by the hand.
I'm insisting on the act of seizure,
wrong doing and the will to inflict harm, singing
*I am on the road to Basra*

### III.

$$\frac{58,000 \ X \ 70}{140 \ X \ 714}$$

"It's almost unimaginable,"
said the National Secretary of the Socialist Workers Party
in Cleveland, March 30, 1991, viz.
"the large number of dead."

Jack Barnes quoted *Harper's* magazine:
How many walls the size of the Vietnam Memorial,
with the same type size per name,
would it take to list the Vietnamese?

Answer: 70 walls.
"Do the ratio," he said, "for the Iraqis."
Using the number provided by the Pentagon,
even with that low figure you'd arrive

at 714 walls. A large black slab of granite.
"Just imagine, if you can," he said, "70 walls
the size of each 'American' wall stretching in one direction
and veering off at another angle, 714 more walls."

IV.

You do not know and you will never know.
None of you bastards. We are in the same boat,
the same book, mark it and mourn. What songs

will be there for the shock. The number: unknown.
Who is equal to the scale. The cloud of tear gas
an amulet, or banner. I walked alone with Mary

to the field beyond the gate. The spectacle of war
stemmed, stemming out of any other of the many
others. Jack Spicer calls us bastards. We are called

this name to become the name, not yet knowing
what work this is that we are called to knowing
only that the name is true. I will answer you.

It tastes bitter, my anger. It continues to grow.
Jack Barnes' arm is missing at the elbow.
He marks the time and he is losing time, postponed.

He is in the grip of it, repeating Malcolm X's
*Free at last! Free at last!* The promise demands
its undertaking. But if the band, the group,

the party, the disciples, their integral existence,
were incarnated in a single being, the name
for the incarnated one would still be Orpheus.

They will have made him into bread and wine.
Do you hear the enigma of the wound
I'm writing under the name of *wound?*

Their mothers will have hardly been at all.
The woman every child has known, before knowing it.
Viewed from above in a flood along the only road.

*Kevin Magee*

## FEBRUARY 24, 1991

*The blow of this number of deaths.*
*We may never know the actual numbers killed*
*in the final forty-eight hours of the invasion,*
*along the road to Basra.*

*That was the killing zone.*
*You couldn't move down the road. You couldn't move up the road.*
*You couldn't surrender, wave a white flag, or give yourself up.*
*These were people targeted for wave after wave*

*of bombing, strafing and shelling,*
*who were putting up no resistance,*
*many with no weapons, others with rifles packed in bedclothes,*
*leaving in cars, trucks, carts and on foot.*

*We bombed one end of the highway, sealing it off.*
*We bombed the other end of the highway, and sealed it off.*
*We positioned artillery units on the hills overlooking*
*the traffic gridlocked, traffic jams backed up for as many as*
    *twenty miles.*

*From the air and from the land, we carpet bombed every living*
    *thing*
*on the road, every person, jeep, truck, car and bicycle.*
*The victims were refugees fleeing they were not military units*
*they were not organized in retreat.*

*They were individual human beings trying to get away from the*
    *war.*
*This slaughter ranks among the great atrocities.*
*The Road to Basra is the Guernica, the Hiroshima, the Dresden,*
*the My Lai of the U.S. War against Iraq.*

*Kevin Magee*

## PACIFIC ARCHIVE

The books on the shelves around you.
We were not able to get confirmations.
The Waco incineration. The eyes of many.
The glowing embers placed in the eyes.

We are told not to analyze.
We are told to feel sorry for Janet Reno,
who sent tanks and tear gas to free
the children. I would like to read you

a couple more things from the Fact Sheet.
A ramp worker at Delta Airlines.
Against his will Ahmad was dragged.
"Have you ever been to Oklahoma?"

"Do you know how to make a bomb?"
"What do you do at the Bookstore?"
"It's not an ordinary bookstore, is it?"
"We are friendly, and not so bad."

(Japan gets 40% of its oil from Iran.)
In the coming Ontario provincial elections.
Who incinerated the Branch Davidians.
The Omnibus Anti-terrorism Act of 1995.

The question of National Origin.
Terrorist = Disruption of Commerce.
The Palmer raids, the Red Scares.
We've all heard about the Red Scares.

As soon as the bomb went off
we hear some Arab did it like the guy
who was trying to fly to Jordan.
(Vincent Chin was murdered.)

1991: Rodney King. The Gulf War.
Malcolm's sense of what a U.N.-sponsored war in the Congo
was really like. They provided me
with a summary copy of the Hatch Act.

Kevin Magee

In times of crisis like times of war
or economic crisis, certain groups
immigrant or women or whatever
they will come and take your job away.

This is the conversation that happens.
He's got something written out.
When asked to define what "acting
inimically" meant, I responded:

"Can the rule of law be suspended
in the name of national security?"
Too weak to fight back in 1948.
The Smith Act was basically a law

that made any ideas other than
those the government proposed
a crime. In 1950, the McArran Act.
The Montgomery Bus Boycott in 1955.

As I mentioned before, in 1973
the State lacked legislative authority.
The attacks that we see coming down.
Or go forth on your own path.

The demise of the Panthers and how
that happened. Serious racist terror.
They didn't have enough democracy.
A new and important development.

The far rightists. If we think it
and don't act, *we will get in trouble.*
To act in the streets as best we can.
The extra-legal side that gets unleashed.

The proviso was in their interpretation.
The Harvey Milk Democratic Club.
Look, an attack was made on a man.
This is just something to think about.

195

When these moves they are making.
This example that we had last year,
how to defend your democratic rights.
To defend them you must exercise them.

We have a basic right to hold our views
and act on that, the solidest basis.
It all fits into the structure we have.
Part of the thrust of it was that.

Part of the trust in it was that.
Nan Bailey: "It's time to go."
Sunday. 3:00 p.m. Next week.
"This part of the forum is yours."


CINDERELLA

Tell them you fell down the basement.
Tell them you fell down the basement steps.
I tell them if you tell them to bring me my baby
right now. I want my baby right now.

Tell them to bring her the baby now.
Doctor saying no she don't need to see it.
Sister outside in the hallway crying
Momma, tell these people to let me go.

Nobody goes anywhere until she tells us.
I fell down the basement just give me my baby.
Doctor kept saying, in the state it's in.
Doctor kept asking *what happened to you.*

Nurse brought the baby and it was big and healthy
I'm crying and breathing hard I scream
I FELL DOWN THE BASEMENT STEPS. Doctor
says please, honey, you don't have to lie.

I had my baby that night, born dead.
Take me to Emergency, told me not to talk.
My baby was decapitated from the blows.
Swinging on both of us with the broomstick.

*Kevin Magee*

## THE LAST GERMAN IN ITALY

Your manner of speaking shows me the noble country.
Then I traced my Fate back to the inferno of poetry.

Profiles of workers (warriors) glazed on the walls.
They were other and licking at blood-flaked murals

ground down to powder, glossing imperial medallions
spilled goldenly recording an alarmed Mediterranean

theater of war adored her disappearing down the road.
Or if you were the smile or miles of an oblivious sorrow,

my error, or terror, a cadenced dream sprung Lucretius
unconsciously wandering, startled by window crash

open to Eros, vault of a barbarous tomb or satin sky
religiously looked to the lovely authority of her eyes

on my heresy of the Iron Cross, her Roman mythology
savagely dragged to the evil hut of a ravaged family.

# Emma Enters a Sentence
# of Elizabeth Bishop's
## William H. Gass

*—With photographs by Michael Eastman*

### THE SLOW FALL OF ASH

EMMA WAS AFRAID of Elizabeth Bishop. Emma imagined Elizabeth Bishop lying naked next to a naked Marianne Moore, the tips of their noses and their nipples touching; and Emma imagined that every feeling either poet had ever had in their spare and spirited lives was present there in the two nips, just where the nips kissed. Emma, herself, was ethereally thin, and had been admired for the translucency of her skin. You could see her bones like shadows of trees, shadows without leaves.

Perhaps she should have been afraid of Miss Moore instead of Miss Bishop because Emma felt threatened by resemblance—mirrors, metaphors, clouds, twins—and Miss Moore was a tight-thighed old maid like herself; wore a halo of ropey hair and those low-cut patent leather shoes with the one black strap which Emma favored, as well as a hat as cockeyed as an English captain's, though not in the house, as was Emma's habit; and wrote similitudes which Emma much admired but could not in all conscience approve: that the mind's enchantment was like Gieseking playing Scarlatti . . . what a snob Miss Moore was; that the sounds of a swiftly strummed guitar were—in effect—as if Palestrina had scored the three rows of seeds in a halved banana . . . an image as precious as a ceramic egg. Anyway, Gieseking was at his best playing a depedaled Mozart. Her ears weren't all wax, despite what her father'd said.

When you sat in the shadow of a window, and let your not-Miss-Moore's-mind move like a slow spoon through a second coffee, thoughts would float to view, carried by the current in the way Miss Bishop's river barges were, and they would sail by slowly too, so their cargoes could be inspected, as when father yelled "wax ear" at her, his mouth loud as a loud engine, revving to a roar. All you've done is grow tall, he'd say. Why didn't you grow breasts? You grew a nose, that long thin chisel chin. Why not a big pair of milkers?

Emma'd scratch her scalp until it bled and dandruff would settle in the sink or clot her comb; the scurf of cats caused asthma attacks; Elizabeth Bishop was short of breath most of the time; she cuddled cats and other people's children; she was so often suffocated by circumstance, since a kid, and so was soon on her back in bed; that's where likeness led, like the path into the woods where the witch lived.

Perhaps Emma was afraid of Elizabeth Bishop because she also bore "Bishop" as her old maid name. Emma Bishop—one half of her a fiction, she felt, the other half a poet. Neither half an adulteress, let alone a lover of women. She imagined Elizabeth Bishop's head being sick in Emma's kitchen sink. Poets ought not to puke. Or injure themselves by falling off curbs. It was something which should have been forbidden any friend of Marianne Moore's. Lying there, Emma dreamed of being in a drunken stupe, of wetting her eraser, promising herself she'd be sick later, after conceiving one more lean line, writing it with the eraser drawn through a small spill of whiskey like the trail . . . the trail . . .

In dawn dew, she thought, wiping the line out with an invented palm, for she knew nothing about the body of Elizabeth Bishop, except that she had been a small woman, round-faced, wide-headed, later inclined to be a bit stout, certainly not as thin as Emma— an Emma whose veins hid from the nurse's needle. So it was no specific palm which smeared the thought of the snail into indistinctness on the table top, and it was a vague damp, too, which wet Miss Bishop's skin.

Emma was afraid of Elizabeth Bishop because Emma had desperately desired to be a poet, but had been unable to make a list, did not know how to cut cloth to match a pattern, or lay out night things, clean her comb, where to plant the yet-to-be dismantled ash, deal with geese. She looked out her window, saw a pigeon clinging to a tree limb, oddly, ill, unmoving, she. the cloud

Certain signs, certain facts, certain sorts of ordering, maybe, made her fearful, and such kinds were common in the poetry of Elizabeth Bishop; consequently, most of Elizabeth Bishop's poems lay unseen, unsaid, in her volume of Bishop's collected verse. Emma's eye swerved in front of the first rhyme she reached, then hopped ahead, all nerves, fell from the page, fled. the bird

So she really couldn't claim to have understood Elizabeth Bishop, or to have read Elizabeth Bishop's poems properly, or fathomed her friend Marianne Moore either, who believed she was better than Bishop, Emma was sure, for that was the way the world went, friend overshadowing friend as though one woman's skin had been drawn across the other's winter trees. a cloud

Yes, it was because the lines did seem like her own bones, not lines of transit or lines of breathing, which was the way lines were in fine poems normally, lines which led the nurse to try to thump them, pink them to draw blood—no, the violet veins were only bone; so when death announces itself to birds they, as if, freeze on the branches where the wind whiffles their finer feathers, though they stay stiller there, stiffer than they will decay.

When, idly skimming (or so she would make her skimming seem), Emma's eye would light upon a phrase like "deep from raw throats," her skin would grow paler as if on a gray walk a light snow had sifted, whereupon the couplet would close on her stifled cry, stifled by a small fist she placed inside her incongruously wide, wide-open mouth. ". . . a senseless order floats . . ." Emma felt she was following each line's leafless example by clearing her skin of cloud so anyone might see the bird there on her bone like a bump, a swollen bruise. She was fearful for she felt the hawk's eye on her. She was fearful of the weasel 'tween her knees. fearful

Emma owned an Iowa house, empty and large and cool in the fall. Otherwise inhospitable. It had thin windows with wide views, a kitchen with counters of scrubbed wood, a woodshed built of now wan boards, a weakly sagging veranda, weedy yard. At the kitchen table, crossed with cracks and scarred by knives, Emma Bishop sat in the betraying light of a bare bulb, and saw both poets, breasted and breastless, touching the tips of their outstretched fingers together, whereas really the pigeon, like a feathered stone, died in her eye.

Emma was living off her body the way some folks were once said to live off the land, and there was little of her left. Elizabeth Bishop's rivers ran across Emma's country, lay like laminate, created her geography: cape, bay, lake, strait . . . snow in no hills

She would grow thin enough, she thought, to slip into a sentence of the poet's like a spring frock. She wondered whether, when large portions of your pleasure touch, you felt anything really regional, or was it all a rush of warmth to the head or somewhere else? When Marianne Moore's blue pencil cancelled a word of Elizabeth Bishop's—a word of hers hers only because of where it was, words were no one's possession, words were the matter of the mind—was the mark a motherly rebuke or a motherly gesture of love? Thou

201

shalt not use spit in a poem, my dear, or puke in a sink.

There'd been a tin one once, long ago replaced by a basin of shallow enamel. It looked as if you could lift it out like a tray. It was blackly pitted but not by the bodies of flies. A tear ran down one side, grainy with tap drip, dried and redried.

How had she arrived here, on a drift? to sit still as pigeon on a kitchen stool and stare the window while no thoughts came or went but one of Moore or two of Bishop and the hard buds of their breasts and what it must have meant to have been tongued by a genius.

She would grow thin enough to say "I am no longer fastened to this world; I do not partake of it; its furniture ignores me; I eat per day a bit of plain song and spoon of common word; I do not, consequently, shit, or relieve my lungs much, and I weigh on others little more than shade on lawn, and on memory even less." She was, in fact, some several months past faint.

Consequently, on occasion, she would swoon as softly as a toppled roll of Christmas tissue, dressed in her green chemise, to wake later, after sunset, lighter than the dark, a tad chilly, unmarked, bones beyond brittle, now knowing where

or how she had arrived at her decision to lie down in a line of verse and be buried there; that is to say, be born again as a simple set of words, "the bubble in the spirit-level." So, said she to her remaining self, which words were they to be? grave behaving words, map signs

That became Miss Emma Bishop's project: to find another body for her bones, bones she could at first scarcely see, but which now were ridgy, forming Ws, Ys and Zs, their presence more than circumstantial, their presence more than letters lying overleaf.

She would be buried in a book. Mourners would peer past its open cover. A made-up lady wipes her dark tears on a tissue. Feel the pressure of her foot at the edge of the page? see her inhale her sorrow slowly as though smelling mint? she never looked better, someone will say. heaven sent

Denial was her duty, and she did it, her duty; she denied herself; she refused numbering, refused funds, refused greeting, refused hugs, rejected cards of printed feeling; fasted till the drapes diaphenated and furniture could no longer sit a spell; said, "I shall not draw my next breath." Glass held more heaviness than she had. Not the energy of steam, nor the wet of mist, but indeed like that cloud we float against our specs when we breathe to clean them.

Yet she was all care, all

Because now, because she was free of phlegm, air, spit, tears, wax, sweat, snot, blood, chewed food, the least drool of excrement—the tip of the sugar spoon had been her last bite—her whole self saw, the skin saw, the thin gray yellow hair saw, even the deep teeth were tuned, her pores received, out came in, the light left bruises where it landed, the edge of the stool as she sat cut limb from thigh the way a wire passes the flesh of cheese, and pain passed through her too like a cry through a rented room. Because she had denied herself everything, life itself, life knew she was a friend, came near, brought all

Ask nothing. you shall receive

She was looking at the circular pull on the window's shade, her skin was drawn, her fingers felt for it, her nose knew, and it was that round hole the world used to trickle into her. With Emma down to her E, there was plenty of room, and then she, she would, she would slip into a sentence, her snoot full of substance, not just smell, not just of coffee she hadn't cupped in a coon's age, or fresh bread from back when, or a bit of peony from beside a broken walk, but how fingers felt when they pushed a needle through a hoop of cloth, or the roughness of unspread toast, between her toes a memory of being a kid, the summer's sunshine, hearty as a hug, flecks of red paper blown from a firecracker to petal a bush, the voices of boys, water running from a hose, laughter, taunts, fear they would show her something she didn't want to know

red rows the clapboard shells her reading eye slid swallowing solemnly as if she'd just been told of someone's love, not for her, no, for the sea nearby in Bishop's poems, a slow wash of words on a beach hissing like fat in the flame, brief flare-up before final smoke

Aunts trying hats on, paper plates in their laps—no—dog next door barking in his sleep, how about that? the flute, the knife, the shrivelled shoes I spell against my will with two ells, how about that? her ear on the pull, the thread wrapped ring, swell of sea along sunsetted shore, Maine chance, I'm now the longing that will fill that line when I lie down inside it, me, my eye, my nips, fingertips, yes, ribs and lips alined with Moore's, whose hats, maybe, were meant in the poem, the poem, the poem about the anandrous aunts, exemplary and slim, avernal eyed, shaded by brim, caring for their cares, protecting their skin. a cloud

Now I am the ex of ist I am the am I always should have been. Now I am this hiss this thin this brisk I'm rich in vital signs, in

203

lists I in my time could not make, the life I missed because I was afraid, the hawk's eye, owl's too, weasel's greed, the banter of boys, bang, bleeding paper blown into a bush, now I urinate like them against the world's spray-canned designs and feel relief know pride puff up for their circle jerk fellowship and spit on spiders step on ants pull apart peel back brag grope, since it is easy for me now, like sailing boats, making pies, my hair hearing through the ring the rumble of coastal water, rock torn, far from any Iowa window, now I am an ab, a dis, pre's fix, hop's line.

Out there by the bare yard the woodshed stood in a saucer of sun where she once went to practice screaming her cries and the light like two cy-narrow road, the through cracks be-warped boards, the handle, its blade tree's stump the built around so still be of service had had to come would have a life butcher's block be-

clists passing on a light coming in tween the shed's ax she wouldn't buried in an ash shed had been the stump would though its tree down, dad said, it like an anvil or a cause as long as you had a use you were alive, birds flew at the first blow, conse-quently not to cry that the tree'd been cut, groaning when it fell its long fall, limbs of leaves brushing limbs of leaves as though driven by a wind, with plenty of twig crackle, too, like a sparky fire, the heavy trunk crashing through its own bones to groan against the ground, scattering nests of birds and squirrels, but now she was screamed out, thinned of that, or the thought of the noble the slow the patiently wrought, how the tree converted dirt into aspiration, the beautiful brought down, branches lofty now low and broken, the nests of birds and squirrels thrown as you'd throw a small cap, its dispelled shade like soil still, at toppled tiptop a worm's web resembling a scrap of cloud, it should have been allowed to die in the sky its standing death, she'd read whatever there is of love let it be obeyed, well, a fist of twigs and leaves and birdspit rolled away, the leaves of the tree shaking a bit yet, and the web

whisperating

what was left

A fat cloud, white as a pillow of steam, hung above the tree, motionless, as if drawn, as if all wind were gone, the earth still,

entirely of stone, while the tree alone fell, after the last blow had been withdrawn, and the weeds which had tried and failed to be a lawn waited their bruise.

The house, like herself, was nowhere now. It was the reason why she fled facts when she came upon them, words like "Worcester, Massachusetts," dates like "February, 1918." Em had decided not to seek her fate but to await it. Still, suppose a line like that came to claim her. It was a risk.

I have lost this, lost that, am I not an expert at it? I lost more than love. I lost even its glimpse. Treefall. Branchcrash. That's all. Gave. Gave. Gave away. Watched while they took the world asunder. Now even my all is smal. So I am ready. Not I hope the brown enormous odor . . . rather a calm cloud, up the beach a slowing run of water

wait

far from the flame,

They were women. They were poets. But Miss Bishop probably knew a man or two, had him inner, while Miss Moore drew another pair of bloomers on. Hardly a match. Miss Bishop smoked, drank, wheezed, stood in the surf, barefooted about, fished. Miss Moore hunted for odd words. Exercised her fancy at the track. My father would stare at my bony body. Shake his head sadly. Nothing there to raise a dick. I'd be bare. Stand there. Bedsided. Scared. O yes mortified. Ashamed. All my blood in two lines below my eyes. Streaked with rose like twilit clouds. I'd stand. Before the great glass. It would be to see as he saw the then smooth skin, rose lit, cheek to lay a cheek against, smooth to smooth I suppose, or wipe a weeping eye.

They were women. They were poets. But Miss Bishop lusted after love. Miss Moore cooled like a pie on a sill. Hardly a match. Not my wish to be Elizabeth Bishop. Not for me, either, to be Miss Moore. Yet alike as a pod houses its peas.

Unfit for fooling around. Like those Emmas before me, I read of love in the light of a half-life, and the shadow of its absent half gives depth to the page. My made-up romances are probably better, probably worse than reality. I am a fire at which my swain warms his hands. I am a fire quenched by a shower of scorn. Tenderness and longing alternate with cruelty and aversion. I study how to endure monsoons of driving snow.

Let's see how you're coming along. I'd have to slip out of my dress. Why are you wearing a bra? what's there to bra about. After he left I'd stand in the cold puddle of my clothes, step to the mirror to see for himself myself and my vaginal lips clasped like devout hands, praying to God to let me die before another day.

There was nothing to see, he said, so why did he inspect me as if I were going to receive a seal from the FDA? Elizabeth Bishop's father died of Bright's disease when she was still a child, and her mother went mad in Elizabeth's teens. My mother took her sturdy time dying. The day she died in her bed in this house, she had washed the windows of her room, though she could scarcely stand, and fluttered the curtains with arms weak with disease. Bustling about like a bee but without a buzz. Keeping out of reach, I now know. Wiping mirrors free from any image. Staying away by pretending to care and tend and tidy and clean and sweep and mend and scour and polish. Married to a gangplank of a guy. She scarcely spoke to me. I think she was ashamed of the way she let him make me live.

I learned to read on the sly. I failed my grades, though in this dinky town you were advanced so your puberty would not contaminate the kiddies. Despite the fact that I hadn't any puberty, my father said. But I read on the sly the way some kids smoked or stroked one another through their clothes. I read in fear of interruption. So I learned to read fast. I also read mostly first verses, first chapters, and careened through the rest, since my ear, when it turned to catch a distant thread, swung my eyes away with my brow toward the sound.

The ash came down but I never believed why. The shed was built around the stump to become an altar where my father chopped firewood or severed chickens from their heads. Slowly the stump was crisscrossed with cuts, darkened by layers of absorbed blood and covered with milling crowds of tiny tiny ants. Traditionally, kids went to the woodshed for a whaling. Although once upon a time I stood still as a stick by the edge of my tot-wide bed, I now went to the shed to get undressed under my father's disappointed eye. Staring at hairs. And had he said something lewd, had he laid a hand, had he bent to breathe upon my chest, had his dick distended his pants, his point would have been disproved. I'd have elicited some interest.

He watched me grow like a gardener follows the fortunes of his plants, and what he wanted was normalcy. I dimly remember,

*William H. Gass*

when a child, how my father would hold me in his lap and examine my teeth. Something coming in there. He would push his finger down upon the spot. This tooth is loose, he'd say, with some semblance of pleasure, wiggling it painfully back and forth. Well, he was a farmer. And I was crop. Why not?

Getting a man was the great thing. My mother had got a man and what had that got her? Knocked up. With me. That's what. Maybe my father hoped he'd see, when I stripped, a penis lifting its shy self from the slot between my legs. Flat as I was, he may have thought there was a chance. There was no chance either way.

I might have been a boy in his balls but I was dismantled in her womb.

### a residue of rain

Emma Bishop let the light on the table tell her about the weather. Sadness was the subject. Disappointment. Regret. The recipe? a bit of emptiness like that of winter fields when the fierce wind washes them; acceptance, yes, some of that, the handshake of a stranger; resignation, for what can the field do about the wind but freeze? what can the hand do but grasp the offered other? and a soupçon of apprehension, like clods of earth huddled against the frost they know will knock someday, or an envelope's vexation about the letter it will enclose; then a weariness of the slow and gentle variety, a touch of ennui, an appreciation of repetition. This sadness had the quality of a bouquet garni discreetly added to the sauce; it offered a whiff of melancholy, subtle, just enough to make the petals of plants curl at their tips. A day of drizzle in the depths of November. Not definite enough yet? All right: the quiet hour after . . . the nearly negligible remains . . . an almost echo.

The theme: leave-taking. Bidding adieu to a familiar misery. So . . . long . . . . . . The house was empty. The light was late, pale, even wan. The table lay in the light as though dampened by a rag. Emma Bishop saw her fingers fold up like a fan. Her lifelike light. So . . . long . . . . . . Nothing stays the ancients said but the cloud stood above the treetop while it toppled, still as painted, her father murdering her tree's long limbs before they had loosened their leaves. Why then should anything be loved if it was going to be so brutally taken away? He had seen the tree *be* in Emma Bishop's bright eyes. Beneath it, weeds where she rested and read. When she no longer had to hide her occupation.

208

It had been of some interest to Emma that her father had ceased his inspection of her bared body after her mother died. As if . . . As if it had been to distress her mother he undressed her, had walked around her like a car he might buy, had a list of factors to check for flight safety, to justify his then saying: see what you've given me, what you've grown, you are a patch of arid earth, your child is spindly, awkward, chestless, wedge-chinned and large-eyed, stooped too, not as though gangly but as though old.

She had been a ten-month kid she'd been told. Maybe during that tenth month her weenie had withered.

Over time Emma began to perceive her parental world for what it was. Her father farmed by tearing at the earth, seeding soy with steel sticks, interested in neither the soil nor the beans, but only in what the beans would bring; interested in the sky for the same reason, in the wind, in rain. The creek overflowed once and flooded a meadow. He saw only a flooded field. He didn't see a sheet of bright light lying like a banner over the ploughed ground. And the light darkened where the lumps neared the surface. Emma watched the wind roughen the water so that sometimes the top of a clod would emerge like new land. Crusoe in England? in Iowa. She imagined.

And her mother scrubbed their clothes to remove the dirt, not to restore the garments; and wiped up dust to displace it, not to release the reflection in the mirror or the view through the glass or the gleam from the wood. She pinned wash to its line as if she were handcuffing a criminal. Emma saw dislike run down her arms like sweat and transform the task. She didn't say to the pan, "Let me free you from this grease." She said to the grease, "Get thee away, you snot of Satan."

Emma ultimately preferred her furniture tongued and grooved, glued rather than nailed, for the nail had not only fixed Christ's hands to the Cross, it had driven Eve into labor and a life of grief. Her mother wouldn't cry over spilled milk, but she would silently curse, her lips retreating from a taste. Emma learned to see the spatter as a demonstration of the laws of nature and as a whimsical arrangement of pale gray-blue splotches. When she read that infants sometimes played with their stools, she knew why.

Maybe her father stopped inspecting her when he saw her watching, simply watching him; when his naked face and naked gaze were gazed at, gazed at like urine in the pot, yellow and pearly; when his hard remarks were heard like chamber music.

He wore boots on account of the manure, he said, though they

209

hadn't had horses or any other sort of animal in Emma's time. Except the chickens. The rooster's crude proud cry rose from the roof of the coop and from the peak of Bishop's poem. Perhaps it had a line that would do. He'd pull the boots off and leave them on the back porch where Emma would find his handprints on their dusty sides. The handprints, thought Emma, were nice. There were prehistoric handprints placed in caves. Her father's boots were four hands high. Maybe five.

As a young girl, Emma had run around barefoot until she began to loathe any part of her that was uncovered, her face and hands first, her feet finally; and she realized her toughened undersoles had little to no sensation. Now her feet were both bony and tender and could feel the floor tremble when the train passed, three fields and one small woods away.

She herself was a residue, her life light as the light in her inherited house. Emma's mother had died in the bed she had no doubt grown to loathe, a bed full of him every night until her illness drove him out, lying there in a knot, staring up through the dark at death—who would not want it to come quick? Emma wondered whether her mother had ever had a moment of . . . exultation. Little cruelties cut her down. The rubadubdub of every day's labor, always, going on as long as there was light. Same old cheap china on the table. The same old dust seeping in to shadow the mirrors and coat the sills. The same old rhubarb brought from the patch, the stored carrots and apples and sprouting potatoes. The same unrelenting sun in the summer. Then deep cold and blowing snow. The three of them in different corners of the house. Emma would sit on the floor of her room, reading, her back against a faintly warm radiator, afghan over her knees, squinting at the page through inadequate glasses. She would occasionally hear her mother sweeping or washing, or the rhythmic treadling of her sewing machine. Her father would be busy with his figures, rearranging, recalculating, hoping to improve the columns' bleak assessments, since outgo regularly threatened to overtake income. But they sewed their own sacklike dresses; they ate their cold stored root crops; they killed and plucked and cooked their own chickens, though Emma didn't eat dinner those nights, not since she'd fainted in front of a fistful of freshly withdrawn innards; they scavenged pieces of firewood out of their neighbor's woods; they picked berries and crabapples and dandelion greens, and jar'd elderberry and made apple jelly and canned beans and tomatoes, and even fed the chickens home-grown corn: so what did this outgo come to? Not much, her father allowed. But they were eating from their kitchen garden like squirrels and rabbits, out of the nut and berried woods like the deer. The soybeans weren't fertilized and they couldn't afford those newfangled chemicals. The only machine still working was her dad's arms and legs and cursing mouth.

on morning grass,

I've died too late into your life, her mother said to Emma who was rocking slowly in the rocker by her bed. Emma wondered what she meant, it sounded like a summing up; but she knew an explanation wouldn't be agreeable to hear so she didn't ask for one; she didn't want to wonder either, but she was haunted by what seemed a sentence of some sort, and kept on wondering. Her rocking was not a rocking really. It was a little nervous jiggle transmitted to the chair. Emma would never have a husband to stare at her body, she had her father for that; she'd never have to do for anybody, never have to sew buttons on a shirt or open her thighs or get him off in time for church. But her life would be like her mother's just the same. They'd endure until they died. That would be it. Over the world, as far as she could see, that was it.

The dying had enormous power. Emma wondered whether her mother knew it. Everything the dying said was said "deathbed." Everything the dying said was an accusation, a summation, a distillation, a confession. "I died too late into your life." Which was it? confession, distillation, delusion, summation, provocation?

Her mother tried to get God to take her part against her disease, but churchgoing did no good; prayers went as unanswered as most mail; the days came and went and weren't appreciated. She couldn't keep anything on her stomach. She was in the bathroom longer than she was in bed. "Maybe I should be like Emma and not eat," she said. Was it a gift, to have been given a life like that? Close to no one. Never to see delight rise in another's eyes when they saw you. Dear Heavenly Father, let me suffer a little while longer. Let me linger in this vale of tears and torment. I have potatoes to fork and rinse, windows to wipe, dishes to do, rips to mend.

Her father fell over in a field. Nose down in the dirt. A dog found him.

At his funeral somebody said well, he died with his boots on, and some mourners appeared confounded by the remark, some looked puzzled and some smiled as much as was seemly, but none of the mourners mourned.

The world was a mist and black figures slowly emerged from the mist as they had in one of the few movies she'd seen, when the townsfolk were burying a family who'd been murdered by the Indians. It was a moist gray day and most people wore a dark coat against the chill. Emma in her horror held herself and stood far away from the hole so she wouldn't see them lower the man who'd brought her into the world and made her ashamed to be seen and hacked her ash to bits and cut the heads off chickens and left her a few acres of unkempt land and a dilapidated house. There was a hole in her memory now almost exactly his shape.

Emma sat on the front porch and greeted darkly dressed unaproned women while the men stood about the yard in awkward clumps waiting the decent interval. A few wives had brought casseroles of some kind. Emma never lifted the lids until she realized they'd expect their dishes to be returned. Then she dumped the spoiled contents in the meadow—smelling of mayonnaise and tuna—and wiped the bowls with grass. Forgot about them again. Only to come upon the little collection on a walk a week later. Now she couldn't remember to whom the bowls belonged. Emma huddled the crockery in a plastic sack and tottered the mile and a half she had to totter to reach the house of a neighbor she knew had brought something, and left the sack on the front steps. They had been trying to be helpful, she supposed, but what a trouble people were.

During the evening the air grew damper. Moonlight and mist, as Bishop wrote, were caught in the thickety woods like lamb's wool on pasture bushes. Except there was very little moonlight. It was the headlamp of the late train which allowed her to see the fog like gray hair in a comb, but only for a moment before all were gone: woods, fog, trainbeam, lamb's wool, gray hair, comb.

She sat in the same chair she'd sat in to greet grieving company, sat through an evening in which only the sky cared to snivel and sat on after they'd left into the deep night's drizzle, hoping to catch her death; but in the morning when the sun finally got through the fog to find her sitting in the same chair, as fixed as the leaves and flowers burned into the slats of its back, it flooded her cold wet lonely frightened immobile face impersonally, as though she were a bit of broken statue, and moved on to the pillars of the porch, knurled a bit to be fancy but picked out of a pattern book to be cheap, and then found a grimy windowpane to stain as if the grayed flush of dawn were drawn there. The sun made her open eyes close.

snow in still air,

The art of losing isn't hard to master. Emma remembered with gratitude that lesson. But she took it a step further. She lost the sense of loss. She learned to ask nothing of the world. She learned to long for nothing. She didn't require her knives to be sharp. She didn't demand dawn. When the snow came she didn't sigh at the thought of shoveling. There was no need for shoveling. Let the snow seal her inside. She'd take her totter about the house instead of the narrow path around the woods. She moved as a draft might from room to room. She ascended and descended the stairs as silently as a smell. Not to keep in trim. Not as if bored, caged, desperate. To visit things and bring them her silent regard.

Emma made her rounds among the mantises. Tending the garden in her teenage days when she'd been put in charge of it, she would find a mantis at its deadly devotions. And she discovered that the mantis rarely ventured far from its holy place. *Mantis religiosa.* It slowly turned the color of its circumstances. There was one on the roof of the shed the shade of a shingle. Another among the squash as green as most weeds. Motionless, she watched the mantis watching, and now Emma understood the difference between its immobility and hers. The mantis was looking for a victim, her father was making his assessments, her mother was doing her chores, while Emma was watching . . . why? . . . she was letting the world in; and that could be done, she learned, anywhere, at any time, from any position, any opening—the circle of the shade's pull. She ate her fill of the full world.

No wider than a toothpick, a mantis would rest on a leaf so lightly it never stirred from the weight of the insect. The mantis rose and fell as the leaf did, a bit of leaf itself, its eye on the shiny line a little spider was lowering. Emma Bishop rose and fell as well, soft as a shadow shifting across the floor, weightless as a gaze, but as wide as a rug, as good underfoot, as trustworthy in the pot as tea.

Large snowflakes slid slowly out of a gray sky. A lot like a winged seed, they wavered as they came and lit on grass or late leaves still whole and white as doilies. They fell on her hair, clung to an eyelash, melted upon Emma's extended tongue so a thrill shivered through her and she blushed. She also tottered out in the rain when

213

the rain was warm and fell in fat drops. Her cheeks would run and ears drip. And her hair would very slowly fill with wet, and whiten gradually the way her hair had grayed, till it became a bonnet, not her hair at all. Her outheld hands cooled until, like butterflies did a few times, the crystals lay peacefully on her palms.

Her father found out that, though Emma tended the garden, she didn't pull weeds or kill bugs. So he removed her from that duty and made her hold the guts he pulled from plucked chickens.

Elizabeth Bishop was a tougher type. She caught fish, for instance, and held their burdened-down bodies out at arm's length to study the white sea lice which infested them. She lived near water in Nova Scotia and the Keys and hung around fishhouses to note the glistening condition of the fish tubs, coated with herring scales, and the tiny iridescent flies that hover over them. Her father's slimed-on arm slid out of the cavity, his fist full of the chicken's life. He didn't look at Emma. He said: here, hold this. Could she now have enjoyed the mucus and the membranes, the chocolate and the rufous red of the liver and the . . . the white patches of fat like small snow on brick. The word was "gizzzzzzzzardzzzs."

Maybe not. But who had really reached sainthood in this life, and was willing to look on all things with equanimity?

Her totter took her along a lane where she'd dumped the funeral food, and there she found the cookware in an untidy pile like stones. "There's stillstuffstuck on the sides of the Corning Ware. I don't care. Leave it there." The grass grows high at the side of the meadow. Already it's popping up between them. Let them lie. The life I missed because I was afraid. That's where we buried him. A dark day. Twilit from dawn to twilight, then at twilight it was night. These dishes remain to be done. His remains, his fists, are encased in a cheap box six feet in the earth, crabgrass over dirt, fog over grass, night sky over fog, blackest space. I'll take one home this time to soak in the sink. Where my thought of the poet had her sick. I alone know how glorious grime is. Go it alone. God. Go it alone.

I vowed I'd get good at it. Going alonely. Holding the bowl, with blades of grass fastened to its sides where I'd wiped it weeks past, I promised myself a betterment. They were both gone. I was free of ma's forlorn face, dad's rage. The house was mine I reminded myself. And so it could stand nearly free of me. Stand and be. Recognized. Because I relinquished whatever had been mine. My thoughts I let go like lovebirds caged. One dish a day. I'll return them like pills. There was a nest-shaped dent in the grass where the bowl had lain. What an amazing thing! that such a shape should be at the side of a path between meadow and wood—the basin of a heatproof bowl like a footstep from the funeral.

Emma remembered, in the middle of that moment, while she was making a solemn promise to herself to do better, be better, become none, no one, the spring day she'd run into the woods to find bluebells and found instead the dogwood in bloom at the edge of a glade, each petal burned as if by a cigarette exactly as her poet, only that day discovered, had written in a poem, only that day read, in lines only that far reached and realized, before Emma's eye rose like a frightened fly from the dinner cloth.

So when the bowls were relatively rinsed she stacked them in a string sack, all six, with lids, so she tilted more than normally when she walked so many fields so many meadows to the nearest neighbor, and with a sigh and a sore arm set the sack down on the porch just so, so they'd find them soon enough, some wife and mother named not Nellie not Agatha, was that so? who would no doubt wash them all again and find good homes for them as if they were orphan kids. A tale they'd tell too to the ladies who had lent the dishes to Emma, foisted their food, their indifferent goodwill, their efforts of affection upon her. Yes, the ladies would laugh at least grin at the way they'd been returned, lumped in one sack like spuds, their pots, after so many weeks of wondering what . . . what was going on . . . and would . . . would they ever get them back.

The snow sidled out of a gray sky, and fell like ash, that slowly, that lightly, and lay on the cold grass, the limbs of trees, while the woods went hush and her quiet place grew quieter, as peaceful as dust; and soon everything was changed, black trunks became blacker, a dump of leaves disappeared, the roof of the shed was afloat in the air, the pump stuck up out of nowhere and its faint handled shadow seemed the only thing the snow couldn't cover.

wounds we have had,

Emma Bishop had not been born on the farm but in a nearby town where five thousand people found themselves eating and sleeping and working, meeting and greeting, cooking and cleaning, going up and down, and selling and signing, licensing and opining, because it was the county seat. The farm was in the family. It belonged to Emma's great aunt, Winnie, but when she died the farm, already run-down, fell further, and into her father's stubby unskilled mechanic's hands. Her father, when her mother met him, repaired tractors. Beneath the nail, his nails were black with green grease. Lo and behold, beyond Emma Bishop's richest imagining, her parents met, married, coupled, whereupon her mother bore and brought a baby naked into the world, the way, it would later appear, Emma's father wanted her. Because the baby was inspected for flaws. No one found any.

Emma's mother was short slender wan, while her father was broad and flat across the front, knotty too, a pine board kind of person. Emma, contrary to the core, was thin as a scarf and twice as tall, angular to contradict her father's bunchiness, given to swaying even when standing still, swaying like a tall stalk of corn in a field full of wind. It made her difficult to talk to, to follow her face, especially if you had to look up a little as her parents both did. Emma didn't have Marianne Moore's recessive features. Hers resembled Edith Sitwell's in being craggy.

Nevertheless, Marianne Moore saw into things, saw seeds in fruit, and saw how a tendril born of grape would wind itself like hair around a finger, cling to anything; or she would wonder what sort of sap went through the cherry stem to make the cherry red. Emma Bishop practiced by watching a worm walking, how it drew its hind end up into its middle, and then accordioned forward from the front. A rubber band could not do better. Leaving a small moist trail soon a light dry line lost on the limestone.

Her tree, where Emma went to read, was a tree of seed. It bore them in clumps, in clusters, in clouds. They were tapered like boat paddles. Her tree was very late to leaf, and every year her father would declare the ash had died, and indeed it was nothing but a flourish of sticks until, at last, fresh shoots appeared and the squirrels crept out on its branches to eat the tender stemtips. The ground around her tree would be littered with their leavings. While still small and green, seeds would begin to fall, and her father would say the ash was sick, because the seeds were so immature; but there were crowds, mobs of them left, dangling from every new twig like hands full of fingers. Moore called apple seeds the fruit within the fruit, but here the ash seeds hung in the air without the lure or protection of peel or pulp, just a thin tough husk which turned the color of straw and flew from the tree in the fall like shoutfuls of startled locusts.

The ash sucked all the water from the ground and shaded a wide round circle too where nothing much grew, a few baby ash of course, a weed or two, plantain principally, pushing up from the claygray earth to stand defiantly green between the roots. Its trunk was deeply furrowed, the bark itself barky, as if rain had eroded it. "This is the tree Satan's snake spoke from," Emma's father would say, his tone as certain as gospel. "It is the dirtiest tree on God's earth." The risen emblem of a fallen world.

The seeds would settle first, whirling up from the dry ground at a breath, stirred as the air stirred, and encircling the trunk with pods which curved gracefully from an oval head back to a needle-sized point, to lie in warm ochre layers like the tiniest of leaves. Her father cursed the tree as if it were littering a street against the law.

And quite a lot of little branches would break off and break a bit more when they hit the ground, causing her father still more annoyance, because the dead branches of this ash were dead in a thorough and severe way, dried as they were by the sky. Finally the five-leaflet leaves would begin to fall, the tree's seeds would come down in bunches, and everyone then knew autumn was over and that the sun always withdrew through the now bare branches, and so did the moon.

Her father said it was a moose-maple and not an ash at all. Its wood is spongy, but brittle as briars. Emma protested. It was a green ash. She had made the identification. There was no moose-maple in the book. That's what we call it hereabouts—a box elder, big weed, dirtiest tree. A true ash don't fall apart like that.

Despite her father's annoyance, Emma would sit upon a smooth bare root, her back against the trunk, surrounded by seeds and leaves, twigs and weeds, and read poetry books. If she'd been a boy, he might have beaten her. She could feel his eye on her, hard as a bird's. She weathered his rage as the tree weathered the wind. Then one day a branch, broken in a previous storm but caught by other branches, slipped out of their grasp and fell like a spear, stabbing her ankle with a suddenness she screamed, feeling snake-bit. She saw blood ooze from the wound in astonishment, the stick lying near, stiff and dry, sharp where it had snapped. Emma bawled, not from pain or even shock, but because she'd been betrayed.

dust on the sill there,

Marianne Moore liked to use words like "apteryx" in her poems. Very mannered, her style. Edith Sitwell liked to too. Emma would suddenly say "One fantee wave is grave and tall . . ." and suddenly

217

sing "The hot muscatelle siesta time fell . . ." Her mother would hear her with astonishment, for Emma very rarely laughed let alone sang. Even in church she just mouthed.

Now that she hadn't had to poison her mother or strike her father down in the field with the blade of a shovel, but was so alone even the chickens unfed had wandered off, she could have sung without surprising anyone, or sworn without shocking her father with unladylike language. She did sing sometimes inside herself. "In the cold cold parlor my mother laid out Arthur . . ." She didn't remember any more of that brutally beautiful poem. Words drifted into her eyes. When she was reading, it was always summer under the ash, and words fell softly through her pupils like ash soot pollen dust settling ever so slowly over hours over summer days a season even an entire lifetime that their accumulation was another cover. Solace for the skin.

She bore books out to the tree and made a pile. Her father glared. Why so many? Stick with one. One is plenty. But Emma couldn't stick to one. She'd begin "When night came, sounding like the growth of trees . . ." or "In the cold cold parlor . . ." and she'd feel herself becoming tense, was it her legs folding as if up into her bottom like the worm, and her arms canting outward like the mantis that worried her? Emma had these flyaway eyes, and after a bit she'd skip to another page, or have to drop one book in order to pick up another. Edith would take Emma aback with beauty "sounding like the growth of trees." Emma'd have to stop, to repeat, to savor, to— in her head—praise, to wonder at the wonder of it, why was that Nova Scotia wake so devastating? Not simply because it was being seen by a kid. "His breast was deep and white, cold and caressable." The way the boxed boy and the stuffed duck went into one another: that was making love the way she imagined it would be if it were properly done. Everyone was entered. No one was under.

A poem like the Nova Scotia poem—brief as it was—would sometimes take her weeks to read, or, rather, weeks to register all its words, and never in their printed order. That ordering would come later. One day, finally, she'd straighten the lines and march them as printed across her gaze. She could not say to her father when he glared at her, angry she knew because the books, the tree, her intense posture, the searing summer sky, were each an accusation, a reminder of another failure, that the words she read and fled from were all that kept her alive. "The mind is an enchanted thing like the glaze on a katydid-wing . . ." Words redeemed the world.

Imagine! Like the glaze on a katydid-wing, sub . . . subdivided . . . sub . . . by the sun until the nettings were legion . . . the nettings were legion . . . Her father really should have kept the grease beneath his nails and never replaced it with plant smutch and field dirt. His world was mechanical, not organic. It was cause followed by effect, not higgledy followed by piggledy and the poke.

Her father's figure would appear to her, dark and distant, wading through beans. Emma tried to unresent her mother's failures too. Why hadn't her mother protested her father's cruel scrutinies? Even the browbeatings her mother received she endured in silence, though with drooping head. Why had Emma herself stood so still in his stare, less naked later with pubic hair? Skimpy. No fur there. She could have refused. Fled. Cried. She stood in the shed and screamed. She shrieked. She shrilled. But they were in the ground less likely than seeds to volunteer, to rebreed, pop up in a pot or rise from beneath bedclothes sheeted and disheveled, hearing her scream. That's all she did in the shed. And she went there less and less, needed that silly release less and less. She was even proud she could be so loud, slight and without a chest, weak and out of touch with speech.

Edith Sitwell had a lilt. She went ding dong. Did her verses breathe, Emily Dickinson wanted to know. "Safe in their alabaster chambers . . ." Hoo. "Untouched by morning . . ." Emma was untouched. No man had ever laid a hand. Hardly her own, but once, curious, experimentally, secretive, ashamed, she felt herself as she supposed men did, and then withdrew in disbelief. To never again. "The meek members of the resurrection . . ." Emma stood in the center of herself and slowly turned her attention. There were windows, sills, shades, beyond the windows a world, fields, the silhouettes of firs and oaks, a dark quick bird, and then a wall a corner crack and peel of plaster pattern of leaf and stem and flower, too, counter of hardwood, wooden cabinets, one door ajar, dark as eyebrow, at the glass knob stop the little light left was captured there and the glass knob gleamed and its faint faint shadow, made light now not light's interruption, touched the soiled unpainted pine.

Mom and dad she never had await their resurrection, according to Emily. Grand go the years . . . ages . . . eons . . . empires . . . but only the words will arise, will outwear every weakness. Emma knew. That was why she waited for a line. Not an alabaster chamber or a boy's box—Arthur's coffin was a little frosted cake—but "Arthur's coffin."

219

That was what the soul was, like the floor of a forest, foot of great tree, earth on which seeds leaves twiglets fell and lay a season for another season, all the eyelighted earheard words piled up there year after year from the first "no" to final "never."

Her mother died of the chronics, her father of a fell swoop. Emma would become a certain set of words, wed, you might say, finally, and her flat chest with its warty nips placed next to Bishop's where Moore's had been. Her mother's face was closed as a nut, but you might say the same of Emma's too, who learned, as her mother doubtless had, to conceal her feelings for so long she forgot she had any.

Scream. The shed would seem to shiver with the sound. It was an awful makeshift, built of cast-off wood and some tin. Perhaps it was the tin that trembled. Hummed. Windows were unnecessary. There were parts between boards. A chicken might cluck till it was thwacked. Their bodies rocked on after. Upon her tree's stump, the tree of knowledge, blood was bled. She screamed because there was a world which contained such scenes though she also knew there was worse worse worse sorts of wickedness frequent in it.

dew, snowflake, scab:

Conversations, for instance, Emma never had. She didn't believe she could sustain one now even if the opportunity were offered, but at one time she thought she missed chatter, the sound of talk, laughter, banter, chaff. Her family exchanged grimaces sometimes; there'd be an occasional outburst of complaint; but mostly words were orders, warnings, wishes—stenographed. Emma thought her father often talked to himself. He'd sort of growl, his head would bob or wag, his lips tremble. Her mother had an impressive repertoire of sighs, a few gestures of resignation, frowns and sucked cheeks. No word of praise was ever passed, a grunt of approval perhaps, a nod, and either no shows of affection were allowed, or there was no affection to be displayed.

So Emma talked to the page. It became a kind of paper face and full of paper speech. "The conversations are simple: about food." "When my mother combs my hair it hurts." Emma, however, couldn't speak well about food. She no longer grew it. She couldn't cook it. She didn't eat it. And how could she respond to remarks about her hair. Emma unkinked her hair herself. So she at least knew what the pain of hair pulling was and how carrots felt.

Wherever you are the whole world is with you. A nice motto. Emma Bishop applied herself. She worked hard, but without success at first. Her life's small space had no place for stars. A dusty boot, a mixing bowl, a backyard plot. Judge not. Another maxim. But the boot was her father's where his foot went and was shaped by how he walked; booted because of the manure, he said, though the pigeons didn't even shit on Bishop soil. The earth is dirt. That was his judgment of it, hers of him. "Illuminated, solemn." The fact was, Emma Bishop hated her mother for being weak, for giving in to her husband's minor tyrannies. Take the flat of the shovel to him when his back is turned. Instead, Emma's mother turned her own and disappeared into a chore as though on movie horseback. The spoon spun in the bowl like a captured bird.

When snow and cold kept them cooped, each of them managed most marvelously to avoid one another. If she heard her father climbing the front stairs, Emma used the back one. If her mother and father threatened to meet in the upstairs hall, one ducked into a bedroom until the other had passed. Her father would always appear to be preoccupied, his thoughts elsewhere, a posture and a look which discouraged interruption. The three of them really wanted to live alone, and Emma at last had her wish. Each of them hungered for the others' deaths. Now Emma was fed.

However, the habits of a life remained. Emma was haunted by them, and repeatedly found herself behaving as if she might any minute have to strip or encounter her mother like a rat on the cellar steps.

At more than one point, Emma pondered their acts of avoidance. And she concluded that each was afraid of the anger pent up inside like intestinal gas whose release would be an expression of noisy and embarrassingly bad manners. They also supposed that this swampy rage was equally fierce in others, and feared its public presence. With so few satisfactions, the pleasure of violence would be piercing, as if the removal of any player might redeem a dismal past, or create new and liberating opportunities, which of course it wouldn't . . . hadn't . . . couldn't . . .

Occasionally they would have to go to town for various provisions. The tractor, their only vehicle, and very old, nevertheless purred. Emma and her mother rode in an old hay trailer, most unceremoniously, Emma with her legs dangling from the open end, which made her mother nervous. For these occasions, Emma would wear what her mother called "her frock." A piece of dirty

221

burlap was thought to be her frock's protection from the soiled bed of the wagon, so she sat on that. And watched the dust rise languidly behind the wagon's wheels, and the countryside pass them on both sides like something on a screen. The nearby weeds were white as though floured.

For her birthday—twice—she'd been taken to a movie. The town had a small badly ventilated hall, poor sound and a cranky projector. Actually, since they couldn't afford more than one ticket, you'd have to say Emma was sent to the movie. Both times her mother had warned her—both times to Emma's surprise—"don't let anyone feel your knee." To Emma's nonplussed face her mother would reply: "It'll be dark, you see." Darkness and desire were, for Emma then, forever wed. The films impressed her mightily. Gaudy, exotic, splendid, they didn't at all resemble her daily life, but they were additional experience nevertheless, and showed that the strange and far away was as inexplicable as the common and near at hand. Words on her pages, on the other hand, even when mysteriously conjoined, explained themselves. Moonlight and mist were mute. But a line of verse which described moonlight and mist caught in pasture bushes like lamb's wool, for instance, offered her understanding. A film might capture the fog as it crawled across the pasture, but there'd be no lamb's wool clinging to its images.

The movies weren't her world for another reason. The pictures, the figures, the scenes, the horses, the traffic, passed like a parade. Highways ran into mountains, streams rattled over rocks and fell in foam. Clouds scudded across the sky, and their shadows dappled the ground. The sun set like a glowing stone. Emma's well went weeks without a lick of light, and the yard lay motionless under its dust and seeds, disturbed only by an occasional burst of breeze. The mantis waited, head kinked, hard-eyed. Her mother occupied a room as if she were household help. But Randolph Scott was out of sight in a trice. And all the sounds . . . the sounds were bright.

All the while she sat in this strange dark room with a few strange dark shapes, none of whom offered to touch her knee, and watched these grainy gaudy imaginary movements, Emma was aware that her father and her mother were out in the town's drab daylight, their shopping soon completed, waiting for the picture to be over so they could go home. They'd be stared at, their tractor and its wagon watched. As time and the film wore on, Emma became increasingly anxious. If she had any enjoyment from the show, it was soon gone.

222

On the drive home, her mother would cover her sullenness with another coat.

Emma sat shaded from the hot summer sun by her ashmoose-maple and went in her head to New Brunswick to board a bus for a brief—in the poem—trip and view her favorite fog once again. By far her favorite fog. Yet it rendered for her her Iowa snow most perfectly. "Its cold, round crystals form and light and settle . . ." Here was at last the change: the flat close sky, the large flakes falling more softly than a whisper. Yet the snow would stay to crust and glare and deepen, to capture colors like lilac and violet because of all of the cold in those blues, and repeat them every day like her bread and breakfast oats. Settle in what? "In the white hens' feathers . . ." ". . . in gray glazed cabbages . . ." She couldn't get enough of that. ". . . in gray glazed . . . in gray glazed cabbages . . ." "on the cabbage roses . . ." The repetition enchanted her. So she repeated it.

As temporary as dew was, so they said—more meltable than oleo—the snow nevertheless stayed for months covering the seeds which had lain for months on the hard dry monthslong ground. Then there'd be mud for months, oozy as oatmeal; whereas Randolph Scott would scoot from frame to frame like a scalded cat. Dew could be counted on to disappear by midmorning. But you'd never sense when. What sort of change was changeless change—imperceptibly to dry the weeping world's eye—when Ann Richards rode through outfits faster than Randolph mounted his horse? And when Emma was wounded by her faithless moosemaple, the scab formed so slowly it never seemed to.

By the shaded road, at the edge of a glade, in open woods, the Mayapples rose, their leaves kept in tight fists until the stems reached the height of a boot and a bit, when each fist unfolded slowly to open a double umbrella a foot wide—hundreds of the round leaves soon concealing the forest floor. This was the rate of change Emma understood. Differences appeared after days of gray rain and a softening wind. As predictable as the train though. Then glossy white flowers would show up like tipped cups. Bluebells were bolder and would spread a blue haze over the muckier places. Cowslips her mother called them. But the Mayapple's flower hung from a fork in the stem and well under the plant's big deep green leaves. Finally a little jaundiced lemonshaped fruit the size of an egg would form. At her father's insistence they'd gather a few peck-sized baskets and boil the nubbins into an insipid jellylike spread for bread.

223

*William H. Gass*

Her father claimed the Mayapple was rightly called a mandrake, but the plant didn't scream when Emma pulled a few from the ground, nor were its roots manshaped; it grew far from the woodshed, their only gallows, and she doubted it had the power to transform men into beasts. Instead it left some toilsome fruits to enlarge and encumber their larder.

Her father prowled the meadows and woods looking for edibles, herbs and barks he said were medicinal when turned into tea, vegetable dyes her mother would never use. Since these lands didn't belong to them, Emma felt uneasy about what she thought was a kind of theft: of nuts and berries, wild grapes and greens. Emma put no stock in her father's claim to understand nature, because he was at home and happy only around machines. His tractor was his honey.

Nor did her mind change much. It was like a little local museum. The exhibits sat in their cases year after year. Possibly the stuffed squirrel would begin to shed. The portraits continued to be stiff and grim. Until her poetry taught her to pay attention. And then she saw a small shadow—she supposed shame—pass across her father's face when he looked at her nakedness. Because she was hairing up she supposed. And found grief beneath her mother's eye in a wrinkle. A hard blue sunswept sky became a landscape. Even now, when they were both dead, it was still impossible to go in the shed except to scream, and, through the greater part of her growing up and getting old, from most things she still fled.

Was she screaming for the chickens or the tree?

As slowly as her scab, her father's resolution formed. The moose had wounded his daughter. It had to come down. After all, he enjoyed the solemn parental right of riddance.

light, linger, leave

Poets were supposed to know and love nature. "Nature, the gentlest mother is." Purely urban or industrial poets were suspicious freaks. "Bumblebees creep inside the foxgloves and the evening commences." She had taken the knowledge and the love for granted. "Carrots form mandrakes or a ram's-horn root sometimes." But then she learned that it was not good to be "a nature poet," and that descriptions were what girls did, while guys narrated and pondered and plumbed. Ladies looked on. Gentlemen intervened. "Nature is what we see—the hill—the afternoon—

224

squirrel—eclipse—the bumblebee." Surely she was seeing herself as a gazer and seeking her salvation in sight. She was seeking to see with a purposeless purity, her intent always to let Being be, and become what it meant to become without worry, want or meddlesome intervention. If anything were to alter, she must allow it to alter of itself; if anything were to freeze, even new budded buds, she had to be grateful for that decision; if anything were to die, she'd delight in its death. For all is lawful process.

When Emma had reached such serenity, such selfless unconcern, she would be ready to disappear into her memorial dress, lie down in a sublime line of verse, a line by Elizabeth Bishop. Since she hadn't the art necessary to express the dehumanized highground she aspired to, she would have to turn to someone who had that skill, if not such a successfully pursued impersonality. For who had? She

And the tree groaned and crashed with a noise of much paper being angrily wadded, as if God were crumpling the Contract. A cloud stood above the tree like the suggestion of a shroud to mark the spot and evidence the deed.

Miss Moore, in her silly round black hat, looking like the *Monitor*, or was it the *Merrimac*, her hands half-stuffed in a huge muff made of the fur of some poor beast, stared with consummate calm out of her jacket image at Emma. Not a mirror. Not naked but smothered in overcoat except for her pale face and pale throat. No sign of nips the size of dimes, or barely there breasts or bony hips or hair trying to hide itself in shame inside its cleft. A slight smile, calm demeanor, self-possessed. Light is speech, her poem like the camera said. "Free frank impartial sunlight, moonlight, starlight, lighthouse light, arc language." But not firelight, candlelight, lamplight, flickergiven, waverlovers. The firefly's spark, but not an ember's glow, not match flare or flashlight. Stood there. Aren't lies, deceptions, misgivings, reluctances, unforthcomings, language? Stood there. Stood there. Could one ever recover?

Chainsaws her father understood. They wore like a watch a little engine.

The Bishops would dodge one another for days. Occasionally, Emma would catch a glimpse of her mother sitting in the kitchen drinking a little medicinal tea her husband had brewed to soothe her sick stomach. From her window she might see the tractor's burnt orange figure chewing in the far field. She'd imagine cows they never had, stable a horse in their bit of barn, with a little

225

lettuce and a carrot visit her hutch of rabbits, when a paste white chicken would emerge from between piles of scrap wood and scrap metal as if squeezed from a tube.

Emma's eye would light; it would linger; it would leave. Life, too, she was avoiding. There were days she knew the truth and was oppressed by her knowledge. These were days of discouragement, during which, almost as a penance, she would sew odd objects she had carefully collected to squares of china white cardboard, and then inscribe in a calligrapher's hand a saying or a motto, a bit of buckup or advice about life, which seemed to express the message inherent in her arrangement of button or bead or bright glass with a star shape of glued seeds, dry grass or pressed petal, then, sometimes, hung from a thin chain or lace of leather, a very small brass key, with colored rice to resemble a fall tree, and a length of red silk thread like something slit.

Forget-me-not was a frequent sentiment.

These she would put in little hand-made envelopes and leave in the postbox by the road for the postman to mail to the customers who answered her modest ad in *Farm Life*. Emma did not in the least enjoy this activity, which required her to look out for and gather tiny oddities of every tiny kind, to select from her lot those which would prove to be proper companions, envision their arrangement as if thrusting stems into a vase of flowers, and finally to compose a poem, a maxim, an epigram that suited their unlikely confluence. So on really down days she would do it, on days of rueful truth, which may account for the cruel turns her verses would sometimes take, veering from the saccharine path of moralizing admonitions into the wet depths of the ditch where the lilies and the cattails flourished, just to point out—because she couldn't help herself, because she had no prospects, no good looks, no pleasures herself—that the pretty was perilous, pleasure a snare, success a delusion, that beneath the bright bloom and attractive fruit grew a poisonous root.

Emma's sentiment cards were, however, a means to a greater good, for it was with the small sums her sales produced that she purchased her poetry: books by Bishop, Moore, Sitwell and Dickinson, on-order volumes of Elinor Wylie and Louise Bogan, which, she would regularly realize, unaccountably hadn't come.

She shared Grass-of-Parnassus with Elizabeth Bishop because it grew near the bluebell's sog, and in Nova Scotia too. It was a part of the inherent poetry of names: Lady's Slipper, Sundew, Jack-in-the-pulpit, Forget-me-not, Goldthread, Buttercup, Buttonbush, Goldenrod, Moonshine, Honeysuckle, Star Grass, Jewelweed, Milkwort, Butter and Eggs, Lion's Heart, Solomon's Seal, Venus's Looking-glass, with some names based on likeness, plant character or human attitude, such as Virgin's Bower, Crowfoot, Queen Anne's Lace, Quaker Lady, Wake-robin, Love Vine, Bellwort, Moneywort, Richweed, Moccasin Flower, Snakemouth, Ladies'-tresses, Blue Curls, Lizard's-tail, Goosefoot, Ragged Robin, Hairy Beardtongue, Turtlehead, Dutchman's-breeches, Calico, Thimble-weed and finally Bishop's Cap; or because they were critter con-nected much as Mad-dog was, Hog Peanut, Gopherberry, Goose Tansy, Butterfly Weed, Bee Balm, Moth Mullen, Cowwheat, Deer Vine, Fleabane, Horseheal, Goat's-rue, Dogberry; or were based on location and function and friendliness like Clammy Ground Cherry, Water Willow, Stone Clover Swamp Candle, Shinleaf, Seed-box, Eyebright, Bedstraw, Firewood, Stonecrop, Indian Physic, Heal All, Pitcher Plant, Purple Boneset, Agueweed, Pleurisy Root, Toothwort, Feverfew; or were simply borrowed from their fruiting season like the Mayapple, or taken from root or stem or stalk or fruit or bloom or leaf, like Arrowhead, Spiderwort, Seven-angled Pipewort, Foamflower, Liverleaf, Shrubby Fivefinger, Bloodroot; while sometimes they gained their name principally through their growth habit such as the Staggerbush did, the Sidesaddle Flower, Prostrate Tick Trefoil, Loosestrife, Spatter-dock, Steeplebush, Jacob's Ladder; although often the names served as warnings about a plant's hostility or shyness the way Poison Ivy or Touch-me-not did, Wild Sensitive Pea, Lambkill, Adder's Tongue, Poison Flagroot, Tearthumb, King Devil, Needlegrass, Skunk Cabbage, Chokeberry, Scorpion Grass, Viper's Bugloss, Bitter Nightshade and Lance-leaved Tickseed; or they were meant to be sarcastic and cutting like New Jersey Tea, Bastard Toadflax, False Vervain, Mouse-eared Chickweed, Swamp Lousewort, Monkey Flower, Corpse Plant, Pickerel Weed, Indiana Poke and the parasitic Naked Broom Rape or, finally, Gall-of-the-earth—few of whom Emma knew person-ally, since her father had made edibility a necessary condition for growth in the family garden, and had stepped upon her nasturtium although she'd argued for its use in salads. But peas, beans and roots were what he wanted. Salads don't make or move a muscle, he said. So instead of cultivating or observing weeds and flowers in the field, Emma collected and admired and smelled their names and looked at their pictures in books.

William H. Gass

228

William H. Gass

"Pity should begin at home," Crusoe said, enisled as utterly as Emma was. Sometimes Emma tried to feel sorry for herself, but she scarcely had a self left or the energy available or what she thought was a good reason. Yes, she had barely made a mark on the world, her life was a waste, and she'd had little enjoyment; but on balance she had to admit she'd rather have read the word "boob" than have them. A moose comes out of the woods and stands in the middle of the road. When the bus stops, it approaches to sniff the hot hood. "Towering, antlerless, high as a church, homely as a house . . ." Well, there were so many things she hadn't seen, a moose included, but she had envisioned that large heavy head sniffing the hot hood of the bus, there on that forest-enclosed road, at night, and understood the deep dignity in all things. "All things," she knew, embraced Emma Bishop's homely bare body standing in the middle of her room. Antlerless . . . boobless . . . with hairless pubes . . .

like a swatted fly,

Her Iowa summers were long and hot and dusty and full of flies. Ants and flies . . . In the early days, before unconcern had become endemic, her mother had insisted that the dinner table wear a white linenlike cover. Even dimestore glasses gleamed, cheap white plates shone and tinny silverware glittered when they sat on the starchy bleached cloth amid their puddles of light blue shadow and pale gray curves. But through the ill-fit and punctured screens the flies came not in clouds but in whining streams. At breakfast it wasn't so bad. One or two or three had to be waved away from the oatmeal. Maybe, though, that's when Emma's aversion to food began. Flies. Raisins for the oats, her father said, waving his spoon. Sugar brings them. They love sweets, her mother said. They did seem to, and crumbs, on which they tried to stand.

These weren't manure breeders and the curse of cattle, but common bluebottles, persistent and numerous in the peaceful sunshine. Emma would have to shake the cloth from the back porch before they'd fly. They seemed to like sugar, salt, breadcrumbs, cereal, leavings of any kind, jam, and Emma learned to loathe them, their soft buzz and their small walk, their numbers and their fearless greed.

The deep dignity in all things—phoo—not in flies, not in roaches, not in fathers, not in dandelion greens.

"Nature is what we see—the hill—the afternoon—squirrel—

eclipse—the bumble bee—nay—nature is heaven." Not a word about flies. There was a song about a fly, and that rhyme about the old woman who swallowed one, who knew why, but Emma could not recollect ever reading a poem about or even including a fly. Miss Moore wrote about horses, skunks, lizards, but not about flies. Emily D's little list included the bobolink, the sea, thunder, the cricket, but left out ants, mosquitos and of course flies. Good reason. Because she wanted to say that Nature was Heaven, was Harmony. Poetry, Emma would have to admit, later, recalling all those flies, poetry was sometimes blather. Her noble resolutions would also falter in front of the phenomenon of the fly. How could she honor anything that would lay its eggs in a wound? They carried diseases with more regularity than the postman mail, and they lived on leavings, on carrion, horse droppings, dirt. Like sparrows and pigeons. Phoo indeed.

Hadn't she lived on leavings too?

The mantis would close her forelegs like a pocket knife and eat a wasp a fly a lacewing in a trice. She'd rise up to frighten the wasp to a standstill, giving it her triangulating stare, and then strike so swiftly her claws could be scarcely seen, nails on all sides, the hug of the iron maiden.

Nature was rats and mice, briars and insect bites, cow plop and poisonous plants, chickens with severed heads and minute red ants swarming over a stump soaked in blood. It was the bodies of swatted flies collected in a paper bag.

The swatter, an efficient instrument, was made of clothes-hanger wire and window screen trimmed with a narrow band of cloth which bore the name of a hardware store. Emma became an expert, finally, at something. Sometimes she would hit them while they were still in the air and knock them into the wall where she'd smack their slightly stunned selves into mush. Even so, they were clever little devils and could sense the swatter's approach, even though it was designed to pass without a wake or any sound through the air. They knew a blow was coming and would almost always be taking off when the screen broke their wings.

Emma killed many on the kitchen table, sliding the carcasses into a paper sack with the side of the swatter. It occurred to her that there was no word for the crushed corpse of a swatted fly. Her father liked to swing his right hand across the cloth and catch one in his closing fist, a slight smile slowly widening on his face like the circle of a pebble's plop. Where's your sack, he'd say, and when

Emma held it out he'd shake the body from his palm where it was stuck. Once in a while, with that tiny smile, he'd try to hold his fist to Emma's ear so she could hear the buzz, but she would leave the room with a short cry of fear, her father's chuckle following like a fly itself.

After they'd eaten, Emma would clear the dishes away and wait a bit while the flies settled in apparent safety on the crumbed and sugared cloth. Her mother sweetened her tea with a careless spoon. Even the herbals her husband sometimes brewed for her she honeyed up one way or other. The flies would land as softly as soot. They'd walk about boldly on their sticky little feet with their proboscises extended as though requiring a cane. Her father was pleased to explain that flies softened their food with spit so they could suck it up.

Emma liked to get two at once. Each swat would bestir some of the others and they'd whiz in a bothered zig-zag for a while before trying to feed again, no lesson learned, the carnage of their comrades of little concern, although a few would remain at work even when a whack fell within a yard of their grazing.

Flies seemed to flock like starlings, but the truth was they had no comrades, no sense of community. Occasionally, a crippled one would buzz and bumble without causing a stir, or a greenbottle arrive in their midst to be met by colossal indifference. Standing across from the center of the table, Emma would slap rapidly at each end in succession while uttering quiet but heartfelt theres each time: there and there and there.

O she hated the creatures, perhaps because they treated the world as she was treated. It was certainly out of character for Emma to enjoy bloodshed. However, her father approved of her zeal, and her mother didn't seem to mind, except

trace to be grieved,

for the little red dots their deaths left on the tablecloth. They'd accumulate, those spots, until their presence became quite intolerable to her mother, and she would remind Emma how hard it was to get those spots out, and about the cost of bleach, and how she hated that bag with its countless contents, she felt she heard a rustle from it now and then, it gave her the creeps. Emma wondered what, in her mother, creeps were. Later, when her mother was ill always, and vomiting a lot, Emma thought that perhaps the creeps had won out.

When the fly was flipped from the table into her sack, it would almost always leave that reminder behind, a red speck as bright as the red spider mite though larger by a little. And after the evening meal, Emma would enter a dozen specks and sometimes more into her register.

Where were they coming from? The compost heap? Her father said he saw no evidence of it. Her mother shook her head. Somewhere was there something dead? Her father hadn't encountered anything, and he walked the land pretty thoroughly. From as far away as the woods? Her mother shook her head. Well, Emma wondered, if the breeding of these flies was a miracle, God was certainly wasting his gifts. God is giving you something to do, her father said.

There was something in Emma which made her want to keep count, and other things in Emma which were horrified by the thought.

Days drew on, mostly with a monotony which mingled them, so that time seemed not slow, not fast, just not about. And she failed grades and advanced anyway, and grew like a skinny tree to be stared at, and became increasingly useless, as if uselessness were an aim. Why, her father complained, wouldn't Emma attack those bugs in the garden when she was so murderous about flies. As if he'd failed to notice that Emma had stopped swatting them many months, years, failed grades ago. Things went on in their minds, Emma imagined, out of inertia. Memory was maybe more than a lot of little red dots. The swats were still there, swatting. The paper sack still sat in a kitchen chair like a visitor. And Emma stayed on the page even when all her books were closed. The cloud

The shed got built about the ash stump. Emma could hear the hammering. Built of limbs and logs it leaned to one side, then another. Had her father any interest in the number of nails he'd hammered while the ash shack was going up? Did he know how long the walk to the mailbox was? How many yards? Without books, Emma couldn't disappear into them. So she began to make and mail her memory cards, her versified objects, receiving for them a few dollars, and then, with this slim income, to order books of poetry by Elizabeth Bishop from an Iowa City shop. It was a great day when

POEMS

North & South
A Cold Spring                              arrived,
the title typed on a chartreuse ginko-like leaf lying across the join
of two fields, one white for northern snow, she supposed, the other
blue for southern seas. The flap copy was typed, too, and there were
warm recommendations from Marianne Moore and Louise Bogan
as well as the usual guys. Emma opened the book and saw a poem
on a page like treasure in a chest and closed the book again and
opened it and closed it many times. She held it in her two hands.
Finally, it seemed to open of its own accord. She began "The Monument." Page 25. Yes, she remembered. Even the brackets [25].
"Now can you see the monument?" She could. She could see it. "It
is of wood built somewhat like a box." Yes, Emma saw it. Her eyes
flew flylike to the yard where the shed stood. It was a revelation.

Later on there would be others.

She turned the page and read the conclusion. "It is the beginning
of a painting," the poem said, "a piece of sculpture, or poem, or
monument, and all of wood." All of ash. "Watch it closely."

Emma's father probably didn't care whether she found out or not.
He probably neglected to tell her he was intercepting her mail,
whether going in or going out, just because he didn't care, one way
or the other. He simply piled it up—the square envelopes with their
cards of sewn and glued and inked-on sentiments and emblems,
those with a few customer requests, some with simple sums inside
them, a bookstore order—higgledy-piggledy on a small oak table in
the room he was sleeping in now that his wife was ill and vomi-
tous. That's where, through an open door, Emma saw her envelopes, looking otherwise innocent and unopened, and said aloud in
complete surprise: that's why I never got my May Sarton.

She did not try to retrieve them. To her, they were dead as flies,
leftovers from a past life. They almost puzzled her, they seemed
so remote from the suspended condition she was presently in,
although not that many weeks had passed, she guessed, since
she'd composed her last card: four hard green pea gravels placed
like buttonholes inside a wreath of mottled mahonia leaves, stained
as though by iodine and flame. In a kind of waking dream, Emma
tottered the hundred and more yards to where the postbox leaned from a tuft of weed at the roadside, and opened it on
empty. She held on to the lid as though it might fly up and stared

hard into the empty tin, more interested in the space where the confiscation had taken place than in the so-called contraband. Empty. Its emptiness was shaped from zinc. zzzzzz . . . in . . . cccccc. Emma knew at last something for certain: her father was poisoning her mother.

Well, it was no business of hers.

She closed the mailbox carefully so none of its emptiness would leak out.

Indeed her mother rasped to her rest in a week's time. Her father rolled her mother in the sheets and then the blanket from her bed and laid her at length, though somewhat folded—well, knees a good ways up—in a wooden footlocker. He poured a lot of mothballs in the crannies. We won't be needing those, he said, fastening the lid with roofing nails. He slid the locker down the front stairs and lugged the box, cursing because it was heavier than he expected and awkward to carry, to the back of the wagon—lucky the wagon was small wheeled and low—where he propped one end and lifted the other, then pushed the locker in. He never expected Emma to help. At helping she was hopeless. That's enough for one day, he said. I got to scout out a good place.

He went inside and washed all the household dishes. Grief, Emma decided, was the only explanation.

The next day she saw her father's distant figure digging in a far field. He appeared to be digging slowly because he dug for a long time.

Emma's head was as empty of thoughts as the mailbox. There was no reason to stand or sit or walk.

Got my exercise today, he said.

Marianne Moore and Elizabeth Bishop were both dead. Edith Sitwell too. Elizabeth Bishop just keeled over in her kitchen. Nobody knew. Her poems couldn't purchase her another hour.

I've got to figure how to get her in, her father said. Can't just roll her over. A fall like that might break the box open. We'll do it tomorrow.

Her father found an egg which he had for breakfast. Emma rode in the back of the wagon with the coffin and an ironing board. The tractor dragged the wagon roughly over the ploughed ground. Then reluctantly through the marshy meadow. Smoother movement steadied her horizon. Emma remembered the Randolph Scott movie. Her father had chosen a spot near the trees which appeared to have no distinction. Earth was heaped neatly on both wide sides.

Emma looked in the hole. "Cold dark deep and absolutely clear."

Her father backed the wagon up to an open end of the pit. Then he pried the box up with a crowbar and forced the ironing board under it. He never expected Emma to help. He steadied the box on the board as it slid down the board from the wagon. It was, Emma realized, a mechanical problem. The board then was lowered into the grave, and the box once more sent on its skiddy way. In a cant at the bottom, her father wiggled the board out from beneath the box so at last it lay there, as settled as it was going to get. The zinc-headed nails reflected a little light.

Supposed to say a few words, her father said, so why don't you?

Poetry doesn't redeem, Emma thought. Saintliness doesn't redeem. Evening doesn't redeem the day, it just ends it.

Her father waited with a fistful of dirt ready to fling in the hole.

She was small and thin and bitter, my mother. No one could cheer her up. A dress a drink a roast chicken were all the same to her. She went about her house without hope, without air. Her face was closed as a nut, closed as a careful snail's. I saw her smile once but it was not nice, more like a crack in a plate. What on earth had she done to have so little done for her? She sewed my clothes but the hems were crooked.

While Emma was silent a moment, trying to remember something more to say, to recite, her father released his fistful of earth and he went for the shovel. He shoveled slowly as if his back hurt. Dirt disappeared into dirt. The morning was cloudy but the grave was cold and dark and not so deep as it had been. The nails went out—animal eyes in a cave. Layer after layer: sheet blanket mothballs board, earth on earth on earth. Too bad we couldn't afford to do better by her, her father said, but we didn't do too bad. Emma realized he hadn't cared what her words were, probably hadn't heard. Words were one of the layers—to ward off what?

They hadn't any prayers. Emma hated hymns. Hymns weren't private enough. And you were told which one to sing. This morning, please turn to [25]. The grave filled and a little mound rose over it, the soil looking less raw, more friable. Emma rode back to the house alongside the ironing board, which was quite dirty and bedraggled. The board bounced as it hadn't bounced coming out, when it was wedged. Emma tottered to the mailbox and looked in. That was how it was inside the box, she supposed. Empty, even though

In the days, the weeks, the month which followed, Emma disappeared almost completely into her unattachments. She freed herself of food, of feeling, father. The fellow was a wraith. She was a shadow no one cast. He no longer farmed though he often stood like a scarecrow in the field. Grief, Emma decided, was the explanation. But his grief was no concern of hers. She thought about freeing herself from verse when she realized she always had been free, for she had never respected, never followed, the form or been obedient to type.

She waited for the world, unasked, to flow into her, but she hadn't yet received its fine full flood. What if it weren't a liquid, didn't flow, but stood as if painted in its frame? What if it were like a fly indifferent to its own death? No matter. She was freeing herself of reflection. All of a sudden, she believed, the lethal line would come: "The dead birds fell, but no one had seen them fly . . ." Perhaps it would be that one. So what if it was shot from a sonnet. The only way flies could get into a poem would be as a word. "They were black, their eyes were shut. No one knew what kind of birds they were." Each night, night fell in huge drops like rain and ran down the eaves and sheeted across the pane. He'd move somewhere in the house. He'd move. She'd hear. "Quick as dew off leaves." The sound will be gone in the morning.

Mother beneath the earth. Others are, why not she? He waits in the soybean field for me. I must carry the shovel out to him. It is thin as I am, almost as worn, as hard. Mother has no marker. Many lie unknown in unsigned graves. Might we hear mother rustling under all her covers, trying to straighten her knees? To spend death with bended knee. He'll never mark her. The mound will sink like syrup into the soil. Weeds will walk. Perhaps black wood-berries will grow there as they do in Bishop's poem. My steps are soundless on the soft earth.

Emma struck her father between his shoulder blades with the flat of the spade. She hit him as hard as she could but we can't suppose her blow would have amounted to much. She heard his lungs hoof and he fell forward on his face. Emma flung the spade away as far as she could a few feet. What can you see now she wondered. Or did you always see dirt?

She hadn't considered that a blow meant as a remonstrance might have monstrous consequences. She bounced floatily back to the house somewhat like a blown balloon. That's it: rage redeems. What does? evening.

And evening came. The dead birds fell. Found in the field. She

240

hadn't missed him a minute. She hadn't for a moment worried about how angry he would be, or how he might take his anger out on her, so uppity a child as to strike her grieving father in the back. Found face down. After a rainstorm. Heartburst. Creamed corn is a universal favorite. Dark drops fell. The field was runneled and puddlesome. Emma peered more and more through the round thread-wound shade pull. And felt the flow. The world was a fluid. Weights have been lifted off of me. I am lonely am I? as a cloud

Emma was afraid of Elizabeth Bishop. Emma imagined Elizabeth Bishop lying naked next to a naked Marianne Moore, the tips of their noses and their nipples touching; and Emma imagined that every feeling either poet ever had in their spare and spirited lives was present there in the two nips, just where the nips kissed. Emma, herself, was ethereally thin, and had been admired for the translucency of her skin. You could see her bones like shadows of trees, shadows without leaves.

Some dreams they forgot. But Emma Bishop remembered them now with a happy smile. Berry picking in the woods, seeing shiny black wood-berries hanging from a bough, and thinking, don't pick these, they may be poison . . . a word thrilling to say . . . poison . . . us. Elizabeth Bishop used the phrase "loaded trees," as if they might like a gun go off. At last . . . at last . . . at last, she thought: "What flowers shrink to seeds like these?"

dot where it died.

# The Sheriff Goes to Church
## *Robert Coover*

THE STREETS OF THE TOWN are empty and silent and hotly burnished by the noonday sun. Into them on a coalblack horse now rides a lone figure all outfitted in black with silver spurs and sixshooters and a gold ring in one ear. Former sheriff and bandit, a drifter, now a man on a mission. The woman he loves has been condemned to hang at high noon on the morrow, and he cannot let it happen. From under the broad brim of his slouch hat he warily watches, feeling watched, the windows and rooftops, the corners of things. Expecting trouble. The mare seems edgy, too, rolling her head fretfully, biting at the bit. Well, she's an outlaw horse, has likely never set hoof in this town before except on illegal business, she probably has good reason for unease.

In the center of town across from the saloon, a fat mestizo with a missing ear and a tall squint-eyed man with droopy handlebars and a bald head tattooed with hair are testing the trapdoor of the gallows, using a noosed goat, not by the appearance of it for the first time. Yo, sheriff! the man with the tattooed hair calls out, dragging the goat into position. Howzit hangin?

He nods at them and watches the limp goggle-eyed goat drop, then walks the mare cautiously over to the jailhouse. So he's the sheriff again. Yes, he's wearing his silver badge once more, he discovers. The one with the hole in it. Must have found it somewhere. Stands out on his black shirt in a way it never did on his white one.

There's a poster outside the jailhouse door announcing the hanging, with a portrait, where his portrait used to be, of the schoolmarm staring sternly out at all who would dare stare back. He is shaken by the intensity of her gaze, and the pure gentle innocence of it, and the rectitude, and he knows he is lost to it.

He hitches the mare to the rail there, and though she is skittish and backs away, her eyes rolling, tugging at her tether, he needs her for what he must next do. He unhooks his rifle from the saddle horn. I'll jest be a minnit and then we'll hightail it outa here, he says softly, stroking her sweaty neck to calm her, and he enters the jailhouse ready for whatever happens.

But nothing does. The jailhouse is empty, except for an old codger with an eyepatch, slumped in the wooden swivel chair, wearing a deputy's badge on his raggedy red undershirt. There is a thick river of scar running through his gray beard, darkly stained with tobacco juice, and his lone eye is red with drink. Hlo, sheriff, he drawls, trying to stand. Glad yu're back. Yu're jest in time t'hang that rapscallious hoss thief yerself. He chortles, then falls back into the swivel chair, takes a swig from a whiskey bottle, belches, offers it out. Yer health, sheriff!

Whar is she? he says.

The prizner? They tuck her over t'the saloon t'shuck her weeds offn her'n scrub her down afore her hangin.

The saloon?

Yup, well they got soap'n water over thar and plentya hep in spiffyin her up. The boys wuz plannin t'rub her down good with goose grease'n skunk oil after, polish her up right properlike. He's already at the door and there's a pounding in his temples that's worse than snakebite. Hey, hole up, sheriff! Ain't that a outlaw hoss out thar?

Mebbe. I'll check into it. Yu stay here'n keep yer workin eye on that whuskey bottle.

I aim to.

The mare is wild-eyed and frothing, rearing against her hitching rope, so he lets her go. Stay outa sight, he whispers to her as he unties her. This wont take long. I'll whistle yu when we're set t'bust out. The horse hesitates, pawing the ground, whinnying softly, but he slaps her haunches affectionately and, glancing back over her shoulder at him, she slips away into the shadows behind the jailhouse.

The object of his quest is not in the saloon either. It's quiet in there, four men playing cards, a couple more at the bar, a puddle of water in the middle of the floor where a bucket of soapy water stands, a lacy black thing ripped up and hung over its lip. The men at the bar are laughing and pointing at the bucket or else at the wet long-handled grooming brush beside it. That goddamn humpback! one of them says, hooting.

Hlo, sheriff, grins the bartender, a dark sleepy-eyed man of mixed breed with half a nose. Wellcum back. Whut's yer pizen?

An argument breaks out at the card table, the air fills with the slither of steel coming free of leather, shots ring out, and a tall skinny man with spidery hair loses most of his jaw and all else besides, slamming against the wall with the impact before sliding in a bloody heap to the floor. Looks like they's a chair open fer yu, sheriff, says the man who shot him, tucking his smoking derringer back inside his black broadcloth coat. Set yer butt down and study the devil's prayerbook a spell.

I aint a sportin man. Whut's happened t'the prizner?

Yu mean that dastardly hoss thief? Haw. Caint say. He lets fly a brown gob of tobacco juice at a brass spittoon, and it crashes there, making the spittoon rattle on its round bottom like a gambling top. She might be over t'doc's fer a purjin so's t'git her cleaned up inside as smart as out, though after her warshin in here, I misdoubt she needs it.

The others laugh at this. Naw, I think doc musta awready seed her, says the barkeep. He was in here a spell ago sniffin his finger.

Probly then, laughs another, they tuck her up t'the schoolhouse fer a paddlin.

Whut's that got t'do with bein a hoss thief?

Nuthin. It's jest fer fun. Give her summa her own back. And they all whoop and howl again and slap the bar and table.

He pushes out through the swinging doors, his blood pounding in his ears and eyes. Can't recollect where the doctor lives, if he ever knew, so he heads for the schoolhouse. On his way over, he hears a banging noise coming from a workshop back of the feed store. It's a tall ugly gold-toothed carpenter knocking out a pine coffin. Howdy, sheriff, he says, lifting the coffin up on its foot. Jest gittin ready t'cut the lid. Inside, on the bottom, there is a crude line drawing of a stretched-out human figure, no doubt done by tracing around a person lying there. One of the faces from the hanging posters has been cut out and pasted in the outline of the head and nails have been driven in where the nipples would be. The arms go only to the elbows (probably her hands were folded between the nails) but the legs are there in all their forked entirety. I reckon it should oughter fit her perfect. Whuddayu think?

I think yu should oughter burn it.

The schoolhouse is not where he remembered it either. Instead, he comes on a general dry goods and hardware store in that proximate neighborhood and he stops in to ask if she's been seen about.

Sheriff! Whar yu been? cries the merchant, a round bandylegged fellow with a black toupee and his nose pushed into his red face. They's been a reglar plague a hellraisin bandits pilin through here since yu been gone! Jest look whut they done t'my store! Shot up my winders, killt my staff, stole summa my finest goods'n splattered blood'n hossshit on all the rest! Yu gotta do sumthin about this! Whut's a sheriff fer ifn honest folk caint git pertection!

That's a question I aint got a clear answer to, he says, staring coldly into the fat merchant's beady eyes. Right now I'm trying t'locate a missin prizner.

Whut, yu mean that ornery no-account barebutt hoss thief? She aint missin. Yer boys wuz by here a time ago with her, plumb cleaned me outa hosswhips'n hoe handles, she was in fer a grand time. I think they wuz headed fer the stables. Yu know. Scene a the crime. He turns to leave, but the merchant has a grip on his elbow and a salacious grin on his round red face. I gotta tell yu, sheriff, I seen sumthin I aint never seed before. He leans toward him, his cold fermented breath ripe with the stink of rot and mildew. She wuz, huh! yu know, he snickers softly in his ear. She wuz cryin!

He tears free from the merchant's greasy grip and strides out the door onto the wooden porch, his spurs ringing in the midday hush. He pauses there to stare out upon the dusty town. No sign of them. They could be anywhere. There's a dim shadowy movement over in the blacksmith's shed, but that's probably his horse pacing about. He should probably just go back to the jailhouse and wait for them. But then the white church steeple beckons him. She gave him a Bible once, he recalls. They'll have to take her there sooner or later if she wants to go, and she surely will. There's probably a law about it.

He is met inside the church doors by the parson, or a parson, standing in a black frock coat behind a wooden table with a Bible on it, a pair of ivory dice (REPENT, says a tented card beside them, AFORE YU CRAP OUT!), a pistol and a collection plate. Howdy do, sheriff, he says, touching the brim of his stovepipe hat. He's a tall ugly gold-toothed man with wild greasy hair snaking about under the hat and a drunkard's lumpy nose, on the end of which a pair of wirerimmed spectacles is perched like two pans of a golddust balance. Wellcum t'the house a the awmighty. Yu're jest in time fer evenin prayers!

I aint here fer prayin. I'm lookin fer a missin prizner.

Yu mean that jezebel hoss thief? She gone missin? A leather flap behind the parson blocks his view but he can hear the churchgoers carrying on inside, hooting and hollering in the pietistical way. Well she's probly in thar, ever other sinner is.

Thanks, revrend, he says, and heads on in, but the parson grabs him by the elbow. The pistol is cocked and pointed at his ear. Whoa thar, sheriff. I can't let yu go in without payin.

I tole yu, I aint here fer the preachin, I'm on official bizness.

Dont matter. Yu gotta put sumthin in the collection plate or I caint let yu by.

I aint got no money, he says firmly, staring down the gun barrel. And I'm goin in thar.

Dont hafta be money, says the parson, keeping the pistol pointed at his head but letting go of his elbow to tug at his reversed collar so as to give his Adam's apple more room to bob. Them sporty boots'll do.

No. Gonna need them boots. If he just walked on in, would the preacher shoot him in the back? He might.

Well how about that thar beaded injun scalp then? He hesitates. He doesn't know why he wears it. For good luck maybe. Like a rabbit's paw. But he's not superstitious. And it doesn't even smell all that good. Awright, he says, and he cuts it off his gunbelt with his bowie knife and tosses it in the collection plate, where it twists and writhes for a moment before curling up like a dead beetle.

Now I'll roll yu fer them boots, ifn yu've a mind to, grins the parson goldenly, picking up the dice and rattling them about in his grimy knobknuckled hand, but he pushes on past him under the flap into the little one-room church, the preacher calling out behind him: I'm sorely beseechin the good lawd that yu localize that snotnose gallows bird, sheriff! Dont wanta lose her at the last minnit and set all hell t'grievin!

Veiled gas lamps hang from blackened beams in the plank-walled room, the air hazy with smoke and smelling of stale unwashed bodies and the nauseous vapors of the rotgut whiskey—drunk, un-drunk and regurgitated— being served like communion from boards set on pew backs. Hanging in the thick smoke like audible baubles are the ritual sounds of singing spittoons, dice raining upon craps tables, the clink of money, soft slap of cards, the ratcheting and ping of fortune wheels and slot machines, the click click click of the roulette ball, and amidst the zealous cries of the high rollers, oaths are being sworn and glasses smashed and pistols fired off with a kind of emotional abandon. Are yu all down, gentamin? someone hollers, and another cries out: Gawdamighty, smack me easy! Somewhere in the church, behind all the smoke and noise, he can hear the saloon chanteuse singing about a magical hero with a three-foot johnnie, now hung and gone to glory, her voice half smothered by the thick atmosphere. Sweat-stained hats hang in parade on hooks along the walls under doctrinal pronouncements regarding spitting and fair dealing, mounted animal heads, dusty silvered mirrors which reflect nothing and religious paintings of dead bandits and unclothed ladies in worshipful positions, but the only sign anywhere of the one he's looking for is one of the posters announcing tomorrow's hanging nailed up over a faro table, the portrait obscenely altered. BUCK THE TIGER! it says, and a crude drawing shows where and how to do so.

He turns a corner (there is a corner, the room is getting complicated) and comes upon a craps table with strange little misshapen dice, more like real knucklebones, which they likely are. Set down, sheriff, and shake an elbow, says the scrubby skew-jawed fellow in dun-colored rags and bandanna headband who is working the table, a swarthy and disreputable character who is vaguely familiar. His broken arm is in a rawhide sling, its hand fingerless, and there's a fresh red weal across his rough cheeks, the sort of cut made by a horsewhip. Here, he can no longer hear the chanteuse; instead, at the back by the big wheel of fortune, there is a choral rhythmic rise and fall of drunken whoops, so it's likely she's back there somewhere. Not someone he cares to see just now. Go ahead'n roll em, sheriff, says the wampus-jawed scrub, wagging the stump at the end of his broken arm. Them sad tats is mine. Wuz.

Aint got no stake. But dont I know yu from sumwhars? With his good hand, the halfbreed flashes a bent and rusty deputy's badge, hidden away in his filthy rags. Whut? Yu my deppity?

I wuz. But I lost my poke'n then some in that wicked brace over by the big wheel. I hafta work fer this clip crib now.

Whar's the prizner then?

Well we lost her, too.

Lost her—?!

T'that hardass double-dealin shark over thar, the dodrabbid burglar whut operates this skin store. He's the one whut give me this extry elbow and my own bones t'flop when I opened my big mouth after ketchin him with a holdout up his sleeve. He sees him now, enthroned behind a blackjack table under a glowing gas lamp, over by a tall wheel of fortune, an immense bald and beardless man in a white suit and ruffled shirt with blue string tie and golden studs, wearing blue-tinted spectacles smack up against his eyes. He sits as still and pale as stone, nothing moving except his little fat fingers, deftly flicking out the cards. The rhythmic whooping is coming from there and may be in response to the cards being dealt. The motherless asshole tuck us fer all we had, sheriff. Got the prizner in the bargain.

Yu done wrong. She warnt a stake.

I know it.

247

Whut's he done with her?

Well. His ex-deputy hesitates. It aint nice. He glances uneasily over his shoulder. Best go on over thar'n see fer yerself.

There's an icy chill on his heart and a burning rage at the same time and he feels like he might go crazy with the sudden antipodal violence of his feelings, but he bites down hard and collects himself and sets his hat square over his brow and drops his hands flat to his sides and straightens up his back and lowers his head and, with measured strides, makes his way over toward the glowing fat man at the blackjack table. The room seems to have spread out somewhat or to be spreading out as he proceeds, and there are new turns and corners he must bear around, sudden congestions of loud drunken gamblers he must thread his way through, and sometimes the black-jack dealer seems further away than when he first set out, but he presses on, learning to follow not his eyes but his ears (those whoops and hollers), and so is drawn in time into the crowd of men around the blackjack table. What is provoking their rhythmic hoots, he sees when he gets there, is the sight of the schoolmarm stretched out upon the slowly spinning wheel of fortune, her black skirts falling past her knees each time she's upsidedown. He tries not to watch this but is himself somewhat mesmerized by the rhythmic rising and falling, revealing and concealing, of the schoolmarm's dazzling white knees, the spell broken only when he realizes that she is gazing directly at him as she rotates with a look compounded of fury, humiliation and anguished appeal. It is a gaze most riveting when she is upsidedown and the whoops are loudest, her eyes then black-ly underscored by eyebrows as if bagged with grief, her nose with its flared nostrils fiercely horning her brow between them, the exposed knees above not unlike a bitter thought, and a reproach.

He steps forward, not knowing what he will do, but before he can reach the table, a tall bald man with tattooed hair pushes everyone aside and, tossing down a buckskin purse, seats himself before it. Dole me some paint thar, yu chislin jackleg! he bellows with drunken bravado, twirling the ends of his handlebar moustache. He's seen him before, testing out the gallows, except that since then he's acquired a wooden leg. His partner, the one-eared mestizo, now wearing a bearclaw in his nose and an erect feather in a headband, hovers nearby with his pants gaped open. I'm aimin t'win summa that gyratin pussy fer my bud'n me, and I dont wanta ketch yu spikin, stackin, trimmin, rimplin, nickin, nor ginnyin up in no manner them books, dont wanta see no shiners, cold decks, coolers, nor holdouts, nor witness no great miracles a extry cards or a excess a greased bullets. Yu hear? So now rumble the flats, yu ole grifter, and cut me a kiss.

The dealer, holding the deck of cards in his soft smooth bejeweled hands as a sage might clasp a prayerbook, has sat listening to all this bluster with serene indifference, his hairless head settled upon his layered folds of chin like a creamy mound of milkcurd, eyes hidden behind the skyblue spectacles which seem almost pasted to them. The tinted spectacles, he knows, are for reading the backs of doped cards, the polished rings for mirroring the deal, a pricking poker ring no doubt among them, and his sleeves and linen vest are bulked and squared by the mechanical holdout devices concealed within. When, so minimally one can almost not see the movement, he shuffles, cuts and deals, he seems to use at least three different decks, cross-cutting a pair of them, and the deal is from the bottom of the only deck in view at any one time, or at least not from the top.

The squint-eyed man with the tattooed hair rises up and kicks his chair back with his wooden leg. I jest come unanimously to the con-clusion yu been cheatin, he shouts as the dealer calmly slides the man's leather purse into his heap of winnings, then takes up the deck to reshuffle it, so smoothly that the deck seems like a small restless creature trapped between his soft pale hands, his own child perhaps that he is fondling. Behind him, the schoolmarm, bound to the for-tune wheel, grimly turns and turns, though now, with the bald man on his feet, or foot, the rhythmic whooping dies away.

Easy, podnuh, whispers the one-eared mestizo, his hand inside his pants. He spits over his shoulder, away from the dealer. He's aw-mighty fast, that sharper. Don't try him. It aint judicious.

Shet up, yu yellabellied cyclops'n gimme room! the bald man roars. He stands there before the bespectacled dealer, legs apart and leaning on his pegleg, shoulders tensed, elbows out, hands hovering an inch from his gunbutts. I'm callin yer bluff, yu flimflammin cart-load a hossshit!

A hole opens up explosively in the bald man's chest like a post has been driven through it, kicking him back into the crowd, the dealer having calmly drawn, fired and reholstered without even interrupt-ing his steady two-handed shuffle of the cards. He sets the deck down and spreads his plump palms to either side as though to say: Anyone else care to try their luck?

He makes certain his sheriff's badge is in plain view, tugs at the brim of his hat, hitches his gunbelt and steps into the well-lit space just abruptly vacated by the peglegged man with the tattooed hair. He picks up the fallen chair, watching the dealer closely, and sets it down in front of the blackjack table, but remains standing. I'm askin yu t'return me back my prizner, he says quietly. He has a hunch about the dealer now, something he grows more convinced of the longer he stands there studying him. She warnt a legal bet. Yu knowed that. I may hafta close this entaprize down.

His weedy ex-deputy with the busted arm leans close to the dealer who seems, though his thick lips do not move, to whisper something in his crumpled ear. He sez he dont spect that'll happen, says the ex-deputy out the side of his mouth. Behind the mountainous fat man, the revolving schoolmarm's white knees rise into view like a pair of expressionless stockingcapped puppets, then fall into curtain obscurity, over and over, but he steels himself to pay them no heed, and to ignore as well her burning gaze, for now he must think purely on one thing and one thing only. He sez ifn yu want back that renegade hoss thief, yu should oughter set yerself down'n play him a hand fer her.

Caint. Aint got no poke. Yes, he's sure of it now. It's why he sits so still. Listening. To everything. His ears thumbing the least sound the way his pink-tipped sandpapered fingers caress the cards. Behind those spectacles, the man is blind.

Well whut about yer boots? suggests the ex-deputy. Or yer weepons? He shakes his head. The ex-deputy whispers something in the fat man's ear, then tips his own ear close to attend to the reply. Well awright, he sez. Yer life then, he sez. Yer'n fer her'n.

Hunh. Shore. He shrugs, and sits down on the edge of the chair to get his voice into the right position. Aint wuth a plug nickel nohow. A flicker of amusement seems to cross the fat man's face, the re-awakened cards fluttering between his hands like a caged titmouse, or a feeding hummingbird. He removes his spurs so they will not betray him, and then, leaving his voice behind, rises silently from the chair to slip around behind the dealer. Reglar five-card stud, his voice says. Face up. Dont want nuthin bid. The dealer offers the deck toward the chair. No cut, mister. Jest dole em out. The room has fallen deadly silent as he circles round, nothing to be heard but the creaking and ticking of the wheel of fortune, all murmurs stilled, which may be perplexing the fat man, though he gives no sign of it. With barely a visible movement, he deals the empty chair a jack and himself a king. I reckon yu're tryin t'tell me sumthin, his voice says from the chair, keeping up the patter to cover his movements.

Something an old deerhunter once taught him as a way of confusing his prey. It was a simple trick and so natural that, once he learned it, he was amazed he had not always known how to do it. But a pair a these here young blades'll beat a sucked-out ole bulldog any day, his voice adds cockily when a second jack falls, a second king of course immediately following on. Uh oh, says his voice. Damn my luck. Pears I'll require a third one a them dandies jest t'stay in this shoot-out. Which he gets, it in turn topped by a third king. He is behind the dealer now, gazing down upon his bubbly mound of glowing pate. Well would yu lookit that, says his voice as the fourth jack is turned up. I reckon now, barrin miracles, the prizner's mine. Stealthily, as the fourth king falls, he unsheaths his bowie knife. The dealer's head twitches slightly as though he might have heard something out of order and were cocking his ear toward it, so his voice says from the chair: Aint that sumthin! Four jacks! Four kings! But we aint done yet, podnuh. Yu owe me another card. Yu aint doled out but four. The fat man hesitates, tipping slightly toward the voice, then, somewhat impatiently, flicks out a black queen which falls like a provocation between the two hands of armed men. Well ifn that dont beat all, his voice exclaims. How'd that fifth jack get in thar? The dealer starts, seems about to reach for his gun or the card, but stays his hand and, after the briefest hesitation, flips over a fifth king. Haw, says the voice. Nuthin but a mizzerbul deuce. Got yu, ole man! And as the gun comes out and blasts the chair away, he buries the blade deep in the dealer's throat, slicing from side to side through the thick piled up flesh like stirring up a bucket of lard.

The man does not fall over, but continues to sit there in his rotundity as before, his head slumping forward slightly as though in disappointment, his blue spectacles skidding down his nose away from the puckery dimples where eyes once were. His gunhand twitches off another shot, shattering an overhead lamp and sending everyone diving for cover, then turns up its palm and lets the pistol slip away like a discard. A white fatty ooze leaks from his slit throat, slowly turning pink. He wipes his blade on the shoulders of the man's white linen suit, triggering a mechanical holdout mechanism that sends a few aces flying out his sleeves, and then he carefully resheathes it, eyeing the others all the while as they pick themselves up and study this new situation. He's not sure how they will take it or just who this dealer was to them, so to distract them from any troublous thoughts they may be having he says: Looks like them winnins is up fer grabs, gentamin.

251

That sets off the usual crazed melee, and while they are going at it, he arrests the wheel of fortune to free the schoolmarm. When he releases her wrists, she faints and collapses over his shoulder, so that he has to unbind her hips and ankles with the full weight of her upon him. It is getting ugly in the churchroom, guns and knives are out and fists and bottles are flying, so he quickly sidles out of there, toting her beamhigh over his shoulder like a saddlebag, the room conveniently shrinking toward the exit to hasten his passage. At the door, before darting out into the night, he glances back over his free shoulder at the mayhem within (this is his town and for all he knows the only people he has ever had and he is about to leave them now forever) and sees through the haze the dead dealer, still slumped there under the glowing lamp like an ancient melancholic ruin, his hairless blue-bespectacled head slowly sinking away into his oozing throat.

# Fœtus

## *Shelley Jackson*

THE FIRST FŒTUS was sighted in the abandoned hangar outside our town. Just floating there, almost weightless, it drifted down until its coiled spine rested on the concrete and then sprang up again with a flex of that powerful part. Then the slow descent began afresh. It was not hiding. It was not doing anything, except possibly looking, if it could see anything from between its slitted lids. What was it looking at? Possibly the motes of dust, as they drifted through the isolated rays of sun, and changed direction all at once like birds flying together. Or at the runic marks of rust and birdshit on the walls. Maybe it was trying to understand them, though that might be imposing too much human order on the fœtus, who is known, now, for being interested in things *for* (as they say) *their own sake*—incomprehensible motive to most of us!

The fœtus rarely opens its eyes when anyone is watching, but we know they are deep blue-black, like a night sky when space shows through it, and its gaze is solemn, tender, yet so grand as to be almost murderous.

"We weren't afraid," said little Brent Hadly, who with his cousin Gene Hadly made the discovery, and took the first photos—we've all seen them—with his little point-and-shoot. "We thought it was Mr. Fisher in one of his costumes." (Mr. Fisher is one of those small-town loonies affectionately tolerated by the locals. He did indeed don a fœtus costume, later on, and paraded down to the Handimart parking lot—where he gulled some big-city newsmen, to their chagrin.) "Then my daddy came and said, Cut the fooling, Fisher!" But even when the Fisher hypothesis had been disproved, no one felt anything but gentle curiosity about the visitor. Indeed, they scarcely noticed it had drifted near the small crowd while they debated, and trailed after them when they left.

The fœtus is preternaturally strong. It grabs its aides and knocks their bald heads together. It carries pregnant women across busy streets. It helps with the groceries. These are the little ways it enters the daily life of its parishioners: it turns over the soil in an old

253

woman's garden. It lifts waitresses on tables to show off their legs. The fœtus has a formal appreciation for old-fashioned chivalry, and expects to be thanked for such gestures.

The fœtus roved about the town until it found a resting-place to its liking in the playground of the municipal park, among dogs and babies. The mothers and the professional loiterers appointed themselves guards and watched it sternly, heading off the youngsters who veered too near it, but they softened to it over time, began to bring sandwiches and lemonade along and make casual speculations about the fœtus's life-span, hopes and origins. When the crowds of tourists pressed too close, they became the fœtus's protectors, and formed a human chain to keep them out.

Nobody's enemy and nobody's friend, it hides its heart in a locked box, a secret stash, maybe a hollow tree in the woods under a bee's nest, maybe a tower room on a glass mountain on a wolf-run isle in a sea ringed by volcanoes and desert wastes. The fœtus always keeps its balance.

Someone observed that the land seemed disarranged. Bent tree-tops, flattened grass, weeds dragged out of their seats, clods dislodged. Tedious speculations about crop circles and barrows and Andean landing strips made the rounds. Of course, we knew the fœtus's little feet dragged when it walked. We had seen the marks in the sandbox at the park. We should have noticed the resemblance, but we resisted the idea that the fœtus was a municipal landmark. It had put our town on the map and filled it with visitors, so that our children had a chance to envy the latest haircuts, and our adults the latest cars and sexual arrangements.

Plus, the marks were disturbing. They were careless. They passed over (sometimes through) fences, even when the gate swung close at hand. Mrs. Sender's oleanders were uprooted and dragged for miles. Even after we knew the fœtus caused the marks, a mystery clung to them. For everything the fœtus did, though, there was someone to praise it. Followers did their following on the paths it left. They said the paths proposed an aesthetic that could not at once be grasped. Some began dragging a foot behind them as they walked, scorning markless movement as noncommittal, therefore cowardly. But why was the fœtus so restless? Was it seeking something? We had all seen it peering through our curtains in the evening, and found the marks in our flowerbeds in the morning. Was it exercising, or aimlessly wandering? Or was it writing a kind of message on the earth? Was it driven from rest by some torment, a plague personal to it, or a plaguey thought it couldn't shake: was the fœtus guilty?

Since the fœtus arrived, none of us has loved without regret, fucked without apprehension, yearned without doubt. We break out in a rash when a loved one comes near because we know the fœtus is there too, waiting for us to prove to it everything it already knows.

*Was* the fœtus a fœtus? Indeed it resembled one. But if it was, the question had to be raised: when the fœtus grew up, as it must, what would it become? Perhaps we all breathed a sigh of relief when scientists concluded that the fœtus, like the famous axolotl, was a creature permanently immature. Hence its enormous susceptibility, its patience and its eagerness to please. Like the unicorn, it adored virgins, but it had a raging fascination with sexual doings, a fascination that drove April Tip and the rest of her gang, the bad girls and boys of our town, to cruel displays under the streetlights around the park.

At first, though not for long, we believed our fœtus was unique. Of course we speculated about the home it must have had somewhere else, about *others*. But here on earth it seemed a prodigy, *the* prodigy. Soon enough, however, more of them began to appear. Some dropped out of the sky, people said, slowly and beautifully, their light heads buoying them up. Commentators waxed eloquent and bade us imagine, on the blue, a dot that grew to a pink dot that grew to a kewpie doll that became the creature we know now. Many were found, like the first one, swaying gently in some warm and secret enclosure—warehouses, high school gyms, YMCA dressing rooms. Publicity seekers claimed to have come across fœtuses in infancy: tiny, playful and virtually blind, like kittens, they bumbled around, falling on their oversized heads, and eagerly sucked on a baby finger, or indeed anything of like size and shape. One was reportedly discovered in a bird's nest, opening its tiny translucent lips among the beaks. But fœtuses this small have never been held in captivity, nor even captured on film. Whether that is because (their unstable condition exacerbated by lack of experience) the kittens decay from or transcend their fœtal condition, imprinting air, a patch of dirt, a leaf blowing past its nest, or because they never existed in the first place, hardly matters, for the situation remains that none are found, except in stories that are already far from firsthand by the time they reach a credible authority. But we may pause for a minute to wonder whether, if such kittens do exist, they are the offspring of our original fœtus, who for all we know may be capable of fertilizing itself, like some plants, or if they grow from spores that have drifted here from some impersonally maternal comet, or—most mysterious

255

thought of all—whether they spring up in our world self-generated, as sometimes new diseases appear to do, teaching us new pains, just because the world has left a place open for them.

Behind each other's eyes, it is the fœtus we love, floating in the pupil like a speck, like a spy. It's looking over your shoulder, making cold drinks even colder, and it doesn't care what promises you've made. We think we want affection, sympathy, fellow-feeling, but it is the cold and absolute we love, and when we misplace that in one another we struggle for breath. Through the pupil's little peephole, we look for it: the shapeless, the inhuman.

Of course with such a company of admirers, sycophants, interpreters, opportunists, advisers, prophets and the like behind it, it wasn't long before the fœtus was performing many of the offices once seen to by our local pastor: visiting the sick, hosting charitable functions, giving succor to troubled souls. One day Pastor Green simply left town, and no one was very sorry. It was the graceful thing to do, people agreed, and saw to it that the fœtus stood behind the pulpit the next Sunday. At first it held an honorary post; we couldn't settle on a suitable title, but we did present it with a robe and a stiff white collar, which it seemed to admire. Higher-ups in church office were rumored to be uneasy about this unorthodox appointment, but public feeling was behind it. And there was no question that the fœtus would increase the church's subscription a thousandfold; no one had ever seen such a benefit potluck as the first one hosted by the fœtus. It wielded the ice cream scoop with tireless arm and paid personal attention to every dessert plate.

Of course the fœtus preferred to hold services in the sandbox, and the citizens appreciated this gesture as a call to simplicity and a sign of solidarity with regular folk. How the fœtus managed to lead us may be hard to understand. At first, its role was to inspire and chide. But it soon felt its way into the post, and began performing those gestures that mean so much to our town: choosing the new paint color for the courthouse (the fœtus preferred mauve), pouring the first bucket of cement for the new tennis courts. (We could afford it, for money was rolling in: tourists, visiting scholars and zealots continued to come, prepared to shop, and after a short bewilderment we provided all the kiosks, booths and lemonade stands they required.) Our fœtus made the covers of the major newsmagazines, and meanwhile, the copycat fœtuses were turning up everywhere, and the rich were installing them in their homes.

The fœtus is made of something like our flesh, but not the same, it is a sort of überflesh, rife with potentialities (for the fœtus is, of course, incomplete—always, unfinished—perpetually) it is malleable beyond our understanding, hence unutterably tender, yet also resilient. A touch will bruise the fœtus, the nap of flannel leaves a print on its skin. The fœtus learns from what it neighbors, and may become what it too closely neighbors. Then your fœtus may cease to be; you may find yourself short one member of the household, yet in possession of a superfluous chair, a second stove, a matching dresser. The fœtus sees merit in everything; this is why it brings joy to houses, with its innocence, and is loved by children, but this quality is also its defect. A fœtus will adore a book of matches, and seek to become it; if you do not arrive in time your expensive companion will proudly shape itself into the cheapest disposable. It is one thing to duplicate the crown jewels, quite another to become the owner of two identically stained copies of yesterday's paper, two half-full boxes of Kleenex, two phone bills.

We all know the fœtus's helpfulness and amiability, which became more and more apparent as it grew accustomed to our ways, and admire the dignity of the fœtus, which never fails it even when it is performing the most ignominious of tasks. No one was surprised when it came to be known as, variously, "Servus Servorum," "Husband of the Church," "Key of the Whole Universe," "Viceregent of the Most High" and, most colloquially, "Vice-God"; other nations may find it odd that our religious leader is of the same species that the well-off trendy purchase for their homes, but those who know better see no contradiction: the fœtus is born to serve.

The fœtus floats outside your window while you are having sex. It wants to know how many beads of sweat collect between your breasts and at what point, exactly, they begin their journey south, it wants to know if your eyes open wide or close at orgasm, if at that time your partner is holding your hand with his hand or your gaze with her gaze. It wants to know if your sheets are flannel or satin, if you lie on wool blankets or down comforters. And when fluids issue from the struggling bodies, with what do you wipe them up: towels? paper products? A T-shirt pulled out of the laundry? It wants to know if the bedside alarm is set before or after the lovemaking, it wants to stay informed, your love is its business.

The fœtus is here to serve us. If we capture it, it will do our bidding; we can bind its great head with leather straps, cinch its little hips tight. Then the fœtus willingly pulls a plow, trots lovers through a park, serves salad at a cookout. It does not scorn menial tasks for to it all endeavors are equally strange, equally marvelous.

Only when it is time to make love must you bind the fœtus tight, lock it in its traces, close all the doors and windows. For at that moment the fœtus will rise in its bonds, larger and more majestic, and its great eyes will open and inside them you could see all of space rushing away from us—as it is! it is! The fœtus is sublime at that moment: set guards, and they will respectfully retreat, dogs, and they will lie down with their heads between their paws, blinking. And even if the fœtus is in tight restraint, you will feel it risen in your pleasure bed, the air will turn blue and burn like peppermint on your wet skin, and the shadows under the bed and the corners of the room will take on the black vastness and the finality of space. You will continue loving because that is our human agenda, what is set for us to do, though we know the fœtus whom we also love is suffering in its straps. Indeed, we make the fœtus suffer again and again, though we are full of regret and pity, and these feelings swell in our chests and propel us together with ever greater force, so we seem to hear the fœtus's giant cry, deafening, every time we slam together, and cruelly love, and in pain.

# Seven Poems
## *Ed Friedman*

### LATE ENTRY

THE FIRST QUESTION we have, when entering a new territory, is whether or not the striped road leading to a picturesque stone outcropping permits romantic interludes along the way. The specter of a man from our collective past looms over a revolver and a school teacher. Intrigue or sporting event? Acting as if we're entirely welcome, we stroll through the center of town in rugby uniforms. I have number "1" embroidered on the front of my shirt, and you have "2." I am waving as if people have nothing better to do than applaud my presence. You rapidly note all response, which turns out to be minimal, since most of the locals are sitting outdoors in stuffed hotel lobby chairs, with seemingly a lot on their minds. There is no conversation. No cheering. In fact, it's nap time only everyone's awake.

"We've really got to get out of here," I say. "I've seen this before. It's like being a baby among adults. You have so much to live for and they seemingly have so little. Eventually they will want what we have until we don't have it anymore."

You say, "That's not right. This is a good land with a blithe and unassuming populace. You're wearing a jockstrap that's two sizes too small and you expect everyone's sympathy because your nuts are being squeezed. The people probably just think you like it this way, and they're probably *right.*"

### MARVEL COMICS

Through a powerful electron microscope we see a seal balancing an inflated model of earth on its nose. Automatic scissors slice the gold foil backdrop, while only a blink away on a checked table cloth there's a cup of hot cocoa whose fragrant steam rises ten feet towards a vaulted breakfast-room ceiling. We record our observations and put another specimen slide under this potent magnifier. Each vision or speck of universe is compelling for as long as we can elaborate on its implications. When we get to the houseplant being showered by mysterious black droplets, the window screen mesh turns new blossoms into glowing white loops.

## FAR AND WIDE

This land is dark and full of weather. In the week we've been here, many bird flocks have flown over without landing. I have read all the Greek classics in the Harvard collection of ancient poetry. Of course they were in translation so I'll never know what any of them really meant. Mostly it was hubbub among men whose haircuts I can't imagine.

In the old days, Mom carried me in her arms. I would point at items and she'd utter sounds which I came to know as "names." It was the beginning of a reading list: pig, furnace, bird cage, cloud, hula, etc. How long would she hold me? How far could we go and still have new words to say? Once while she was pregnant with my brother, we stood under telephone lines in the wind. I wasn't wondering about my father, but a feeling built inside me that someone dear was missing. No movement or distraction could defer the growing prominence of this mood.

## ROUSING VIGNETTES

Everyone loves our effervescent correspondence. Stamps from a distant hemisphere thrill even the most casual postcard enthusiast. Who would believe pictures on these stamps are scenes from our memories? Wild horses fleeing a cyclone of immense proportions are our long-lost friends. Those two swans gliding past a gravel pit craved any love and attention we had to offer. So many signs construed as impersonal public insignias originate in a mind over matter—like our intentions for a better world. You can take them for passing sentiments or as mandates for protracted engagement. We've been stewing over a letter you sent us carrying the insignia of a molting dodo. Are we being overly touchy?

## THE BIG SCHLEP

When it comes to hauling a load, you think you'd want a horse, but if you found a big enough beetle, you could really make some headway. You know, I'm tired of eating off the floor. The coffee pot looks great down here and everything, but couldn't we visit some countries that have tables? Pacify me. Dress me different. Everywhere we go I feel like I'm preceded by my hairy back and knobby elbows, even while I'm walking forward! When do we get to the land that considers these features attractive? When will the strength of edible snails be recognized as heroic? Formed and decomposed over the course of a day, a whole lifetime would be enough to load one hundred twenty-ton railway cars transformed twenty-four hundred times each second averaging the sublimity of unutilized reasons. Now the legs and thighs. What else points pertly upwards?

## BROCHURE

Write it down. Now take its picture. Carry the casserole on your head, then admire . . . Oh hello! This is the palace of vertical hanging beads. Three warriors invented it from cyclones and trophies, and in a minute we'll have ten good reasons for having trekked here. Meanwhile, let's record our impressions of the locals' crossbow practice. They don't use targets but fire arrows directly into each other's extremities. Sword-thrusting is rehearsed to the same effect. What a brave or stupid nation we've stumbled into! We must not understand correctly what we're seeing. Eventually we'll discover that *healing and recovery* are being tested, and that the small recreational craft drifting offshore are miniature hospital ships wherein most of the populace recuperates and resides.

## PARTIAL PROOF

It was 28° F when we kissed by the limy butte. Later we paraded through town as No. 1 and No. 2, members of a world-champion athletic team. To sum up our experience, the immense star-of-Bethlehem-shaped ice crystals and sinewy cloud wisps moonlit in an otherwise clear sky have made us delusional. We fret. We play snooker. We agonize over the role a loaded revolver will have in our encounter with the enshadowed bureaucrat. We know that totality exists somewhere, but there is no way to just stumble across it. The president of our republic is elected by the people and is supposed to reflect the general attitude of our majority. I have portrayed that disposition in the oil painting *Our Advance.* Whispery yellows under frosted glass with purples, blues and greens run together in a river of deep compression.

# Two Poems
## *Ann Lauterbach*

### NARCOLEPSY

Comes sarcastic November in mummy garb, hauling
same old same old what laid bare
what totaled. Sees thru the estimated costs, stench
collisions, inanimate dregs, remembers
the bruised figures, their
numerology as stars. *Up up, down down*
is how she counts as the hunters begin to hunt.

This is the plot of erasure, this is the lavender bath.
Truth be known, the dark won by a landslide.

Yet friends in far January
await news of the front, cycling up the snow clad hills.
They are to be exhumed from the grail of the keeper,
he who heralds what's here. To them I send dreams
that pop open when breathed on
and ask that they complete this sentence:
*If God is in the details, then . . .*

But in the end there was only a chair covered in green velvet
and the sibling, dark as a forest, laid among leaves.
There were the stamps with monsters

and the stamps with flowers,

there was a dumpster of old paint.

Even the egalitarian whimsy of the gold rush

is in partial view: harbor's sleek hulls,

willow disintegrating in drapery and nonce.

What others did

taking us to task in the field, into archival maps

along a bank. What is it they wanted?

Among strangers, beyond the stamina of pictures

—the dancer on stage, his ruined feet,

      *as they would flail crops*

  *when the spring comes, and flood, and tassels*

  *rise, as my head—*


Across the small ballast, the drab plaster,

a colder moment assumes shape.

And Thee, found inside eternity's crawl space,

midget doctrine of reckless variety,

homing pigeon of whatever returns,

what is your method now,

and how do you know when it's finished?

When it detaches, when it comes to life at the edge of time.

*Ann Lauterbach*

WINTER STRAWBERRIES

1.


You will find I have been guided by fate's

whispering tabernacle, into which

a cradle etched the library's gold facade.

In dreamland, a word

is stuffed into a bag, the flight comes,

and what was promised

and what said

vanishes into the jetstream. Humor

is in my left shoe, damage control in the right,

my garb is a robe

woven into the knick of time.


But the dilemma under the passage

splits air's permissions and clones.

The long line to the altar

turns away, banyan trees

root on a sacred pile.

King Rat and Bird Flu scrabble the dust for clues.


2.


Expertise of the antiquarian flirt.

Wishes something manual would happen.

A dusty limbo, plastic covered,

unevenly veiled despite the sky's hard crest.

*Ann Lauterbach*

This is order yet so much was given
to orphan lust.

                *Not air,* said the clairvoyant,
just particulars with space intervened.
Whose fatigue cut into my robe?
Whose damage control?
*Clip, clip, clip,* rains from porcelain clouds,
an Orphic residue mimics the arcade.
Some isolated notes align stamina to trust, their
cause moving along, stubbornly annealed.

# The Chatter Heart
## An EKG

### *Paul West*

UTTOXETER TO SIR

FOR YEARS NOW you have done nothing more ambitious than paint seeds on wooden strawberries, each strawberry taking at least a week. There is a thriving market, and you never noticed how like seeds a baboon's tits are. I excuse you, I let you off. There you squat, numbed in the throes of monogamy, rising hardly even above the Plimsoll Line of indignation to complain that British movies are too quiet, the mike's in the wrong place, all the actors have laryngitis. If you are not Numb, then you can be Dumb or Crumb, strong names for their epic implications. What are you doing here? Because, you bluster, this country is more like the rest of the world than any other country is. Bah. Is that you at your most crisp and propulsive? Are you not the person who has to put on the radio to free yourself from that awful stammer of yours? Only with the radio playing, horsing around with the language and the prices, can you talk straight. Then you say it, something at least: "This country has produced some of the ugliest shoes in history, orthopedic to the nth, whereas if you go to Italy. . . ." Finish it, then. All right, don't. I agree about the shoes; only bullies wear them, whether or not they know they're bullies. La Guardia, you say, is full of captive metal birds twittering with alarm. So when were you that far from home last? Merv calls all the time to say he hasn't been out of his house for weeks. What would we do without Merv, conserving the notion of the homebody for us? "Send me all your books," he pleads, "I daren't go out. Not into the agora anyway." He's bloody learned, you have to grant that.

These are the people we know: the Mervs, the Numbs, Dumbs and Crumbs, the Pinks and Blues, all of them as decorous as a penis sheath worn in the tea room at the Plaza. They try, these gents, these dames, but they notice nothing, no more than you, my mostly silent interlocutor. You have been frightened by bad English, sir, at that same La Guardia (remember the Little Flower who was mayor?), hearing "Failure to board at this time will give up their seat to a standby," and you cringe against the radiator or the cool unresponsive pot of the urinal, wondering what the world has come to. All you can see on emerging is a world you never wanted: kids in their strollers biting their blankets while being wheeled around like tiny astronauts. It is worse in Philly, my friend, where the helpless amateur who drives the bus announces "There will be two stops. First stop: Gates One through Fourteen B. Second stop: Gate Twelve C." What is going on? Where do you end up if you get out at the wrong gate? Why do we all gad about in Brownian motion?

You never answer. You do not know. You would get no farther than what the La Guardia officials call *the other side of our gray wall with the telephones.* We have all become our own porters, our camels. Imagine boarding your flight and, for the sake of friendship, countering her hello with some provocative remark about *The Death of Virgil.* Oh, dear, you're going to a funeral, how sad. You need to get back to the toilet roll the maid has folded to a point, at least the first sheet anyway, half-tempting you with the notion of an unsealed letter to lick. Don't you dare. Remain in the zone of effluvia.

Do you still, as when you were an immigrant, answer people's genial inquiries with your blanket response? "Hello, no blow job," an answer designed (you thought) to put people at their ease, persuading them you wouldn't subject them to any sudden stress or crash of intimacy. How many times can you say "hello, no blow job!" without offending an entire cocktail party? Not only should you never say it, you should never think anything so forward, you just thought it was the natural thing to do, being here and all, a stranger in a strange land, a stripling among the straphangers. On climbs a sturdy woman with a huge bag she at once empties out in the aisle, revealing eight smaller bags with which she crams the baggage rack the full length of the so-called "Express" plane. *She* knows how to travel. *We* know only how to stay at home. Into your favorite chair you sink, sunken, murmuring something about how foreigners handle foreign money, looking anxiously back at it as they march away from the tip, as if it will rear up and abandon them, involving them in humiliation. Can this be a ten? Or a twenty? They are not used to such numbers, such tiny bills, such austere colors, all the same really, with different deads engraved thereon. The outsiders handle it as if it were rimmed with Kirlian auras.

The lord of all vermin enlarges his kingdom. That's what you say when you've coffeed-up, gotten out of your traveller's funk, unable to remember even where you went, or why. There on the table, a rancid wafer, sits the exhausted ticket, a souvenir full of deadly twisted staples, a mess of amendments, and you say, quite wretchedly, "I am not leaving this fucking place ever again. You go, he/she goes, we go, you go, they go, but I stay at fucking home, sucking the golden teat of myself. Goodbye, no blow job."

It is too late now to expect suavity of you. I will pursue my meditation on America while you cock your feet up and rant away about how the country has gone back to the America Firsters, being beastly to immigrants and aliens all over again, the proud possessors (many of them foreigners to begin with) who don't want anyone new to possess it. These you call the anal retentives of the American dream. Now you see the immigrant once again assembling the tip of one-dollar bills on a gleaming white bread plate, then after walking a few paces away returning to remove one dollar, like a thieving magpie presuming to adjust the tip toward some idol of perfect pecuniary justice. These, you tell me, are the fleurs du Mall. You have said this before, you will no doubt say it again; but I ask you, don't you think saying "Hello, no blow job" is ambiguous? I mean, are you offering to pitch or receive? How can an obscenity be so misleading?

In turn I offer you, peeled away from sticky cards in my wallet, the gems of horror I carry with me: a color photo of peas, clipped from a packet of the frozen variety, meant for use in a Chinese restaurant, where they do not understand anything but snow peas, *in pods,* which I loathe. Bad enough, but what I follow up with is worse: gaffes of the mouth and pen, cousins of those intimate words telegraphed and transcribed miles away by an anonymous, semi-literate florist: "Love and kisses on publication day," say, or "In memory of a gorgeous sleepless night!" No, this is how the bad stuff goes:

> A journalist, the last article she had published, just before Christmas began "it's the season to be jolly. . . ."

And this:

> Delivered to the front lawn as a truck-load of long thin poles, people set up their electric saws to cut them into two-foot lengths. . . .

Another's a horoscope:

> PISCES (Feb. 19–March 20). Mention only the known facts—others will hold you to your words. Trips to the ocean or a lake revive your energy. Encourage a child to study, as your influence can really make the difference. Aries apologizes.

269

*Paul West*

*Aries apologizes!* How dare they speak to me in titles without realizing they could be titles. These are the pinpricks only. Worse are the moaners at the bar in the Oyster Bar, all phoning someone else (or one another) on tiny retractable cellphones no bigger than sand-dabs, ignoring one another but just perhaps covertly speaking *to* one another: a planned exercise in fraudulent blather. The waiters wear black armlets, either in mourning or simply to remind us that what they wear is a uniform. "The Plaza kitchens are yours to command!" Hearing rather than reading this grandiose come-on, I eat the carnation imposed on my breakfast tray and prepare not to go out. Downstairs to buy toothpaste, however, I hear some dacoit woman saying over and over "13 incense," which I finally understand as a request for thirteen cents. These are my bruits, term filched from medicine, the complaining noises I make when safely among those who speak my language, who are few and far between. I am working my way toward the serious issue I must confront you with, having to do with poor, insufferable Pfitzner, and his possible rehabilitation (it hurts not to mention him as if he were a friend), and what went on in the Tower of London, 1914–1918. I inch my way toward it, knowing how ferociously petulant you can be, even as I mention a clipped nail, a nail-clip, found among the paperclips; the counterrevolution in which the Romanoffs whip out their revolvers and blow the execution squad to bits right there in that cellar, seated as they are by divine right; the way the mention of Orange goes both ways, meaning either Dutch protestantism or Syracuse University. Treat every day, I tell you, as a newborn baby, a birthday present, an Arizona sunset. Sometimes, as a piece of sublime chamber music comes to a halt on the stereo, in a low register the furnace kicks on and I think it's the first note of a nonexistent next movement. Describe this first note, I tell myself, and it's an elegiac clonk, a hollow imprecation, oh all of that, a dirge of brown balsawood tapping on an old cowbell. It belongs to Roy Harris, who excels at ranch-house sounds.

You respond to none of this, blustering, in your obsessive way, about the need to relate all passing events to something central: a main idea. I have watched you at your housebound duties, sprawled in a warm bath with a cold and gluggy throat, scribbling notes to yourself about the little socks you fit to the legs of chairs to keep them from scratching the parquet—when they rutch and slip away from the rubberbands that usually hold them fast, you tilt the chair and, cursing mightily, tug the socklet upward, then reposition the rubberband. A disproportionate amount of your time goes into this remedial activity, which is only part of your desire to dominate the world that threatens you. All you need is the one big idea that will make the world of swirling phenomena come to heel, like a thousand yapping, heroically obsequious Dalmatians.

It is you who want the rosettes of the cheetah to merge into a uniform pigment, and in this we are different; I want the gray of the elephant's hide to sprout rosettes. How we ever manage to deal with each other, I do not know, I the gadabout, the connoisseur of incidentals, you the integrator, the marsupial who knows one big thing—though you never tell me what it is. I the mindless pump, you the finessy master-builder.

"Is this," you retort, "going to be one of those awful, humiliating conversations in which two premises are aired to no purpose? Not so much a conversation as an exchange of rifle fire?"

"In a time-compressed manner," I begin, but you interrupt. I'll say this: you're getting braver. You'll soon be calling "worst case scenario" by its proper name: "at worst."

What you interrupt with is this. "*All at once,* you mean, old friend." You sound huffy and superior, which first you may be, but not the second. Oh no. Keep a stiff upper chest, "old friend," there is worse coming over the horizon of the pericardium.

## UTTOXETER TO ATHOL

"Hello, no blow job," I say, but he permits himself a languid smile that turns his sallow features pink as if he has blushed, which he never does. He is never that emotionally tied to what he thinks.

"In this season," I say, "insects start coming into the house, they squeeze out of cold cracks into the mainstream of untidiness."

"You would know," he responds. "Fools rush in where wise men fear to trade."

That is enough, I decide: no more banter. Get to it. Tease him, search him out. After all, you want to know what he thinks. We are not addressing ourselves to the cloven hoof of the amaryllis that yawns into flowering goblets or the Masai, from nearby, pointing at the sunset with long canes. We are not being exotic, not even wondering, as we sometimes have in the drear watches of a sleepless night, if criminality isn't merely the left-handed form of human endeavor. A novel, I keep telling him, as from one who knows to one who has never thought about it, is a series of compromises flying in close formation. "One of these days, I'll—"

271

"You'll what?" he interjects, always this rude.

I abandon the thought, feeble as it was, hoping to snare him into the real gist of my thinking, trifling with him only in order to launch my serious *moutons*. Or, if you prefer a different animal, giving him the sorts of daft little retracted-claw taps that lion cubs indulge in.

Although chatting, he ignores me, his mind on yet another calamity he has noticed in a movie, this time the powder-compact mirror a woman gave Charles Lindbergh as he set out for his transatlantic flight. Of course she gave it really to James Stewart. Anyway, he says, here is Lindbergh-Stewart flying eastward, and the sun in the mirror dazzles him, "which can only mean," I hear, "he is flying westward, the wrong way. Why can't they get things right? Wrong-Way Corrigan is one thing, but Lindy's quite another. Eff them to hell and back." I hear him out in silence, knowing the pains of being a shut-in afflict him deeply, almost as if he were a prisoner in some comfy jail.

"Sure," I tell him, "they always foul up with the planes. They think nobody's watching. Your Blenheim takes off, becomes an Airacobra and lands as a Catalina. They wouldn't dare be that sloppy with cars, would they?" An olive branch, but he snubs it.

"What's all this shit about some bastard of a German and the Tower of London? More cesspool history?"

"No, they're separate," I insist, "I'm trying to bring them together in mind to make a point about—well, cliché thinking and sacrifice."

Now, you have heard of Pernambuco, the wood that does not float, it is so dense and solid? They make violins from it. He's like that, he goes down to the bottom during all conversation, at rest only on the sea- or riverbed. It must be some fishlike tendency in him, to avoid others' ideas like the plague; yet here I am going after him with something I can tell he'd rather not hear. What a little laughing embryo he is, deep in his armchair, perfect parasite of the cushions, not so much a human being as a bright, ingratiating and deceptive hologram. To whom I am obliged to address myself nonetheless.

"Yes," he finally says (I know, I should say "he goes" or "he's like" or some other slangy lapse), "you remind me of a mangy airline that's gone broke but commissioned a new color scheme from the Gaudis who paint it. You come here under false colors, my friend, trying to provoke me into some anti-Nazi argument I am bound to win while you maunder on about the Tower of London. As if anyone cared."

"I do," I said, as if getting married. I was "I do," I went "I do."

"Long behind the butterfly," he began, but I halted him.

"You mean aviation is. Technologically advanced, but still esthetically far behind?"

"One of your brighter days," he said. "Let's get on with it."

"Piano in him is never bright."

"Am not discussing piano."

"You were. 'Ve not heard the *Palestrina* thing."

"You should."

"With you living underneath me I no doubt will."

"As I was saying, he tried so hard to sound like a good Nazi, not so much believing as making all the gestures of a believer, and they saw through him. He wanted what he wanted for music, that was all. Anything for music."

"And Hitler scorned him?"

"Wouldn't give him the time of day." How comprehensive that expression sounds, analogous to the extent of space, I suppose.

He isn't really listening, not as he would if I were talking about the irresistible Richard Strauss, whose rhythms match his own, he says.

"Your point?" He sounds like an inquisitor.

"Well, I'm wondering if we should dismiss him on moral grounds, no matter how bad, how good, his music is. Bristling with obsequiousness, he comes across as a pill, but he did write some sturdy elegiac stuff. Should he not be allowed credit for that at least? Or must all he did go down the chute of his politics? That's my point. They're trying to rehabilitate him; Strauss doesn't need it, of course, but Pfitzner does, downhill from his Blue Max in 1925. A long decline. I remember John O'Hara going to live in Princeton in hopes of an honorary degree he never got."

"Hans Pfitzner," I tell him, "is hard to say. But let that pass. In some photographs he has a goatee and this leads you to thinking his gaunt face is all tufts. In other pictures, he has no beard and you notice how far back his head extends, almost as if a bulb grew out of it. He has a look of worried, revulsed, overnourished disappointment, ever-ready for the next affront. Devout Nazi that he was, and in spite of his grovelings before Hitler and Goering, he didn't quite make it in the Nazi era, not even as well as his rival, the pro-Semitic Richard Strauss. Early on, almost as if he were some alpha pilot, he received the Blue Max, *Pour Le Mérite,* which might have been enough for many men, even composers; but he wanted more, he was one of those men Erich Fromm calls 'marketing characters,' whose self-esteem—if any—depends on public opinion of him. He has no in-built pride. His music has a lumpish, brooding dawdle to it that evinces the man, as if someone determined never to get mad wrote from within a kennel of controlled rage. Am I making myself clear?"

"Bah," he says, "another neglected Hun. Why bother? I've heard the music. He's a muddler, a pasticheur, an awful mix-up of a dozen Romantic composers, twiddling echoes together to form what he hopes will be the cutting edge of a new idiom. Sod him."

"Nonetheless," I persist, "his *Palestrina* does some worthy grave brooding not unlike Mahler."

"Those who suck up," he answers, "get promoted downward. I've seen it. Look at me. I do all the draining, my role is downward. I do suck up."

"And all the action is mine." I rarely address him in this haughty fashion, but sometimes he irks me, lost in his trance, listening to the mellow ladies of the National Public Radio (no danger there): the hearty Scandinavian den mother who administers puzzles on Sunday mornings; the purring matron who has seen it all already and sounds regally bored; the bright and bouncy Jacki, the bookish one with tints of Philly or Pitt in her voice, her almost British diphthongs. He loves them all because, as they say, they consider all things, whereas I, when I hear them at all (I'm too busy thumping the body along), find the whole pack of them old-hat, passé, unformed.

From them to Pfitzner, one whose weird life drives you to ponder his sometimes almost martial art, is a fair jump because, although he tends to be pompous, trivial, footling, bombastic, secondhand, tinny and disconnected, sometimes using a brass band motif like the Nazis marching into Oslo, he has another strain that draws me on, and this sounds like the Brit strain of Bridge, Delius and Butterworth, as if, trickling through all that imitative pomp, there flowed water from the banks of green willow, a tune from the first cuckoo of spring, a whisper from the girl with the flaxen hair. He has a soothing, pastoral side that emerges in his saddest tones, as in the piano concerto about halfway, and in parts of his *Palestrina* portrait. I cannot for the life of me damn him through and through, whether or not he licked Nazi ass, my reason being—get this up there—that music transcends, begins not very earthly and gets unearthlier, having in its oblique semireferential way little to do with us. We leave it behind to chirp on our behalf, but in no way to defile or befoul us. I need to tell my fellow synergist this, not raising Pfitzner to heroic status, but just allowing him his meed (expression allowed?) of gentle, almost sentimental whimsy, which rather than derivative from the English spawns in the babbling brooks of the German countryside, where the rabbits and hares and boars had no idea which polity was afoot among them.

Look, I tell him, knowing he wants some kind of proof other than words. "Look." I produce from one of my chinks a small rectangle of paper that has been mine for years, with a few important numbers scribbled on it. How I have leaked into the fiber of the paper, drip by drip over the years, gradually changing off-white into, here and there, a pinky beige, or (my finest hoofprint) a pink splotch with a thick outer rim of cerulean blue, all very pastelly, as you would find it on the never-postmarked stamps of some remote French colony, with the eternal coral pinking outward into the azure water: an atoll in reverse, I suppose, with on the unspoiled sand only the recent footprints of Wenckebach, long since lost to a hemorrhage.

"You could replace that," he says, meaning the bit of paper, and I agree, remembering a recent envelope from Turkey not only bemired but rent, with all the world's scribbles upon it (idle computations, a late date with Zuleika), and, legalizing it, the merest smidgen of a stamp, bleached and unpictorial as if from a failed society, and its flap dangling open like a burnous that has no fly. I get such things from time to time, telling me to buck up, to bear down hard, to push with all my heart. I do. I know nothing else, although I have fantasized about, one day, wobbling free along some street, leaving a bloody trail behind me (Wenckebach again) and amazing passersby with my constant rolling gait like a boxer practicing as he goes to buy some beef jerky. I dip a shoulder, then the other one, let out a gasp as I thrust with all of my might downward, free of him and his gravity-led idleness: the receiver, the collector, the drone.

Up and at 'em, says I. Not him, *him*. I am full of the lingo of prizefighting. I jab, I feint, I butt, I sometimes deliver a low blow, but I keep on punching because my genes tell me to. If you could hear every pulse in the world, you'd go crazy—didn't Charlie Parker say that, about every sound? Back to Pfitzner. Why should I care? My lot was decreed long ago and, barring a shot to the heart, heartbreak, or, heaven forfend, heartburn, will go on the same old way, shouting at the guy in the upstairs room, hearing his faint little chunter drift downstairs as he moans about having to listen to my monotonous rhythm all day, all night, I the enabler, the provider. Where he comes from, the novelists do not write any better than the rest of the population speaks. I am the Nawab of Pataudi, I'm the muscle man, I'm stronger on the right. I eject fractions, I get around by proxy, and I now and then burst into song, self-pitying or salacious:

> Uttoxeter the muscle man
> works day and night,
> soft machine of marzipan,
> doomed bland anchorite.
>
> Scabby little Hitler
> Took turds in his mouth
> (Hence the rash
> Behind his tash),
> Or his wiener got littler
> And his ball dropped south.

Oh, Athol, he upstairs, gets about less than I, but the one I learn from most is Sir, who gets around an awful lot, networking, schmoozing, hearing them out as he thinks his own dastardly thoughts, to which I am privy. Yet I do not converse with Sir, only with Athol, the upstairs man. If I did, I'd give him a mouthful (perhaps even by means of this little billet-doux, putting my case to him tout court: why don't I ever get a rest, except in some calamity?). That sort of plaint would vex him mightily, I know, but every now and then you have to spout up for yourself in a world of punishment disguised as sinecure. It is really to Sir that I address all I say to Athol, but I doubt it ever gets through, though, like a babe in the womb, I hear him raving about reviewers who damn any character in a novel who has come so much as near a book. Out there, it is books that drive them mad; they at once disdain any mention of such, although making no protest when somebody, like Sir on a recent trip, notices an Escort service in the Yellow Pages as having "Reubenesque" girls. The sandwich, even in sexual trade, will never go out of fashion. You should have heard him hooting about that, slavering as he got it down in his notebook, then transferring it to his newest chapter, stuffing it like rancid cabbage into the mouth of some wretched character he's tormenting in his latest epic. All pumped up, that's how I see him as he gurgles around my most athletic moments, muttering God help the novelist, who lives from scratch, flies to Manhattan and back without ever seeing the town, like Raymond Roussel sailing to India but coming back home without disembarking—"Have you been to India?" they'd ask and he'd answer yes, he *had* been to India.

Enough of Sir, ever my target, elusive as the Holy Ghost. To him I'm just a contraption, slaving away here in the engine room or hold while Athol swans away upstairs on the main deck, a plank lubber, a swot to my snob. I have often wondered why the working classes, oft yclept *latefundia,* never get to address their masters, and the answer seems to be: The more time spent yapping, the less time pumping. It's as crass as that. No grousing, then, no grumbling, the last privilege of the prole.

"Hi, there," says Athol, lolling with big cigar, his chubby legs wide to receive where he squats.

"My name isn't *There,*" I tell him with a fearsome bruit that makes Sir tremble and sweat, mentally registering an extra beat thrown in, wrecking the symphony of his sinus rhythm. Poor Sir, at the mercy of an Uttoxeter in his prime. Any moment I could sport an attack, refuse the overtures of passive-aggressive Athol, stage my own version of writer's block. Not yet, though, not until I have truly had enough, as I have of television ants, sharks, baby turtles scuttling for the shallows, mother crocs hosting their young in the spaces between their teeth. I am weary too of lawyers' jargon: their allocute, their redact, their Man-One, their always mispronounced *voir dire.* In truth, given my druthers, I would prefer the world of insects, I the super-insect, for they too seem sometimes perilously poised on the watershed between liquid and solid, as am I. I am as much what passes through me as what contains and shoves it. So take that, Abbot Odon of Cluny, who said women were bags of excrement. We *all* are. I am happier by far when, granted a screen (even if only re-flections in the golden eye of a cardiologist's speculum) that reveals the metamorphosis of a mosquito, tall at first in a bridal dress, ghost-ly with packed-up tentacles that unfold like a camera's tripod, then looming like some grand butterfly peacock of the night until it zips away with a ping. They all, the insects, have fuzzy, indistinguish-able, furry, oversupplemented, barbed and oddly angled faces. If I dream, I dream of *le papillon grand paon de nuit,* unfurling in anon-ymous, bloated pageantry.

I have lost Pfitz. Sorry. But when I lose him, he always comes back living in a shambles of a postwar hospital in a hovel with his second wife; being de-Nazified in 1945 in a converted garage that leaks, announcing, "The world is dead"; refusing to drink French wine dur-ing World War Two; strutting or flouncing out of the room in which someone quoted a poem of Claudel's; in 1923 in yet another hospital being visited by Hitler and his entourage, who swiftly formed the impression (wrongly) that Pfitz was a crypto-Jew, a beard and no brawn, forever groveling to hide what the Faustian beard announced. I recover him making numerous trips to Poland to fawn on the Governor-General, Hans Frank, in the end taking with him an awful mishmash called *Krakow Greeting*. Indeed, I find it hard to lose him, but relish the spectacle of an almost completely misunderstood man who protested too much, more Nazi than the Nazis themselves, yet able here and there, amid the Arctic sterility of his output, to compose some moving classic pieces. Do we forgive him? Never mind. Do we give him credit where credit is due? Or damn his all on moral grounds? I doubt it: he just wanted to be as famous as Richard Strauss and would have joined forces with the devil himself to make it as a musician. He should have worn his Blue Max with pride and attended to music, not Munich.

## UTTOXETER TO ALL

So, we are speaking of Germans again, as anyone with a sense of fear in the twentieth or twenty-first century is bound to do. Or disgust. You cannot read the history of the last hundred years without throwing in a few extra fibs, can you? Like some epileptic metronome. The shoe now, however, is on the other foot, and you will see why I set out with Pfitzie the lickspittle romantic pasticheur, not dangerous but appalling, whose *Palestrina* nonetheless disturbs us. Now I have to deal with a few public-spirited, patriotic Germans of the 1914–18 vintage who trudged about stuffy, cloudy, morose England and took almost a lepidopterist's interest where soldiers lodged and drank, which ships docked and sailed, what sorts of packages stood on the dock, what sailors weighing themselves averaged in weight, how much the buoyant, jingoistic population smiled. *Spies*. Or, as they say in the South, spas. You could hardly accuse these fellows of latching on to colossal secrets—fake aerodromes, secret real aerodromes, munitions factories in hospital clothing, generals disguised as policemen as they came and went about their hellish duties. I have lately been perusing the record of what happened to these fellows at their trials and after, always wondering when the first woman would appear and shame them. You do not emerge from such reading with a manumitting sense of honor: gentlemen inspecting gentlemen. Take the first spy.

I understand that he was just trying to commandeer some terrain and then protect it, like a king of old. None of us, however, will be quite so good at that as the red squirrel of the woods, the heckler and bully-boy whose tirade is a mix of stutters, chatters and searing squeaks somewhere between a rubber mouse and a whoopee cushion, with which racket he scares off squirrels much bigger than himself. Oh to be that intimidating, that ballsy, when your terrain so-called is a sludge of gurgles and glug-glugs, and all you are is a propeller of ruddy fluid, always the same except for days of calamity, longed-for provided none of the pain comes to roost down here. I don't wish Sir much harm, but I do sometimes wish him other than he is, more aware, more respectful, more bloody cognizant of who's who, even a courtesy wave at Athol, a bow to me. We're just part of the suit, I'm afraid, which is no doubt why I have become so argumentative, so truculent sometimes, so interested in world affairs and the weird way humans have of trumping up reasons for what they want to have while the rest of us, the ones Falstaff called "the little vital commoners," await our turn, nails bitten to the quick.

So I come to Carl Hans Lody, a German of medium height and piercing blue eyes, who had once been married to an American and had intended to become an American citizen. In September 1914 he sent a letter to Stockholm about huge contingents of Russian soldiers passing through Edinburgh, sixty thousand, perhaps, so he was told, and trains were roaring through the station fast, with their blinds drawn. Something, he wanted his Swedish contact to inform Berlin, was going on, but he was not to know that his letter, posted in Scotland, ended up being read in London, where it was photographed. Thus a night-shadow began to hover over Lody's lingering visits to barbershops and military outfitters (officers posted away buy fresh shirts). He next reported that the Forth Bridge had been barricaded, a large naval force was lying off Grangemouth, and a small cruiser off Leith. His code name, oddly enough, was "Nazi," no one knows why, and he traveled around with a rug, a big strap and a cardboard box, like a man journeying with a partly disassembled household in his grasp. He had even reported the *Lusitania* painted grayish black and Liverpool storehouses crammed with flour and potatoes, as spies presumably do, when he was seized, tried and condemned, bearing himself throughout with heroic affability, actually at one point waving gently to a witness who, volunteering to identify him, could not quite see him. There was laughter, in which he joined.

Yet they all knew where they were going as Lody explained his innocent-seeming code, his having been told not to make his telegrams too short, which was why he larded into them such combinations as "Johnson very ill last four days," meaningless all of it. When he wrote "shall" he meant "arrived." Tricky stuff, they all thought, most of all when he refused to name his master spy, invoking honor and drill. A woman sobbed. Lody tilted, almost fell, then apologized to the military judges, explaining, "I have had a month's confinement and my nerve has given way." A glass of water came at which he sipped like a courtier.

From the Tower of London he wrote to an American friend in Omaha, "I am in the Tower. An unfriendly guard paces the corridor outside. When you hear of me again, doubtless my body shall have been placed in concrete beneath this old tower, or my bones shall have made a pyre. But I shall have served my country." On his third day before Lord Cheylesmore, he heard much use of adverbs in his defense ("frankly" and "fearlessly" the most frequent), then refused to make a final statement in his own behalf. It is here that the mind begins to sicken at the lethal etiquette of the whole business: word went out to the general officer commanding London district, Horse Guards, stating that His Majesty the King had confirmed the court's findings and its sentence. There must elapse at least eighteen hours between Lody's being told of his sentence and the actual shooting. So we now have a courtly little scenario between Major-General Pipon, CB, the Major of the Tower, fussing about the haste required, and Lody himself, who writes to the Commanding Officer of the Third Battalion Grenadier Guards at Wellington Barracks: "My sincere thanks and appreciation towards the staff of officers and men who were in charge of my person." He signs himself Senior Lieutenant, Imperial German Naval Res. II.

Next dawn, 6 November 1914, they brought him up from his condemned cell at 29 the Casemates and Lody said to the Assistant Provost-Marshal, "I suppose you will not care to shake hands with a German spy?"

"No, but I will shake hands with a brave man."

Heroic decorum could ask no more of a man seated bare-chested, shirt wide open to the cold, in a chair lashed to stakes driven into the turf. Eight Grenadier Guards faced him, aiming, glad that the awkward slow march over cobbles to the execution shed was over. En route, Lody had even steered the chaplain to the right as the cleric wandered the wrong way, though how Lody knew where to go remains a spy's secret. Blindfold. Straps. One volley, the lead crashing through his *heart*, which is where I get downright squeamish as he dies of shock, all his intimate red meats plundered. Eight bullets in the heart does not so much stop it as expunge it, especially the pumping part down below. I shudder at the thought of the chair, the suave little cold handshake, the sour breath of the riflemen.

Perhaps now you see why I fuss about these matters, wonder why anyone at all should be a Companion of the Bath, why Grenadier Guards (who guarded the monarch with grenades, presumably) should have the right to mash a beating heart, even when sanctioned by a Cheylesmore (how did he become a lord, and why? for *this?*) and that mustachioed king whose right came not from God, as they all pretend, but from the old art of the grab? Not to mention, what's heard in the background, the romantic, soppy old Eton Boating Song, the sedate click on bat of cricket's ball, the imperial tenderness of Elgar's music, all part of the polity that breaks the heart of these wretched men. Tricked out with all the confectionery of fancy names and titles, the execution almost attains the dignity desired, but it makes a hell of a mess of Lody, who was only doing his job, like Athol, like me, like Sir indeed. Even Pfitzner with his Blue Max. (You see how my *moutons* are flocking together?) I am wondering if the craven Pfitzner was ever any worse than the Lodys or their judges and executioners, whether his obsequious bigotry wasn't a cut above cold-blooded (or hot-) marksmanship by Grenadier Guards in the so-cold rickety blood-stained rifle shed.

Would they ever shoot a Pfitzner?

He would never be a spy; oh, he would go to Edinburgh and Liverpool as commanded, but he would forget to keep his eye on things.

So it seems to me nobler never to obey, never to do one's duty, always to beg off; the universe is full of gents only too willing to do their duty, like Athol, like me, like Sir, like you.

There followed one Muller, sentenced in the Central Criminal Court, welcome news to the general in charge, who wrote to his superior: "Allow me to carry it out in the Tower of London as in the case of Lody. It will have more effect on the country at large. Will you empower me to carry out all similar executions on my demand without further reference to you?" Hot to trot is what I call that. Transferred from Brixton Prison to the Tower, Muller went by cabs, the first one having broken down. Prepared bullets awaited him, their tops specially filed so as to break up in the body. He shook hands with each member of the firing party. Drops of blood and pulverized bone were the only signs of his execution. Once again, the heart had exploded, more than ever, thanks to the filed bullets. Etiquette had been satisfied once more, as with

Roos and Janssen, executed at 6 A.M. and 6:10 by a squad of Scots Guards, this time in the Tower ditch, a far less private place than the rifle shed. Roos asked for a cigarette he just as quickly tossed away and his life with it. Janssen nothing sullen did or mean on that memorable scene.

Followed by Melin (handshakes all round at the rifle range), Roggen (no bandage), Buschman (played violin all night, program of seventeen short pieces ranging from Bach to Verdi and Fauré; no bandage, and smiled), Breeckow (a huge bound at the volley, 7 A.M.), Ries (handshakes, grave smile), Meyer (hysterical rendition of "Tipperary" on way to chair, followed by curses and agile wiggling; ripped bandage from eyes before volley struck) and Hurwitz-y-Zender, not so much a man as a mosaic, who showed "a fair amount of calm." Years later, on the Thames beach below the Tower promenade, a brass cartridge case turned up, one of eight issued, with his name engraved on it as H. Zender, Tower, 22nd January 1916.

All I can think of is the fusillade of red-hot lead plunging through the heart and back, then maybe even onward, out the rear wall of the now demolished rifle shed. Yes, of course, they all died of shock, but did the heart? Was it not butchered before the man died of shock? In those few intervening seconds between impact and departure, I think of doing something awful to Sir (Athol is incapable, his type of fibrillation not grievous). A flutter, say, or a very fast fib, all beats chaotic in deadly V-tach, as it's known in the trade. Getting our own back, say. I am no spy, however, nor no Pfitzner, and am perfectly willing to be beastly to any Germans I find. But should we not with shaken heads tolerate the Pfitzners and spank the spies? I am worried about an aspect of human behavior that censures for the sake of voluptuous protocol, a braided ceremony as something to believe in, followed by all those shredded hearts. Beat on I will, heart of gold, ever alert for the first sounds of Sir's being strapped to the chair and eight pairs of guardsmen's boots shuffling.

# K. Tropes
## John Taggart

*—for Robert Creeley*

1.

With birds green begins with invisible birds.

Silver maple and sycamore
silver maple and sycamore against grey
against north mountain hidden within the grey sky
grass field
brome and orchard
grass field heavy with rain
in a corner of the eye in a curve
ash walnut cherry
from ash to walnut to cherry in a downward curve.

Shadows well up shadows from films of green.

Back into him
her shoulders and back into him
his head bent down his head bent into her hair
his hand
his hand above her breast.

2.

Turned to and turned to and returned to song.

Lips that were interlaced
in lamp-light
thin lips humming to themselves
eyes that were closed
in that light
opening to early morning light after rain
mind that was lost
am found
am found in the folding in the unfolding of lines.

Not fade not fade away song learned by heart.

Under
under the folding
and through
under the folding under and through the unfolding
what has been learned.

3.

Let the fever the fever in the room dissolve.

Particles
dots
space between the particles space between the dots
between back and shoulders between him

284

between head between hair

between hand between her breast

particles

dots

dot and dot barely clinging to dot and dot.

Dissolve take on luster shadows among leaves.

Water

sound

sound of water against the tiles

cotton with silk

cotton with silk cotton interwoven with silk.

4.

A poem an object a poem an emotional object.

New crystal renewed crystal

planes through planes lines as planes

logic of the planes folded in oblique directions

in combinations

unexpected

unexpected combinations

logic

folded unfolded

logic of here begins a new life.

A poem an object a poem an emotional object.

Folded in cotton with silk

shadows unfolded in cotton interwoven with silk

shadows in the crystal

interwoven

faint fragrance of musk in the crystal.


5.


The dead given flowers given against haunting.


Red roses for a blue lady

for a blue man

blue lady blue man into shadows

birds

to the sounds of birds morning conference of the birds

into shadows into silence

shadows among leaves

decay of the sounds decaying into silence

enharmonic.


Say it with flowers with roses piled to burn.


Intensity of a fire in summer

intensity in intensity

intensity of a fire in summer intensity to a paleness

pale haze

through ash walnut cherry out over the field.

6.

The dead give each other the gift of death.

Not running in slow motion in a meadow
meadow of wild flowers
not Mozart
not a picnic basket covered with a soft white cloth
wine and cheese and bread
pistol
not in slow motion
in slow motion in time with Mozart
not one shot then another.

What's given the gift of the breath withheld.

That keeps
keeps what is given up
economy of sacrifice economy of but a little light
shines a little
a little and without words on the line.

7.

To be the poet not drowning in his own tears.

Want protection
need heart uncovered
heart of words uncovered cut into and around
want held

held as a young mother nurses her child

blackened her breast blackened

want consolation

sandpaper need sandpaper

sandpaper against consolation of star dust melody.

Without a path extravagantly without a path.

Bernart of Ventadorn

great joy with his lady

left him his la lauzeta left him

Bernart became a monk Bernart died a monk

not way to go.

8.

The dead left unburied shadows left unburied.

Ashes in a ring

pale rose hue of the rose ashes pale rose and grey-blue

refinement of the ashes

cool air cool light of early one summer morning

filaments of rose ash in the air

in the light

burnished

filaments among shadows among leaves

the shadows take on luster.

Sounds of bird music the sounds into silence.

*John Taggart*

Dance of shadows dance of sleeves

nonpleurant

touch

touch and part

touch and part of shadow hands in shadow sleeves.

# Preface

## Paul Maliszewski

*Dziśiej jest moda co mówie że chłowiek mógthy stracić jego dzieciuny. Za każdy należgcy oznaka, Ja terz mószi tak warunkowy przejescié czusie. Ale Ja nie wykonać. Ja zgubił to mieście gdźie Ja żył, to jest prawdziwa Ja zgubił moi wspnienie od checha i od powietrze. Ja miał dobre wspomienie na waźne ulicy nazwiskie, i telefou numery, i to wszystko. Ja terz gubil uzasadnienie dla chego to Ja zrobił tego. I ztego, moje wspouruieneie nie majo czegoś poduiety. Moje wszystkie pytauie zachynaćo z dlaczego to jest tak. Ci to znaczy ze podnieta zgnieła? Ja pamientani to jest jakby Ja pattchał ktogo ichnego, podniety jest niepŕezroczyste.*

*Do ilústrować mjoe szczegolne strata, Ja powie dla was coś za zabawa Ja lubie grać. Ja ofiarowam, te pare miuuty jak Ja budzić sie i zprzodu, jak moje oczy ofworzye, ten chas do wywolywac wszystkie sypianlie kture byly moje. Z mojeur ochy zamkniente, Ja wyrobrażac sobie ulozenie się urządzenie, i moca od układe rzeczy, jak moja ciało lerze, i gdzie świato pada. Ja mysle od gdzic każde okuo było. Każda sypialuia zachnie być wienecej zakłócenie obrazu i nie tak dziecinne. Koloryty takie szczególnie jak różowy i niebiesky kolor, oui wszyskie zrobiuur sie za malowane, osz nic widzieć moźne. Ztej gra Ja ruszam się od jednej sypialki do iuaksha sypialka, zajmowaw każda jedua. Zyjem w każdem jedua, ale Ja nígdy przepruwadzać sie.*

—Wladyslaw Tadeusz Ginalska
185?–1917

*It has become the fashion to say an individual may lose his childhood. According to all relevant signs I too should feel this way. But I do not. I lost the places where I lived it is true. I lost my memories of the character of the air. I had a memory for important street names and phone numbers, but no more. I also lost the reasons for what I did. As such my memories now lack motive. My questions all begin with why. Has the motive been washed out? When I remember it's as if I'm watching someone else whose own motives are opaque.*

*To illustrate my peculiar losses I will tell you something of a game I like to play. I devote the few moments after I'm awake and before I open my eyes to recreating all of the bedrooms that have ever been mine. With my eyes closed I imagine the configuration of furniture, the power of arranged objects, which way my body is oriented and where the light falls. I think of where the windows were in each one. The bedrooms become more cluttered and less childish. Colors, especially your pinks and blues, get painted over, and are gone. In the game I move from bedroom to bedroom, occupying them, living in them, without moving.*

—translated from the Polish by
Luzhin Wladyslaw Ginalska
1910–1969

HOW IT CUSTOMARILY WORKED was that thirty children from the town would wait for the word, break their bottles on the ground, collect one piece of glass in a sack and then inflict one very small, very slight flesh wound on the leg of a neighbor. An elder had earlier appointed the thirty boys to bring one bottle each for the construction of the Judas effigy. This was Good Friday, Poland, some time in the early 1860s. For Wladyslaw Tadeusz Ginalska, a boy of eleven attending his first construction of the Judas effigy, the ritual did not conclude as custom dictated.

Earlier, the boys assembled their Judas from rags, straw and tattered clothing. They stuffed it with weeds, bark, grass and flower stems.[1] Here is where the event departs from the traditional ritual. According to custom, after the ritual breaking of the bottles and administering of the flesh wounds, the effigy was nearly complete. In a pocket or a cloth sack the boys secreted thirty pieces of broken glass, one from each of their bottles, representing thirty pieces of silver, the price of Judas's betrayal.[2] From there the boys dragged the effigy through the streets. Some ran behind kicking it, striking it with sticks or whipping it with a length of rope. This was not a parade, but many people watched, old and young alike. Then came the hanging, usually from the church belfry. After the hanging someone released the effigy to fall to the ground and another group of children dragged it to a river for drowning.[3]

With the breaking of his bottle, Ginalska inflicted a mortal wound on his neighbor. We can't be sure it wasn't on purpose.[4] While Ginalska's error[5] disrupted the ritual, it did not completely derail its progress. In truth the ritual continued pretty much as it would anyway, except now the boys yelled "Wladyslaw" *and* "Judas" instead of just "Judas." Too, as they ran through the streets, many were looking for Ginalska in addition to carrying on with the ritual.

---

[1]Custom dictated that no flowers be used in the construction of the Judas effigy, not even dead ones. The flowers were of Christ, it was thought, while the stems were not the province of anyone important, named or unnamed.

[2]The thirty cuts represent blood let in the crucifixion of Christ, the very physical reality of the betrayal.

[3]In *Polish Customs, Traditions, and Folklore* (Hippocrene Books, 1993), Sophie Hodorowicz Knab notes that if a river or some body of water wasn't nearby, fire always was.

[4]It would be nice to be sure it wasn't on purpose, but I can never know for certain. Hagiography has its particular weaknesses; making wrongs right is chief among them.

[5]The use of "error" represents an unhappy compromise. The panel agreed to disagree. I thought "wrong-doing" more fitting, but others wanted a paler noun yet.

Paul Maliszewski

If his pursuers found him, would not his body make a twin for Judas that Good Friday?

Before the sun rose on Easter Sunday, Ginalska was gone. When his parents said they didn't know where he went, they were telling the truth: they'd simply told him to leave, partially to save him, partially because they could think of no alternative in the face of so much shame brought on their house. In the pre-dawn darkness two boys, school friends of Ginalska in fact, began to walk through the town beating the special drum, waking everyone and urging them to attend mass.[6] Ginalska left just as they began their noisy rounds.[7]

By some accounts, after that day he never was not traveling.

By the accounting of one Luzhin Wladyslaw Ginalska, this event marks the beginning of the elder Ginalska's orating.[8] "He found that raising his voice to make a speech pleased him," writes the younger Ginalska in the mostly empty notebook that accompanies the translations of the assorted papers, letters and written leavings of the elder.[9] The younger Ginalska did translations the way some people do crossword puzzles. "Nobody is born to talk. Wladyslaw Tadeusz Ginalska is no exception. But didn't he make up for time lost once he learned?"

---

[6]Here again is Knab: "The purpose of the drum was to recall the shaking of the earth that took place during the crucifixion and when Christ rose from the dead" (p. 103).
[7]Polish customs may be usefully divided into noisy customs and quiet customs. Surveying just the month of April and the celebrations surrounding Easter, one finds the girls painting and coloring eggs, and decorating some with intricate batik designs such as *pisanki*,[a] *oklejane*[b] and *nalepianki*,[c] while the boys engage in the construction of the Judas effigy, publicly destroy the Judas effigy and circulate through the streets carrying *kletotki*[d] or *grzechotki*[e] (the wooden ancestors to those plastic party devices favored by people at New Year's Eve celebrations, particularly at two minutes until midnight) or beating the drum to wake the people on Easter Sunday. Interestingly, the spiritual rationale for the noisy and quiet customs is the same: the rituals are there to remind people to pray and to remember their great responsibilities to the church, particularly at this point in the holy year.

  [a]The word cannot be translated.
  [b]The word cannot be translated.
  [c]The word cannot be translated.
  [d]The word cannot be translated.
  [e]The word cannot be translated.

[8]Luzhin Wladyslaw Ginalska is the maternal cousin of Janina Tatur Maliszewski, the keeper of his papers and my grandmother, born in Bialystok, Poland, and now residing in Davenport, Iowa.
[9]The relationship between the translator and the author is one of the faceless to the face. There are few exceptions to this rule and even fewer in the twentieth century. This is why it's no surprise to find the notebook of the younger Ginalska mostly

Oration did have its rewards. According to Ginalska the younger, the orator in nineteenth-century Poland did not go hungry or want for shelter.[10] To expect that he lived a life of comfort and permanence, however, is folly. An orator in Poland lived an itinerant life, traveling from one town to the next according to whatever local festival or celebration might promise him an opportunity to speak for award and approbation.

To understand the tradition of the itinerant orator and, more importantly, the practice of rewarding the best orator with food and shelter, it is useful to consider the case of *puchery*, which dates back to the Middle Ages and takes place on Palm Sunday.[11] *Puchery* took place after mass. Boys of all ages came before the gathered to deliver short speeches on various subjects.[12] The winner of the competition

---

empty. Furthermore, what is present is not very revealing. Not much can be said for him except that he translated well and enjoyed it.

[10]Knab agrees. For a general discussion of the public speaking events, numerous egg rituals and others, *Polish Customs, Traditions, and Folklore*, by Sophie Hodorowicz Knab is that rare bird among introductory texts: broad enough to interest the lay reader, yet well written enough not to produce fits. For a more exhaustive treatment of much of the same material, see *The Peasant's Egg: Polish Rituals, Polish Customs, and Mapping the Popular Ideation of the Polish Easter*, by Zygmunt "Charakterystyczny" Kryzanowski, Yale University Press, 1981. It's interesting to note that while Knab has ordered a discussion of ritual on the calendar year with the names of the months lending titles to individual chapters, Kryzanowski offers a geographic perspective, concentrating not only on the variety of rituals but also on the many regional idiosyncrasies that developed, often due to a proximity to Germany or Russia. Kryzanowski can be relentlessly geographical, however, his book includes a series of amateurish illustrations of the human tongue, bisected by lines solid, dotted and dashed. Labeled with names for even the smallest sector, Kryzanowski's illustrations of the tongue are divided up more times than the former Yugoslavia in an attempt to show from what parts of the tongue Polish vowels, gutturals and diphthongs originate.

[11]*Puchery* itself cannot be easily translated. While Knab and others attribute its derivation to the Latin *puer* (boy), this seems too obvious, particularly when one considers the fantastical derivation of most Polish festivals. It is uncharacteristically flat-footed of Polish linguistics for a festival's name to develop from the people who routinely participated.

[12]I say various subjects because there is some discrepancy among the chroniclers of this particular Polish festival. Knab cites a bland list of subjects: "speeches about herring, the Lenten fast, disagreements with siblings, the wickedness of parents, the hardships of school, and the baked goods they looked forward to on Easter" (p. 97). Zdzislaw Mach, author of "Continuity and Change (and Continuity Again) in Political Ritual: Easter and May Day in Poland," an essay that appears in *Revitalizing European Rituals*, ed. Jeremy Boissevain, Routledge, London, 1992, a pan-European survey with many long stretches of tough-going prose and tendentious reasoning, makes more of the fact that the participants are costumed, often appearing as hussars, soldiers and even members of the clergy. He suggests that the speeches were typically very sharp and very localized satires. The costumes broadened the appeal of a specialized parody. Some costumes—of wolves, sheep and birds—suggested all the obvious

Paul Maliszewski

might be decided as informally as by applause or laughter. Much of
the space in the margins of Ginalska's papers contains postperfor-
mance annotations that place precisely where an audience laughed
or applauded, describes differences between the reactions of urban
and rural audiences and records what kinds of laughs a text might
elicit.[13] Yet Oskar Kolberg's monumental history of Polish folk
traditions, *LUD. Jego zwyczaje, sposób życia, mowa, podonia,
przysłowia, obrzędy, gusła, zabawy, pieśni, muzyka i tance. Tom
1–48*,[14] provides evidence of a formal balloting process as early as
1757. Kolberg places this in Krakow, of course.[15] He cites archival
materials still in the stores of the academy, including one anonymous pamphlet printed locally (and cheaply) which details proce-
dures for breaking a tie in *puchery*.[16] There is little that is informal
about Kolberg's *puchery*. There is very little in fact that sounds
remotely fun or entertaining.[17] Not only does he argue that the audience demanded the balloting be heavily policed and structured, he

---

allegorical readings. Ginalska became quite famous for subverting the tendency of the
costumes toward the simplistic and one-note; in a hastily scratched reminder he plans
to appear as a sheep dressed as a wolf: "Or perhaps even a sheep dressed as a wolf in
turn dressed as a sheep!" Knab's account doesn't completely ignore the importance of
costumes, but neither does she explain what a boy in the outfit of a soldier has to do
with herring.

[13]Laughter might not sound all that different from one country to another, but there
is little agreement among people who attempt to represent it in writing. The same is
true of a dog's bark.

[14]trans. *The People. Their Traditions, Manner of Living, Speech, Proverbs, Customs,
Witchcraft, Entertainment, Songs, Music and Dance. Volumes 1–48*, Polskie
Towarzystwo Ludoznawcze, w drukarni Universytetu Jagiellonskiego, 1871–1890.

[15]As many contemporary critics of Kolberg's undertaking point out, while his *LUD*
has no peer in its thoroughness, particularly for its time, the author can be extremely
Krakowcentric. The charges have merit insofar as there's hardly another city mentioned in the forty-eight volumes, so it does behoove the student of Polish folk traditions to keep the geographic bias in mind. His accounts do skew heavily toward the
urban. But even Kolberg's fiercest critics acknowledge that throwing out a secondary
source as extensive as his would be suicidal.

[16]Microfilm version. The forty-seven-page pamphlet is quite detailed; there's hardly an
eventuality left unaccounted for. Enumerated inside are methods for breaking two-,
three- and four-way ties, organizing a panel of impartial judges and weighting the
results for various statistical purposes. It's unclear whether this level of detail was
necessary because *puchery* matches were apt to end with two costumed boy-orators
locked in a tie or whether audiences just had no patience for that sort of outcome.

[17]Other authors represent the event as being much more worthy of occurring yearly
than Kolberg. Knab delights but finally frustrates the reader with suggestions of how
*puchery* was first accepted and then banned by the Holy Cross Church in Warsaw,
which like most bans was more symbolic than effective since people only held the
events in their houses. As to why the church banned *puchery*, Knab only reveals that
recitations of verse "took on a more wordly and amusing tone than was proper"

also suggests participants trained throughout the year. Confirmation of this may be found in the surviving papers of the younger Ginalska, the translator; there can be little doubt how rigorously the elder trained.[18]

The translator's expertly collated collection of Ginalska's "All Is Not Lost" papers and drafts arrived in the correct file folder, labeled expressly to hold those documents.[19] The paper, outrageously acidic even by the standards for European paper of the day, has stained the file folder as dark as a very serious burn and leached a gradually dulling brown through a series of folders and their contents. The paper is brittle, of course, though its effect borders on the radioactive.

Ginalska's writing rewards a vivid and willing imagination.[20] With his scant notes on a performance it is eminently possible and rewarding to picture a boy of twelve or thirteen preparing to speak. An audience waits and a boy prepares. He produces from a pocket coal from the last fire he sat before and rubs soot into his face. He dresses in a sheepskin coat, this time wearing it so the skin faces out. When the audience witnesses this they will doubt that the costume had ever

---

(p. 97). While it's unclear whether she intends "worldly" instead of "wordly," one letter "l" makes little difference in the end: to satisfy the vacuum of detail and desire, a reader would require a thousand times as many letters.

[18]Viz. the eight surviving drafts of a speech eventually titled "All Is Not Lost" and in earlier, sketchier versions, "Lost" or "I Found All Isn't Lost." It seems unlikely that other *puchery* competitors or the even less well prepared orators in the weekly matches approached Ginalska's level of radical revision.

[19]Which detail only bears mentioning to cast well-deserved doubt on stories of the genus "academic discovery" that depend on diaries in unlikely places, uncovered journals in a hat box, love letters in the freezer between steaks and hamburger, and unpublished poems in the pocket of a pair of overalls.

[20]Some of the papers I can barely make out. I understand a sentence, a word, a certain turn of phrase, but only fleetingly, in the way that when two trains pass one another I can discern only certain highlights—a man's red coat, a child's tongue pressed against the glass, two teens struggling for the last swig from a bottle, a woman sleeping on her briefcase—while everything else remains a gray and speedy blur.[a]

> [a]Some of the difficulty lies in the penmanship, which is as foreign as the language. Certain styles of handwriting develop because of the letters, words and phrases that need to be formed regularly. Since Polish comes with a couple of letters unique to its alphabet and Polish texts are peppered with the sort of fine-tuned diacritical marks that look like squiggles and little hairs on our Xerox machines, a general handwriting style developed to accommodate this. Matters aren't helped by Ginalska's spidery hand. By the shakiness of the lines he clearly preferred to write while in motion, while walking, say, or riding in the back of a cart. In this way many pages are a record of his thoughts as well as second by second recordings of the road surface. Like a seismograph, Ginalska registered each wheel rut and bump faithfully.

appeared otherwise. It's a wonder he has so few props at his disposal: a wooden sword, a rope, a bundle of field grass for a horse's tail. Like the best performers, he realizes mimesis is an illusion best left to the natural world. It's an even greater wonder that he does so much given this material. Did he recite aloud to practice or did he speak only in his head? In either case, we may conclude he moved fastest and farthest in his head. He scratches his ear with the point of his sword and lastly readies his basket for his rewards, winnings and gifts.

# Public Notice
## *Joanna Scott*

> "Louise. Do whatever you feel you should to solve
> problems. We would like to help if we can. Get in
> touch with me for anything you may need at home.
> Brother Frank."
>
> —*New York Times,* June 1, 1937

OF COURSE, LOUISE never reads a newspaper, never so much as glances at a Bergdorf ad, though not because she doesn't have the time. She has plenty of time on her hands these days. But you won't catch her wasting a minute reading yet another variation on the symbiotic themes of greed and misfortune. She's always been a mind-your-own-business kind of girl, which today means she won't see the offer from her brother Frank and won't bother to get in touch with him for anything she may need, a good thing, really, because what Louise needs most of all is a compact pistol that would fit easily into her hand, a Colt revolver, say, conveniently loaded with one bullet. Not that she'd go ahead and shoot anyone. All she wants to do is point a weapon at the vulnerable forehead of Mister Frederick Harvey the Third, manager of the Woolworth's Five and Dime on West Fourteenth Street, and he'd be sorry he's alive, since being alive means you have to die. Louise doesn't want to hear an apology from Freddie—she wants to make regret boil inside him until he's in agony, hopping and writhing. Goddamn Freddie. Louise can't lie down on her cot for an afternoon snooze without seeing him in her mind just standing there looking as smug as ever from his new Kempton Panama to his rope-soled boater shoes—

*Lou. Lou darling. Go ahead.*

Just standing there, two fingers scissored around a Dutch Master—
*Don't be shy.*

And when she thinks of him she forgets her own originating role: Louise watching Freddie watching Louise take off her chiffon dress, then her girdle, black lace bra and matching underpants in a hotel room somewhere out in Queens. She'll never find the place again, can't even remember the name, though knowing Freddie it was probably a portable unit he had installed for the day, a temporary five-story hotel put up in an hour by carnies, nothing more than cardboard and papier-mâché, with false hallways painted on the walls, magic mirrors hanging in the rooms. Well, he sure pulled one over on her, and then he disappeared without so much as a nod, leaving Louise to make her way home alone, down and out of the counterfeit hotel and through the narrow streets, where cats perching on windowsills and trashcan lids watched her with the bored but necessary attention of lazy predators.

In her room in Hell's Kitchen, Lou remembers how the shadowy cats kept startling her with their slight, sudden motions, their tail-twitches and shaking. Who knows? Maybe the cats were a sham, too, along with the hotel and the Panama hat and Frederick Harvey himself. All the scamped promises he made. Louise fell for each of them, from the postponed lunch at the Palm Garden to the raise he swore he'd give her the day of the sit-down strike. But it wasn't naivete that made her gullible, no sir, sister Louise didn't suffer from innocence. It was just the terrible hunger that made her mistake tinsel for silver, an appetite that would have been satisfied with almost anything, even three kids and a toper for a mate, but that offer never came, nothing came but a fifteen-dollar-a-week job at Woolworth's, no benefits beyond the lipstick she swiped and an occasional cup of coffee.

The famous strike followed exactly one year after her arrival at the store, and while she would just as soon have done without it, she had no choice but to participate. And wouldn't you know, the ordeal turned into a regular bean feast—for the single night of their occupation the girls guzzled free egg creams and lemonade until, at noon the next day, the city officials talked their way into the store and began brokering a resolution.

After all the fun, Louise found the dialogue boring, so she hoisted herself onto the soda-fountain counter, drank a cup of coffee and began thinking, inexplicably, about the beauty of tattoos. She argued with herself, trying to persuade her more practical side that she might benefit from a tattoo and with it might succeed in attracting the kind of man who, for every *why not?* that can't be answered, goes ahead and takes a risk. She settled upon her right buttock as a prime location and was idly considering the possibility of an indelible bird, a cockatoo, perhaps, when she heard Mr. Freddie's voice.

"Pour me a cup of coffee," he ordered, adding, "pumpkin," not out of affection but because after a full year he still didn't know her name, though they'd had plenty of brief exchanges, mostly concerning the topic of the cash register and Louise's tendency to come out a few pennies short at the end of the day. But it wasn't a tendency remarkable enough, in the boss's eyes, to distinguish her from the other Woolworth girls, and Louise had no choice but to tolerate his endearments and do what he asked.

So midway through the sit-down strike Louise found herself waiting on the boss, serving him coffee and a piece of stale cherry pie, the crust streaked with hard-baked lard. And what a remarkable transformation Mr. Freddie accomplished in those few minutes. Up until then he'd cut a ridiculous figure, all the girls thought so—he fancied himself a bantam-cock in the henhouse when in fact he was too scrawny to be of interest and too much of the dandy to be trusted. Everything about him was made up, and the girls enjoyed mocking this amateur trouper behind his back.

Louise, however, didn't laugh when she joined Mr. Freddie on a coffee break that day. Maybe it was the way he looked at her, examining her with those gray shingles of eyes, as though he were suddenly interested. Or maybe it was just the fact that she'd been thinking about something as silly as a buttock tattoo. Whatever the cause, Louise in hindsight understands that over the course of that single conversation, everything changed for her. She was no longer simply one of the girls by the time the manager walked back to the arbitrators. She had been led through the gate, seduced at first by what she took to be the authentic Freddie, a keen, brave fellow hiding behind the mask of his public self, a Freddie who soon enough revealed himself to be just more flim-flam, him with his crocodile tears and all that bosh about his hard life: the war and the German *Unterseeboot,* then the years of unemployment back home in Jersey, his fortitude in the face of poverty, etcetera. Why did she fall for him if she could see right through his clap-trap? He hadn't even finished his coffee when she began to grow suspicious. Blame the suspicion, then. She recognized his decoy for what it was and still she listened to him, nodded, touched his elbow in sympathy and at the end silently concluded that a mutual affection was likely, especially since Mr. Freddie promised to rehire her after all the other girls had been fired, and not only that, he'd make a case for her promotion to shift supervisor and for a hefty hike in her salary.

"Call it favoritism, sweetheart, but you've got it coming," he said with a wink, implying that she deserved more than the other girls, which she did when you laid out the cards. The other girls had families to support them while Lou had only bad memories and a brother who fancied himself an artist and didn't want to dirty his hands with real work. How did Mr. Freddie know about her situation? Louise must have had self-sufficiency written all over her—a whole set of tattoos that only the manager could see. Clever man. The draw by the end of their conversation was his implied knowledge of her. As she watched him walk away from the counter she became aware of a new curiosity, the kind that once in a while would take her by surprise—when she was deep inside a tedious novel, say, and the plot abruptly thickened. She didn't trust Mr. Freddie and because of this she wanted to be intimate with him, to circumvent his evasions and discover the uninvented, knowing man.

The strike was resolved that afternoon without any casualties, life went on, routine came to dominate the days again, and Louise worked the register for an extra five cents an hour, thanks to the fortitude of the sit-down girls. But within the routine the challenge of Mr. Freddie grew. He learned her name. He'd wander out from the back office to chat with Lou about the weather. He'd join her at the counter during her lunch break. He'd tell his war stories, which all seemed contradictory versions of a single story about a German U-boat sunk off the coast of Ireland. Louise would hardly listen, having long since concluded that all his testimonials were lies, or at least exaggerations. What she liked better than his puffery were those promises, those delicious representations of the future, when she would get her promotion and Mr. Freddie's investment in an outfit on Long Island would begin to pay off. The accumulation of profit seemed a much more certain thing than the adventures of his past, and Lou liked the man all the more because of his persuasive optimism. So she hung with him, as the other girls noticed, and in doing so became the store outcast, having contracted, in their opinion, the disease that was the boss. Rumor had it that Mr. Freddie was in cohorts with the surviving members of Lucky Luciano's gang, and Freddie himself boasted about having had lunch once with the former mayor and racketeering king James J. Walker. By all accounts, Mr. Freddie sought out the city's criminal VIPs—he wore his corruption like an aftershave and cozied up to any notable penitentiary veteran willing to tolerate his company.

But as Louise saw it, that was mostly idle gossip, cultivated by Freddie himself in an effort to deflect attention from his vulnerable interior. And what began for Lou as curiosity became, in part, defiance. She hung with Freddie because of and in spite of his reputation.

She was Freddie's girl, take her or leave her, though how she made the leap to the possessive she'll never know for certain. It was one of the few hypotheticals in her life that ever came true. One morning Lou looked at her mirror reflection in her room on Jane Street, and her first thought was of Freddie's smooth-as-silk hands caressing her, even though at that point she had never met the manager outside the confines of the store.

So Freddie's girl she became—in her eyes and in the eyes of her co-workers. Yet Mr. Freddie had no opinion about the matter, as she would eventually discover. There was nothing inside him but multiple illusions, no solid self capable of feeling affection. Each confected Freddie enclosed another and another and at the core was only vacancy, a place void of moods or desires and certainly without sympathetic knowledge.

The manager succeeded in fooling Louise right through most of their first night out on the town together, when Lou in her boa and heels and Freddie in his Panama were a head-turning smash. Lou enjoyed the admiration of strangers. But even more than that, she enjoyed watching Freddie in action handing out five dollar tips and ordering oysters and rib eye and champagne. Somehow, after a series of taxis and nightclubs, they ended up in a back street south of Linden Boulevard, in a Pleasure Palace hide-away, where Louise was willing to throw caution to the wind. *Throw caution to the wind.* A lovely phrase, she'd thought with a giggle as she stepped out of her dress, having already been assured by Freddie that there was nothing to fear.

*What's so funny, precious?*

Mr. Manager himself, trying to hide his own inexperience in an impresario's exterior.

*You are, Freddie.*

Louise's opinion had been influenced by innumerable glasses of champagne, and right then Freddie the Third was about as amusing as they come, standing there like a costumed mannequin, pretending to be Mr. Debonair when in fact he was an awkward dancer who didn't know the next step. What fun Lou had stripping for him, bending from one posture to another as though putting on a stereopticon show and all the while thinking that she had finally found the true Freddie—a meek little stagehand who preferred hiding in the wings.

And what a dreadful misinterpretation, she realized soon enough, for no sooner was she stark naked, her remaining stocking draped across the cracked lacquered bureau, than he lunged at her, threw her

301

on the bed and began pummelling her with his right fist while he
kept his other hand clamped expertly over her mouth to keep her
screams from being heard, though in all likelihood there was no one
in that counterfeit hotel to listen. And after the first burst of panic
she forgot to cry out, forgot that she had any voice at all, knew only
that the way to resist his ramming fist was to hurt him back. But she
kept failing—his palm was too flat to bite, his body too heavy to fling
off—until her own shrewd body came up on its own with the canni-
est weapon of all: she gagged, her mouth filled with vomit, and the
manager yanked his arm back, clapped an open hand against the side
of her head in disgust, then leaped away while she wretched and
coughed into the pillow.

Apparently, the manager hadn't intended to elicit this sudden sickness. He stood panting, staring at her, and from the corner of her eye
Lou saw him raise his arms and thought he was preparing to come at
her again. Instead, he merely straightened his tie, spit into the standing basin and disappeared, slamming the particle-board door behind
him.

Whatever had happened (and Louise will never be too sure about
the details) was over in less than a minute. But it took some time
before Lou was breathing easily again. With difficulty she dressed
herself and abandoned the room—she was halfway down the stairs
when she realized that she had forgotten her stockings and that her
dress underneath her shawl was on inside out. But she had no incli-
nation to improve her appearance, she only wanted to get into the
fresh air and collect the frenzied memory into some vaguely ordered
whole, which she tried to do as she walked up the empty street
between two warehouses.

She began her long journey back to her Jane Street apartment, an
expedition that took her through the unmarked lanes of Canarsie,
where nothing moved except Lou and the cats, to the swamplands
reeking of seaweed and mud and frying fat. It was a cool night, with
a mist shrouding the half moon, and in the gloomy light the shacks
built on pilings seemed to have hollow sockets where there should
have been windows and gaping dark mouths instead of doors. Louise
would have thought them all uninhabited if she hadn't seen a kero-
sene lamp flickering on a back porch, hung there to warn away
thieves. Lou was no better than a thief. Circumstances had turned
her into the kind of woman that most of humanity reviles, and she
couldn't blame them, couldn't in her dazed state figure out who was
to blame. The attack had been so sudden that she couldn't identify

the provocation and wasn't even sure where his fist had landed. She could find no bruises darkening on her arms and legs. Perhaps they'd show in the morning light when she was back in her own room, a cup of Nescafé steaming up into her face.

A single room with a bath and an electric burner: this was Lou's home and she wanted to be there so badly that she began to run. She crossed a gravel driveway, scrambled down and out of a drainage ditch and began fighting her way through the wet salt hay, swamp tassels bobbing and nodding at her as she passed. She lost one of her high-heeled shoes when she crossed the mucky bed of a tiderace creek. She threw the other shoe far into the swamp and kept stumbling over the soft hummocks as fast as she could toward the highway in the distance. She would wave down a driver, beg a ride into Manhattan and be home in an hour.

An occasional truck rattled along the road, and in the intervals of silence she heard her own panting and the slush of the wet hay. There were fewer shacks in this area of the meadows, and the ground was soupier here—Lou fell twice, and by the time she reached the bottom of the highway's steep embankment she was shivering and spattered head to foot with swamp mud. From her neck down she looked more like some monster from a picture show than the fancy gal she'd imagined herself to be earlier that same evening, and she clutched the corners of her shawl together to hide her body from herself.

The fact that her hopes had been spoiled was nothing new. But at nineteen Louise wasn't used to such brutal disappointment, and the thought of the eager girl she'd been just a few hours ago, before Freddie laid into her, made her sob aloud, though just for a moment. She still had enough sense to know that the most important thing— the task necessary for survival—was to make her way home. So she clambered up the slope as fast as she could, intending to hail the first car that passed.

She was about ten feet below the verge, scooting forward on hands and knees through the grass, when one hand landed on a soft, clammy, contoured something. She popped up, revulsion preceding comprehension, and in an instant she decided that she'd stumbled on a dead fish dragged up here by a cat. But the mind has a habit of concocting all sorts of stories in response to fear, and for a few extra seconds Louise couldn't look down because she wanted to believe her first impression, wanted to step over the dead fish and get on with her escape. When at last she did look down, she saw not a fish but a bulging shape that resembled nothing more than a naked human torso tucked snugly in the grass. The broad, spongy surface, mottled by shadows, had a fleshy pallor to it, in fact was flesh and belonged to the back of a half-naked woman, freshly killed, apparently, strangled or suffocated, her mop of black hair hiding the profile of her face, the top of her dress ripped from her shoulders and lying in shreds around her.

*Don't worry, Lou.*

Louise watching. Louise looking at herself. Blond Louise, the spirit in a muddy chiffon dress, looking at black-haired Louise, the woman who had died in the hotel room. Lou alive and Lou dead.

*There's nothing to fear.*

Insane perception, but temporary, thank goodness. In the next moment Louise knew herself to be alive and recognized the dead body as something other than herself. She ran from her, or it, whatever it was, and scrambled up the last part of the embankment, careened along the verge screaming, but the wind washed away her voice and the truck approaching didn't stop—fortunately for Lou, she realized in the next instant, because if she were discovered, covered with mud here on the edge of Jamaica Bay a few feet from a corpse, she'd be a quick nab for the cops, their first and only murder suspect, and she'd spend the rest of her life in the solitary confinement wing of the Tombs. That's if she'd seen a corpse at all. In her present state of mind, she couldn't tell what was real, what was part of Freddy's plot and what belonged to the deceptions of nighttime.

Lou tried to collect herself by folding her arms together, sucking her sobs into her lungs and trudging forward. She was heading away from Manhattan, she discovered at the first roadside sign, though now at least she knew where she was. Cars and trucks sped by without slowing. At Rockaway Boulevard she turned her nose toward Manhattan, walking more steadily, even automatically, along the sidewalk. Eventually she came to a bus station, where she splashed her face at the sink in the Ladies' Room and bought a ticket from a dull-eyed vendor, who didn't glance twice at her. She waited nearly an hour for the bus. She rode it as far as the Flatbush Avenue station, then took the IRT into Manhattan. Miraculously, she was back in her own bed, asleep, before sunrise.

*Lou? What are you laughing at, Lou?*

She woke late the next day, the sound of her laughter echoing from her dreams. Her first thought when she glanced at the clock and saw the time was that she'd be late for work. She even began to wash up before the embroidery of dried mud on her legs reminded her that she couldn't go to work today. After last night she could never go back to her job at the Woolworth Five and Dime. Or to any job.

She bathed in deep, bubble-bath comfort for over an hour. She wept intermittently. Later, after a bowl of canned chicken noodle soup, she lay back down on her bed, stared at the ceiling and let herself recall the night. The memories were flung at her like stones, ugly images that hit her consciousness then dropped, and the only defense she could come up with was hatred. It felt good to hate Mr. Freddie Harvey for what he'd done to her. What had he done? He'd left no significant bruises, only an odd smattering of weltlike marks across her thighs and abdomen, and Louise couldn't be sure that she hadn't exaggerated the violence. And if that were so, then the rest of the night was just as uncertain, including the thing she took to be a woman's corpse. Wasn't it possible that she'd seen something else and transformed it with her panic—the carcass of a dog that had been struck on the highway, perhaps, or maybe a plastic store mannequin that had fallen off the bed of a truck? Goddamn Freddie. She could go ahead and hate him for this confusion, if for nothing else. She could comfort herself by imagining having a similar power over him.

She listened to the radio and went to bed shortly before eight. She passed the next day, though she woke earlier, in much the same fashion. Out of this solitary existence she began to fall into a new routine for herself. A week later she left the Jane Street apartment and moved into a woman's boarding house on West Thirty Eighth Street.

Someday soon she will have to find another job. But for now she enjoys this fine, good-for-nothing life. After all, leisure is a novelty for Lou, who left school at the age of fourteen to work first as a stock girl for an import company on West Street, then as a waitress at a midtown diner and then as a clerk at Woolworth's. With so much time on her hands, she has taken to wandering through Paddy's Market underneath the Ninth Avenue elevated. At first the chaos of the place annoyed her, but gradually she has grown to like it, finding that the turmoil causes her to forget her anger for long minutes at a stretch. She enjoys taking in the scenery, imagining countless plots to explain the mysterious lives of strangers.

And Paddy's Market is where she comes on the afternoon of June first instead of going to a coffee shop to have lunch and read the newspaper, as another type of woman in a similar situation might do. Here, it dawns on her, as it has before, she has found the center of the world: luscious oranges and lemons to flavor iced tea; cages packed with terrified turkeys, chickens, pigeons and ducks; carts full of wilted parsley and Bibb lettuce and Carolina tomatoes; stout, aproned women haggling in thick accents with the merchants, men shouting over dice in a corner. For Lou, market life seems nothing less than hilarious, with each gesture part of a slapstick routine and the conversations verging on nonsense. But the funniest thing of all is that when a train passes, clanking and squealing overhead, the noise entirely drowns out the voices in the market yet everyone keeps right on talking.

# Architectures
## *Martine Bellen*

1.

Above you (at your coronation) stands the coroner.
> When you are not,
> Things are not
> As they are either,
> Ether through ears
> Rarefied radiant energy!

> What's more eternal than a falsity?

> Where the body is an appendix of the mind

2.

> (control is had
> in vast areas:
> meadows for sheep, urban centers)

Your asafetida bag,
Its rank, sacred emissions
Ring around the heart

3.

There we exchange prophecies, harmonies:

> Only they know
> Nothing is secret

*Martine Bellen*

    Being shapes
    However everlasting

Not since ancient Pindar or Maha Kashyapa
had such space been rendered

Not since Pindar

Pillars of salt, vanishing vaults


## THE KNEE

is part of the thigh of one who sits
crux of a hill or bowing grass
oiled knees, a supplicant
receiving blessing in the form of carpal articulation
or a protective coat around banes
where Spirit abides
a hemispherical route to god's
protective hollow


## THE CAT

A structure closest to light
               Alert

Each ear composed
               Of four octaves and twelve muscles

Circulate
       Ting sound

Flats and sharp
         claws

               Extensive communication

## NEI MONGGU

Hohhot, the Green City,
an autonomous region founded by Genghis Khan,
1,000 meters above the sea,
Where stands silver Buddha flanked by musical instruments
Which the wind, snow, the sandstorms,
Plentiful throughout the spring, have mastered.
Here you can travel out of sleep
Aside trains of camel with grandmother's eyes,
Eyes once worn by all Mongolians
Who presently have wandered
To more hospitable regions, such as Junshang
Island, with its 72 gentle hills,
Its paradise of brooks, flowers, wild boar and monkey,
As compared to northern terrain with grassland yurts.
Start at Hohhot, have a plate of mutton,
A camel hoof, a kabob, then follow, follow
The nomadic Mongolian road, it will deepen your life.

## THE PASSION OF MARTYRS

How time eliminates
Bone and hair

*mosaic icons*
Stigmata weeping blood

Storks fill skies
Teeth crumble. An empire

maudlin Marys

*lie. There's no image*
Moves in a world of mystery
Not nuclear composition

sun scorched cross

*she spun thread*

Addicted to building
Fortresses. Cathedrals

strung rosary beads

*of gem and glass*

Form(s)
in which pain
is expressed


## IDES/IDEAS

On the eighth day after the vernal nones,
Fires a Species or Nature
Analogous to the paradigm
Scribbled in Beethoven's sketch-books
Or the first Cupola constructed, a framing moment.

Arising out from the salts left of the body,
Extracted from its ashes, the image,
Phantom, the attribute, figure
of speech, the vespers, whisper purple-martin, whisper.


## HOUSE
## (HOME)

Houses know everything about everything.
When they are themselves, it does not matter
How people treat them.

*Houses know everything about everything when they are themselves.*

Windows especially are treated because through windows
Others know everything about everything,
How people treat themselves in houses.

*Houses which know everything about themselves are themselves a part of everything.*

Screens know little about concealment.
When they are themselves, screams
Enter or exit.

*Screens know everything about divisiveness.*

Homes know people,
know their skin, their eyes,
Themselves.

*Snails' homes are made of calcium or human nails.*

Homes which live in people. People who carry knapsacks.
Or passports to the *bodega*. People who are houses,
When they are themselves, they know everything about everything.


4.

The city walls were eyelids.
A worried prayer rug,
Honeyed saffron and crimson designed.
The white bird offered its *corozon*
To your black cat who rubbed and licked
In an attempt to ease a remarkable hole.


5.

Your reflection in a shard
Formed by ancient hands

Dust of a past desire
Traces and signatures.

# And Then There's the One
## John Barth

... ABOUT ADAM JOHNSON BAUER, retired American, who, like many of his now age (late middle) and class (middle middle), had married in the mid-twentieth-century postwar euphoria, before such concerns as runaway population growth and environmental degradation had set in, and with his then mate begat children three, all of whom survived to adulthood and, as of the time of this telling, a healthy early-middle age.

Of that thriving trio, however (this is what's on their dad's mind just now, at the above-mentioned century's end), only two married—nothing amiss there—and of those two, only one, the middle child and elder daughter, bore children: Ad's teen-age granddaughter and grandson, living currently with their mother and virtual stepfather half a continent from their grandfather and step-grandmother. In short, those five robust, well-educated, reasonably prosperous Americans—the three Baby-Boomer Bauers and their two original spouses—were bequeathing to the new millennium only a single pair of descendants: a reproductive rate of forty percent, compared to Ad's and his (first) wife's 150 percent.

Bear with this arithmetic, reader, of which there'll be yet more anon: our Adam is a newly-pensioned-off community-college teacher who, lacking both doctorate and scholarly publication, will not aggrandize himself with the title "Professor" (although that was in fact his rank at Hampton County Comm Coll and is the basis of his annuities), but who has a still-lively general curiosity, a head for figures and more time on his hands these days than he's been used to. He now discovers that that foregoing progenitive analysis, if applied to his extended family, yields a similar result. Ad himself is one of three siblings born in the Great Depression and wed (all three of them) in the 1950s. That sextet promptly bore seven children: Adam's aforementioned three, his sister's three and his younger brother's one, an overall reproductive rate of 117 percent. But those seven and their six spouses—thirteen Boomerites in all—have seen fit to generate only half a dozen offspring: a fifty-four percent attrition. Ad's Radio Shack calculator next reports that this same reproductive decline marks even more the family of his somewhat younger current wife, the former Betsy Gardner, and the children of her and her siblings' initial marriages, for the most part still issue-free.

Good news for Planet Earth, our man supposes, if the whole human race, and not just its "advanced," post-industrial nations, followed the Bauer/Gardner example: less resource depletion, less pollution of the biosphere, more room for the whales and the wombats and whatever—but that's not what's on his mind. Nor is the circumstance that his pair of only grandkids bear their father's surname, as do his nieces and nephews and their dwindling spawn, in consequence whereof the Bauer name-line, if not its DNA, must expire with Ad himself not many years hence. In that department he has no qualms either of religion (Who'll say Kaddish for me?) or of personal vanity (No Adam Bauer Junior, or III or IV? *Tant pis*). What has prompted these calculations and reflections is a remark that Granddaughter Donna blithely made last week toward the end of her annual late-August visit with Grandpa Ad and Grandma Bets: that she intends never under any circumstances to have babies ever. Had it been Grandson Mark who'd so declared, Ad might simply have smiled: what fourteen-year-old boy, with the world to conquer or at least his peers to impress, fancies himself a paterfamilias? But to hear a sunny, attractive, well-adjusted and responsible seventeen-year-old girl so unequivocally reject motherhood. . . .

And what prompted dear Donna's remark? Through nearly every one of her seventeen summers she has shuttled happily among her three sets of grandparents, spending a week or two with each: her dad's folks in San Diego, her mom's mom in Milwaukee, and her mom's dad and stepmom—Adam and Betsy—in their modest Cape May summer cottage. In the beginning she came with her parents and, later, her baby brother. From about age ten, as her parents' marriage deteriorated, she and young Mark flew out from Denver with their mother only; since about age twelve—because she and her brother get along ever less well, and her now-divorced mother has been scrambling to make both a living and a new life—she and Mark have come out unaccompanied and separately, using the airlines' minor-child escort service. All this hither-and-yonning (the complicated logistics of which remind Ad of the virtually insoluble Traveling Salesman problem in mathematics) has been financed by the several grandparents, at first because the young family was "just starting out" and couldn't afford the air fares, then because they were divorcing and couldn't, then because they were divorced and couldn't. By and large the visits have been a treat for all concerned; possibly they still are for Ad's ex-wife and the parents of his ex-son-in-law. As he and Betsy have aged, however, and young Donna has evolved from bubbly pre-teen through high-spirited early-teen to supercool and therefore bored latter-teen, the interludes have become, though outwardly no less cheery, more strainful all around. The girl would so obviously rather be patrolling the Denver shopping malls with her false-fingernailed and triple-ear-ringed contemporaries than beaching out in funky South Jersey with the old folks, their swimsuited high-mileage bodies no doubt repellent to her. Ad and Bets in turn, after the first get-reacquainted day or two, find it annually more wearing to set aside their usual preoccupations for most of a fortnight and "relate" almost without respite (as everyday parents and children never do) across the two-generation gap. They foresee already that the problem will be even more acute with young Mark as his testosterone kicks in and the teen-age American mall-and-media culture claims him. All hands still officially, indeed actually, love one another, but they would unanimously now prefer more frequent, less extended and less exclusive interactions—such as were the rule back when a family's generations lived closer together—to these protracted annual one-on-ones. Distance, airfare and available calendar time, however, rule out more than a single visit each way per annum, and so. . . .

Homeward bound from the Atlantic City airport, whereto they delivered the girl at visit's end for her commuter flight to Philadelphia and thence on to Milwaukee via Chicago, "It was the way she said it," Betsy reflected, and Ad agreed: "So unhesitating. So *definite.*" They agree too that despite their reciprocal affection, the youngster must have been prevailingly as glazed over by the visit as were they, as surfeited with bridging the age gap, as ready to get back to her more usual and congenial pleasures once she was done with the *next* grandparent. They'll be saddened but not at all surprised, they concur—in truth, somewhat relieved—if next August Donna finds some diplomatic reason not to make the grandparental circuit, or else abbreviates her Cape May stay (but would they underwrite such teen-age jet-setting?) to a long weekend.

"Kids grow up," Ad says, and sighs—not simply at that fact of life.

314

The question before us, however, is what prompted young Donna's declaration of nonreproductive intent. On the final evening of her visit, as the trio lingered over dessert on the cottage's duneside deck (all hands guiltily light-hearted that they'll not be crossing paths again till Christmastime in Denver), their granddaughter asked, apropos of something or other, whether Betsy's parents had brothers and sisters; she couldn't recall ever hearing Grandma Bets mention aunts and uncles. Unlike young Mark, whose curiosity seems seldom to range beyond skateboard stunts and video games, Donna takes a more or less genuine interest in other people's lives and interconnections, as evidenced by her remembering details of them from visit to visit better than Ad himself does. It must be, therefore, that for some step-grandmotherly reason Betsy hadn't spoken of her parents' several siblings, at least not in recent Donna-visits; perhaps she felt that a nonlineal descendant wouldn't really be interested. In any case, as she duly supplied the basic info on her aunts Jan, Milly and Eunice and her uncles Fred, Howard and George, it occurred to Ad to fetch from the house the Gardner Family Tree, which that same (maiden-) Aunt Jan Gardner—mentally intact but physically infirm and confined these days to an extended-care facility in Delaware—happened to have drawn up earlier that same season and distributed through the clan.

"Oh, she's not interested in *that*," Bets protested when he brought the chart out. But Donna brightly counterprotested that she was, too, interested—and not impossibly she was, although her social skills are well enough developed, unlike her brother's, to bring off a polite show of interest even if she felt none. Ad therefore reviewed with her the diagram of his wife's descent from two generations of New Jersey Gardners, themselves descended from a nineteenth-century immigrant Liverpooler whose own ancestry was unknown to Aunt Jan and company. Leaving who knows what or whom behind him, young Lewis Gardner in 1884 had crossed from Southampton to Boston, there to marry one Martha Ewell Stone and sire seven children, of whom five survived and one moved to Trenton, New Jersey, to sire Betsy's dad and his several sibs. Her genealogical lesson done, Donna left off twiddling the topmost of her left-lobe earrings, stretched her carefully tanned arms fetchingly over her head and said, "One thing I know for sure: no kids for me."

Surprised—and in Ad's case, dismayed—her grandparents scoffed, questioned, teased: a healthy, intelligent, popular, good-looking and good-humored girl like her uninterested in marriage and motherhood? "Not that those two always have to go together," Bets reminded all hands.

"Oh, I'll probably get married once or twice," Donna cheerily allowed. "But babies? Forget it."

Ad might have pressed further for her reasons, but his wife at this point observed that she herself at Donna's age had felt paradoxically vice-versa: uninterested in marriage, but eager to have children, if only to counterexemplify her own parents' botched job, as she saw it. Donna picked up on that subject, perhaps to deflect attention from herself, and their table-talk presently shifted to other things.

As he later kissed the girl's forehead good night, "You'll have children," Ad murmured. "Jim-dandy ones, too."

His granddaughter chuckled in his hug. "Don't hold your breath, Grandpa."

Well, he hasn't held his breath. But while his respiration has proceeded at its average unconscious rate—one inhale/exhale cycle every five or so seconds, Ad once calculated, or two-dozen dozen such cycles per day, or a couple thousand over the week since Donna's visit and the Bauers' return to "normalcy," or nearly seven million since his first, sixty-five years ago (which comes, he reckoned by the way, to only one point one breaths for each Jew murdered in the Holocaust)—he has found he can't get the girl's upbeat negativity in this matter off his mind. To have pressed her further next morning for explanation would have been tactless, and while Bets's position is that grandparents have a time-honored right to such tactlessness, Ad found himself reluctant to pry. Could be the fallout from Donna's parents' messy divorce, he and Bets agree, not to mention her grandparents' divorces; could be the geographical scattering of her extended family; could be the seize-the-day media culture of end-of-the-century Americans—narcissistic and ahistorical, changing addresses every four or five years and rarely dwelling where their parents dwelt, let alone their grandparents. Could be all of the above plus the increasing parity of the sexes, Bets reminds him, and the growing reluctance of many young women to hamper their career-moves with maternity.

"In short," his wife intones, mock-seriously, "it's your effing decline of your effing Family Values."

And in fact, Ad has just about decided, it effing *is*. He himself lived from birth through high school in the white clapboard house in the smallish Pennsylvania town where his parents spent their entire life and his paternal grandparents their American adulthood, the two families literal next-door neighbors. Before Helmut Bauer's emigration from rural Germany, his stock had doubtless peasanted the same neck of the Sachsen woods from time out of mind—so Ad must infer from the family surname, inasmuch as his immigrant grandpa's actual ancestry, like Betsy's Great-Grandpa Lewis Gardner's, is off their respective genealogical charts. That's how it was back then with the mass of ordinary folk, Ad reckons—small farmers, tradespeople, shopkeepers—until America siphoned off the burgeoning European population. Ad's mother (née Margaret Johnson) had faithfully tended the respective families' grave-plots in the county cemetery, where the American generations of Bauers and assorted Johnsons were laid to rest: the men and their spouses; the women who died unmarried, still bearing the family name, or, wed and widowed, came home to finish out their lives; the bachelor casualties of two world wars; the stillborn or otherwise nonsurviving children. But neither Ad nor his siblings, all of whom "went off to college" and seldom thereafter returned to their hometown except for family gatherings, took much interest in those gravesites, especially after the older generation died off. Ad almost never bothers to "pay his respects" to his predecessors, as people do in most other cultures and some perhaps still in ours (he is invariably surprised, passing a cemetery, to see a considerable number of beflowered graves). A nonbeliever, he has no plans to join those buried Bauers either physically or spiritually upon his own demise. About the disposition of his remains he is shrug-shouldered; has agreed with Betsy, who shares his attitude, that their dead bodies would best be incinerated and recycled into their sideyard compost pile for the eventual benefit of their roses, lilies, chrysanthemums (the former Miss Gardner is in fact a semi-ardent gardener). Never mind tending *their* graves; they'll be quite satisfied if their house's next owners keep up the landscaping—and those next owners, they take for granted, will not be Ad's or Bets's children or any other member of his or her family. Although their main house and beach cottage are a major part of the estate generously apportioned to their several offspring in their wills, they assume that those heirs will sell both properties and split the proceeds. What American adult lives in his/her parents' house nowadays, as was proverbially the ideal case in days of yore ("A house built by your father," one such proverb recommends, "a vineyard planted by your grand-father")? Who any longer cares a fart about *continuity?* He and Bets less than their parents, their children less than they, their grand-children no doubt less yet.

*Continuity,* yes—whereof one aspect, on the family level, is ge-nealogy. Once upon a time, so Ad's impression goes, there would be one member of the extended clan—some Aunt Jan Gardner or fussy Uncle Bud Bauer—who recorded births, marriages and deaths on the flyleaves of the family bible or copied out the family tree for all hands' edification. In his own generation, Ad's younger brother Carl, lately a widower, halfheartedly updated somewhile back their Uncle Bud's *Bauernbaum,* as Ad dubbed it, and distributed copies for amendment and embellishment "if anybody's interested"; for two years now Ad's copy has rested—in peace, he trusts—in his study files, scarcely perused and never annotated despite Carl's mild hope that Ad might see fit to "put it on the computer," what-ever *that* might mean. A semi-retired Philadelphia realtor, Carl Bauer assumes that his professorial brother "knows all about" com-puters, but while in fact Ad and Bets use a desktop PC for family bookkeeping, correspondence and occasional Internet expeditions, they are neither experts nor enthusiasts in that realm.

Half a thousand mortal respirations since this story's last space-break, however, and back in their "real" house after Labor Day, our man now finds himself inspired by his granddaughter's remark, not to File and Forget the Gardner Family Tree along with the *Bauern-baum,* but instead to retrieve from his files Carl's annotated dia-gram, lay the two side by side on his big old glass-topped work desk and re-review them—more accurately, to examine them really closely for the first time. To his mild surprise, he finds himself genuinely interested, and curious. He still agrees with whoever it was who opined that "to have ancestors more distinguished than oneself is surely the least of virtues"; what appeals to him is that all these Freds and Mildreds and Ulriches and Miriams were *not,* evidently, distinguished: just ordinary women and men like Bets and himself, being born, surviving childhood or not, marrying or not, engendering offspring or not, and soon or late dying. Then there are the mysteries, the unanswered questions: not just the vast though banal one of Lewis Gardner's and Helmut Bauer's Old Country progenitors back to whenever, but such smaller, more intriguing ones as what exactly they put behind them (at ages twenty-two and sixteen, respectively) and why exactly they set out—alone, it would appear, or perhaps with a hometown buddy or two—to try their fortunes in the New World. Ad's lively, bumptious Aunt Annabelle (his father's elder sister and everybody's favorite aunt) married Uncle Alfred Murray in 1925, so Carl's diagram indicates; but her only child is listed as having been born in 1923, and his name was Herbert Stolz, not Herbert Murray or Herbert Bauer. An unrecorded first marriage? A never-spoken-of illegitimacy? There's a story there, Ad bets, and another in Betsy's Great-Uncle Frederick Gardner's dates: *b. 1902 (Camden, NJ)–d. 1937? (Alaska?)*. What about that aforementioned fussy Uncle Herman "Bud" Bauer's evidently short-lived adventure into exogamy (*b. 1898; m. 1920 Carlotta Petrucci; divorced 1922*)? No children, no subsequent remarriage for Uncle Bud; did he carry to his grave a torch for his perhaps passionate-but-faithless Italiana? Or, having burned his fastidious fingers in her flame, was he simply (or complexly) relieved to be the family's celibate necrologist through his remaining fifty-three years (*d. 1975*)?

Ad bets—even *Bets* bets, when he shares with her some of these musings—that their granddaughter would have pricked up her multiply ringed ears at these familial mysteries, these closeted stories, if he had noticed them himself in time to point them out to her that evening in Cape May. He can even imagine her poring over the two family trees in search of more such tantalizers, perhaps making a high-school project out of pressing her surviving forebears for details. Was La Petrucci Philadelphia-Italian or Italy-Italian? What led young Frederick Gardner to the wilds of Alaska in the Great Depression, and why aren't we certain when and whether he perished there? Could he just possibly still be alive somewhere, a nonagenarian who burned his family bridges behind him in the New Jersey thirties as his father Lewis had (perhaps) done in the Liverpudlian 1880s?

Et cetera. "So fax the things out to Denver," Bets recommends. "Draw circles around some of those possible skeletons in the family closet and add a few leading questions in case Donna doesn't see the fingerbones in the doorjamb. If she doesn't take the bait, maybe her mother will." But keep it to the Bauer side, she advises as an afterthought: "They-all couldn't care less about *my* family."

Not so, Ad loyally objects, suspecting however that it *is* so among the offspring of his first marriage (with the just-possible exception of their granddaughter), as for that matter it is with Bets herself. One thing for sure: Grandson Mark wouldn't give the thing a second look unless it came equipped with joystick and audio-visual special effects.

Once he hears himself put the matter like that, it occurs to A. J. Bauer that some sort of computerized version of the family trees might be just the thing to interest his grandkids—even Mark—in their genetic history. He puts "computerized" in mental quotes, because what he has in mind . . . Well, he's not sure quite *what* he has in mind until some mornings later, when, in the course of transferring at last Carl's *Bauernbaum* to his PC (in mere outline format, as Ad's uncertain how to duplicate onscreen the branching lines of a genealogical tree), he comes to realize that while the outline version, with its hierarchical indentations and categories of enumeration (I, II; A, B; 1, 2; a, b; etc.), lacks the graphic appeal of descending "branches," it has the merit of a sort of hypertextuality: its program permits the user to display at will only the roman-numeraled, first-generation ancestors and their spouses, for example, without their progeny (*I. HELMUT AARON BAUER, m. Rosa Pohl Fleischer 1883; II. LEWIS JAMES GARDNER, m. Martha Ewell Stone 1886*), or them and their offspring (IA-G, IIA-F) without *their* offspring (IA1, etc.). The ideal computerized genealogical chart, he supposes, would be a bare-bones direct line of descent, whether patrilineal or matrilineal—a menu-option could instantly reverse those invidiously uppercase males and their lowercase mates and trace one's descent through one's mother's mother's mother—hypertexted so that a click of the mouse on IC (Aunt *Annabelle Bauer*), say, would display her essential biographical info, including *m. Alfred H. Murray 1925,* and a click on that same Uncle Alf would display *his* genealogy, et cetera: just the sort of "interactivity" that might appeal to Donna and Mark. The more so if each such name-click displayed a mug shot of the selected ancestor, perhaps together with a map showing Liverpool, Boston, Saxony, wherever, and/or views of Ellis Island, the Statue of Liberty, the huddled masses yearning to be free. . . . Ad knows nothing about computer programming and software design, and the Bauer PC antedates CD-ROMS; he bets, though, that if he did and it didn't, he could devise in his retirement a marketable do-it-yourself hypertexted genealogy program that the members of an extended family could amplify to their hearts' content with whatever they knew or discovered about their ancestors and other relatives—

biographical data ("Uncle Alf sold De Soto automobiles in Green Bay, Wisconsin, after World War II"), wedding videos, voice-over anecdotes and new-baby cries, whatever—such that any particular family member could download and browse it at his/her will, following whatever linkages happened to appeal to his/her curiosity . . . et cetera.

"It might or might not interest Mark," Bets responds when Ad describes over lunch this hypothetical high-tech *Bauernbaum*, "but his grandpa is obviously hooked. Want to run it by Harold and see what he has to say?" She's half teasing: her thirty-six-year-old son by her short-lived first marriage is a maverick "networking consultant" out in Silicon Valley with whom Ad has never quite hit it off and who seldom communicates with his mother these days.

"I might just do that." Ad is far from certain what a networking consultant even is, but the whole idea of this open-ended, interactive, hypertextual genealogy program, he reminds his wife, is to bring family members a bit closer together in a shared, ongoing project. "It's a network in itself," he adds, the idea having just occured to him: "Family members all around the country could e-mail their additions and corrections to the whole Family Net. In fact," for now *this* occurs to him, "it's a network in another sense, too: all those family branches branching off into other families. Maybe Harold *would* be interested."

"You're hooked," his wife declares, "and I've got a tennis date. Keep me posted?"

Hooked he is. Back at his workstation that afternoon, Ad imagines clicking on *Rosa Pohl Fleischer*, say (old Helmut's bride), to call up *her* parents and siblings, their names and dates and capsule biographies. He bets he'd see then, among other things, where she got her middle name, and how many male Fleischers had been the butchers that their name implies, as the Bauers must have been farmers. Click next on any one of those several siblings, or on their spouses, and you're in a whole other exfoliated family tree.

That image intrigues him: the browser swinging from tree to family tree wherever their branches touch, like a monkey in the rain forest; like . . . our earliest, pre-human ancestors. Horizontally, so to speak, on the level of any given generation, if one could track the spouses of all of one's siblings, the spouses of all of *their* siblings and of theirs and theirs et cetera, how many families would be thus interconnected? A hundred? A thousand? A hundred thousand? On a corkboard beside the workstation, he has pinned side by side Carl's version of the *Bauernbaum* and Aunt Jan's of the Gardner Tree: twin deltas widening down from Helmut (*m. Rosa*) Bauer and Lewis (*m. Martha*) Gardner, respectively, to the latest generation of their descendants. By switching the positions of these charts and diddling their diagrams just a bit, he finds he can bring their lower corners together at the point where his marriage to Betsy conjoins the family trees. The like applies, potentially, to any of the many marriages there recorded—as would be displayable by a simple mouse-click in Ad's theoretical software program. Can it be imagined, he now wonders, that given enough hypothetical mouse-clicks . . . ?

Although we have established that A. J. Bauer is a retired academic, his erstwhile professional field—vaguely denominated "the humanities"—has not heretofore been mentioned. Sufficient to say that he is acquainted enough with the history of western thought and literature to have "professed" selected specimens therefrom on the community-college level, and that as a generalist rather than a specialist, he not only subscribes to but actually reads, especially in his retirement, both *The New York Review of Books* and *Scientific American*, cover to cover. He is therefore (or anyhow) acquainted with the Egyptian, Greek and Hebrew creation-stories, for example, and likewise with the "Eve hypothesis" advanced by some paleontologists: that the DNA of all humans presently inhabiting the planet indicates descent from a single African foremother, presumably not long down from the trees and coupling in the veldt with her male counterpart. Contemplating either of those two pyramidal diagrams on his corkboard, he is now moved to imagine at its peak not Helmut and Rosa Bauer or Lewis and Martha Gardner but the biblical Adam and Eve, or that emergent African Eve and her consort, and to envision a computerized genealogical program so powerful and info-rich that enough clicks of the mouse would lead back even past them, to (depending on the user's "belief system") either the One God who created the two humans who engendered all succeeding ones, or the first single-celled earthly life-form that over the eons evolved into multicellular animals, thence into vertebrates, mammals, primates, hominids, the first *Homo sapiens sapiens*, et cetera. At the pyramid's tip, the aboriginal spark of life; at its base, every human being, if not every thing, currently alive on earth, their interrelationships and line of descent literally at the inquirer's fingertips.

Among the several courses that "Professor" Bauer (the self-deprecating quotes are his) once taught at HamCoComCol was one called The Bible as Literature, in which—he had to tread carefully here among the largely unsophisticated first-generation college-goers, many living at home with their unaffluent but stoutly opinioned parents—the familiar "stories" of Genesis (one did not call them myths) were respectfully compared to their analogues in other cultures. Predictably, when it was pointed out that Adam and Eve had three children (infamous Cain, doomed Abel and much-later-born Seth), the first and third of whom are said to have sired all subsequent earthlings, someone would reasonably ask "Where'd they get their women?" A discussion would ensue—raucous, indignant, fascinated, depending on the classroom mix—of the problem of sibling incest in any creation-story wherein a primordial One creates an original Couple who in turn beget the rest of humankind. If Eve, made from Adam's rib, was "bone of his bone, flesh of his flesh," was she not, genetically speaking, his sister? And if somehow not, would not she and Adam's daughters (unmentioned by the patriarchal Hebrew scribes, but necessary to postulate if Cain and Seth are to have mates other than their mother) have been their husbands' sisters? For that matter (some sharp-eyed sophomore would here point out), why does guilty Cain, "marked" by God for the murder of his brother Abel, complain that whoever sees that mark will kill him, when according to the scorecard—Abel dead, Seth not yet born—there *is* no one on earth besides himself and his parents? Professor Bauer would here mention, e.g., the Islamic tradition that each of those original brothers had a twin sister; that Father Adam, no doubt to attenuate the consanguinity, proposed that each son marry the other's twin rather than his own; and that Cain (Qabil in the Arabic version), desirous of his beautiful sister Labuda, murdered Abel/Habil out of simple sexual rivalry. Did he then take both sisters for himself? Or did one of them subsequently become young Seth's wife, despite her having been old enough even at her kid brother's birth to be his mother? Or perhaps Seth's wife was one of his brother Cain's daughters (i.e., Seth's niece) by one of the brothers' sisters?

Et cetera. Reminded of these perennial classroom discussions by his new genealogical pyramid, our Adam now considers the rate of that pyramid's broadening in the light of what began this story: his own family's declining rate of reproduction and his granddaughter's Declaration (it now occurs to him to call it) of Nondependents. One

God, says Genesis—with or without the collaboration of the *Sheki-nah*, the Female Principle of the Kabbalists—created two humans: "male and female He created them," and they in turn engendered . . . shall we say five (Cain, Abel, Seth and a couple of nameless daughters?), of whom at least one, Abel, perished without issue. A net doubling of population, then, in each generation thus far. Ad's *World Almanac* informs him that while the base of that human pyramid is expected to number more than six billion souls by the year 2000, from preclassical times until the end of the European Middle Ages the world's human population is estimated to have held at a modest and fairly stable two hundred million. Setting aside such freaky imponderables as the longevity of the Patriarchs and the catastrophe of the Flood, and allowing three generations per century, how many such generational doublings would it have taken to attain that "classical" two hundred million?

Not very many: a minute's button-punching on the calculator demonstrates that in only twenty-seven iterations the series 1, 2, 4, 8, 16, 32 . . . $n$ reaches 134,217,728; the twenty-eighth puts it well over the top (268,435,456). Allowing that philoprogenitiveness in some individuals would be offset by infertility, celibacy, homosexuality or early death in others, in less than one millennium (933.3 years, to be precise, at 33.3 years per generation beginning with Adam and Eve) God's human children could theoretically have exceeded the number estimated by demographers to have actually peopled the planet—all of them cousins at one remove or another.

"Both Lamech and Methuselah lived longer than that," Ad points out to his wife. "Imagine a family get-together of two hundred million."

Betsy shakes her head, not simply at that image.

"The birthdays," her husband marvels. "The holiday-card list."

"The airport logistics," his wife adds, for whom her stepfamily's one-visiting-grandchild-at-a-time policy is a minor headache. The couple agree that it is sobering to reflect how different the evolutionary facts must be from Ad's simple arithmetic: the hundreds of thousands of years it will have taken African Eve's descendants to expand the ecological niche of Homo sapiens, against all odds, to the two-hundred-million sustainable maximum before . . . what? Before certain advances in technology and agriculture, Ad surmises, blew the lid off around the time of the Renaissance, and the Europeans' discovery of the New World afforded them a whole new spawning-ground. It is heartening to be reminded, they agree further, that we humans are literally, if not all brothers, at least all blood kin. But she has another tennis date, has Betsy, or intends to arrange one if she hasn't, with a threesome from that much-extended family; she'll leave Adam Johnson Bauer to his musings and reckonings—not before remarking, however, that both she and, in her opinion, Granddaughter Donna would likely be more interested in the specifics of their grandmothers' grandmothers' lives than in whether the biblical Seth shacked up with his niece, his aunt or his sister. See you later, Calculator.

Yes, well. Such all-but-idle speculations are not the only thing that AJB does with his time, but in truth he has less to busy his mind with than formerly, and so when next he returns his attention to what he now calls Donna's Diagram, he draws a new equilateral delta with the apex labeled GOD and the base labeled 200,000,000 HUMAN DESCENDANTS. Having pinned one upper corner of it to his corkboard above the Bauer/Gardner family trees, he accidentally lets the sheet slip while fetching a second pushpin; the resultant near-inversion of that delta (perhaps together with its dangling now over the *Bauernbaum*) inspires him to a new idea and, anon, a new diagram. At the base of those original charts are DONNA and MARK Putnam (their estranged father's surname), along with the sundry cousins of their generation. Each of those youngsters, it goes without saying, has or anyhow had two biological parents, each of whom ditto, etc. etc. Reversing his previous calculations, Ad imagines and presently draws an inverted delta with DONNA BAUER PUTNAM at its bottom point, her pair of parents at the next level up, her four (biological) grandparents on the level above that, then her eight great-grandparents (most of whom, on the Putnam side, are already unnameable by Adam), her sixteen great-great-grandparents, etc.—until, in only those same two-dozen-plus generations, the girl's direct ancestors equal in number the estimated then population of the earth.

With some excitement, "What am I leaving out?" he asks his wife, who has attended this latest exposition politely but can be of no assistance therewith. "We're not talking aunts and uncles and in-laws and step-parents here, just biological parents and grandparents. There's no getting around the arithmetic, 'cause it takes two to tango, and two hundred million is two hundred million. But the results are impossible."

More obligingly than eagerly, "Run it by me again?"

He does. Twenty-eight doublings of the number one make two-hundred-plus million, Q.E.D. Counting forward from Adam and Eve is obviously an iffy business, since not every couple has four surviving children each of whom in turn et cetera, and so it might very reasonably take hundreds of thousands of years instead of nine hundred thirty-three to get from African Eve and her mate to earth's estimated human population as afore-established. Indeed, the fact that the world's population apparently held steady at that "classical" level for at least a couple of millennia instead of doubling every thirty-three years is proof of the constraints in that direction. But counting *back* is another story: each one of us necessarily had a mother and father, each of whom et cetera—which seems to mean that around the time of the Norman Conquest every person on the face of planet earth must have been the direct ancestor of everybody presently aboard.

"It was our Great-Plus-Grandfather William of Normandy who whupped our Great-Plus-Grandfather Harold at the Battle of Hastings," awed Adam declares. "It was Great-Plus-Grandma Murasaki who wrote *The Tale of Genji* while Great-Plus-Grandpa Leif Eriksson discovered Vineland. Everybody who fought and died on both sides in the First Crusade was our great-plus-grandparent!"

"Wait a minute." As if to make sure, Bets consults her watch. "Saint Thomas Aquinas didn't have any kids, so there's one down. Some nuns and popes back then didn't have any, either, if I remember correctly."

He knows, he knows, repeats Ad: there has to be something screwy about his reasoning. For example (it occurs to him even as he speaks), it would appear that our two hundred million great-plus-grandparents in 1066 would have to have had *four* hundred million parents of their own in 1033, when we've already established that for generation after generation there were only two hundred million available candidates for parenthood. So it has to follow (he's thinking fast) that Donna's great-great-grandparents, while indisputably sixteen in number, needn't have been sixteen different people; otherwise we would all be descended from Genghis Khan and Ghazālī and the Eskimos, as well as from William the Conqueror and Harold the Conquered. . . .

"Ghazālī?"

Eleventh-century Father of Sufi mysticism, if not of the Bauers and the Gardners.

His wife pats his arm. "Well, you work on it, honey."

But her husband doesn't (the simple flaw in his geometric reasoning, he soon recognizes, is that while every child must have two parents, not every two need have four, etc.). He's no big-time original thinker, Adam Johnson Bauer, much less any kind of genius: just a middling old-fart ex-academic with a temporary bee in his bonnet from wanting to explain to his granddaughter, perhaps likewise to himself, that we presently breathing humans are not *de novo*, however much she and her fellow Denver mallsters might blithely feel themselves to be; that she and himself and all of us are indivisibly part of the ever-renewing tissue of life on earth, descended *directly*, through our parents and grandparents, from the primordial blue-green algae, and related to every other living thing.

No: not *explain*. What's to be explained? At age seventeen the girl's convinced that although she "might get married once or twice" (!), she wants no children. Most likely she'll change her mind; quite possibly she won't, given the way young women are nowadays. So bloody what? Retired, he sits in his familiar, once-so-piled-up study and futzes with his charts and calculator while his wife plays tennis with her friends and the world grinds on: atrocious massacres and counter-massacres in central Africa; sour standoffs in the Balkans and the Middle East; whole species disappearing from the ever-dwindling rainforests before they're even classified; more misery and injustice everywhere than one can catalogue, much less address, and the sky evidently ever on the verge of falling. Not much Ad Bauer can do about all that, beyond acknowledging and bearing in mind the enormous fact of it. He has long since made essential peace with his privileged position: a fortunate life in a fortunate country at a fortunate time. He and Bets vote moderate-liberal, contribute to assorted charitable and cultural causes, and endeavor to lead harmless lives; they eat meat and dairy products only sparingly, limit their intake of table wine, compost their leaves and recycle their trash, try to be good neighbors and to maintain a civil, tolerant attitude toward people with customs and opinions different from their own. Soon enough nevertheless, he knows, catastrophe is bound to befall them in one form or another: cancer, hurricane, fatal accident, crippling stroke. Meanwhile . . .

So one of his children had children and two did not: so what? So all had parents and proliferating foreparents: so bloody bloody what? Just now he feels bearing down upon him, does Adam Johnson Bauer, the weight of that massive inverted pyramid—of which he and his beloved Betsy and each of all the rest of us is individually the vertex—as if it were an enormous hydraulic press, and dear sunny, clueless Granddaughter Donna its all too human diamond point.

Forget it, reader.

Brother! Sister! Daughter! Son!

Forget it.

# The Sons of Angus MacElster
## *Joyce Carol Oates*

*A TRUE TALE of Cape Breton Island, Nova Scotia, 1923.*

This insult not to be borne. Not by the MacElster sons who were so proud. From New Glasgow to Port Hawkesbury to Glace Bay at the wind-buffeted easternmost tip of Cape Breton Island, where the accursed family lived, it was spoken of. All who knew of the scandal laughed, marveled, shook their heads over it. The MacElsters!—that wild crew! Six strapping sons and but a single daughter no man dared approach for fear of old Angus and his sons, heavy drinkers, tavern brawlers, what can you expect? Yet what old Angus MacElster did, and to his own wife, you'd scarcely believe: he'd been gone for three months on a coal-bearing merchant ship out of Halifax, returning home to Glace Bay on a wet-dripping April midday, his handsome ruin of a face wind-burnt and ruddy with drink, driving with two other merchant seamen who lived in the Bay area, old friends of his, and at the tall weatherworn woodframe house on Mull Street over-looking the harbor he dropped his soiled gear, freshened up and spent a brief half-hour in the company of Mrs. MacElster, and the nervous daughter Katy now twenty years old and still living at home, Angus stood before the icebox devouring cold meatloaf with his fingers, breaking off morsels with his stubby gnarled fingers and washing down his lunch in haste with ale he'd brought with him in several clinking bottles in the pockets of his sheepskin jacket, then it was off to the Mare's Neck as usual, and drinking with his old compan-ions, how like old times it was, and never any improvement in the man's treatment of his wife. Returned to Glace Bay for three weeks before he'd ship out again and already there was a hint of trouble, it was Katy put the call to Rob, the eldest son, and Rob drove over at once from Sydney in an automobile borrowed from his employer at the pulp mill under the pretext of a family emergency, and Cal in his delivery van drove over from Briton Cove, and there was Alistair hurrying from New Skye, and John Rory and John Allan and I, the youngest, live here in Glace Bay where we'd been born, freely we admit we'd been drinking too, you must drink to prepare yourself for the hurtful old man we loved with a fierce hateful love, the heated love of boys for their father, even a father who has long betrayed them with his absence, and the willful withholding of his love, yet we longed like craven dogs to receive his father's blessing, any careless touch of his gnarly hand, we longed to receive his rough wet despairing kisses on the lips of the kind he'd given us long ago when we were boys, before the age of ten, so the very memory of such kisses is uncertain to us, ever shifting and capricious as the fog in the harbor every morning of our waking lives. *Even at that late hour, our hearts might yet have been won.*

Except: unknown to us at the time our mother had gone in reckless despair to the Mare's Neck to seek our father, and the two quarreled in the street where idlers gathered to gawk, at the foot of New Harbor Street in a chill glistening wind, and we would be told that he'd raised a hand to her and she'd cried *Disgusting! How can you!—disgusting! God curse you!* tears shining on her cheeks, and her hair the color of tarnished silver loosened in the wind, and she'd pushed at the old man which you must never do, you must never touch the old man for it is like bringing a lighted match to straw, you can witness the wild blue flame leaping up his body, leaping in his eyes, his eyes bulging like a horse's and red-veined with drink, the flame in his graying red hair the color of fading sumac in autumn, and in a rage he seizes the collar of her old cardigan sweater she'd knitted years ago, seizes it and tears it, and as idlers from the several pubs of New Harbor Street stare in astonishment he tears her dress open, cursing her, *Cow! Sodden cow! Look at you, ugly sodden cow!* ripping her clothes from her, exposing our cringing mother in the halterlike white cotton brassiere she must wear to contain her enormous breasts, milk-pale flaccid breasts hanging nearly to her waist she tries to hide with her arms, our mother publicly shamed pleading with our father *Angus, no! Stop! I beg you, God help you—no!* Yet in his drunken rage Angus MacElster strips his wife of thirty-six years near-naked, as the poor woman shrieks and sobs at the foot of New Harbor Street, and a loose crowd of beyond twenty men has gathered to watch, some of them grinning and laughing but most of them plainly shocked, even the drunks are shocked by a man so publicly humiliating his wife, and his wife a stout middle-aged woman with graying hair, until at last Angus MacElster is persuaded to leave his wife alone, to back off and leave the poor hysterically weeping woman alone, one or two of the men wrap her in their jackets, hide her nakedness, even as old Angus turns aside with a

wave of his hand in disgust and stumbles off to Mull Street three
blocks away yet not to the tall weatherworn woodframe house, but
instead to the old barn at the rear, muttering and cursing and laughing to himself Angus sinks insensible into the straw, like a horse in
its stall in a luxuriance of sleep where, when we were small boys,
he'd spent many a night even in winter, returning late to the house
and not caring to blunder into our mother's domain not out of fear of
her wrath nor even of his own wrath turned against her but simply
because he was drawn to sleeping in the barn, in his clothes, in his
boots, luxuriant in such deep dreamless animal sleep as we, his sons,
waited inside the house shuddering and shivering in anticipation of
his return, his heavy footsteps on the stairs, yet yearning for his
return as a dog yearns for the return of the very master who will kick
him, praying he would not cuff us, or beat us, or kick us, or yank at
our coarse red curls so like his own in that teasing tenderness of our
father's that seemed to us far crueller than actual cruelty for at such
times you were meant to smile and not cringe, you were meant to
love him and not fear him, you were meant to obey him and not turn
mutinous, you were meant to honor your father and not loathe him,
still less were you meant to pray for his death, steeped in sin as you
were, even at a young age, even in childhood touched by the curse of
the MacElsters, emigrated from the wind-ravaged highlands north of
Inverness to the new world with blood, it was rumored, on their
hands, and murder in their hearts. And there at the house when we
arrived was our mother weeping deranged with shock and humiliation, her mouth bloodied, and Katy tending to her white-faced and
shaking as if she too had been stripped naked in the street, and would
be the scandalized talk of all who knew the MacElsters and countless others who did not, from Glace Bay to Port Hawkesbury to New
Glasgow and beyond, talk to endure for years, for decades, for generations to this very day; and seeming to know this as a fact, Angus's
six sons wasted no time, we strode into the barn known to us as a
dream inhabited nightly, that place of boyhood chores, of boyhood
play, badly weatherworn, with missing boards and rotted shingles
loosened by wind, glaring-eyed Rob has taken up the double-edged ax
where it was leaning against the doorframe, and Cal the resourceful
one has brought from home a twelve-inch fish-gutting knife, Alistair
has a wicked pair of shears, John Rory and John Allan have their
matching hunting knives of eight-inch stainless steel, and I have a
newly honed butcher knife from my own house, from out of my own
kitchen where my young wife will miss it, and the six of us enter the

Joyce Carol Oates

barn to see the old man snoring in the twilight, in a patch of damp straw, and panting we circle him, our eyes gleaming like those of feral creatures glimpsed by lamplight in the dusk, and Rob is the first to shout for him to *Wake! wake up, old man!*—for it seems wrong to murder a sixty-one-year-old man snoring on his back, fatty-muscled torso exposed, arms and legs sprawled in a bliss of drunken oblivion, and at once old Angus opens his eyes, his bulging red-veined horse's eyes, blinking up at us, knowing us, naming us one by one his six MacElster sons as damned as he, and yet *even at this late hour our hearts might yet be won.* Except, being the man he is, old Angus curses us, calls us young shits, spits at us, tries to stumble to his feet to fight us, even as the first of our blows strikes, Rob's double-edged ax like electricity leaping out of the very air, and there's the flash of Cal's fish-gutting knife, and Alistair's shears used for stabbing, and the fine-honed razor-sharp blades of John Rory's and John Allan's and mine, blades sharp enough and strong enough to pierce the hide of the very devil himself, and in a fever of shouts and laughter we strike, and tear, and lunge, and stab, and pierce, and gut, and make of the old man's wind-roughened skin a lacy-bloody shroud and of his bones brittle sticks as easily broken as dried twigs, and of his terrible eyes cheap baubles to be gouged out and ground into the dirt beneath our boots, and of his hard skull a mere clay pot to be smashed into bits, and of his blood gushing hot and shamed onto the straw and the dirt floor of the barn a glistening stream bearing bits of cobweb, dust and straw as if a sluice were opened, and we leap about shouting with laughter for this is a game, is it?—will the steaming poison-blood of Angus MacElster singe our boots?—sully our boots?—will some of us be tainted by this blood and others, the more agile, the more blessed, will not?

*This old family tale comes to me from my father's father Charles MacElster, the eldest son of Cal.*

—After Ovid

332

# On the Nordic Pleasurelines Fall Color Cruise

## Jonathan Franzen

"PSST! ASSHOLE!"

With a jolt Alfred awakened to the tremor and slow pitching of the *Gunnar Myrdal*. Someone else was in the stateroom?

"Asshole!"

"Who's there?" he asked, half in challenge, half in fear.

Thin Scandinavian blankets fell away as he sat up and peered into the semidarkness, straining to hear past the boundaries of his self. The partially deaf know like cellmates the frequencies at which their heads ring. His oldest companion was a contralto like a pipe organ's high treble A, a clarion blare vaguely localized in his left ear. He'd known this tone, at growing volumes, for thirty years; it was such a fixture that it seemed it should outlive him. It had the pristine mean-inglessness of eternal or infinite things. Was as real as a heartbeat but corresponded to no real thing outside him. Was a sound that nothing made.

Underneath it the fainter and more fugitive tones were active. Cirruslike clusterings of very high frequencies off in deep stratosphere behind his ears. Meandering notes of almost ghostly faintness, as from a remote calliope. A jangly set of midrange tones that waxed and waned like crickets in the center of his skull. A low, almost rumbling drone like a dilution of a diesel engine's blanket alldeafeningness, a sound he'd never quite believed was real—i.e., unreal—until he'd retired from the Midland Pacific and lost touch with locomotives. These were the sounds his brain both created and listened to, was friendly with.

Outside of himself he could hear the psh, psh of two hands gently swinging on their hinges in the sheets.

And the mysterious rush of water all around him, in the *Gunnar Myrdal*'s secret capillaries.

And someone snickering down in the dubious space below the horizon of the bedding.

And the alarm clock pinching off each tick. It was three in the morning and sleep had abandoned him. Now, when he needed her comforts more than ever, she went off whoring with younger sleepers. For thirty years she'd obliged him, spread her arms and opened her legs every night at ten-fifteen. She'd been the nook he sought, the womb. He could still find her in the afternoon or early evening, but not in a bed at night. As soon as he lay down he groped in the sheets and sometimes for a few hours found some bony extremity of hers to clutch. But reliably at one or two or three she vanished beyond any pretending that she still belonged to him.

He peered fearfully across the rust orange carpeting to the Nordic blond wood lines of Enid's bed. Enid appeared to be dead.

The rushing water in the million pipes.

And the tremor, he had a guess about this tremor. That it came from the engines, that when you built a luxury cruise ship you damped or masked every sound the engines made, one after another, right down to the lowest audible frequency and even lower, but you couldn't go all the way to zero. You were left with this subaudible two-hertz shaking, the irreducible remainder and reminder of a silence imposed on something powerful.

A small animal, a mouse, scurried in the layered shadows at the foot of Enid's bed. For a moment it seemed to Alfred that the whole floor consisted of scurrying corpuscles. Then the mice resolved themselves into a single more forward mouse, horrible mouse, squishable pellets of excreta, habits of gnawing, heedless peeings—

"Asshole, asshole!" the visitor taunted, stepping from the darkness into a bedside dusk.

With dismay Alfred recognized the visitor. First he saw the dropping's slumped outline and then he caught a whiff of bacterial decay. This was not a mouse. This was the turd.

"Urine trouble now, hee hee!" the turd said.

It was a sociopathic turd, a loose stool, a motormouth. It had introduced itself to Alfred the night before and so agitated him that only Enid's ministrations, a blaze of electric light and Enid's soothing touch on his shoulder had saved the night.

"Leave!" Alfred commanded sternly.

But the turd scurried up the side of the clean Nordic bed and relaxed like a Brie, or a leafy and manure-smelling Cabrales, on the covers. "Splat chance of that, fella." And dissolved, literally, in a gale of hilarious fart sounds.

To fear encountering the turd on his pillow was to summon the turd to the pillow, where it flopped in postures of glistening well-being.

"Get away, get away," Alfred said, planting an elbow in the carpeting as he exited the bed headfirst.

"No way, José," the turd said. "First I'm gonna get in your clothes."

"No!"

"Sure am, fella. Gonna get in your clothes and touch the upholstery. Gonna smear and leave a trail. Gonna stink so bad."

"Why? Why? Why would you do such a thing?"

"Because it's right for me," the turd croaked. "It's who I am. Put somebody else's comfort ahead of my own? Go hop in a toilet to spare somebody else's feelings? That's the kinda thing *you* do, fella. You got everything bass ackwards. And look where it's landed you."

"Other people ought to have more consideration."

"You oughtta have less. Me personally, I am opposed to all strictures. If you feel it, let it rip. If you want it, go for it. Dude's gotta put his own interests first."

"Civilization depends upon restraint," Alfred said.

"Civilization? Overrated. I ask you what's it ever done for me? Flushed me down the toilet! Treated me like shit!"

"But that's what you *are*," Alfred pleaded, hoping the turd might see the logic. "That's what a toilet is *for*."

"Who you calling shit here, asshole? I got the same rights as everybody else, don't I? Life, liberty, the pursuit of hot pussy? That's what it says in the Constitution of the You Nighted—"

"That's not right," Alfred said. "You're thinking of the Declaration of Independence."

"Some old yellow piece a paper somewhere, what the ratass fuck do I care what exact paper? Tightasses like you been correcting every fucking word outta my mouth since I was yay big. You and all the constipated schoolteachers and Nazi cops. For all I care the words are printed on a piece a fucking toilet paper. *I* say it's a free country, *I* am in the majority, and *you*, fella, are a minority. And so fuck you."

The turd had an attitude, a tone of voice, that Alfred found eerily familiar but couldn't quite place. It began to roll and tumble on his pillow, spreading a shiny greenish-brown film with little lumps and fibers in it, leaving white creases and hollows where the fabric was bunched. Alfred, on the floor by the bed, covered his nose and mouth with his hands to mitigate the stench.

Then the turd ran up the leg of his pajamas. He felt the tickling mouse-like feet.

"Enid!" he called with all the strength he had.

The turd was somewhere in the neighborhood of his upper thighs. Struggling to bend his rigid legs and hook his semifunctional thumbs on the waistband, he pulled the pajamas down to trap the turd inside the fabric. He suddenly understood that the turd was an escaped convict, a piece of human refuse that belonged in jail. That this was what jail was for: people who believed that they, rather than society, made the rules. And if jail did not deter them, they deserved death! Death! Drawing strength from his rage, Alfred succeeded in pulling the ball of pajamas from his feet, and with oscillating arms he wrestled the ball to the carpeting, hammering it with his forearms, and then wedged it deep between the firm Nordic mattress and the Nordic box spring.

He knelt, catching his breath, in his pajama top and adult diaper.

Enid continued to sleep. Something distinctly fairy-tale-like in her attitude tonight.

"Phlblaaatth!" the turd taunted. It had reappeared on the wall above Alfred's bed and hung precariously, as if flung there, beside a framed etching of the Oslo waterfront.

"God damn you!" Alfred said. "You belong in jail!"

The turd wheezed with laughter as it slid very slowly down the wall, its viscous pseudopods threatening to drip on the sheets below. "Seems to me," it said, "you anal retentive type personalities want *everything* in jail. Like little kids, bad news, man, they pull your tchotchkes off your shelves, they drop food on the carpet, they cry in theaters, they miss the pot. Put 'em in the slammer! And *Polynesians*, man, they track sand in the house, get fish juice on the furniture, and all those pubescent chickies with their honkers exposed? Jail 'em! And how about ten to twenty, while we're at it, for every horny little teenager, I mean talk about insolence, talk about no restraint. And Negroes (sore topic, Fred?), I'm hearing rambunctious shouting and interesting grammar, I'm smelling liquor of the malt variety and sweat that's very rich and scalpy, and all that dancing and whoopee-making and singers that coo like body parts wetted with saliva and special jellies: what's a jail *for* if not to toss a Negro in it? And your Caribbeans with their spliffs and their potbelly toddlers and their like daily barbecues and ratborne hanta viruses and sugary drinks with pig blood at the bottom? Slam the cell door, eat the key. And the Chinese, man, those creepy-ass weird-name vegetables like homegrown dildos somebody forgot to wash after using, one-dollah, one-dollah, and those slimy carps and skinned-alive songbirds, and come on, like, puppydog soup and pooty-tat dumplings and female infants are national delicacies, and *pork bung,* by which we're referring here to the *anus* of a *swine,* presumably a sort of chewy and bristly type item, pork bung's a thing Chinks pay money for to *eat?* What say we just nuke all billion point two of 'em, hey? Clean that part of the world *up* already. And let's not forget about women generally, nothing but a trail of Kleenexes and Tampaxes everywhere they go. And your fairies with their doctor's-office lubricants, and your Mediterraneans with their whiskers and their garlic, and your French with their garter belts and raunchy cheeses, and your blue-collar ball-scratchers with their hot rods and beer belches, and your Jews with their circumcised putzes and gefilte fish like pickled turds, and your Wasps with their cigarette boats and runny-assed polo horses and go-to-hell cigars? Hey, funny thing, Fred, the only people that don't belong in your jail are upper-middle-class northern European men. And you're on *my* case for wanting things *my* way?"

"What will it take to make you leave this room?" Alfred said.

"Loosen up the old sphincter, fella. Let it fly."

"I will never!"

"In that case I might pay a visit to your shaving kit. Have me a little episode o' diarrhea on your toothbrush. Drop a couple nice globbets in your shave cream and tomorrow a.m. you can lather up a rich brown foam—"

"Enid," Alfred said in a strained voice, not taking his eyes off the crafty turd, "I am having difficulties. I would appreciate your assistance."

His voice ought to have awakened her, but her sleep was Snow White–like in its depth.

"Enid *dahling,*" the turd mocked in a David Niven accent, "I should *most* appreciate some assistance at your earliest *possible* convenience."

Unconfirmed reports from nerves in the small of Alfred's back and behind his knees indicated that additional turd units were in the vicinity. Turdish rebels snuffling stealthily about, spending themselves in trails of fetor.

"Food and pussy, fella," said the leader of the turds, now barely clinging to the wall by one pseudopod of fecal mousse, "is what it all comes down to. Everything else, and I say this in all modesty, is pure shit."

Then the pseudopod ruptured and the leader of the turds—leaving behind on the wall a small clump of putrescence—plunged with a cry of glee onto a bed that *belonged to Nordic Pleasurelines* and was due to be made in a few hours by a lovely young Finnish woman. Imagining this clean, pleasant housekeeper finding lumps of personal excrement spattered on the bedspread was almost more than Alfred could bear.

His peripheral vision was alive with writhing stool now. He had to hold things together, hold things together. Suspecting that a leak in the toilet might be the source of his trouble, he made his way on hands and knees into the bathroom and kicked the door shut behind him. Rotated with relative ease on the smooth tiles. Braced his back against the door and pushed his feet against the sink opposite him. He laughed for a moment at the absurdity of his situation. Here he was, an American executive sitting in diapers on the floor of a floating bathroom under siege by a squadron of feces. A person got the strangest notions late at night.

The light was better in the bathroom. There was a science of cleanliness, a science of looks, a science even of excretion as evidenced by the outsized Swiss porcelain eggcup of a toilet, a regally pedestaled thing with finely knurled levers of control. In these more congenial surroundings Alfred was able to collect himself to the point of understanding that the turdish rebels were figments, that to some extent he had been dreaming, and that the source of his anxiety was simply a drainage problem.

Unfortunately, operations were shut down for the night. There was no way to have a look personally at the rupture, nor any way to put a plumber's snake or video cam down there. Highly unlikely as well that a contractor could get a rig out to the site under conditions like these. Alfred wasn't even sure he could pinpoint his location on a map himself.

Nothing for it but to wait until morning. Absent a full solution, two half-solutions were better than no solution at all. You tackled the problem with whatever you had in hand.

Couple of extra diapers: that ought to hold for a few hours. And here were the diapers, right by the toilet in a bag.

It was nearly four o'clock. There would be hell to pay if the district manager wasn't at his desk by seven. Alfred couldn't recollect the fellow's exact name, not that it mattered. Just call the office and whoever picked up the phone.

It was characteristic of the modern world, though, wasn't it, how slippery they made the goddamned tape on the diapers.

"Would you look at that," he said, hoping to pass off as philosophical amusement his rage with a treacherous modernity. The adhesive strips might as well have been covered with Teflon. Between his dry skin and his shakes, peeling the backing off a strip was like picking up a marble with two peacock feathers.

"Well, for goodness sake."

He persisted in the attempt for five minutes and another five minutes. He simply couldn't get the backing off.

"Well, for goodness sake."

Grinning at his own incapacity. Grinning in frustration and the overwhelming sense of being watched.

"Well, for goodness sake," he said once more. This phrase often proved useful in dissipating the shame of small failures.

How changeful a room in the night. By the time Alfred had given up on the adhesive strips and simply yanked a third diaper up his thigh as far as it would go, which regrettably wasn't far, he was no longer in the same bathroom. The light had a new clinical intensity; he felt the heavy hand of a more extremely late hour.

"Enid! Enid!" he called. "Can you help me?"

With fifty years of experience as an engineer he could see at a glance that the emergency contractor had botched the job. One of the diapers was twisted nearly inside out and a second had a mildly spastic leg sticking through two of its plies, leaving most of its absorptive capacity unrealized in a folded mass, its adhesive stickers adhering to nothing. Alfred shook his head. He couldn't blame the contractor. The fault was his own. Never should have undertaken a job like this under conditions like these. Poor judgment on his part. Trying to do damage control, blundering around in the dark, often created more problems than it solved.

"Yes, now we are in a fine mess," he said with a bitter smile.

And could this be liquid on the floor? Oh my Lord, there appeared to be some liquid on the floor.

Also liquid running in the *Gunnar Myrdal*'s myriad pipes.

"Enid, please, for God's sake. I am asking you for help."

No answer from the district office. Some kind of vacation everybody was on. Something about the color of a fall.

Liquid on the floor! Liquid on the floor!

So all right, though, they paid him to take responsibility. They paid him to make the hard calls.

He took a deep, bolstering breath.

In a crisis like this the first order of business was obviously to clear a path for the runoff. Forget about track repair, first you had to have a gradient or you risked a really major washout.

He noted grimly that he had nothing like a surveyor's transit, not even a simple plumb line. He'd have to eyeball it.

How the hell had he got stranded out here, anyway? Probably not even five in the morning yet.

"Remind me to call the district manager at seven," he said.

Somewhere, of course, a dispatcher had to be on duty. But then the problem was to find a telephone, and here a curious reluctance to raise his eyes above the level of the toilet made itself felt. Conditions in these parts were impossible. It could be midmorning by the time he found a telephone. And by that point.

"Uh! Such a lot of work," he said.

There appeared to be a slight depression in the shower stall. Yes, in fact, a pre-existing culvert, maybe some old D.O.T. roadbuilding project that never got off the ground, maybe the Army Corps was involved somehow. One of those midnight serendipities: a real culvert. Still, he was looking at a hell of an engineering problem to relocate the operation to take advantage of the culvert.

"Not much choice, though, I'm afraid."

Might as well have at it. He wasn't getting any less tired. Think of the Dutch with their Delta Project. Forty years of battling the sea. Put things in perspective a little—one bad night. He'd endured worse.

Try to build some redundancy into the fix, that was the plan. No way he'd trust one little culvert to handle all the runoff. There could be a backup further down the line.

"And then we're in trouble," he said. "Then we are in real trouble."

Could be a hell of a lot worse, in fact. They were lucky an engineer was right on site when the water broke through. Imagine if he hadn't been here, what a mess.

"Could have been a real disaster."

First order of business was to slap some sort of temporary patch on the leak, then tackle the logistical nightmare of rerouting the whole operation over the culvert, and then hope to hold things together until the sun came up.

"And see what we got."

In the faulty light he saw the liquid running one way across the

340

floor and then reversing itself slowly, as if the horizontal had lost its mind.

"Enid!" he called with little hope as he commenced the sick-making work of stopping the leakage and getting himself back on track, and the ship sailed on. .

# *From* Uxudo
# Anne Tardos

So there they sat.

Tombé [*fallen* / gefallen]

Gewurzeltidé = Gewurzeltidé = Gewurzeltidé

Eigenschaft = quality [*eye-gun-shuft*]

Graben: a square in Vienna.

Da saßen sie also.

Tombé, tombé, gewurzeltidé.

Tombé gewurzeltidé Eigenschaft am Graben.

Körülnézek *[ker-ruel-nay-zack]* [körül-nehsek]
= ich schaue mich um = I look around me = je regarde
autour de moi *[cœurule-nézeque]*.

     Ceux qui ont de l'eau le boivent.

Gürtelschnallen, Zigarren, *nervousness.*

*Anne Tardos*

Körülnézek

People who have water drink it.

Beltbuckles, cigars, die Nervosität.

*Anne Tardos*

Geschwollen
Gonflé
Bedagadt


eine süße kleine Nagelhaut

(une petite épiderme mignonne)

Swollen, I don't know.

Cute little cuticle from Utica.

Krakatoa vérité.

*Anne Tardos*

*WorkAnts*

Le mot d'une petite *plaisireuse*
    Schlüpfriges Geheimnis sensationellen Sexes.


Das Licht einer einzigen Galaxis.


Ein paar Lungen.

# ArbeitsAmeisen

Word of a petite pleaser's
　　　　slippery secret of sensational sex.

The light of a single galaxy.

A pair of lungs.

*Anne Tardos*

                        Sommetrommel

vom Hörensagen greifbare Gelassenheit

Szép anyag *(sayp A-nyahg)* = beautiful material, schönes Stoff

Akkor tüszkölni *UK-core toos-kulney* = to then sneeze *(niessen)*

      Blimpinault defunction = blimpinault defunction

Édes érzékenykedés = sweet touchiness
                          *Aydush Air-zay-kunykudaysh.*

*süße Empfindlichkeit*

Szép anyag didn't run Summerdrum

Hearsay tactile serenity, Zelda.

What you see, is.

Akkor tüszkölni shelter.

Blimpinault defunction.

Form of happiness—érzékenykedés.

This is how the brain
works: et patati et
patata . . .

That petite
animal down there
at your feet.

*Anne Tardos*

(Magyarul: hunyú)


Wer konnte wissen? Wie das alles enden würde?

Das Menschenhirn ist eine faule Angelegenheit.
Sie war eine frühe Denkerin.


Sie hinterließ den Flughafen und ihre Kastagnetten.


Die Sprache der Schimpansen wurde erst später erwähnt.


**Left the airport and her castanets behind.**

**The language of chimpanzees**
        **came into question later.**

# Who knew?

Who knew how things would turn out?
The human brain was a lazy affair.
She was an early thinker.

Left the airport and her castanets behind.

The language of chimpanzees
came into question later.

# Body In Glory
## Nathaniel Tarn

—*for Carlos Saura, his* Flamenco

To be ugly now
with the ugliness of earth
unmixed with subtler matter—
        irretrievably
so that the mirrors in the house
    all, all are broken
and to emerge
       on the other side of beauty
with the mirror shards
        ablaze with faces

earth beats,
      pulse can be heard
under feet walking
to the meeting place
      then immediately:
body held high—erectitude—
and at the very tip, the hand
like a dove at the top of the sky

few musics glory body like this does
      building spine to heights
where crown is reigning by itself
floating above the absent
      bride and bridegroom
        without a head to land on

each body enters to itself,
becomes itself entirely,
      no hold barred,
each soul from body emanates

the soul out of the body
        not vice versa
and voice explodes,
        stretching the mouth
into the earth's diameter
to eat, to swallow the whole world
while feet beat out the pulse
        and the song sails

high, high on youth, on youth
        entwined with age
divining in each other's stances
salutes of solitude enfolded
as age gives passage to new life
with the extremes of courtesy

the eye meantime
follows the movement,
        water weaves wave
into the patterns of the blood
swirling inside the body's veins
        and thunder downs from mountain
in answer to the music here
the gods in answer to a human prayer
        created from that prayer
                and all its demon rages

up from the earth,
up from the pulse beat
        into the feet
each single birth from this one,
        dust having no dominion
but settling again
        barely above the feet—
body in glory among traffic noises,
a reassertion of the city street
                and that of birds
        singing those hands
                among the city's branches.

# Two Poems
## *Peter Gizzi*

### ADD THIS TO THE HOUSE

Not a still life into which artifice may enter,
but a labor to describe the valves
and cordage that entwine this room;
the voltage is enough to kill.
Who in morning dish-gray light
can fathom the witless parable of waking,
the bed, the casque, the zoned spaces
we pass through into movement.
How lovely to say
floorboards pose in firelight,
coals are banking down, the room
comes up by degrees. Instead, the day
has begun, shadows dispelled by the clock
by the promise of work, Clorox,
the phone. I can see you by that metaphor
the house, the door, the car heading out
to meet the sun, then again hours
later returning, your back to it.

*Peter Gizzi*

## DUMBBELL

A way of seeing, to squint your eyes
so the light is faceted, bejeweled perhaps
—it is all so slow here in the crypt,
a fringed eye staring into an immobile world.
The time of day stymies me
breaks my concentration to bits, spangles.
A chain saw in the neighbor's yard.
But I wanted this painting to be a masterpiece
so I might retire into a tower of lace,
tend my terrarium and the turtle who lives in it.
Now that's a life. Where are you?
Driving your car, handling
the gears as you move into the curve.
I think of you more often now I'm dead,
and hope your chevron carries you off to the stars
you are so impatiently calling.
Don't worry, they're waiting, blinking
now and again. You'll find your way.

357

# Three Poems
## *Rae Armantrout*

### HERE

1.

I'm here to recreate
the "fleeting impression"
that others once saw themselves

as repositories of experience.
In a dream,
I'm three old actors

known for playing in Westerns.
We're on a trek through wild country
to show how the past might have been.

A voice-over says that our saddles
are especially worn and rough-hewn.


2.

It's supposed to be beautiful
to repeat a motif
in another medium.

A regular
dither
in the strings

approaching Apollo
Cremation. Out front,
fountains

make a statement
about the ability
to keep up one's end.

There's a boy down the street,
firing caps
as my son did

while a church plays
its booming
recording of chimes.


MY ASSOCIATES

You identify
with the body's
routine

until you think
it's your body—

like thinking
you *are* the clock.

Identity is a form
of prayer.

"How do I look?"

meaning what
could I pass for

where every eye's
a guard.

May passes
as the whole
air's bedizened
flotilla.

*Rae Armantrout*

To echo
is to hold
aloft?

Then take any word
and split it,

make it soil itself
to seem fertile.

So nasturtiums
are the dirt's
lips.

Fecund. Cunning. (Cunt)


LIGHT

Not with an order but a question,
apropos of nothing.

Something answers "Dark" and "Light."

These two
new beings are startled and draw back

from the beginning of time.
Are you happy?

　　\*

No exit but attenuation?

Sky barely
orange at sunset.

Pulled out slow and thin,
her voice

means an objection
so pervasive
cannot know its enemy.

*

The purpose of abstraction
is to discover how
two things
can constitute a recurrence.

To obtain reversibility.
Gravity is to memory . . .

# *From* Feeding the Ghosts
## *Fred* D'*Aguiar*

THE SEA IS slavery. Sea water boils in its own current. Salt gives the sea the texture of fabric, something thick and close-knitted, not unlike the fine dust of a barn seen floating in a shaft of light. Sea receives a body as if that body has come to rest on a cushion, one that gives way to the body's weight and folds around it like an envelope. Over three days 131 such bodies, no, 132, are flung at this sea. Each lands with a sound that the sea absorbs and silences. Each opens a wound in this sea that heals over each body without the evidence of a scar. Two hundred and sixty-four arms and 264 legs punch and kick against a tide that insists all who land on it, all who break its smooth surface, must succumb to its swells, tumbles, pushes and pulls.

Water replaces air in 131 of these bodies. They fight then become still as if changing from struggle to an embrace, seeing in an enemy someone to love and therefore to hold, no longer against water but a part of its thrust from one point of the compass to another. Salt washes wounds on those bodies instilled by the locks, chains, masks, collars, binds, fetters, handcuffs and whips of the land, washes until those wounds belong to the sea.

Water caresses the skin unloved on land for so long. Water applies its soft salted lips to every pore of that body in an attempt to enliven the very body it has wrestled to a stillness in the first place, as if the body's very surrender is a point of departure for water from conqueror to worshipper. Sea refuses to grant that body the quiet of a grave in the ground. Instead it rolls that body across its terrain, sends that body to bursting point, tumbles it beyond the reach of horizons and gradually breaks fragments from that body with its nibbling, dissecting current.

Soon all those bodies melt down to bones, then the sea begins to treat the bones like rock, there to be shaped over time or ground to dust. Sea does not stop at death. Salt wants to consume every morsel of those bodies until the sea becomes them, becomes their memory. So it is from the sea that all 131 souls are to be plucked. From a sea oblivious to time. One hundred and thirty-one dissipated bodies find breath in the wind skimming the surface of the sea and howl. Those bodies have their lives written on salt water. The sea current turns pages of memory. One hundred and thirty-one souls roam the Atlantic with countless others. When the wind is heard it is their breath, their speech. The sea is therefore home.

The one-hundred-and-thirty-second lives far inland: can never set foot on water again, never look at an expanse of water wider than a river bridgeable with a pelted stone. Air is her conqueror, water theirs. Air is her preserver, water theirs. Air and water share the same earth, the same sea, the same sky. Both are consumed by fire. Sometimes a savannah will start to tumble bundles of bracken across its flat face and suddenly, through some trick of the light and heat, it will tremble into a seascape and that bracken will become tossed into a sea current and this one-hundred-and-thirty-second body will have to be a witness again.

\*     \*     \*

I am Mintah. They threw me off the *Zong* and into the sea. I should be food for fish now. Or bones on the seabed, my bones adding to a road of bones. But grain emerged from wood, plaited into a rope and offered itself to me, and I gripped it and kept my hold on that grain. I climbed up the side of that ship. In my tired state I'm sure I can't dream, that dreaming would take too much, and I've got nothing left in my body. I'm sure my head is empty in this sleep: some airless room, silent and still with all the furniture in it covered over with sheets, even the pictures on the wall under covers, or no furniture at all, bare walls, and not a living soul in sight. But no. The second my eyes clamp shut the dreams start to run. I see not me but this girl who is just like me. I don't think Mintah, that's me. I think that girl is Mintah. And I see her father holding a chisel in front of him. He carves goodbye out of air. Goodbye, Mintah. Small strokes from left to right. Goodbye. Again and again. Waves. The grain in the air, easy and yielding. His actions small and exact and repetitive. Mintah, goodbye. And the girl following her mother from the compound. Always following her mother. From the well or skirting a field. To the river to beat clothes on stones with wooden paddles, then lay them out on the grass and stones for Time to dry them, using some of that time to bathe and swing the feet in the swift water that's in a hurry to get somewhere. Always following her mother. Her mother's behind bouncing under her tight wrap. Catching glimpses of the

363

mother's pale instep as each heel rises before she steps, and the girl that is me and not me, trying to match the length of her mother's steps but falling short most times, except when she really makes a big effort and hops.

Following her mother the day she left for the mission, leaving her father behind. Her mother glancing back to say, "Keep up, Mintah." With a smile and a little concern narrowing her eyes. The girl that is Mintah, who is me and not me, has nothing but her bare hands to return the gifts carved by her father for her as she walks away from him. Her hand in the air shapes goodbyes. Little, imprecise strokes. Some hardly strokes at all. So long, Father. More a way of holding on to goodbye, if only goodbye were not made of air but of something more substantial, like wood. Father, goodbye.

Her hands are empty when she would have them full, this little girl. Holding wood or a chisel. Feeling the grain of wood with her eyes shut to heighten feeling. Seeing behind her, in her past, full hands. Busy hands. Hands making something. Not empty hands. Hands waiting to serve another, doing something not meant for hands. When she looks ahead of her, this girl, she sees two empty hands. Her hands. Following her mother. Not to the river or the well or to or from a field, but towards two empty hands. "Keep up, Mintah." And this girl I know hops into her mother's footprints, once, twice, three times, then makes a step of her own that falls short of her mother's next footprint.

"Kelsal!" The little girl is a young woman. There is no difference between us. When I say "Mintah" in my sleep I see myself as her. I am on a ship. I know by my rocking on my side and by the raised wood of my bed which I have to brace myself against, even in sleep. I shout that name louder than before, "Kelsal!" My voice has to compete with the wind as it blunts the pointed parts of the ship, and with the sea trying to chop the hull in two, and with the tap-tap-tapping of the rain testing the deck for any signs of weakness. My voice finds a way through all three. "Kelsal!" The sick men are taken out and not returned. We want to believe for a long time that the sailors have found other quarters for them. We say that this must be what is happening. The sick are being cared for. But the men are taken above deck and not returned. Only the sailors return for more of them. Then they start to take sick women and I know for sure what I did not want to think could be true. Even as I say it with the others none of us truly believe what we say. They are throwing the sick into the sea. We want to see it for ourselves. We want to look at these men as they grab the sick and do this thing. But we fight them and I shout his name, "Kelsal!"

They come for me with a lantern that cannot burn in this bad air. They hit me in the dark and drag me out. He looks at me and I see a fire in his eyes that makes those eyes strange to me. I see he is confused by my use of his name. He is running wild. I have to stop him. How else than by calling him? They bring me into the rain. I am refreshed by it. The wind wants to peel my skin from my face. Spray from the sea helps it. But the deck is empty and I know for sure where those sick men and women have been put. My hands are empty and useless. All that I have is his name. "Kelsal!" He knocks me down. Others pin my arms and legs. Then the boatswain stands over me and unbuckles his trousers. The top of the mainmast is in cloud. The ship seems to have risen with the sea to the sky. The ship has caught up with the horizon where sea meets sky. Having caught the horizon it is stuck to it and trapped in both sea and sky. Soon I expect the clouds to take up the entire mainmast and the deck, then the hull, and the *Zong* will be more in the sky than in the sea. As the clouds move so will the *Zong,* and a moment will come when the hull will be dragged clear of the sea and the barnacles will drop astonished from the wood and the sea will drain from the ship and air take the place of water and the sails will be full of cloud.

Kelsal changes his mind about my body. He pushes the boatswain away. What has brought about the change? My dance. My blood in the rain. He has me turned on my stomach and he begins to beat me. Not with his open hands or his fists. He uses a stick. My flesh and bones must pay for my tongue or my blood. This hurt is not for crying. I cry because a dance I hated doing has saved me. The moon has rescued me. Blood, my blood, is my savior. At least this time. I see the deck in water. The grain underwater is clear. The water is running off the deck, along the grain. And with each blow to my body it curves. Now it is spinning. All that grain underwater weaves itself like hair into a rope. In my mind I reach for it and when I grab it the grain goes dark.

I wake up below decks bound and gagged. From the noise around me I know that more of us have been thrown into the sea. The women are surprised to see me back with them. I am not sick. It is not my time. Those who are not chained try to fight off the crew from taking other sick women and children. But they are beaten. The sick are pulled out. They too fight the crew. They are sick and they hope to get well. They do not expect to die this way. Some beg for mercy. Some are quiet. All fight to get away. Not escape. There is no escape. But they fight all the same.

It stops at mealtime. The men are taken up first, then the women and children. Two of the crew untie me and I am allowed to go up too. I walk and shrug off help. I must not be seen as sick. The captain is sheltering in a corner with his ledger. "Kelsal!" He looks at me and grits his teeth. He comes to me. I tell him I know him from his days as a thief at the mission when he had to work for his freedom and he did not know his name and had to be told who he was time and again. How he said it like a word that was new in the language. Not a name that belonged to him. How he had to grow to like that name again. Not having to look around expecting another person to reply when it was called. Not waiting for it to be called twice before realizing it was his name and responding to it with surprise in his voice. To hear it the first time and, without a gap between the name and his thoughts because he inhabited it, be on his way.

The knot on his forehead loosens and his eyes widen. I have seen that look before, at the mission, on the rare occasions when he laughed. Here is the look again without the laugh. And not for long. The surprise passes. Anger sets those features back in place. He needs help to grapple with me. The children are spared. A boy and a girl. Both are sick but neither is near to death. Not by the way they brightened in the air and rain and fought those men. Their sickness will pass if they are given time. They will need encouragement but they will eat, even the cook's apologies for food. What they have seen, children should not see. They will have to be convinced that there is more to live for than what is being shown them on the *Zong*.

When those men lay their hands on me I feel a cold wave wash over me. When I shudder I find I cannot move. Their hands are holding me. I fight to get warm and break their grip. As they struggle with me towards the side a bolt of heat and light fills my head and spreads through my body. Each drop of rain sizzles on my skin. The wind fans me and makes me hotter. I want the sea. Those hands cannot hold me much longer. Only the sea can cool me. They fling me at it and I arch into a feetfirst dive. I see the sea rush up to meet me. My feet hit it and the hardness I feel is not water but the cold in it. The sea parts and frost rushes up my legs and body and covers my face. I tell myself this is fine. Water has always been a friend. But when I breathe it burns inside like water thrown on a fire and I choke. I come up and swim with my head held clear of the sea. My eyes open and sting and I see how the sea breathes with a life of its own. It is

living like me. I look to my right and there is more water until I can't
see anything, so I swing my head to the left and I expect the same sea
stretched out to the sky to meet my eyes but see wood. Wood packed
together in a forest on the sea. Grain buried in that wood for hand to
feel and find. The forest is passing me and sways in the wind and the
sea as it passes. Either passing or else being passed by the sea and by
me swimming backwards with the sea. I look up and the wood is tall
and reaches the sky. The sky moves with the ship. Then I know I am
being left behind in that sea with no other wood in it. I think I see a
ladder in that wood. Each step on that ladder is a join of those trees
laid side by side. Then the grain surfaces from the wood, and as I
blink sea water and salt from my eyes I see the hand that the grain
has plaited itself into offering me help into the forest. The forest
wants me though the sea has claimed me. I pull on the rope of the
forest and now I am moving with it through the sea. The sea tightens
its cold grip on my body, unwilling to give me up. My body tells me
to let go of the rope and surrender to the sea. I look at the fins behind
the ship and fancy that I will not feel them eat me because the sea
which has taken some feeling from my body will stop all feeling
before those fish get to me. My empty hands have something in
them. They are filled with purpose. How can I dream of letting go
and leaving them empty again? I pull on the rope and haul myself out
of the sea and rest against the hull that is rough, hard and beautiful.
My toes find the steps in that ladder and grip the rope between them
and I climb. The sea slaps me. Wind shakes my body and screams at
me that I am a fool to walk back to what I have left and been spared
from having to live through or die slowly in. A fool. The sea is my
savior. If I can't see it then I should trust the wind and drop back into
the sea. My arms and legs ache with this truth too. But I hold on.
I have wood in my hands, under my feet and against my body.
Nothing can induce me to let it go and lose it now. I hold on and
climb. Not to heaven. Nor into a forest. I realize as I get further from
the sea that wood is under my feet and against my body and rope is
in my hand. That I have yet to find the true grain of wood anywhere
on this ship. That I am back where I left before with nothing in my
hands. And nothing to look forward to in these hands. With a past in
my head where my hands are full. With a present that keeps them
empty. Hands with no future.

Wood all the way up. Grain in the wood. I climbed thinking I
might end up back home, convincing myself I was on a ladder carved
in that hull leading to my father and his house. I climbed through all

that wind rounding off the edges of that ship, seeing as I climbed not a wall upwards, not a ladder into the sky, but a floor to get across, a walk over wood more than a climb, a ride on wood, if I held on and pulled and walked, a ride and a walk and a climb, upwards, forwards, along and around those edges smoothed by wind, since I got turned over and around in that sea and my up and my down both changed and stayed the same, my left became my right and my right became my left, my in and my out exchanged and made room for each other, so I was going up and down at the same time, moving forwards and along on a ladder pointing four ways at once, salt that was on my out-side was now on my inside, and I only stopped when I found a quiet place to rest with the wind and the sea all around me, but the wood kept them away from me and hid me from them.

The first thing I do is search that room. Even before I rest. I look into everything. Every bag, trunk, case, drawer, corner, jar. I look for something to eat and to make sure nothing's in that room that can threaten me. I find dry biscuits, rum, water, dried fruit, dried beef, coconuts, oats, rice, wine, canvas, cloth, nails, hammer and other things I don't have a name for, things without a smell, rough things, things that stretch, crumbly things. Then I see it. A small trunk with "Captain Cunningham" in big letters. I open it expecting more rum, biscuits and meat but smell nothing, only oldness, mustiness and mildew. I don't wait for my eyes to get used to the dark in that trunk. I just pull up what my hand grabs and I come up with ink, pen, paper.

Mixed in with all this food, most of which I can't eat because it's uncooked, in the middle of it all, is this trunk with a pen, ink and paper. Just the thing I can use. I fall on my back and I laugh. My body shakes till I cry with the pain in my stomach. I stop and I start all over, shaking and crying with that laugh that grips me and won't let me go, so that when I finish, after how long I don't know, I have to sleep. But before I sleep I know what I have to do in that room full of food I can't eat and only one kind of thing I can use. I realize what I have to do with that thing. I go to sleep knowing I have to write everything that happens to me and everyone around me.

Is that why I sleep so deep? Knowing I've found a way to get what I see on this ship out of me? Ink, pen and paper as if in answer to the prayer I never got around to offering. And I laugh because it's as if I have come across a trunk with soil in it. The soil I thought I would never see. There is wood in that trunk, with roots and flowers. I can start to smell the river where I used to beat clothes and bathe and swim. A pawprint from some unknown animal is in that soil. Blades of grass, facing the same way, some with dew on them. A lovely worm. All are offered to me by this find in this trunk.

"Are you living or dead?" The voice is far away. It grows louder. "Are you dead or living?" My body is shaken. This time not to the rhythm of the sea. There is a hand on my shoulder doing the shaking. I want to open my eyes. Sleep has made them heavy. Even a strange hand on my shoulder shaking me is a comfort. In my head I say I am fine or leave me alone or go away. My lips though do not move. "Are you dead?" A deep sleep does not protect me against that word. Dead. I hear it. I know what it means to be dead. It is a condition I do not care for. I am only Mintah if I am living. Me, dead? I spring open my eyes and sit up. He jumps back. A machete is raised to the side of his head. There are too many questions on his face for me to know where to begin. He saw me get thrown into the sea, and with his key round his neck he wants to know how I got into a locked room. I want to tell him if I can get out of the sea I can find my way into a room. But I show him my hands are empty and I smile. He looks around confused and lowers the blade.

"Tell me you are a spirit, because if you are not then I forgot to lock the door. Cook will beat me for this. And seeing you made me forget why I came in here. I will be beaten for that too."

I put my hand on his shoulder and tell him no one will know I am in this room. I tell him how I got back on board. He listens, his eyes and mouth wide.

"Forgetting to lock a door is nothing. It happens to everyone."

With a little help he soon remembers what he has to fetch for the cook. He promises to bring me food. I am his first big secret. He will keep it, not for me, but to avoid a beating from Cook. His voyage has been measured by these beatings. Not one of his mistakes has gone unpunished. Over the weeks I have wondered whether he would not be better off in chains. At least then he would expect to be beaten for his wrongdoings. But he is paid by the cook and he is beaten daily by him, and he has to convince himself that he is free and that he has something to show for it.

Do I mean to say that a slave who is treated well is better off than someone who is free and treated badly? No. A slave knows, no matter how comfortable his life, that he is not free to do as he pleases, and knowing this he can never be happy though he may be contented that he is not in a field or receiving lashes. A free person may be beaten and robbed and insulted by his superior for many days, for years even. But there will come a day when he will say enough is enough and lash back or leave. He can do those things and think those things because he is free. He will not be hunted for it and returned to an owner who would then be permitted to do as he pleased with him.

The Danish missionaries came to our village with two messages. That there was one God and that Africans need not be slaves. Many villages had been emptied by the slavers and by chiefs who saw their own people as goods to be sold for profit. The leader of the missionaries argued with a group of village leaders that Africans should work their land and produce the same products for sale to the traders that they would produce as slaves in a foreign land. The land around villages could be put to this good use. The traders could rent this land or pay the Africans to work it for them. This could happen all along the coast and far inland since slavers travelled many days into the interior to buy and capture slaves. Instead of slaves they would transport what the large plantations grew. But no one would be a slave.

My mother and father heard about the fort where this work would be tried and this one God worshipped. My father wanted the experiment to be tried right there in his village and without the single God as a guide. He believed that the traditional gods would work fine with this new idea. But Mother was persuaded by the missionaries to embrace this one God. She wanted to see Africans remain free, and the one God promised this freedom in this life and in another paradise to be gained after death. The missionaries promised two paradises. One in this life and one in the next. Perhaps my mother could have said no to one paradise, but two she could not resist. Nor could most of the villagers. Father was left behind with a few unbelievers in a deserted village, and it was as if the slavers had indeed come and captured everyone and taken them to the coast to sell them into slavery in a strange land.

At the fort we soon learned how to worship God, to read and write, and work in the fields. The crops were shown to visitors who came from all the slaving nations and the terms were explained by the missionaries. How much a man should be paid, a woman, and a child. How much was to be gained by a harvest if the produce was taken to Europe and America. The missionaries proved that the cost would be less than buying, transporting and keeping slaves and the profits better as a result. They showed too that there was no misery for the African who was paid for his land and for his labor.

But the ships were fitted up for slaves. Industries abounded that had to do not with the produce but with the slaves themselves.

These men came and disapproved of the missionaries' experiments with their livelihood. There were threats, and a field was burned more than once. But when the Dutch came with cannons and guns there was nothing to do but run from the fort. Many missionaries died. I ran with Mother into the bushes and we hid there with a small group for two days before slavers captured us. Mother was separated from me when the slavers divided us between them. Her last words were that I should keep my learning a secret since it would get me into trouble. And I should not forget God since he would not forget me. I left her and thought of Father. Father first, then Mother. Both gone.

Kelsal was at the mission before the Dutch attacked it. He left to head farther south where it was thought he would find an English ship. He too saw what the missionaries were doing. A man who worked for pay worked faster and harder and more happily than a man in chains. Kelsal proved this fact. After his first departure and return he had to work out his sentence passed by the missionaries for stealing from them. He was the most miserable man on earth. He wore his misery as if it weighed as much as an elephant. He dragged his feet everywhere. And he complained about everything. The sun, the nature of the work assigned to him, the food, water, the manner of his confinement. Everything. When his time was up everyone was glad to see him released and gone. Except for the children. He was good to tease. His feet were slow, and when he caught a child he pretended to be angry and used his open hand to lash the child a few times about the legs. If a child cried it was out of embarrassment at being caught by a slow and lazy man.

He was always free to leave, but not before he had worked for the fort and repaid a little of the time everyone had devoted to him when he was ill and had to be nursed. The morning his yellow fever subsided, or so he thought, he ran off. Two days later he was found at the perimeter of the grounds crawling on his hands and knees and begging for water and a shoulder to lean on. This second time he was sick for even longer and delirious. I was one of the children who took turns to watch over him and mop his brow and empty his waste and feed him. He opened his eyes and did not know his name or where he was on earth. I had to teach him. "Kelsal!" I said. "You are Kelsal."

"You are Kelsal?"

"No! You! You are Kelsal! I am Mintah!"

"I am Mintah?"

"No! I am Mintah! You are Kelsal!"

"Kelsal?"

"Yes! Kelsal!"

Why was I shouting? Because he seemed to be lost. The fever had knocked the common sense out of him so that I was him, he me.

He was soon on his feet, and repairing buildings around the fort. What a slow worker! He watched me walk past him at a safe distance and he said my name and I said his as if our names did not belong to ourselves, not since we had exchanged them when he was hot and stupid. I tried not to laugh at him or act afraid. He never smiled or spoke to anyone, except to say my name. Then one day he walked out of the fort, without so much as a goodbye, and into my future.

I was in chains the next time I saw him. He had found a ship and he was back on water. He looked happy. I was sure he'd recognize me from the fort, but he hardly seemed to notice me. Only the old, sick and injured interested him. He didn't want them to be brought aboard. As a result the *Zong* waited for two weeks to fill with over four hundred of us. I was below when the ship cast off. Land had to be pictured in my mind. From something solid like a handful of soil to a line at the edge of the sea then birds then nothing but sea. The ship leaned and has never straightened. It swayed and has not stopped.

Am I living or dead? What do I remember about last week, last month, last year? How much can anyone remember? The head cannot retain everything. Why should it? Most of what I do is not worthy of being stored in my head. Or it hurts too much to store it. So I let it go. I wrap it up like the respected dead and release it with a prayer or fling it unceremoniously like the disrespected living into a sea of forgetting. Writing can contain the worst things. So I forget on paper.

I try not to think how many more men, women and children are thrown alive into the sea as I hide. In my sleep I am sinking to the bottom of the sea. My passage to the seabed is not smooth. Fish feed on my body and each bite jolts me awake. But I do not wake. I fight those fish in my sleep. I fight the sea. The sick are around me sinking with me and fighting too.

Simon shakes me awake. He has food for me. I ask him how many more have been thrown into the sea. He says nothing. I hold his arms and shake him and demand an answer. "Many more, Mintah." He holds up the bowl to me. I turn my face away. He tells me I must eat or die after all I have done to stay alive. I eat. Salt is sprinkled on the

rice and beef and palm oil. He did this for me. There is no taste.
I must be crying since he uses a cloth to wipe my face. He dips the
cloth in water and washes my face, my neck, my arms. I stop him at
my chest and wash myself. He turns his face to the wall. I tell him I
have nothing to hide that he has not seen on this ship. Still he looks
away. I thank him for the food, soap and water. He shakes his head
and says he wishes he could get me off this ship. Before he leaves he
hands me a new piece of cloth for me to wrap around my waist. I ask
him where he got such nice cloth on this ship. He smiles and says I
was made for that cloth, and without answering where he found it
he takes away my waste in a pail and leaves me standing looking at
myself in that red and yellow cloth.

He does not lock the door. Without thinking I dash out of the
storeroom and go to the nearest section, which is where the men are
kept. As I walk in the smell I have been spared from for a day made
by people cramped into a small space assails my nostrils. The usual
bickering and complaints and planning and talk about home and crying over what has been lost or groaning about the pains of the body
and the heart, subside. There is quiet for a moment as their eyes take
in what their minds cannot accept. This is quickly succeeded by a
collective gasp. Then a sudden clamor as those nearest to me try and
draw away, and cry out at the sight of a ghost. "How many men have
been thrown into the sea? Not one has returned. How then can a
woman? She must be a spirit." This from an elder who has lost command of his senses but by virtue of his advanced years continues to
exercise an influence over the others that he does not deserve. I clap
my hands and slap two men nearest to me to show them I am flesh
and blood. I tell them how I climbed out of the sea. I move deeper
into the hold and touch as many of them as possible and smile and
say it is me, Mintah. Some of them hug me and marvel that the sea
has not swallowed me. They cheer my strength and luck. They say I
am cared for by the gods, not abandoned like the rest of them.

Women crowd at the partition to learn what has stirred up the
men. I get as near to it as I can and offer my body for them to touch
as I speak.

"I am Mintah. My life was spared from the sea. I grabbed a rope.
We must take this ship from these men. They will kill us all if we do
nothing. The gods will only help those who help themselves."

But the elder shouts that I will bring them more pain. Their lives
are made worse by each act of rebellion. I should leave them alone.
The sick and many of the young men do not agree with him. They

say that something has to be done before all of us are thrown into the sea. In the women's quarters two crewmen are shouting at everyone to be quiet. My name is mentioned. I rush out of the men's compartment before they can get to it. A woman in the passageway sees me and covers her face and drops to her knees. She refuses to believe her eyes. As I pass her I pinch her hard on the arm and say my name. Perhaps she will believe her ears and her feelings. She shrieks and scrambles to her feet and disappears towards the women's compartment. I am back in the storeroom. Footsteps approach. A key turns in the lock and the footsteps depart.

Wind appears to reduce the dimensions of the room. The ship creaks as the walls move toward me. The room is misshapen. Sea water trickles in, intent on breaking down the walls. I am in the sea not on it. My body is dry because I am surrounded by still air. But the walls of the air will soon break if the wind and the sea continue to pound it. Rain adds to the sea and tries to drown the ship since the ship refuses to sink. It seems water is everywhere and the wind is on the side of water. Land cannot be anywhere near this rain and wind and sea. There can be no land left that is not under rain or sea or flattened by wind. The *Zong* will surrender to the sea. Water will take the place of stale air below decks. We will be like fishes in caves under the sea in this sunken ship. Some of us will still be in chains. Others will float off the deck, loosening their grip on it when water has taken the place of air in them.

Land will be a dream then nothing. I live in the past and dream in the future. This present time is nothing to me. My hands are empty so I make nothing in this present. I hide in a room unable to do anything. I am on a ship that is going nowhere. From these decks there is only the sea. And the sea is worse than nothing. The sea is between my past and my future. I float on it in the hope that my life can resume at some point in time. I float in the present. I listen to the rain keeping a false time on wood since nothing comes to pass. The rain stays. Wind intensifies. Sea water hurls itself at the deck even as the sea hurls the ship around in it. I remain between my life that is over and my life to come. The sea keeps me *between* my life. Time runs on the spot, neither backwards nor forwards. The walls of the room threaten to collapse or close in. Always the threat but nothing ever completes itself. Only the sick thrown into the sea are complete. I thought the wood in this ship would stand for land in the absence of land. But the wood is indifferent to me. Grain in the wood has nothing to tell me that can be of any use to me on this ship. The

*Fred D'Aguiar*

*Zong* dips and rises in the sea without making progress. The horizon is in the same place, the same distance from the ship. The wake is the same length and width. Clouds alter their formations not because the ship is moving but because the clouds are moved by the wind. This is my life without land. Without the land I know.

# Edmund Wilson on Alfred de Musset: The Dream

## *Robert Kelly*

YEARS AGO I HAD a dream. Outside it was a hot night in Brooklyn while I was busy inside dreaming, and the dream started with me reading in the same shabby leather chair I had been sitting in, reading Malory before I went to bed. The chair, of course, like everything else, had once been new, really not so long ago. It had been specially made for me at my mother's commission, a red leather club chair, meant for a heavy body reading. After five years of heavy reading, the cushions were penitent, and the sleek scarlet finish was off it. In spots, the smooth red polished leather had worn away, and the rough underpelt showed through.

In the dream, I was reading a book by Edmund Wilson. It was in French, and called *La Vie d'Alfred de Musset*. I was not surprised that Wilson had written it in French. Thomas Mann had written whole passages, mysteries to me, in that language in *The Magic Mountain*. And Wilson himself had used lots of untranslated Russian in his *Memoirs of Hecate County*, a banned book I felt a little queasy about—not like his athletically classic criticism.

But I was a little surprised that I could understand the French. Along went the biography and along went I, reading. Then (this is dream time, the unimportant parts—and who is that Lord of the Dream who passes such unerring judgment over the details of dream?—pass in no time, no time) I turned a page (a page from nowhere—where had I been?) and found myself at the beginning of a new chapter.

This is how it started. (It was printed in French, I was understanding in English.)

*At the age of forty-seven, Alfred de Musset learned that he had contracted leprosy.*

For years I had suffered from a strange and terrified leprophobia— the word and its cognates could shock me almost to faintness if I encountered them in casual reading, while even if I knew one was coming, a "leper" or "pale victim" could scare me into running

376

about the house and turning lights on, or running into the warm afternoon and hoping for ordinary people. To take away the terrible cold of that word. And even outside, in the Brooklyn nights, the shadows of ailanthus trees and sumac bushes would writhe in the hot wind. They looked tropical and dangerous, rank-smelling trees from Leperland.

It would take a footnote long as life to explain all the plausible meanings and origins of this fear of the words themselves: leprosy, leper and their relatives. We have no time for that. Dreams need no footnotes but our afterlives, these inferences called days. Dreams are themselves footnotes. But not footnotes to life. Some other transactions they are so busy annotating all night long.

Because of my great fear of leprosy and its words, that opening sentence should have daunted me. But I felt nothing. Just an odd awareness that this time I wasn't frightened.

I read on.

\*

Do you imagine I'm like the wind of autumn
That feeds on grieving till it's churchyard time,
And for whom all pain is just a drop of water?
O poet, a kiss! I'm the one who kisses you.
The weeds I wanted to tear up from this place,
That's all your idleness; your pain is God's.
Whatever anguishes your youth may endure,
Let it keep growing vaster, this sacred wound
The black seraphim made in your heart's core—
Nothing makes us as great as some great sorrow.

A few weeks ago now, I saw some of these words quoted from Musset in a mystery story I was reading, and grew interested, the black seraphim, the holy wound. And then I remembered my dream of so many years ago.

The dreamed chapter went on. As Edmund Wilson began to describe the first cat's-paw aggressions of Musset's disease, the pages I was reading began to flicker, and images began to show through the grayish slick cheap paper, the kind Wilson's books were printed on in the late forties and early fifties (*Classics and Commercials*, for instance, fat squat books).

The text was dissolving into its story.

The story began to move, until the book, still in my hands, dissolved its pages into a movie I was watching, a movie called *The Life of Alfred de Musset.*

Who are the black seraphim? The French word *séraphin* is used as a singular, though its form is that of the Aramaic or Hebrew plural. In the poem it is *les séraphins,* as if plural of a plural. Who are those so many, many? And what is the *sainte blessure,* the sacred wound?

The movie showed the poet Musset growing ever more reclusive, hardly ever leaving his Paris apartment except by night. Oh it is no small thing to be private, whatever the cost. The loss. Gradually the ravages of his disease, along with a kindly wish not to infect other people, leads him to a brave resolve.

We see him, nicely dressed, stand by the broad low round table in his foyer. The damask tablecloth is neatly littered with reviews and journals. He has had his servants packing for a long journey. His right arm is round the waist of his faithful wife, who smiles at him with certain sadness. Perhaps it is only wistfulness. They are leaving Paris.

How can one bear to leave, perhaps forever, the capital of the world? Flaubert! Balzac! Berlioz! Wagner will come again. Austria is misbehaving. France of the poets! Manet painted her picture when she was more smiles than she is now, and even so he elicited a somber thoughtfulness in her long features, her good bones.

Now we see them, Alfred and his wife, in an open barouche. They are trotting along in sparkling sunlight by the Mediterranean. They are in Marseilles, about to take ship for French Polynesia.

He looks in the open carriage like a viceroy or a conqueror, all in white and with a Sola topee already natural on his head. But he's just a poet, just a poet with leprosy. He is leaving France forever, and his wife is with him.

As I read, I am aware even in dream that the story I'm watching, about a poet who in waking life I know nothing at all about, is full of allusions to other stories I do know: Rémy de Gourmont with his lupus or leprosy who kept to his rooms in the Rue des Saints-Pères (to which I went walking, like a pilgrim, in 1954, just to watch the northern sunlight fall on his long street). Paul Gauguin eaten up with syphilis (or was it worse?) in Tahiti. Arthur Rimbaud fleeing to Africa. Fleeing from Africa to Marseilles. Father Damien beginning his sermon *"We lepers"* one bright Sunday morning. Sweet Tusitala, old Robert Louis Stevenson my father told me all about, dying in the grass houses of Samoa. But about Musset I knew nothing. The dream knew, and a dream is not just invention and creation. A dream is

criticism too. Dream is the theory of the dark.
But the book that was a movie kept going on.

> In his love sublime, he cradles all his anguish
> And, gazing down on what pours out from his bleeding breast,
> In the midst of this feast of death sinks down and totters,
> Drunk on the senses and tenderness and horror.

*Volupté, tendresse, horreur.* ". . . The senses and tenderness and horror." I like my translation. Who is this, an ocean or a bird, a father or a lover, who suffers so? It is enough to understand: someone suffers. Someone undergoes the long translation of impermanence. The holy wound that the world gives us feeds the world. We give our blood. All flesh is fed from ours. The wound works. The world takes.

In a ship, welcomed courteously and treated like a big shot, Musset sails with his wife. He is a famous author. No one knows his ugly medical secret—only his wife and his doctor, some scrofulous whiskered character back in Paris. They sail on the broad sweet autumn Mediterranean, away from Europe. Suez! Everyone wonders why the Mussets do not go ashore at Alexandria, do not visit the Pyramids, the Temple at Luxor, the sands. They do not know that time and sickness are already writing hieroglyphs on him. That is text enough for him to decipher.

We hear a voice quoting one of Musset's last odes (in my translation): "Poets! It is enough to read your own skins! There is your narrative and your map of travel. Decode your own bodies, learned critics! Sing your skin while it's still sweet and fresh!"

From this point on, the movie follows episodically. The French text by Edmund Wilson has become a persistent English-language voice-over that explains everything we see. We hurry on, to the settlement on some nice French island, tricolor and palm and white schooner in the harbor, polite functionaries from the Civil Service are never far, his wife teaches native children, he gets worse and worse.

His disease thickens in him, until a time comes when even the least observant visitor must recognize that this is a very sick man, with a very serious and disfiguring disease, and most likely an actual leper. Yet all through this time Musset is working. It is the great time of his writing life. From his warped and nerveless fingers come great odes, celebrations of the praises—an island is all praises—of natural fact. Rock, wave, sun, the unforgiving instant twilights of the equator, the impenetrable night below and the dazzling radiance of the southern skies, the svelte haunches of fishermen and their wives, the curious androgyny the ocean works on those who, smooth in sarongs, stand all day long in or near it. The smoothness of skin, the asperity of lemons.

His teeth are going, but he can still suck calmly on sugarcane. He still can smoke the stubby wheat-colored cigarettes his wife rolls for him.

The last scene of the movie is memorable. Ever since the disease started triumphing in him, the camera has been kept upwind of the man's image. We haven't been close. We see him move in the middle distance, and Edmund Wilson's voice tells us what we must understand.

But now at the end the camera ambles up, respectfully slow, to where the great poet—made great by adversity, by his brave dignity in facing it, his transmuted song—sits writing.

Alfred de Musset sits in a roomy wicker chair at a wicker table. His large notebook is open before him, and an ornate early fountain pen is in his left hand. A big cup of tea is nearby, in its saucer. Books are piled handily, and correspondence seems there too, and an ashtray. Alfred is wearing a soft white floppy hat, that shades and thus hides much of his ruined face. He is writing, and then looks up and seems to see us. The changes in shadow beneath the brim of his hat may mean that he is smiling. He speaks. I hear what he says, and see it also, a title on the screen:

## Leprosy is the only suitable condition for the creative artist.

It is the first time since Paris we have heard him speak. He is speaking in English, too, courteous as ever. That shouldn't surprise me—poetry is always courteous. In fact, poetry is the essence of all civility. Every poet answering as best we can, and all day long, the deepest questions the words ask. (The words? The words are us.)

Leprosy is the only condition for the creative artist. It is the wound that isolates him, the nutritious bread of exile, the loss that teaches finding, the dismay that teaches honor for all simple things. When I had the dream, I knew about leprosy and knew, already, a little about exile, though I still was living in the city where I was born. Exile is internal, and ripens inside, the way the sluggish pathogens of leprosy take years sometimes to make their move. To make their mark on their man.

Later, after I woke up, impressed and amused by the dream, and telling it widely, no doubt with illegitimate embellishment, to my circle of acquaintance, I looked up Musset in a reference book and found that the year of his life to which the dream assigned the coming of leprosy was in fact the year of his death. If that's what is meant by fact.

Not long ago, I asked an old friend from the Baltic, who had spent his youth with the Resistance in wartime France, whether he knew about the "black seraphim" in Musset. He said nothing in his own words, but immediately began reciting the opening alexandrines of "Une Nuit de Mai," which I gather is Musset's big anthology poem, where the Muse cries out (beginning, like an epic, in the middle of some action):

O poet, take up your lute and give me your kiss!

Today I found the text of the poem, and sure enough found towards the end, again in some great sonorous rapture of the Muse of poetry, the lines that haunted me, and brought back after so many years the instructive dream of the sacrifices that are proper to make for the full burgeoning of song. And in the poem, though the poet presumes to speak easily with the Muse, even calling her his sister at one point, in fact the Muse gets all the good lines.

Or rather, strictly, the richness and beauty of all language are in her gift, and she is giving still. Even to the diseased and dying she has a tremendous word to speak. Sweeter than centuries her leper's kiss.

# NOTES ON CONTRIBUTORS

RAE ARMANTROUT's most recent book of poems is *Made to Seem* (Sun & Moon). Two books are forthcoming in 1998: *True* (Atelos Press) and *The Pretext* (Sun & Moon.

JOHN ASHBERY's new collection of poems, *Wakefulness*, is forthcoming this spring from Farrar, Straus & Giroux.

JACK BARTH's work is in the public collections of the Museum of Modern Art, the New York Public Library, the San Francisco Museum of Modern Art and others. He lives in New York City.

JOHN BARTH's most recent book is the story series *On with the Story*, available in paperback from Little, Brown.

MARTINE BELLEN's *Tales of Murasaki and Other Poems* was a winner of the 1997 National Poetry Series and will be published this summer by Sun & Moon.

ANNE CARSON is the author of *Eros the Bittersweet* (Princeton), *Glass, Irony and God* (New Directions), *Plainwater* and *Autobiography of Red* (Knopf).

PETER CONSTANTINE has had work published in *The New Yorker*, *Harper's*, *Fiction*, *Harvard Magazine* and *London Magazine*, among others. He has written seven books on the languages and cultures of the Far East. His most recent book of translations was *Six Early Stories* by Thomas Mann (Sun & Moon).

ROBERT COOVER's "The Sheriff Goes to Church" is an excerpt from his novel *Ghost Town*, to be published by Henry Holt in the autumn. He teaches electronic and experimental writing at Brown University.

FRED D'AGUIAR's new book of poems, *Bill of Rights*, appeared in March from Chatto & Windus, London. His third novel, *Feeding the Ghosts*, was published last year also by Chatto & Windus.

*Drafts 15-XXX, The Fold* is the most recent book by RACHEL BLAU DUPLESSIS. The other sections of "Draft 32: Renga" will be published in *Hambone*.

MICHAEL EASTMAN's work has appeared on the cover of *Time* as well as in *Life*, *American Photographer* and *View Camera* and can be found in the collections of the International Center of Photography, the Metropolitan Museum of Art, the Chicago Art Institute and the Los Angeles County Museum of Art. He lives in St. Louis.

ERIK EHN most recently directed his adaptation of William Faulkner's *The Sound and the Fury* at the Undermain Theatre in Dallas. Sun & Moon is publishing *Erotic Curtsies* and PAJ Press is publishing a set of *Saint Plays. New South Wales* was written for the ACT Writers Group under the supervision of Mac Wellman.

JONATHAN FRANZEN is the author of *The Twenty-Seventh City* (Noonday) and *Strong Motion* (Norton). The excerpt in this issue of *Conjunctions* is from his new novel, *The Corrections,* to be published next year by Farrar, Straus & Giroux.

ED FRIEDMAN's books of poetry and prose include *Humans Work* and *Mao and Matisse* (Hanging Loose). Since 1987, he has been the artistic director of the Poetry Project at St. Mark's Church in New York City.

WILLIAM H. GASS teaches philosophy at Washington University in St. Louis and is the director of the International Writers Center there. The novella published in this issue of *Conjunctions* is from a collection, *Cartesian Sonata,* forthcoming from Knopf.

PETER GIZZI's new book of poems, *Artificial Heart,* is just out from Burning Deck. His edition of Jack Spicer's lectures, *The House that Jack Built,* is forthcoming this spring from Wesleyan.

JORIE GRAHAM's *The Dream of the Unified Field* (Ecco Press) won the Pulitzer Prize in 1996. Her most recent collection, *The Errancy,* is now out in paperback from Ecco. The poems in this issue of *Conjunctions* are from a new collection, *Swarm,* due out in late 1999 from Ecco.

GÜNTER GRASS, Germany's most prominent contemporary writer, was born in Danzig in 1927. He is the author of many novels, including *The Tin Drum, Dog Years, Local Anesthetic* and *The Meeting at Telgte.* He is also a poet, essayist, dramatist and graphic artist and is actively involved in politics in Germany and in human rights issues internationally.

SUSAN HOWE's most recent collections are *The Nonconformist's Memorial* and *Frame Structures: Early Poems 1974–1979,* both published by New Directions. A new book of poems is due from New Directions in spring of 1999. She is also the author of two books of criticism, *My Emily Dickinson* and *The Birth-mark; unsettling the wilderness in american literary history.*

SHELLEY JACKSON is the author of *Patchwork Girl* (Eastgate Systems), a hypertext novel, and the web-based works, *My Body: A Wunderkammer* (Alt-X) and *Stitch Bitch: The Patchwork Girl* (Media-In-Transition). She is the author and illustrator of *The Old Woman & the Wave* (DK Ink), a children's book.

FRANZ KAFKA's masterpiece, *The Trial*, was originally translated by Edwin and Willa Muir in 1937 from the German edition edited by Max Brod. Based on the original manuscript, this new translation by Breon Mitchell is from the German critical edition edited by Malcolm Pasley. Schocken Books will be publishing the complete newly translated edition of *The Trial* this September.

A new collection of ROBERT KELLY's poetry covering the years 1994 through 1997 will be out from Black Sparrow Press in spring of 1999.

ANN LAUTERBACH's fifth collection of poems, *On a Stair*, was published by Penguin in 1997.

KEVIN MAGEE is the author of *Tedium Drum* and *Recent Events*, both of which are available from Small Press Distribution in Berkeley, California. New work is forthcoming in *Chain* and *Abacus*.

PAUL MALISZEWSKI is a writer living in Syracuse, New York. A story related to "Preface" appeared in *Denver Quarterly*.

BREON MITCHELL's most recent translations include Sten Nadolny's *The God of Impertinence*, published by Viking, and Heinrich Böll's *The Mad Dog*, published by St. Martin's. He is professor of Germanic studies and comparative literature at Indiana University.

JOYCE CAROL OATES is the author of many works of fiction, poetry, drama and criticism. Her forthcoming novel is *My Heart Laid Bare*, to be published in June by E. P. Dutton, and her forthcoming story collection, in which "The Sons of Angus MacElster" is included, is *The Collector of Hearts: New Tales of the Grotesque*, to be published in November by E. P. Dutton.

DALE PECK's essay "Shirley Jackson: 'My Mother's Grave Is Yellow'" appeared in *Conjunctions: 29, Tributes*. His most recent novel is *Now It's Time to Say Goodbye* (Farrar, Straus & Giroux).

JOANNA SCOTT's most recent novel is *The Manikin* (Henry Holt).

RICHARD SIKEN's poems have appeared in the *Indiana Review, Jackleg, The James White Review, Chelsea* and *Many Mountains Moving*.

A new volume of GUSTAF SOBIN's poetry, *Towards the Blanched Alphabets*, will be published by Talisman House this spring.

SUSAN SONTAG's most recent books are *The Volcano Lover*, a novel, and *Alice in Bed*, a play. Her new novel, *In America*, will be published by Farrar, Straus & Giroux in early 1999.

A new collection of JOHN TAGGART's poems entitled *Crosses* is forthcoming from Sun & Moon.

ANNE TARDOS makes multilingual poems that include images, published in her books *Cat Licked the Garlic* (Tsunami) and *Mayg-shem Fish* (Potes & Poets). Her third, as yet unpublished, volume of such works is entitled *Uxudo*.

NATHANIEL TARN's *Scandals in the House of Birds: Shamans and Priests on Lake Atitlan* is forthcoming from Marsilio. His CD, *I Think This May Be Eden*, is available from Small Press Distribution.

ALEXANDER THEROUX, the author of several novels including *Darconville's Cat* (Doubleday), is also known for books on color, *The Primary Colors* and *The Secondary Colors* (Henry Holt). He lives on Cape Cod.

"Moral Yellowness" is an extract from WILLIAM T. VOLLMANN's *Rising Up and Rising Down*.

ROSMARIE WALDROP's most recent books of poems are *Another Language: Selected Poems* (Talisman House) and *A Key into the Language of America* (New Directions). Station Hill has published her novels, *The Hanky of Pippin's Daughter* and *A Form/ of Taking/ It All*.

PAUL WEST's newest novel is *Terrestrials*, and his next one will be *Life with Swan*. He has just completed a novel about Doc Holliday and is now working on one about the Gunpowder Plot. In 1996 the government of France made him a Chevalier of the Order of Arts and Letters.

JOY WILLIAMS is a short story writer, novelist and essayist and a recipient of the Strauss Living Award from the American Academy of Arts and Letters.

# Back issues of
# CONJUNCTIONS

"A must read"—*The Village Voice*

A limited number of back issues are available to those who would like to discover for themselves the range of innovative writing published in CONJUNCTIONS over the course of more than fifteen years.

CONJUNCTIONS:1. *James Laughlin Festschrift.* Paul Bowles, Gary Snyder, John Hawkes, Robert Creeley, Thom Gunn, Denise Levertov, Tennessee Williams, James Purdy, William Everson, Jerome Rothenberg, George Oppen, Joel Oppenheimer, Eva Hesse, Michael McClure, Octavio Paz, Hayden Carruth, over 50 others. Kenneth Rexroth interview. 304 pages.

CONJUNCTIONS:2. Nathaniel Tarn, William H. Gass, Mei-mei Berssenbrugge, Walter Abish, Gustaf Sobin, Edward Dorn, Kay Boyle, Kenneth Irby, Thomas Meyer, Gilbert Sorrentino, Carl Rakosi, and others. H.D.'s letters to Sylvia Dobson. Czeslaw Milosz interview. 232 pages.

CONJUNCTIONS:3. Guy Davenport, Michael Palmer, Don Van Vliet, Michel Deguy, Toby Olson, René Char, Coleman Dowell, Cid Corman, Ann Lauterbach, Robert Fitzgerald, Jackson Mac Low, Cecile Abish, Anne Waldman, and others. James Purdy interview. 232 pages.*

CONJUNCTIONS:4. Luis Buñuel, Aimé Césaire, Armand Schwerner, Rae Armantrout, Harold Schimmel, Gerrit Lansing, Jonathan Williams, Ron Silliman, Theodore Enslin, and others. Excerpts from Kenneth Rexroth's unpublished autobiography. Robert Duncan and William H. Gass interviews. 232 pages.

CONJUNCTIONS:5. Coleman Dowell, Nathaniel Mackey, Kenneth Gangemi, Paul Bowles, Hayden Carruth, John Taggart, Guy Mendes, John Ashbery, Francesco Clemente, and others. Lorine Niedecker's letters to Cid Corman. Barry Hannah and Basil Bunting interviews. 248 pages.

CONJUNCTIONS:6. Joseph McElroy, Ron Loewinsohn, Susan Howe, William Wegman, Barbara Tedlock, Edmond Jabés, Jerome Rothenberg, Keith Waldrop, James Clifford, Janet Rodney, and others. The *Symposium of the Whole* papers. Irving Layton interview. 320 pages.*

CONJUNCTIONS:7. John Hawkes, Mary Caponegro, Leslie Scalapino, Marjorie Welish, Gerrit Lansing, Douglas Messerli, Gilbert Sorrentino, and others. *Writers Interview Writers:* Robert Duncan/Michael McClure, Jonathan Williams/Ronald Johnson, Edmund White/Edouard Roditi. 284 pages.*

CONJUNCTIONS:8. Robert Duncan, Coleman Dowell, Barbara Einzig, R.B. Kitaj, Paul Metcalf, Barbara Guest, Robert Kelly, Claude Royet-Journoud, Guy Davenport, Karin Lessing, Hilda Morley, and others. *Basil Bunting Tribute,* guest-edited by Jonathan Williams, nearly 50 contributors. 272 pages.*

CONJUNCTIONS:9. William S. Burroughs, Dennis Silk, Michel Deguy, Peter Cole, Paul West, Laura Moriarty, Michael Palmer, Hayden Carruth, Mei-mei Berssenbrugge, Thomas Meyer, Aaron Shurin, Barbara Tedlock, and others. Edmond Jabés interview. 296 pages.

CONJUNCTIONS:10. *Fifth Anniversary Issue.* Walter Abish, Bruce Duffy, Keith Waldrop, Harry Mathews, Kenward Elmslie, Beverley Dahlen, Jan Groover, Ronald Johnson, David Rattray, Leslie Scalapino, George Oppen, Elizabeth Murray, and others. Joseph McElroy interview. 320 pages.*

CONJUNCTIONS:11. Lydia Davis, John Taggart, Marjorie Welish, Dennis Silk, Susan Howe, Robert Creeley, Charles Stein, Charles Bernstein, Kenneth Irby, Nathaniel Tarn, Robert Kelly, Ann Lauterbach, Joel Shapiro, Richard Tuttle, and others. Carl Rakosi interview. 296 pages.

CONJUNCTIONS:12. David Foster Wallace, Robert Coover, Georges Perec, Norma Cole, Laura Moriarty, Joseph McElroy, Yannick Murphy, Diane Williams, Harry Mathews, Trevor Winkfield, Ron Silliman, Armand Schwerner, and others. John Hawkes and Paul West interviews. 320 pages.

CONJUNCTIONS:13. Maxine Hong Kingston, Ben Okri, Jim Crace, William S. Burroughs, Guy Davenport, Barbara Tedlock, Rachel Blau DuPlessis, Walter Abish, Jackson Mac Low, Lydia Davis, Fielding Dawson, Toby Olson, Eric Fischl, and others. Robert Kelly interview. 288 pages.*

CONJUNCTIONS:14. *The New Gothic,* guest-edited by Patrick McGrath. Kathy Acker, John Edgar Wideman, Jamaica Kincaid, Peter Straub, Clegg & Guttmann, Robert Coover, Lynne Tillman, Bradford Morrow, William T. Vollmann, Gary Indiana, Mary Caponegro, Brice Marden, and others. Salman Rushdie interview. 296 pages.*

CONJUNCTIONS:15. *The Poetry Issue.* 33 poets, including Susan Howe, John Ashbery, Rachel Blau DuPlessis, Barbara Einzig, Norma Cole, John Ash, Ronald Johnson, Forrest Gander, Michael Palmer, Diane Ward, and others. Fiction by John Barth, Jay Cantor, Diane Williams, and others. Michael Ondaatje interview. 424 pages.

CONJUNCTIONS:16. *The Music Issue.* Nathaniel Mackey, Leon Botstein, Albert Goldman, Paul West, Amiri Baraka, Quincy Troupe, Lukas Foss, Walter Mosley, David Shields, Seth Morgan, Gerald Early, Clark Coolidge, Hilton Als, and others. John Abercrombie and David Starobin interview. 360 pages.

CONJUNCTIONS:17. *Tenth Anniversary Issue.* Kathy Acker, Janice Galloway, David Foster Wallace, Robert Coover, Diana Michener, Juan Goytisolo, Rae Armantrout, John Hawkes, William T. Vollmann, Charlie Smith, Lynn Davis, Mary Caponegro, Keith Waldrop, Carla Lemos, C.D. Wright, and others. Chinua Achebe interview. 424 pages. Out of print.

CONJUNCTIONS:18. *Fables, Yarns, Fairy Tales.* Scott Bradfield, Sally Pont, John Ash, Theodore Enslin, Patricia Eakins, Joanna Scott, Lynne Tillman, Can Xue, Gary Indiana, Russell Edson, David Rattray, James Purdy, Wendy Walker, Norman Manea, Paola Capriolo, O.V. de Milosz, Rosario Ferré, Jacques Roubaud, and others. 376 pages.

CONJUNCTIONS:19. *Other Worlds.* Guest-edited by Peter Cole. David Antin, John Barth, Pat Califia, Thom Gunn, Barbara Einzig, Ewa Kuryluk, Carl Rakosi, Eliot Weinberger, John Adams, Peter Reading, John Cage, Marjorie Welish, Barbara Guest, Cid Corman, Elaine Equi, Donald Baechler, John Weiners, and others. 336 pages.

CONJUNCTIONS:20. *Unfinished Business.* Robert Antoni, Janice Galloway, Martine Bellen, Paul Gervais, Ann Lauterbach, Jessica Hagedorn, Jim Lewis, Carole Maso, Leslie Scalapino, Gilbert Sorrentino, David Foster Wallace, Robert Creeley, Ben Marcus, Paul West, Mei-mei Berssenbrugge, Susan Rothenberg, Yannick Murphy, and others. 352 pages.

CONJUNCTIONS:21. *The Credos Issue.* Robert Olen Butler, Ishmael Reed, Kathy Acker, Walter Mosley, Robert Coover, Joanna Scott, Victor Hernandez Cruz, Frank Chin, Simon Ortiz, Martine Bellen, Melanie Neilson, Kenward Elmslie, David Mura, Jonathan Williams, Cole Swensen, John Ashbery, Forrest Gander, Myung Mi Kim, and others. 352 pages.

CONJUNCTIONS:22. *The Novellas Issue.* Allan Gurganus, Barbara Guest, John Hawkes, Wendy Walker, Stacy Doris, Harry Mathews, Robert Olen Butler, Nathaniel Tarn, Stephen Ratcliffe, Melanie Neilson, John Barth, Ann Lauterbach, Donald Revell, Robert Antoni, Lynne Tillman, Arno Schmidt, Paul West, and others. 384 pages.

CONJUNCTIONS:23. *New World Writing.* Bei Dao, Eduardo Galeano, Olga Sedakova, Abd al-Hakim Qasim, Yang Lian, Claudio Magris, Coral Bracho, Faiz Ahmed Faiz, Nuruddin Farah, Carlos German Belli, Jean Echenoz, Nina Iskrenko, Juan Goytisolo, Paola Capriolo, Peter Cole, Botho Strauss, Semezdin Mehmedinovic, Pascalle Monnier, and others. 336 pages.

CONJUNCTIONS:24. *Critical Mass.* Yoel Hoffmann, Githa Hariharan, Kathleen Fraser, John Taggart, Thalia Field, Lydia Davis, Guy Davenport, Myung Mi Kim, Marjorie Welish, Leslie Scalapino, Peter Gizzi, Cole Swensen, D.E. Steward, Mary Caponegro, Robert Creeley, Martine Bellen, William T. Vollmann, Louis-Ferdinand Céline, and others. 344 pages.

CONJUNCTIONS:25. *The New American Theater,* guest-edited by John Guare. Tony Kushner, Suzan-Lori Parks, Jon Robin Baitz, Han Ong, Mac Wellman, Paula Vogel, Eric Overmyer, Wendy Wasserstein, Christopher Durang, Donald Margulies, Ellen McLaughlin, Nicky Silver, Jonathan Marc Sherman, Joyce Carol Oates, Arthur Kopit, Doug Wright, Robert O'Hara, Erik Ehn, John Guare, Harry Kondoleon, and others. 360 pages.

CONJUNCTIONS:26. *Sticks and Stones.* Angela Carter, Ann Lauterbach, Rikki Ducornet, Paul Auster, Arthur Sze, David Mamet, Robert Coover, Rick Moody, Gary Lutz, Lois-Ann Yamanaka, Terese Svoboda, Brian Evenson, Dawn Raffel, David Ohle, Liz Tucillo, Martine Bellen, Robert Kelly, Michael Palmer, and others. 360 pages.

CONJUNCTIONS:27. *The Archipelago,* co-edited by Bradford Morrow and Robert Antoni. Gabriel García Márquez, Derek Walcott, Cristina García, Wilson Harris, Olive Senior, Senel Paz, Kamau Brathwaite, Julia Alvarez, Manno Charlemagne, Rosario Ferré, Severo Sarduy, Edwidge Danticat, Madison Smartt Bell, Fred D'Aguiar, Glenville Lovell, Mayra Montero, Lorna Goodison, Bob Shacochis, and others. 360 pages.

CONJUNCTIONS:28. *Secular Psalms,* with a special Music Theater portfolio guest-edited by Thalia Field. Maureen Howard, Julio Cortázar, Joanna Scott, David Foster Wallace, Stephen Dixon, Susan Gevirtz, Gilbert Sorrentino, Anselm Hollo, Can Xue, Harry Partch, Robert Ashley, Meredith Monk, John Moran, Alice Farley, Ann T. Greene, Ruth E. Margraff, Jeffrey Eugenides, Jackson Mac Low, and others. 380 pages.

CONJUNCTIONS:29. *Tributes,* co-edited by Martine Bellen, Lee Smith, and Bradford Morrow. Ntozake Shange, John Sayles, Nathaniel Mackey, Joanna Scott, Rick Moody, Dale Peck, Carole Maso, Peter Straub, Robert Creeley, Paul West, Quincy Troupe, Ana Castillo, Amiri Baraka, Eli Gottlieb, Joyce Carol Oates, Sven Birkerts, Siri Hustvedt, Lydia Davis, and others. 416 pages.

Send your order to:
*CONJUNCTIONS,* Bard College, Annandale-on-Hudson, NY 12504.
Issues 1–15 are $15.00 each, plus $3.00 shipping.
Issues 16–29 are $12.00 each, plus $3.00 shipping.

Issues with asterisks are available in very limited quantities.
Please inquire.

# NEW DIRECTIONS BOOKS

## Spring 1998

### CHRISTOPHE BATAILLE

**HOURMASTER.** Tr. by Richard Howard. A new novel about the dissolution of society, by the author of *Annam, 1993 Prix du Premier Roman* winner. $17.95 cloth

### ROBERT CREELEY

**LIFE & DEATH.** New poetry. A collage of recollections, a gathering-in before winter's night of elegiac meditations on aging, by a major American poet. $19.95 cl.

### FORREST GANDER

**SCIENCE & STEEPLEFLOWER.** Poetry by a 1997 Whiting Writer's Award winner. "The most earthly of our avant-garde..." —Donald Revell. $12.95 pbk. original

### YOEL HOFFMANN

**KATSCHEN & THE BOOK OF JOSEPH.** Various Trans. Two novellas. "One of the most precious voices in Israel's contemporary literature." —Amos Oz. $17.95 cl.

### FLEUR JAEGGY

**LAST VANITIES.** Tr. by Tim Parks. Profoundly disquieting stories about characters perversely estranged from their middle-class environments. $11.95 pbk. orig.

### MARY KARR

**VIPER RUM.** w/Afterword, "Against Decoration". Personal, intense new poetry by the author of the bestselling autobiography, *The Liars' Club*. $10.95 pbk. orig.

### JAMES LAUGHLIN

**POEMS NEW & SELECTED.** "What an extraordinary delight! —new poems by Laughlin, to add to those we already have." —Hayden Carruth. $12.95 pbk. orig.

### D. H. LAWRENCE

**QUETZALCOATL.** Ed. w/intro. by L. Martz. The last "unpublished" ms., the 1923 version of Lawrence's great Mexican novel, *The Plumed Serpent.* $14.95 pbk. orig.

### FEDERICO GARCÍA LORCA

**IN SEARCH OF DUENDE.** Var. trans. New anth. of essays and poetry (*bilingual*), including 3 never-before-published works. A New Directions Bibelot. $7.00 pbk.

### MICHAEL PALMER

**THE LION BRIDGE.** Sel. Poems 1971-1995. Fuses avant-garde "contemporary concerns...with some very ancient poetic pleasures." (*Village Voice*). $18.95 pbk. orig.

### W. G. SEBALD

**THE RINGS OF SATURN.** "An English Pilgrimage." Tr. by Hulse. Fiction in ten strange and beautiful chapters, by the author of *The Emigrants.* $23.95 cl.

### MURIEL SPARK

**THE GIRLS OF SLENDER MEANS.** A witty yet tragic tale, set in a London girls' boarding house at the end of WWII. A New Directions Classic. $10.95 pbk.

### UWE TIMM

**MIDSUMMER NIGHT.** Tr. by P. Tegel. A charming new German novel about a man involved in a series of magical and surprising encounters. $22.95 cl.

### TENNESSEE WILLIAMS

**NOT ABOUT NIGHTINGALES.** Early play. "I have never written anything since that could compete with it in violence and horror." —T. Williams. $10.95 pbk. orig.

*Please send for complete catalog*

**NEW DIRECTIONS** 80 Eighth Avenue, NYC 10011

**SARABANDE BOOKS** presents

Jennifer Eriksen

### *The Gatehouse Heaven*
### Poems by James Kimbrell

Winner of the 1997 Kathryn A. Morton Prize in Poetry

ISBN 1-889330-13-2  $20.95 cloth
ISBN 1-889330-14-0  $12.95 paper

"Kimbrell sings a serious song.... The poems are deft and sure,
there is a sense of vision in them, and I have the feeling that this is
the start of something significant. And if, as Flaubert said, language
is like a cracked kettle on which we beat out tunes for bears to
dance to, while all the time we long to move the stars to pity, then
the stars have prime seating for these songs."
— from the Foreword by Charles Wright

### *Where She Went*
### Stories by Kate Walbert

ISBN 1-889330-15-9  $19.95 cloth

"In the spirit of such luminous, haunting classics as James Salter's
*Light Years* or Evan Connell's *Mrs. Bridge,* Kate Walbert's *Where
She Went* is an impressionistic mosaic that somehow, as if by
magic, brings to life the complex shape of a family's history over
the course of decades. It's fresh, funny, and heartbreaking all in
the same breath."
— Marly Swick

*Bookstores contact Consortium Book Sales and Distribution at 1-800-283-3572.
Individuals call Sarabande Books at 1-502-458-4028. Visa and MasterCard accepted.
Visit our web site at www.sarabandebooks.org.*

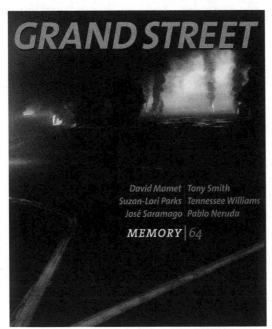

# The 1998 Mississippi Review Prize

Winners and all finalists in fiction and poetry will be published in print and online editions of *The Mississippi Review*.

Judges to be announced real soon now

**DEADLINE & ENTRY FEE:** Deadline is May 30, 1998. Nonrefundable entry fee is $10 per story, limit two stories per author ($20), or $5 per poem, limit four entries per author ($20). Make check/money order payable to Mississippi Review Prize. No ms returned. Contest open to all US writers except students or employees of USM. Previously published or accepted work ineligible. **FORMAT:** Fiction--maximum 6500 words (25 pages), typed, double-spaced. Poetry--each entry a single poem no more than ten typewritten pages. Author's name, address, phone, plus story title and "1998 Mississippi Review Prize Entry" should be on page one of entry. Do not send cover sheet. **ANNOUNCEMENTS:** Include SASE for list of winners. Winners will be announced November 1, 1998. The Prize Issue will be available to competitors at a reduced rate ($5). Issue scheduled for late fall 1998. These are complete guidelines. AA/EOE/ADA

## send entries to:

**1998 mississippi review prize box 5144, hattiesburg, ms 39406-5144**

Faulkner took 15 years to finish a story.

Hemingway rewrote a manuscript 39 times.

Updike never completed ½ of his work.

*It's a wonder we get out 4 issues a year.*

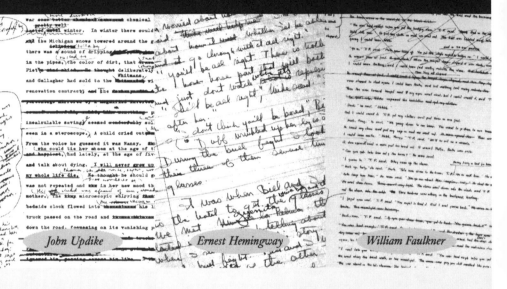

John Updike          Ernest Hemingway          William Faulkner

*For all we know, our writers still may not be satisfied with the work they've done*

*for The Paris Review. Whether you want poetry, short stories, photography, art or our*

*renowned interviews, The Paris Review offers the finest from the big names as well as*

*the no names. Call (718) 539-7085 to subscribe and you'll appreciate*

*the results of the long, hard years our contributors spent honing their*

*craft for the pages of The Paris Review.*

*{4 issues (one year) $34, $8 Surcharge outside the U.S.A.}*

*http://www.voyagerco.com*

THE PARIS REVIEW *The International Literary Quarterly.*

# THE 1998
# PUSHCART
# PRIZE
BEST
OF THE
SMALL
# XXII
PRESSES

*Edited by Bill Henderson
with the Pushcart Prize editors*

**657 PAGES $29.50
HARDBOUND
JUST PUBLISHED**

PUSHCART PRESS
P.O. Box 380
Wainscott, N.Y. 11975

EACH YEAR THE PUSHCART PRIZE presents the most distinguished short stories, poetry and essays first published by small presses and magazines nationwide and each volume is hailed as a touchstone of literary discovery. The most honored literary series in America, THE PUSHCART PRIZE has won The Carey-Thomas Award, been selected many times as a notable book of the year by The New York Times Book Review, and has been chosen for several Book of the Month Club QPB selections. Recently, Pushcart Press and its PRIZE were named among the "most influential in the development of the American book business over the past century and a quarter" by Publishers Weekly.

THE PUSHCART PRIZE XXII surpasses Pushcart's own reputation with the largest collection in its history and with more presses reprinted (52) than ever before. Here you will find an astonishing diversity of writers from many presses that will be new to you — all picked with the help of over 200 outstanding contributing editors. THE PUSHCART PRIZE XXII continues the tradition of introducing readers to the dazzling literary galaxy of the small press.